The Magician's Doll

M.L. Roble

Copyright © 2013 M.L. Roble

ISBN-10: 0988421313
ISBN-13: 978-0-9884213-1-8

This book is a work of fiction. Names, characters, places, and incidents are either the product of the author's imagination, or, are used fictitiously, and any resemblance to actual persons, living or dead, business establishments, events, or locales is entirely coincidental.

Cover design by Candace Foy Chabot
Interior design by Jean Boles

For
J.D. and D.V.

The Magician's Doll

M.L. Roble

Contents

Prologue

The man stood in a clearing in the woods, his head bowed, his hands clasped behind his back. It was night, and above him, clouds covered the moon. All around him the woods were still; not even the crickets chirped. But the air surrounding him hummed; a vaporous light strummed off him in waves. He waited.

A few moments later, a second man walked into the clearing. He was young, barely eighteen, with dark eyes and dark hair. He was tall and walked with assurance, but at the sight of the older man, he paused. As the older man looked up, the young man walked forward and bowed his head.

"I'm sorry, Father," he said.

The older man's chest rose in a sigh. He walked forward until he stood in front of the young man. They were the same height, but the older man had the weight of authority.

"So it's true then," he said. "She's gone."

The young man nodded. "Yes." His head bowed lower, as if too heavy for his shoulders. "Yes," he said again, and this time, his voice held a tinge of despair.

The older man's eyes narrowed. He was silent until the young man raised his head to face him.

"How can this be?" he asked. "You said yourself everything was going well."

"I believed it was."

"Then why did she leave?"

The young man tried to look away, but the older man grasped his shoulder and held him firm.

"Why?" he repeated.

The young man paused. "She discovered the truth."

The older man's head snapped back in surprise. "Impossible. She couldn't have. Not unless someone told her."

The young man said nothing.

The older man's lips tightened; the light around him solidified. He released the young man and stepped back.

The young man swallowed. "Father," he began, but the older man interrupted him.

"So you told her. Why would you do that?"

As the older man spoke, his eyes grew dark. The hum in the air heightened, and the trees rustled as an ominous wind trickled through the leaves and gathered into a whirl. The young man tensed and looked about.

The light around the older man sharpened and pulled tight. Before the young man could react, it shot into his chest, sending him across the clearing into one of the trees. A cry burst from him as he fell to the ground, but he was seized and thrown back into the clearing. He landed in a heap at the older man's feet. "Wait, please!" he groaned.

The older man waved his arms. The light twisted around the young man, lifting him into the air, suspending him. The older man's fingers twirled and tightened. A wisp of light wove free and encircled the young man's throat. The young man's eyes widened and bulged. He grabbed at his throat.

"Father," he choked, "I hoped she would join us."

"When she didn't, why didn't you kill her? You are a young fool!"

"Please stop!" The young man struggled with the grip around his throat. He pulled at his neck, but could not grasp the noose of light. Mustering his strength, he lifted his hand and procured a light of his own. It knocked the older man back just enough to release him. The young man fell to the ground.

The older man's eyes had turned black. "Yes, you are my son and you are gifted, but do not think for a moment that you can defeat me. I can still destroy you."

The young man pulled himself up off the ground. He waited a few seconds, breathing heavily, and then looked his father in the eye.

"But you won't. You need me."

The older man's chin raised a fraction. "I do." He took a deep breath, as if to gather himself, and when he spoke again, his tone was mild. "I am sorry, my boy. I was angry." He gave a dismissive wave of his hand. "The girl, I can let go. We could have harnessed a great deal of power with her, but that is all right. There are always alternatives.

"But you must understand my concern. When your loyalties are swayed by your feelings, and you give away our secrets to those who would betray us, you put our goal at risk."

The young man looked down. "I know that."

"I need you, yes, but I also love you. I want to give you everything, can't you see that? I'm doing this for you, for us."

"Yes, Father."

"Don't you want power greater than any you could ever imagine?"

The young man looked up. "I do," he said. Then again, "I do."

The older man walked forward and put his hands on the young man's shoulders. "I am sorry it did not work out the way you had hoped," he said softly.

The young man's face tightened, but he nodded.

"Can I count on your loyalty?" the older man asked.

The young man's shoulders slumped, his head bowed, but his answer was firm.

"You can."

Chapter One

*I*t was a breathtaking fall picture, the walk to Natalie's home. The sky was a bright blue, and the air crisp and cool. Overnight, the trees had become a kaleidoscope of red, yellow, brown, and orange. They draped over the streets creating tunnels of fall color. Soon the air would be full of burning leaves. It was a smell Natalie loved. Fall was her favorite season.

Today, however, was not a good day. Natalie stomped her way home from school, her head down, her forehead furrowed in frustration. She was a small girl, but at that moment, she moved like a miniature tank, her brown ponytail bouncing behind her.

"Please let me get home quick," she muttered. Her mother had announced at breakfast that the dreaded sign was going up again. Natalie had had to go through the day with a knot in her stomach. The teasing was always worse when the sign went up.

But today during math class, the idea had hit her. If she could get home in time, she could take the sign down before the other kids at school saw it. Her mother would not like it, but sometimes there were things that simply had to be done.

She looked around to see if there was anyone to avoid. So far she was in luck. She hurried along, watching for her favorite house to come into view.

It loomed over the neighborhood, its pointed turret and sharply angled roof tops rising up from the hill at the end of the street. The imposing Victorian was owned by rich, old, Mrs. Blaine. On most days, Natalie liked to stop and imagine what Mrs. Blaine was really like. Everyone knew she was stern and not very friendly, but Natalie sometimes imagined her to be an exiled queen, or a famous actress in hiding, or even a mad scientist with secret experiments.

No time for that today, Natalie thought, as she sped past the Blaine house.

"Natalie Bristol!"

Natalie stopped and spun around, surprised. Mrs. Blaine stood at the gate of her home, leaning on her cane. I didn't even see her there, Natalie thought.

"Why are you just standing there?" Mrs. Blaine asked now. "Come here, please."

"I'm sorry, Mrs. Blaine, but I'm kind of in a hurry." She had a lead on the other kids, but she would lose it if she did not keep moving.

"Don't be silly, child!" Mrs. Blaine said. "I need your help."

Natalie looked down the street. It was empty, but snippets of conversation and laughter echoed down the block. There was not much time. She ran back to Mrs. Blaine.

"I dropped my watch and moving around is hard for me." Mrs. Blaine said. "Please help me find it."

Natalie groaned silently. This could take a while. She glanced down the street again. Other kids were headed in their direction now. She was toast! She got down on her hands and knees and looked hard for the watch. The sooner she found it, the better.

"Here it is!" She held the watch up for Mrs. Blaine.

Mrs. Blaine held out her wrist, and Natalie fastened the watch around it. She stepped back to find Mrs. Blaine's intent gaze on her. Wow, Natalie thought. Mrs. Blaine did not look old, but she sure seemed old.

A strange, yet familiar feeling started to creep over her, but as usual, she fought it back. She shook her head to clear the fog.

Mrs. Blaine smiled. "I hear your mother is open for business again."

Natalie gave a start and looked about. Kids from her neighborhood were walking by now, some staring curiously at her and Mrs. Blaine.

"Mrs. Blaine, I have to go!" Natalie said.

"You young kids are always in a hurry. Okay, then. Thank you, Natalie."

"You're welcome," Natalie said, running out the gate.

I'll never make it, she thought. She ran as fast as she could down the street to her house. As she pulled up to the corner, her heart sank. Three boys waited in front of her lawn, laughing at the sign: Mike Becker, Rory Lindstrom and Larry Walker. It could not have been worse.

Mike straightened at Natalie's approach, a smirk on his freckled face. "So Bristol, your psychic mom's opened shop again?"

"Go away," Natalie said. She walked towards the sign, but the boys blocked her way.

"Oh come on, Bristol," Mike said. "If your mother wants to advertise she's a freak, let her. It's a free country."

Natalie's lips tightened. "Ease off, Mike. I don't want to get into trouble today."

Mike shook his legs in pretend fright. "Oooooh, I'm so scared! Larry, don't I look like I'm scared?"

"You look like you're shaking in your shoes," Larry answered. His red hair stuck up as if electricity had pulled it into the air.

"It must be because Natalie's mom can see baaaad things in the future," Mike said.

"Shut up!" Natalie said.

"I hear she jerks and shakes around when she sees stuff," Rory piped in. "Like this." He jerked his hands, and his bony body shook as if it was having a seizure. Mike and Larry doubled over with laughter.

"I hear her eyes roll back in her head," Larry gasped.

"I hear spit comes out of her mouth!" Mike added.

"Kind of like you when you talk to Suzy Sherman?" Natalie retorted. Suzy was one of the cutest girls in school, and everyone knew Mike liked her. Everyone also teased Mike about the fact that he could barely string two words together whenever Suzy was around.

Mike stopped laughing. "Shut up."

"What's the matter, Mike?" Natalie asked. "You don't think she'll like you with drool coming out of your mouth? I think it makes you look smarter."

Mike scowled. "You think you're so funny. At least I don't have a freak for a mother."

"And I'll bet you're a freak, too," Larry said. "I'll bet you got the freak gene."

"I did not!" Natalie said.

"Ooooh!" Rory said. "So you think you're mother's a freak, too?"

"Shut up!"

"Natalie thinks her mother's a freak," Rory chanted. "Natalie thinks her mother's a freak."

Larry and Mike joined in. "Natalie thinks her mother's a freak..."

Natalie took a deep breath. One, she thought, two...three...four...five...six.

The boys continued their awful chant, "Natalie thinks her mother's a freak..."

"Hey, Larry," Natalie said. "Your mom doesn't seem to care what my mom does."

Larry stopped chanting. "What's that supposed to mean?"

"She's usually my mom's first customer."

Larry's eyes grew round. "She is not!"

"Sure she is," Natalie said. "She comes all the time asking my mom if you're better off in a boarding school."

"She does not!"

"Does too. All I have to say is, the farther the better."

Now she had done it! Mike, Rory and Larry yelled at her all at once. Natalie could not hear what they were saying and could not have cared less. Words spewed out of her in a deluge as she shouted back. The boys brayed louder, but she refused to be outdone and hollered even harder.

She did not know how long they screamed back and forth, but her throat was starting to hurt when her mother's voice cut through the din.

"What is going on out here?"

Mike, Rory and Larry snapped to attention. Their faces were flushed and mutinous, but at the sight of Natalie's mother, their jaws dropped, and their heads ducked.

Natalie, feeling anger rushing red in her face, turned to look as well. As angry as she was, her breath stopped at the sight of her mother.

Serena stepped down from the porch of their home. She wore a drab, brown skirt and a worn blouse, but her honey-blond hair shone like burnished gold, and her vivid blue eyes matched the sky. She had a beauty that glowed fiercely as she looked over the boys and Natalie. Mike, Rory and Larry's heads stayed bowed; Serena's gaze could be blinding when she gave you the full force of her attention.

"Anybody?" Serena asked now. "Mike?"

"Nothing, Mrs. Bristol," Mike mumbled.

Serena looked at Rory. "Rory?"

Rory peeked at Serena from under his floppy, black hair. His mouth moved, but nothing came out. The corner of Serena's lips twitched.

Larry, however, stepped right in. "Natalie said my mother comes to see you. She said my mother wants to send me to boarding school, but it's not true! My mother would never send me away!"

For a second Serena seemed too surprised to answer. Her eyes flicked to Natalie. Natalie sheepishly dropped hers. It *was* kind of a low blow. Serena shook her head at her.

Natalie could not believe it! "But Mom," she protested, "he called you a freak!"

"Larry," Serena said, "I can assure you that your mother does not come to me for advice on which boarding school to send you to."

"I don't need you to tell me that!" Larry shouted. "I don't need some freak psychic telling me it's not true. It's not!" He choked off, turned and ran.

"Hey, Larry, wait up!" Mike yelled.

Natalie and Serena watched as Mike and Rory took off down the street, calling out to Larry who refused to acknowledge them or slow down. As they disappeared from view, Serena turned to face Natalie. She refused to look back.

"Natalie." Her mother touched her shoulder, but Natalie pulled away. She didn't want to be placated, didn't want to talk. If she did anything, she would explode.

Serena was silent for a moment. "Sweetie," she said softly.

"What?" Natalie screamed. "What? What? What?" Her breath became a hiccup, and she looked at her mother, mortified. She wanted to hit something so badly. A tight squeeze gripped her throat. She just wanted to disappear! She spun around and ran for the porch.

As she fumbled at the door knob, her mother's hand appeared, gently opening the door for her. Somehow, this just made things worse. She ran upstairs to her room and threw herself on the bed. She was a horrible person! She was horrible to other people, horrible to her mother, but even worse, horrible about her mother.

"I hate being different!" Natalie whispered into her pillow. She gazed out her window at the bright blue sky. It would be so nice to have wings, she thought. She could forget everything if she could just fly.

Her door opened then, and Serena walked in. Natalie met her mother's eyes and then rolled over. She could not bear to talk now.

Natalie heard Serena sigh and sit down on the chair beside her bed.

"You're angry with me," Serena said. Natalie shrugged. "It must have been a rough day today."

"It's always rough. It's never easy. It's always the same when you put out the sign." Natalie tossed the words over her shoulder at her mother. "You don't understand."

"I do," Serena said. "Of course I understand."

"No, you don't," Natalie said. "If you did, you wouldn't put out the sign."

"Sweetie, please try to understand. This is something I have to do."

Natalie kept her back to her mother.

"Maybe I could get a job," Natalie offered. "Make us some more money."

Serena's voice held a smile. "You're a little young. And we'll be fine."

"If we had more money, then maybe we wouldn't need the sign."

"I'm sorry this is so hard on you," Serena said. The springs on Natalie's bed gave way as her mother sat on the mattress and stroked Natalie's hair.

After a while, Natalie rolled back over. "Why can't you do something different?" she asked.

Serena sighed. "Because this is what I'm good at."

"No one thinks it's real."

"Some people do," Serena said. "What do you think?"

Natalie concentrated on one of the buttons of Serena's shirt. "I don't know," she mumbled.

"You don't know? Well, that's not something you say very often. Maybe you think there's a small possibility that it is."

"No I don't."

"Are you sure?" Serena made an inch between her thumb and forefinger. "Not even a little bit?"

"No," Natalie said.

Serena made the inch smaller. "Not even a teeny, weeny, iota of an itty bit?" she asked, leaning in close to Natalie.

Natalie grinned. "Stop it."

Serena's fingers wiggled now. "Not even a wee wee amoeba of a bit?" she teased, moving her fingers in to tickle Natalie.

Natalie giggled as her mother tickled her. When her mother hugged her, she burrowed her head into her mother's neck and breathed in the sweet scent of honeysuckle.

"Sweetie," Serena whispered to her, "You need to be careful of what you say to people. You really hurt Larry."

"I'm sorry," Natalie said. "I just got so mad. But at least I didn't tell him the truth. I didn't tell him his mom is sick."

There was a slight pause before Serena said, "So you heard about that?"

There was something in Serena's tone, but when Natalie peeked up at her, Serena merely smiled. Natalie rested her head back on her mother's shoulder.

"No," Natalie sighed, "I don't know how I know."

Chapter Two

*P*lease, Mr. Mackey!"

"No, Natalie, I'm sorry, but child labor is against the law."

Mr. Mackey smiled at Natalie and went back to wiping the counter. Natalie climbed up on one of the stools. The soda shop was not very crowded. She had purposely waited until after the lunch crowd so she could have Mr. Mackey's full attention. It was not going too well, but she was not giving up yet.

Mr. Mackey finished wiping the counter and looked over at Natalie. She grinned. Mr. Mackey chuckled and shook his head. He slung his towel over his shoulder and came to stand in front of her.

"Natalie," he said, leaning forward and resting his elbows on the counter.

Natalie leaned forward, putting her elbows on the counter as well. "Mr. Mackey, I promise, I will make your customers the best ice cream sodas they have ever had. They won't ever want to go to anyone else but you for sodas."

"I'm sure you will," Mr. Mackey said. "Of course, I am the only game in town."

Natalie blinked. She had not thought about that. "True," she countered. "But why take any chances? Who knows what competition could blow into town tomorrow?"

"I see your point." Mr. Mackey straightened up, picked up a glass and began scooping ice cream into it. "However, there is still the issue of breaking the law."

"Tell you what, Mr. Mackey. I could do something else, like, sweep the floor, and you could pay me what you want, on the side."

Mr. Mackey laughed. "My goodness, Natalie, you really want a job, don't you?" He finished scooping the ice cream and walked over to the fountain for some root beer. "Does your mother know you're looking?"

"Um, sort of."

"Ah, I see," he said. "Well, I'd love to hire you, but I've already got Mary helping me. I can't take away any of her responsibilities or she'd feel less needed, you know what I mean?" He walked back to Natalie and set the root beer float in front of her. "For you."

Natalie eyed the float and then Mr. Mackey. She had hit a dead end. "Thanks, Mr. Mackey, but I can't. I didn't bring any money."

"It's on me. A girl who works as hard as you deserves some kind of payment. Go ahead, drink up."

As Mr. Mackey walked away to help a customer, Natalie sighed and sipped her float. It was delicious. Mr. Mackey did not really need any help making good sodas. Darn, she thought, Mr. Mackey's soda shop would have been a fun place to work.

It had been a tough day. She had tried the drug store, the candy store, and the bakery, but no one was willing to hire. She was starting to get tired. She had one place left to try and then she was calling it a day.

Natalie finished the rest of her float and hopped off the stool. It was time to move on. "Thanks for the float, Mr. Mackey!" she called out. "Let me know if anything comes up."

Mr. Mackey looked up from a conversation with a customer. "I will, Natalie! Thanks for offering." He waved to her as she walked out.

Natalie closed the door behind her, stopping in the archway to take in the view of downtown. She had heard people say theirs was a small town. She had hardly traveled and could not compare it to any other, but she could never understand why people seemed to want to leave it. She thought their downtown was a great place, with all the cute little stores, and the park in the middle of everything. All the neighborhoods surrounded downtown like a cocoon, making the walk there an easy one. The people in the town were nice, too. Well, the grownups anyway. The kids were kind of mean, but oh, well.

Natalie considered the final store down the block: Stone Sewing and Mending. Maybe Mrs. Stone would hire her.

Janet Stone was a long-time friend of her mother's, and her son, Phillip, was thirteen, a year older than Natalie. Mrs. Stone and Phillip had a lot in common with Natalie and her mother, including that strangeness that made Natalie and her mother different.

Mrs. Stone could sew the most beautiful clothes and mend just about anything. Everyone thought she had magic fingers. There had been whispered rumors of even more wondrous pieces that Janet Stone had created, things that she did not sell in her store, or show to anyone outside of her circle of family and friends.

Natalie, of course, did not believe in any of the things she had heard, but until a couple of years ago, it did make Phillip someone whom she felt she could understand and who seemed to understand her.

Natalie walked down the block to the store and peeked in. Mrs. Stone was working on what looked like a fancy dress with lace. There was no sign of Phillip. Good, Natalie thought. She took a deep breath and entered the store.

Mrs. Stone looked up from her sewing. She had a kind face with twinkly green eyes. She had a way of making people feel at home, and Natalie appreciated the fact that Mrs. Stone always had a fond smile for her. That smile played upon her face now as she saw Natalie.

"Well hello, Natalie! I haven't seen you in a while. This is a pleasant surprise." She got up and hugged Natalie. "What brings you here?"

"Mrs. Stone," Natalie said, "you are my last hope."

Mrs. Stone's eyes widened in surprise. "Your last hope? My goodness, Natalie, should I be seated for this?"

"No, it's okay. I just need a job, and no one seems to have anything available. I could help out with anything you need, and you could pay me whatever you want, on the side, if you like. I don't want you to get in trouble with the law or anything."

"Why are you looking for a job?" Mrs. Stone asked.

Natalie was not sure how to answer that one. She did not want to reveal her hope that an extra income would give her mother a reason to stop her side business.

"Aren't you a little young?" Mrs. Stone asked.

"Well, Phillip's kind of working, isn't he?" she pointed out.

"True," Mrs. Stone said, with a slight laugh. "But he's my son, and it's more along the lines of chores."

Natalie's shoulders slumped. She was getting nowhere today!

Just then, the door to the store opened. To Natalie's dismay, it was Serena. Serena stopped short in surprise at the sight of her with Mrs. Stone.

"Hi, Serena!" Mrs. Stone walked over, hands outstretched, and the two women clasped hands fondly. "Long time, no see. How have you been?"

"Good. It's good to see you, Janet!" Serena looked at Natalie. "I didn't expect to see you, sweetie. What are you doing here?"

Once again, Natalie was at a loss for words. As her silence wore on, Serena's eyebrows went up.

"I was looking for a job," Natalie blurted.

Serena's head tilted back as she nodded slightly. "Ah, yes, I see. Any luck?"

"No, everyone's worried about child labor laws."

"Yes, that is quite an obstacle," Serena said. "Sorry it's not working out, sweetheart, but at least everyone knows you're looking. They'll think of you when something comes up."

"I haven't given up yet," Natalie said, although she was not sure what other alternatives she had.

"I'm sure you haven't." Serena turned to Mrs. Stone. "Janet, there was something I wanted to discuss with you. Is there somewhere we can talk?"

"Of course," Mrs. Stone said. "We can talk in the back rooms. Natalie, I'll send Phillip up here to keep you company."

"Oh, you don't have to do that, Mrs. Stone," Natalie said.

"It's no problem," Mrs. Stone replied.

Natalie meandered around the front of the store, browsing through the lovely sewing projects on display. All the different colors made it a cheerful workplace. She paused in front of the bulletin board near the door. Mrs. Stone had made a pretty fabric one, decorated with ribbons and lace. People liked to put their ads and flyers on it because that background attracted everyone's attention.

Today there were the standard "For Sale" notices, ads for babysitting services, flyers for the community bake sale and a postcard for the theatrical production of "Fiddler on the Roof." But then Natalie noticed a colorful flyer she hadn't seen before.

The Big Top Circus is Coming to Town!

The flyer had pictures of big flowing tents, brightly dressed clowns, and animals like elephants and tigers. The circus had never come to their town before, and Natalie had never been to one. It looked like fun. Maybe the circus could even use some help while it was in town. Natalie leaned in to read the flyer. It would be coming to town for a week during their fall break. The timing was perfect! Maybe they would not be too concerned about child labor laws.

Feeling more heartened, Natalie turned from the bulletin board to find Phillip standing at the counter, staring at her with a wary look on his face.

"Oh!" Natalie started in surprise. "I didn't hear you come."

Phillip shrugged. He was an average-sized boy with sandy hair and hazel-colored eyes. Natalie rather liked his eyes, but right now, they looked a little hostile.

"You didn't have to come out and keep me company," Natalie said, feeling a little defensive.

Phillip shrugged again. "No big deal."

For a while they stood there, saying nothing. What does he expect me to do, Natalie wondered. She went back to the bulletin board.

The circus flyer caught her eye again. The circus would set up at Morton's Field, right near her home. That would make it so much easier for her to work there. There was bound to be something she could do!

"What are you looking at?" Phillip had come out from behind the counter and was standing behind Natalie, trying to see what she was looking at.

"Do you always have to startle me like that?" Natalie asked crossly.

"Sorry, the flyer just looked interesting."

"It's an ad for the circus," Natalie said. "Did you know it was coming to town?"

Phillip nodded. "My mom said something about it. Are you going?"

"I want to. I've never been to one. Have you?"

"Yeah. My dad took me once a while ago. Before he...you know."

Natalie glanced at Phillip. Two years ago Phillip's father had disappeared without a trace. There had been no clues as to what had happened to him, nor had there been any word of him since.

Mrs. Stone had been a wreck during that terrible period, and Natalie's mother had spent much of that time helping her through it.

Phillip, who had always been a bit of a loner, had become sullen and even more withdrawn. He and his father had been very close. His mother mentioned his father every once in a while, but Phillip never did.

"Was it fun?" Natalie asked.

"Yeah, there's lots to do. All the shows and exhibits and stuff. Lots to eat, too." Phillip had a little smile on his face, as if the memory of the circus was a good one.

"It must have been nice, with your dad and all." Natalie said. She remembered Jack Stone had sandy hair like Phillip's, and a big booming laugh that never failed to get everyone else laughing as well.

"Yeah." A shadow fell across Phillip's face. "What about you?" he asked abruptly. "Your dad take you anywhere fun?"

The question threw her for a second. "Um, well, I never saw him. He was gone before I was born."

There was a flash in Phillip's eyes before they hit the floor. "Sorry," he muttered.

Natalie stared straight ahead at the circus flyer. "That's okay."

"I knew that. I don't know why I asked the stupid question."

"Forget about it," Natalie said, wishing he would drop it.

An awkward lull fell between them. Natalie tried to find something else interesting on the bulletin board, but the quiet hung over them like a pall. She considered leaving and waiting for her mother at home.

She was about to say goodbye when Phillip suddenly asked, "Want to see my new maps?" Phillip was a big collector of maps.

"Sure." Maps were not really her thing, but right now it was better than dead air.

Phillip and his mother lived above their store, which Natalie thought was really cool.

"Wow," she said, as she walked into Phillip's room. Phillip had hung a huge map of the world on the wall. It looked like it was made of old parchment, with antique colors and old-style print for the different countries and oceans.

"My dad and I made that," Phillip said. "He found out how to make the paper look old, and Mom helped us with the print. I finally put it up the other night." A fleeting sadness crossed his face and then disappeared.

"I thought it was an antique," Natalie exclaimed. "It looks really valuable."

"Thanks," Phillip said with a grin. He walked over to his desk and pulled out an album. "I've got all sorts of maps. Dad used to travel a lot for his work, and he brought me maps from all the places he visited. Look, they all have the names in the different languages!"

"Wow." Natalie looked on as Phillip flipped through the pages. "Your dad went everywhere."

"Yeah, he did. Look at this one from Russia."

Natalie squinted at the names on the map. "I can't read the letters."

"They have a different alphabet," Phillip said. "I'm going to take Russian someday so I can read what it says."

"That's great," Natalie said. "Do you want to travel someday?"

"Oh, yeah," Phillip said. "I really want to go to China. They have a different alphabet, too. Here's the map of Shanghai. I had one of Beijing, but I lost it. Here, we can take a look at it on the big map."

Natalie followed as he walked over to the large map of the world and traced his finger along China. The map was so cool. She could not believe Phillip and his father had made it.

Natalie moved in for a closer look. There were so many different cities detailed on it. If she looked real close, she could almost see the little roads and pathways between cities.

Natalie blinked. That can't be, she thought. She leaned closer. One little city moved into focus. She couldn't tell which one. "Wow," she breathed. Little buildings on the map were starting to appear.

This is strange, she thought.

"Are you all right?" Phillip's question came from far away.

"I can almost see…" She sounded so faint. There was movement on the map now. The buildings were getting bigger. It looked like the city was rising. "What's happening?" she asked incredulously.

Her hand reached out on its own to the map. As her fingers touched the parchment, a familiar feeling crept over her. One she had been fighting since it first came to her, slowly at first, then with growing power.

"No," she whispered.

"Natalie? What's wrong?" She could barely hear Phillip's question now. She tried to look at him, but she could not move; that feeling was too strong. It washed over her, pulled her under, and she was helpless as Phillip and the world around her faded away.

It was not dark, nor was it light. It was…blank.

The air pillowed around her like a float on water. She tried to fight it. Sometimes she could fight it, but this time it was too powerful.

Something opened and unfurled, inside and all around her. Her head spun and she would have gasped if she could. There was no pain, but nothing was her own.

Then she felt something else: an awareness creeping behind her consciousness, like fire crinkling along the edges of a piece of paper, working its way in.

No, she thought, I don't want to know!

There was no way to stem it. It filled her, working its way through expanded spaces she did not realize she had. She knew things she should not know, but somehow, something was happening to her, and she did *know*.

A distant voice she recognized as her own spoke.

"Phillip, your father's alive."

Chapter Three

$\mathcal{T}$he sun was beginning to set, its last rays peeking behind grayish clouds, when Natalie finally raised her head from her pillow. Serena had checked in on her earlier, but Natalie had refused to look up, blocking out everything Serena had tried to say or do.

There was nothing anyone could do.

Natalie rolled over and faced the ceiling. This last incident had been worse than any of the others. She had lost all sense of what she was doing. It was as if something else had taken over her mind and body.

What was she going to do?

The doorbell rang. Natalie did not move; there was no reason for her to move ever again.

Voices murmured. She recognized Mrs. Stone, and then her mother addressing Phillip. She buried her head in her pillow. Just the people she did not want to see.

Her mother and Mrs. Stone continued to talk, their conversation muffled. Natalie's thoughts wandered. What did it mean, what she had said to Phillip earlier? Why did it have to come from her? Was there anything she could do to stop this? She did not want to have to deal with it. She was a freak.

A rustling sound interrupted her thoughts. She looked over at the door leading to the balcony and froze in surprise. Phillip's face peeked in at her.

"Natalie," he called, "let me in!"

Natalie bolted upright. "What are you doing out there? Are you crazy?"

"Your mom said you weren't talking to anyone, and that it probably wasn't a good time to bother you, but I had to," Phillip said. "Please let me talk to you."

Natalie shook her head. "I don't want to talk," she said tearfully. "I don't want to talk about anything."

"Could you at least let me in?" Phillip asked. "I'd rather not climb back down."

Natalie rose from the bed and walked over to the door to open it. As Phillip entered, Natalie switched on a desk lamp. She sat in her chair and watched him warily. Was he going to try to make her talk about what happened?

"Do you want anything to drink?" she asked.

Phillip brushed off his jeans. "No, I'm okay. Could I just sit here for a second? That was a hard climb." Without waiting for an answer, he plopped down on the floor. "Gotta catch my breath."

For a while they sat there, Phillip's breathing the only sound in the room.

"Does your mom know you climbed up here?" Natalie finally asked.

"No. When your mom said you weren't coming out of your room, I told Mom I'd head home. I actually was headed home when I got the idea to try your balcony." He grimaced. "Didn't know it was going to be a hard climb, but once you're halfway there, there's no going back."

"I can't believe you climbed up," Natalie said.

"I know, right? Like I said, I really wanted to talk to you."

Natalie was silent. Phillip sat for a moment, then got up and walked around the room. Natalie watched him peruse the pictures on her bookshelf. They were mostly pictures of her and Serena; she didn't have pictures of friends. There was one picture, though, that caught Phillip's attention.

"Hey," he said, "this is a picture of when we went on that picnic."

The picture was one of Natalie's favorites. She, Serena, Phillip and Mr. and Mrs. Stone were sitting in the park on a wide blanket with big baskets of food and drink between them. The day had been beautiful and the smiles in the picture were genuine. It had been a fun day. One of the last ones she could remember with the Stones before Mr. Stone had disappeared and Phillip had become withdrawn.

Phillip picked up the picture and contemplated it silently, as if absorbing the happier times caught in the photo.

"It seems like a long time ago," he said. His voice was low and far away. "I really miss him."

The look in his eyes made Natalie drop hers. Please don't make me, she thought.

But Phillip did not say anything. He set the picture down, and quiet settled into the room.

"Wanna see my pocket knife?" Phillip finally asked. "It's really cool."

"Sure," Natalie said.

Phillip sat on the bed by Natalie's chair and pulled something silver out of his jeans pocket. He held it out to Natalie.

"That doesn't look like a knife," Natalie said.

"Haven't you ever seen a pocket knife? All the stuff's inside. Look." Phillip pulled at the knife. Little blades, bigger blades, scissors, even a corkscrew came out.

"Wow, that's really cool!"

"Yeah, it is, isn't it?" Phillip pulled out another section. "There's even a screwdriver. Here, you can have a look." He handed it to Natalie. "You can do just about anything with a knife like this."

"You can't comb your hair with it," Natalie said.

Phillip grinned. "Sure you can. Pull that." He pointed to a section on the knife. Natalie pulled at it and out popped a small comb.

"No way!" she exclaimed. It was really skinny and not much use, but nevertheless, it was a comb. "What can you comb with this, squirrels?"

"I can comb my hair just fine." Phillip took the knife and ran the comb a little awkwardly through his hair. "Yours is just too long."

"I guess. Where did you get it?"

"My father gave it to me. He was planning on taking me camping so I could use it." Phillip slowly pushed the sections back into his knife. "The thing is this," he said softly, "if you know anything about my dad, if there's a chance he's alive somewhere and needs help, I just have to know."

"I don't know anything." Natalie cried. "I swear I don't."

"But what you said earlier," Phillip persisted, "back at my house."

"Stop it!" Natalie put her hands over her ears. "Stop it, please!" She put her head down to block out the sight of Phillip. "Please go away."

She felt Phillip get up and move away quickly. She kept her head low and her hands over her ears. Frightening thoughts she had chased away earlier were trying to come back, and she could not let them. She scrunched her eyes tight and felt tears squeeze from them and trickle down her cheeks.

I'm not going to think about it, I'm not going to think about it, she thought. Please let Phillip go away.

Thoughts pressed along the blockade around her mind. She buttressed against them until they eased, and the panic ebbed away. She uncovered her ears slowly and took a deep breath. She felt a tentative tap on her shoulder and looked up, surprised.

Phillip was still in the room, his face pale. "I'm sorry, Natalie. I won't bother you anymore. I just didn't want to have to climb down. Are you okay?"

"Yes," Natalie mumbled.

"The thing is, Mom's gonna be mad if she finds out I climbed up here. Can you help me sneak out?"

Natalie nodded. She was anxious for Phillip to leave. She got up, and they went to the door. Natalie opened it a crack. Serena and Mrs. Stone's murmuring carried up the stairs.

"I think they're in the living room," Natalie said. "You'll have to go through the kitchen door."

Phillip nodded. They crept down the hallway to the stairwell.

"Be careful," Natalie whispered, "the stairs creak. Stay as far left to the wall as possible."

Phillip moved to the left behind Natalie, and they made their way slowly down the stairs. Suddenly, Phillip grabbed her shoulder.

"What?" Natalie asked.

Phillip put a finger to his lips. "Listen," he mouthed.

Snippets of Serena and Mrs. Stone's conversation floated up the stairwell. Natalie strained to hear.

"What about Phillip?" Serena asked. "Has he started showing any signs?"

Natalie looked at Phillip. Phillip shook his head and shrugged. They edged their way further down the stairs.

"Not yet," Mrs. Stone was saying, "but there's something there. I can't quite put my finger on it, but I think it's just a matter of time." Her voice softened. "He takes after his father."

"Which means you'll have your hands full soon," Serena said. The two women laughed. "I'll work on Natalie," Serena continued. "I'm sorry, Janet."

"These things can't be rushed," Mrs. Stone said. "And it will give me time to figure out how to keep Phillip from running off in search of his father."

"Do you think he'll be all right?"

"I think so," Mrs. Stone said. "I just wish he weren't so withdrawn. He's had to grow up quickly. Sometimes he seems like a little man. And he misses his father."

Natalie snuck a glance at Phillip. His jaw was tight, his attention focused on the conversation.

"I don't know, Janet," Serena said, "I don't like what I'm sensing. With everything that's happened...there's something in the air, I don't know what. I'm nervous about that circus."

"Maybe the circus is nothing," Mrs. Stone said. "Maybe it's just passing through."

"I hope so," Serena said, "but I just have this feeling..." She trailed off. "We've worked so hard to protect what we have here. The last thing we need is something that might draw attention."

Natalie shifted uneasily. This was getting weird. Phillip nodded and motioned to move on. They made their way down to the dining room and passed through to the kitchen. Natalie eased the door open and walked through with Phillip.

When they got outside she asked, "What were they talking about? Do you know what they meant by signs?"

"No," Phillip said, "I sure haven't noticed anything. Has your mom said anything to you about the circus?"

"No, nothing. What are we protecting ourselves from?"

"I don't know. It's all pretty weird."

They stood awkwardly on the lawn as the cool shade of evening washed over them.

"Are you sure you're okay now?" Phillip asked.

The question made Natalie uncomfortable. "Yes. Sorry I freaked out on you."

Phillip was quiet. He looked up at the stars gathering in the sky. "Don't worry about it. I'm sorry, too. Just," he paused for a moment, as if weighing his words, "if you get any more information, will you please let me know?"

Natalie winced and concentrated on smoothing the grass with her shoe. The last thing she wanted was to get more information.

Phillip sighed. "Okay. Well, I'd better get going. See you later, Natalie."

"Bye, Phillip," she replied.

Natalie watched as Phillip edged his way around the side of the house and walked away. He was the closest thing she had to a friend, but she could not do what he was asking.

Feeling a heavy weight in her chest, she turned to look at the house. Through the living room window, she could see her mother and Mrs. Stone talking. Both looked worried. What did they mean earlier, Natalie wondered.

Chapter Four

*T*he circus was in town!

Natalie took in the fall scenery and smiled as she and her mother walked towards Morton's Field. It was another perfect day! Classes had ended yesterday for fall break, and she had a whole week to enjoy, school-free. There was a buzz of excitement in the air as they made their way to the circus.

Morton's Field sat right behind Natalie's house, and it had been so exciting to see the trucks roll in and to see the tents rise like inflated balloons as the circus prepared to open. From her window, Natalie had witnessed all the different animals going through their exercises, and had watched the performers rehearse their routines. It had all looked like so much fun!

"Someone's excited." Serena's expression was indulgent as Natalie skipped along beside her.

"Mom, isn't it great?" Natalie said. "I can't wait to see those elephants! They've got a baby one, and he can sit up and everything. Can we get some cotton candy? I want to see the pretty ladies riding their horses. Ohh, and the man who tames tigers. That one looks really scary!"

"Whoa!" Serena said. "We've got a lot to see today, don't we?"

"Mom," Natalie said, shaking her head, "how are we going to fit in everything we want to do into just one day?"

"Good thing the circus is here for a week!"

The sounds of the circus greeted them as they approached the entrance. Circus people called out everywhere, entreating people to see their varied shows; kids laughed and yelled, begging their parents for cotton candy, caramel corn and snow cones; an elephant trumpeted in the distance, and wild applause followed. Everywhere, people were smiling.

"You look like you could burst with excitement," someone said behind them.

Natalie and Serena turned around as Mrs. Stone and Phillip caught up with them. Mrs. Stone smiled at Natalie. "It's a great day for the circus, isn't it?" Natalie nodded happily.

"The weather certainly agrees with you," Serena said to Mrs. Stone, whose cheeks and eyes were bright and merry.

Mrs. Stone laughed. "It's been pretty busy, and poor Phillip and I haven't had a chance to get out in a while. He's been at me all morning to hurry up." She rumpled Phillip's hair.

"Cut it out, Mom," Phillip grumbled.

"Hi, Phillip," Natalie said.

"Hi." Phillip was stoic, as usual, but for some reason, it did not bother her. The day was too nice, and she could not keep her face from grinning. After a moment, he grinned back.

"That's what I like to see," Mrs. Stone said.

"Shall we head on in?" Serena asked.

"Yes!" Natalie yelled, jumping up and down. Serena and Mrs. Stone laughed, and even Phillip gave a chuckle as they joined the line at the entrance.

"What should we see first?" Natalie asked Phillip, as Serena and Mrs. Stone paid for their tickets.

"Um, I don't know. I guess the animals are always fun to look at."

"Oh, look!" Natalie pointed at a clown performing for some children. He had bright red hair and an even brighter blue and yellow outfit. He teased the children with a flower that squirted water. Natalie and Phillip laughed as the children screamed in delight.

"Come on," Phillip said. They made their way through the entrance onto the circus grounds. "Let's go look at the elephants."

Natalie nodded. "There's a baby elephant. I'm dying to see him!"

"I wanna see the big ones. Sometimes they let you take a ride on them," Phillip said.

"Do they really?"

"The elephants pick you up with their trunks and everything," Phillip said.

"That would be so cool! Let's go!"

"Don't stray too far," Serena called out.

The different attractions flashed by as they ran through the circus. A big carousel circled around carrying colorful horses and sleighs. Concession stands served sno-cones, buttered popcorn and cotton candy. Circus people, costumed in bright-colored outfits, waved to the people. Then there were the tents! They rose over the attractions, shading the audiences that sat underneath, waiting for the shows to start. Everywhere, people talked and laughed. Natalie saw a little baby crying over a spilled ice-cream cone, its mother crooning soothingly as she tried to wipe the baby's shirt.

"Step right up kids! Come see the largest lady in the world!"

Natalie and Phillip stopped in front of a man dressed in bright blue pants, a red shirt and a purple top coat. "A more beautiful woman you will never see—all four hundred and fifty pounds of her!"

"Wow!" Phillip said.

"We'd love to, sir," Natalie said, "but we really want to see the elephants."

"Ah, yes," the man replied, "the elephants! They're right up there past the main tent."

"Great!" Phillip said. "Thanks, sir!"

"Come back later and see the largest woman in the world!" the man roared.

"We will!" Natalie and Phillip yelled back.

They ran through the crowds to the elephant attraction. An elephant lumbered around the corral, the wrinkled gray of its head towering over the line of eager children who were waiting to ride. The elephant uncurled its long trunk, trumpeted a greeting and waved to the people. A padded box lined with ornate material sat on its back.

"Wow," Natalie said, "it's big!"

"Let's get in line," Phillip said.

The first two children in line trotted over to the elephant as it got down on its knees. The handler set up a ladder, and they climbed into the box on the elephant's back. The elephant shifted and pulled to its feet. The children squealed, and grabbed frantically at sides of the box.

"They don't look like they're having fun," Natalie said.

"Just wait," Phillip said.

The elephant shuffled forward, ambling its way around the pen. The children continued to hold on for dear life, but soon, they started to smile. Their heads bobbed around excitedly as they looked around.

Natalie heard one of the children, a little blond girl, say, "You can see a lot of stuff up here!" Both girls squealed in excitement.

"See," Phillip grinned, "told you it was fun."

When their turn arrived, Natalie had to agree. It was scary when the elephant rose to its feet, but once they were up and going, it was exhilarating! The view from the elephant's back stretched far and all around, and the world felt like a different place.

"You're awfully quiet," Phillip said.

She nodded. "It's just so...peaceful up here." She stared at Phillip sitting behind her. He was leaning back against the box, a light breeze ruffling his hair. "You look really relaxed."

Phillip shrugged. "Yeah, I guess. I did this last time when I came with my dad."

Natalie swiveled back around. It was hard, feeling guilty about not helping Phillip with his father. If only the alternative were not so terrifying.

There was a tap on her shoulder. "Have you found out anything about what your mom and my mom were talking about the other night?" Phillip asked.

"No, have you?"

"No."

"Has anything, um, weird happened to you?" Natalie asked tentatively.

Phillip raised his eyebrows. "No, not yet."

"Not yet? You think something is going to happen?"

"I'm hoping something is going to happen," Phillip said.

Natalie stared at him in disbelief. "You're crazy! You don't know what you're talking about, Phillip. It's awful! It's just awful!"

Her voice must have risen because Phillip put a hand on her shoulder. "Hey, calm down. It's okay."

Natalie shifted back around. Her stomach was all shaky. She gripped the sides of the box.

"Are you okay?" Phillip asked.

"No," she said. "I don't understand. Why would you want it?"

"I'd use it to find my father," Phillip said. "You don't understand because you're just scared of what you can do."

Natalie did not have an answer. She *was* scared. More than that, she was terrified. She heard Phillip sigh and shift in his seat.

"You'd be scared too if it happened to you," she finally said. The air around them stilled. Phillip seemed to be holding his breath, waiting.

"It's like you're not you," she said. "Something's got hold of you, and it won't let you go. It makes you see things you don't want to see and tells you things you don't want to know. You don't know where it comes from, and you can't do anything to stop it. It's just doing what it wants with you." She drew in a breath, which was all raggedy and shaky, and the world had become a watery blur. "It's just a horrible feeling."

She tried to fight back the tears. Maybe she was scared and cowardly, but the least she could do was not cry. After a moment, she felt Phillip's hand touch her shoulder, squeezing it. It just made it worse. Her breath came out in a big gasp followed by a stream of smaller ones. Her shoulders shook with each breath. Great, she thought, in despair.

Arms came around her, uncertain and clumsy. She felt Phillip's head on her shoulder, his hair against her cheek. Her sobs settled in surprise.

She did not know how long they sat like that, but all of a sudden, her stomach dropped. She looked up as Phillip said, "Whoa!" and noticed that the world around them was moving. She struggled to get her bearings, and then realized the elephant had lowered to the ground. The ride was over.

"You kids all right?" The man handling the elephant waited for them, a curious expression on his face.

Natalie was a little dazed but said, "Yes, sir." Phillip nodded.

"Did the ride scare you?" the man asked. She and Phillip shook their heads. The man shrugged and helped them off the elephant's back.

When Natalie and Phillip got back on the ground, they walked out the exit. For a while they said nothing. Then Phillip stopped walking. Natalie stopped as well, but was not sure what to say. She and Phillip faced each other, and then for some inexplicable reason, she giggled. It was a strange thing to do, but once she started, she could not stop. After a couple of seconds, Phillip started to laugh as well. Soon they were both laughing uncontrollably. People's heads turned in their direction, but she could not help herself.

"Oh, man," Phillip gasped, wiping tears of laughter from his eyes. He tried to get hold of himself, but when he looked at her, they burst into laughter again.

"I can't stop," Natalie said. It took a few seconds, but between giggles and hiccups, she and Phillip managed to get their laughter under control. They gazed at each other again, smiling.

"Are you okay?" Phillip asked.

"Yes," she answered. And to her surprise, she was.

Chapter Five

W hat do you kids want to do next?" Mrs. Stone asked. "Or did you want to spend the rest of the day here eating?"

Natalie and Phillip looked up from their sundaes. They were seated at a picnic table in a food tent. Mrs. Stone and Serena smiled.

"You're both covered with toppings," Serena said. Natalie wiped her chin with her napkin. Phillip used his sleeve.

"Phillip!" Mrs. Stone exclaimed.

"Sorry," Phillip muttered.

"Thank goodness for washing machines," Mrs. Stone sighed.

"I'm not sure what to do next," Natalie said. "What haven't we seen yet?" she asked Phillip.

"Let's see," Phillip said, thinking. "We saw the tiger show."

"That was so cool, the way they jumped through those fire rings!" Natalie exclaimed.

"I know—right!" Phillip said. "Then we saw the exhibition with the horses. That was pretty cool, too."

"You just liked those pretty ladies," Natalie said.

Phillip blushed. "Did not! It was just neat how they could do all those tricks on the horses."

"Yeah, sure," Natalie laughed.

"You pick the next thing, then," Phillip retorted.

"Hmmm," Natalie said, "what should we do? We saw the House of Mirrors, and the man who did all those tricks with the knives."

"That was really cool, too," Phillip said. "I can't wait to try that."

"Think again, young man!" Mrs. Stone said.

"Aw c'mon, Mom!" Phillip said.

Mrs. Stone gave him a stern shake of her head. Phillip bowed his head over his sundae and ate another bite.

"I'm already tired, listening to everything we just did," Serena said. "Aren't you kids tired yet?"

"Oh, no, Mom," Natalie said, "we haven't seen that much at all."

"What about all those rides you kids were on? And all those games you played?"

"That was hardly anything at all," Natalie said. "Hey, what about the magic show?"

"Yeah," Phillip said, "let's do that one!"

Serena checked the schedule. "Ah, we're in luck. The next show starts in 15 minutes. Hurry up with your sundaes."

Natalie and Phillip finished their ice cream, and they all headed over to one of the big tents. The sun was starting to go down, and the lights of the circus had come on. A line had already formed in front of the tent with a big sign that read:

The Magical World of the Great Beausoleil

"Step right up!" A man wearing a black suit with a top hat stood outside the tent. He beckoned the crowds. "Step right up and prepare to be amazed and enchanted by the magic of the Great Beausoleil! Right this way please." He pulled aside a section of the tent and waved people inside.

"I wonder what we'll see," Natalie said to Phillip as they entered the tent.

"Probably the usual stuff—pulling rabbits out of a hat, sawing a lady in half."

"No way! How does he do that?"

Phillip shrugged. "Magic."

"Yeah, right," Natalie said. "Mom, how does he...."

She broke off mid-sentence. Her mother and Mrs. Stone had just passed into the tent, and both of them had stopped short. Mrs. Stone took in a sharp breath of air that was almost a gasp. Serena put a hand on her arm, as if in warning. They scanned the tent quickly, and a look passed between them.

"Mom, what's wrong?" Natalie asked, but then she felt it. She did not know what it was, but it was something in the air, like a light buzz. Phillip tensed beside her, as if he felt it, too. But they seemed to be the only ones; everyone else in the tent chatted away and went about their business.

"Mom?" Natalie said, alarmed.

Serena looked down at her and smiled. Her blue eyes gazed directly into Natalie's. Almost immediately, the weird feeling faded.

"Nothing's wrong, sweetheart." Serena bent to whisper in Natalie's ear. "Just feeling a bit of the magic of this place, I think."

"Stop teasing me," Natalie murmured. Serena kissed the top of her head.

As they walked towards the seating area, Natalie glanced back at Phillip. He was walking with his mother, her hand on his shoulder. His eyes locked with Natalie's, and she knew that the weird feeling, though gone now, had not been a part of her imagination.

"You're not going to freak out, are you?" Phillip asked her, when they had taken their seats.

"Nope," Natalie replied. She looked at the stage. Heavy, red velvet curtains trimmed with gold tassels lined the front. A small area for the band sat off to the side.

"Well, that's a first," Phillip said.

"Oh, just watch the show!"

Thankfully, the lights dimmed, and they all settled into silence.

Natalie surveyed the people in the audience. "Hey look," she said in surprise, "Mrs. Blaine is here!"

Mrs. Blaine sat in the last row near the aisle. She wore a black dress with a high neckline, which was out of place amongst the sea of jeans and shirts. She had set her cane against the side of her seat, and her ramrod posture only enhanced her odd formality.

"Wow," Phillip said, "you don't see her out very often."

Mrs. Blaine's head swiveled to catch Natalie's gaze. Natalie gave a jolt of surprise. Could she hear them? Don't be stupid, she told herself, she's all the way in the back row.

Mrs. Blaine gave a brief bow of her head in greeting. She acknowledged Serena with a smile, and Serena waved to her in return.

"Mrs. Blaine doesn't seem like the kind of person who would like the circus," Natalie said to her mother.

"Who doesn't like the circus, sweetheart?" Serena said.

"I guess." Natalie snuck another glance at Mrs. Blaine, but darned if her head did not turn to catch her again! Natalie whipped around to face the front.

A spotlight illuminated the middle of the stage. The heavy velvet curtains parted in the middle and rose as a drum rolled louder and louder. Excitement rose in Natalie's chest. Suddenly, the sound of cymbals crashed, and a man stepped out from the curtains and into the spotlight.

The audience clapped as the man took a deep bow. He was tall and broad and had a mustache. His suit jacket was deep red with tails, and he wore it with a checkered bow tie, black pants and a top hat. The smile on his face was cheerful, although Natalie noticed a darker tinge under his eyes, and a slightly weary air about him.

"Allow me to introduce myself," he said now. "I am the Great Beausoleil." The audience clapped again as he made a sweeping flourish with his arm.

"I want to thank you all for coming to my show. You will not be disappointed, for tonight you will experience amazing feats of magic." As he spoke, he held out his hand, palm up, and out of his palm shot a burst of flame. Natalie gasped with the audience in surprise. The flame flickered over his palm, suspended, as if waiting for the Great Beausoleil's next command.

"Prepare for your eyes to be dazzled," he said, bringing his other hand over the flame and covering his palm, "by things that cannot be explained by ordinary means." He rubbed his two hands together and separated them with a flourish. The flame was gone. He pulled his sleeves back and held his palms up to show there was nothing to light the flame.

"Wow," Natalie whispered, as the audience clapped.

The Great Beausoleil took a handkerchief out of his pocket and unfolded it, holding it up between his two hands and showing the front and back to the audience. "Your eyes will see one thing," he said, taking the handkerchief and covering one of his hands with it, "but the next thing they see will be beyond comprehension." The handkerchief shifted and wiggled. Beausoleil whipped away the handkerchief, revealing a dove, fluttering delicately in his palm.

The audience applauded. A woman stepped out from the wings of the stage, wearing a short, black and red sequined outfit with a large, matching headpiece. She carried a small bird cage.

"That's a large headpiece," Natalie heard her mother murmur. Indeed, the piece looked to be at least a third of the size of the lady. It was heavily sequined with long feathers running down the back.

"It looks like she's wearing a red and black peacock," Natalie whispered to her mother. Her mother's mouth twitched as she nodded.

The headpiece must have been as heavy as it looked. The lady wobbled uncertainly under its weight, and it did not help that her heels were high. She tottered over to Beausoleil.

The audience twittered at the unexpected sight. Beausoleil's smile froze. He moved to assist his assistant, but every time he moved in one direction, she tottered in the other. The dove quivered in Beausoleil's hand.

Natalie watched the strange dance between Beausoleil, his assistant and the fluttering bird. The audience had gone completely silent.

In a flurry of wings and feathers, the dove shot from Beausoleil's hand into the assistant's headpiece.

"Augh!" the assistant screamed. The bird cage fell with a loud clatter. The assistant waved her hands wildly around her head as the bird's wings slapped against the giant headpiece. "Get it off me! Get it off me!"

Natalie realized her jaw had dropped. She looked around the audience. Jaws everywhere had dropped as well. Everyone watched, silent and mesmerized, as the giant headpiece slowly tilted backwards.

Oh no, Natalie thought.

The assistant stopped screaming. Her arms made circular motions as she tried to pull against the weight of the headpiece.

"Whoa, whoa!" she said.

Beausoleil, who had frozen in surprise when the bird flew out of his hand, gave a start and reached out to grab the assistant's hand just as one heel left the floor. The audience gasped as the assistant balanced on the remaining heel. Then Beausoleil's grip asserted itself, and the assistant straightened, headpiece, flapping bird and all. The audience sighed in relief.

Inexorably, the headpiece tipped towards Beausoleil.

Uh, oh, thought Natalie.

The assistant's eyes widened. She moved her head and tilted the headpiece to the side. The weight pulled her along, and she tottered with it in her traitorous heels.

Natalie's head moved back and forth, watching Beausoleil and his assistant struggle to the side and then backwards. It was like waiting for disaster to unfold. To her horror, a giggle built up inside her. It would not have been a good thing to laugh, but she must have not been alone, because a snort of laughter broke from somewhere in the audience.

Once one laugh escaped, the rest of the audience could not hold back. A roar of laughter rolled like a wave through the tent as Beausoleil and his assistant jockeyed to balance the heavy headpiece.

It now tilted towards Beausoleil, its precarious height hovering. The assistant fought mightily against its fall, but this time, the balance had tipped too far. A groan escaped her lips.

"Oh, noooo!"

Beausoleil put out his other arm to steady her, but it was too late. The assistant's heels lost its grip on the floor, and she, the headpiece, and the flapping dove toppled onto Beausoleil.

The people in the audience gasped, but even their sympathies could not overcome the comic sight, and everyone laughed as Beausoleil's legs squirmed under the weight of his assistant and her magnificent headpiece.

A stage hand and two audience members ran on stage to help untangle the mess. It took some doing, none of which was helped by the dove, which kept making angry nosedives at the crew, but after several moments, all parties were on their feet, and the headpiece safely removed and placed on the floor. It was, in fact, almost half the size of the assistant.

The manager stepped onstage and whispered furiously to Beausoleil who shook his head. Then the manager, the stagehand, the assistant, and Beausoleil left the stage, the assistant and the stagehand carrying the headpiece. The audience members who had assisted made their way back to their seats amidst appreciative applause.

"What do we do now?" Natalie asked her mother. Phillip and his mother leaned over as well. Phillip had a smile on his face.

"We already got our money's worth," he said.

"Phillip!" his mother said. "That's not very nice." But her mouth struggled to keep her amusement at bay.

Just then, the manager stepped onto the stage, commanding everyone's attention.

"Ladies and gentleman," the manager said, "we apologize for the disruption. I'm afraid that our assistant is unable to help The Great Beausoleil at this time." He gave an almost imperceptible glare to someone offstage. "Given that The Great Beausoleil needs help for some of his other wonderful feats of magic, I'm afraid we will not be able to show you that part of his show.

"However, we do not want you to leave The Magical World of The Great Beausoleil disappointed, so The Great Beausoleil has graciously,"—at this the manager gave another glare offstage— "consented to show you a feat of magic so special, that only a select few have seen it. Just think, ladies and gentlemen, you will be privy to a piece of magic never before seen in a public arena. You may not have realized it when you came here tonight, or when you witnessed the rather unfortunate spectacle up here only a few minutes ago, but, ladies and gentlemen, tonight is your lucky night. Tonight, I present to you, The Great Beausoleil and His Living Doll!"

Chapter Six

With a wave of his arm, the manager gestured to the right of the stage, and exited left. Natalie clapped with the audience. The manager's introduction had been so exciting. A living doll!

"Have you ever seen that kind of trick before?" she whispered to Phillip.

"No," he whispered back, "I've never even heard of it."

The audience continued to applaud, but Beausoleil still had not made his entrance. The clapping died down, and the audience waited with anticipation.

After a few moments, Beausoleil stepped onto the stage. His expression was grim, almost doubtful. In his arms he carried a large doll.

"Wow," Natalie breathed.

The doll was beautiful. It stood almost two feet tall with golden hair that fell in waved ringlets down its shoulders. The curls were decorated by a bright, sky-blue ribbon, its color a perfect match for the doll's eyes which were cat-shaped and framed by long, dark lashes. Its skin was like a porcelain peach, complete with the rosy hues on its cheeks.

"What a beautiful dress," Mrs. Stone exclaimed.

The dress was a satiny white, patterned with blue, pink and green flowers. A blue bow encircled the waist. The dress was light, colorful, and looking at it, Natalie felt as if she were caught outside on a sunny spring day. The dress accentuated the graceful form of the doll.

"Mom, it's so beautiful!" Natalie looked at her mother who was staring intently at the doll. She could not blame her. Once you looked at the doll, it was hard to tear your eyes away.

The Great Beausoleil moved to the center of the stage. He had not spoken. His shoulders were heavy and his face solemn as he set the doll on the floor. He faced the audience.

"May I have a couple of volunteers?" he asked.

Natalie was on her feet. She stepped over Serena's legs and moved quickly into the aisle before anyone else could lay claim to the opportunity of seeing the doll up close.

"Natalie!"

She barely heard her mother's call. The faces in the audience were a blur as they turned to stare at her charging for the stage.

She ran up the stairs to The Great Beausoleil and the doll. When she reached them, she stopped short.

Something hit her from behind. She stumbled forward from the impact, but someone grabbed her arms, holding her back.

It was Phillip. She had run up so quickly she did not realize that he, too, had run up to volunteer.

"Sorry," he muttered. "Why did you have to stop suddenly like that?"

Beausoleil's eyes blinked at her and then Phillip, as if surprised. "Well, it looks like you two are the ones."

The audience laughed. Natalie scanned the audience for her mother. Serena did not look happy. She was on her feet, as if she were ready to run up onstage herself and pull Natalie back to her seat. Mrs. Stone had moved from her chair to sit next to Serena. She did not look happy either. Serena slowly sat back down.

"If you two could please have a good look at this doll," Beausoleil said. "Does it look to you like there's a real person hiding inside a costume?"

Natalie bent to look at the doll. The blue eyes, beautiful and blank, stared into the distance. Natalie peered into the eyes to see if there were any peep holes.

"Do you see anything?" Phillip asked her. He was searching the doll's face as well. "I can't see any holes for breathing or anything."

Natalie shook her head. Up close she could see the perfection of the porcelain skin. Unable to help herself, she reached out to touch it.

"That's it," Beausoleil said, "don't be afraid to really get in there. I want you to be able to prove that this is a real doll. How does her skin feel?"

"It's hard," Natalie said. It was strange that such beautiful-looking skin could be so hard to the touch.

Phillip examined the doll's arms. He tried to bend them, but they only moved at the shoulder sockets; there were no joints in the elbows or wrists.

Natalie checked the doll's legs. They did not bend at the knees. For such a beautiful doll, it was pretty stiff. It was almost disappointing.

"Do either of you think anyone could be hiding inside?" Beausoleil asked.

"No," Phillip said, "it would be pretty hard." Natalie shook her head.

"Thank you for your help," Beausoleil said. "Now if you two could please stand here to the side. I will need to call on your assistance again in a moment."

Natalie nodded and moved with Phillip. It was exciting to think she would be required to help out some more.

Beausoleil stood to the side of the doll. He placed his hand on the doll's head and bowed his head. Quietude settled over him.

The air crackled. It made the hair on Natalie's arms stand up on end. She felt Phillip fidgeting beside her as she stared, spellbound, at Beausoleil and the doll.

Beausoleil had not moved. He was so still; it seemed that he had faded into himself.

Slowly, so slowly Natalie had to blink her eyes to make sure she was not imagining it, the doll's skin seemed to soften. It was as if its hardened porcelain gave way to something warm and pulsating underneath.

"Whoa," Phillip said under his breath.

Something was happening with the doll. The air around it had started to hum.

Then it moved.

The doll's head tilted with a creak. It lifted its arm with a squeak and began to look at its hand. Its arm could now bend at the elbow. Its movements were slow, jerky.

People in the audience gasped.

The doll's head moved at the sound. Everyone fell silent as the doll's scrutiny shifted from its hand to the audience. It surveyed the sea of faces, its head twitching from side to side. Its face showed little emotion, yet when it gazed up at Beausoleil, its voice was plaintive.

"Papa?" it asked.

There was a ripple in the audience. Natalie tore her eyes from the doll and looked around. People were erect in their seats. All eyes were wide and transfixed on the doll. Natalie turned her attention to the stage.

The Great Beausoleil bent and gathered the doll close. His lips whispered near the doll's ear. The doll betrayed no emotion, but its head tilted again, as if in acknowledgement. Beausoleil straightened, holding the doll's hand. He led the doll forward. Natalie noticed the doll's knees bent as it walked, although its steps were stiff and clunky. They stopped at the front of the stage, surveying the audience. Then, without fanfare, Beausoleil spoke.

"Ladies and gentlemen, I present to you my finest creation. A beautiful doll, come to life."

The doll stepped out from Beausoleil's side and curtsied. The movement was lurching, unnatural, but it was more fluid than the doll's earlier movements. The doll's ability to bend its knees and elbows was even more apparent as well. Moment by moment, it seemed that the doll was becoming more and more supple.

"It's a mechanical doll!" someone scoffed from the audience.

"I can assure you it is not," Beausoleil replied. He gestured over to Natalie and Phillip. "Would you two please come forward?" As they stepped to the fore, he said, "Please take a look, and see if you can find anything mechanical about her."

Natalie bent down with Phillip to examine the doll. It was unlike anything she had ever seen. Whereas before the skin had been perfect porcelain, it now looked warmed over, almost like real skin, but not. It was eerie. Eerier still was the way the doll's eyes followed her. Natalie felt its gaze as she inspected the doll's arms and legs, and checked around its dress for anything that might explain its ability to move and talk. She straightened up, finding nothing, only to discover the doll peering at her.

Its eyes were as unnerving as the porcelain. Their color was still a beautiful blue, and they stirred in their mannequin-like sockets. At the same time, there was something more animate about them than inanimate. Their movement, as they took in Natalie, was continuous and deliberate. And they seemed to *see* Natalie. Natalie's stomach churned at the doll's direct gaze.

The doll's head tilted, as if observing.

"What's your name?" it asked.

Natalie's insides reared in surprise. The doll's voice was distant, as if played off a recorder, yet the question was aimed at her. Phillip leaned in quickly to catch where it was coming from. He checked around the doll's head and neck and then shook his head.

"No speakers," he said.

The doll waited for an answer. Creepy, Natalie thought. She wished she did not have to answer, but the doll continued to wait. The silence in the theater was deafening.

"Natalie," she muttered.

"Natalie," the doll said. "That's sooo pretty!" The words were like a sigh.

The doll smiled. Natalie had not realized it could, but sure enough, the corners of its lips curved upwards, and its eyes crinkled around the edges. It was the most human it had appeared so far, and Natalie was mesmerized. A light-headed feeling crept over her as she and the doll regarded each other.

The doll's hand moved then. It rose slowly from its side and held itself out to her.

"Will you be my friend?" it asked.

Natalie's thoughts swirled. She wanted to take the hand; she did not want to take the hand; she should definitely not take the hand, but what was the problem? What if she did?

Her hand moved up from her side.

"Natalie!"

Serena's call was like a giant hand, sweeping through and clearing the cobwebs of her muddled thoughts. It took Natalie a moment to focus, but when she did, she saw her mother had risen to her feet.

Serena gave a small shake of her head in warning. *Don't take the doll's hand!*

Natalie shook off the remaining cobwebs. What had come over her? She turned back to the doll just in time to feel the doll slip its hand into hers.

What an odd feeling, she thought. There was no warm flesh to hold, and yet the hand felt pliable, as if something living pulsated just beyond the cold feel of porcelain.

"Natalie!"

Her mother's voice was a worried cry now. Natalie moved to pull her hand away, but the doll's fingers closed on hers.

Heat rose from her body and moved down her arm through her hand and into the doll. The doll's skin warmed to a blush of pink.

The doll's eyes widened. "Papa!" it cried.

"What..." Beausoleil gasped. "What's happening? This can't be happening!"

The doll was vibrating. At least Natalie thought it was vibrating. It was not moving, but something seemed to bubble inside it, like lava ready to erupt.

"NO!" screamed Beausoleil. He moved quickly and stepped in front of Natalie and the doll, blocking them from the audience. His hand grabbed the doll's arm, breaking its hold on Natalie. He seized the doll by its shoulders and steered it towards the back of the stage, out of view.

It had happened so fast. The stage swayed in front of Natalie's eyes. Then she realized she was the one swaying. Someone grabbed her.

"Honey?" It was her mother. "Natalie?"

She tried to answer, but a chasm had opened. The world was starting to go dark. She would be lost soon.

"Mom!" she called out. "Please, no more. Not again!"

The world swirled and went dark. She had fallen in.

Floating, she was floating. Thoughts and images and bits she did not recognize swirled about, flickering through her consciousness.

Something latched to her: knowledge she did not want. This knowledge was frightening. It was a heavy rock in the pit of her stomach. Or what she thought was her stomach. Nothing felt the way it usually did when she was in this place.

She spoke.

"They are stronger. They are coming. They will arrive."

Chapter Seven

"*I*'m telling you, I don't know what happened!"

"I don't buy that."

"You should ask your little girl what's going on because let me tell you, something happened with the doll tonight that shouldn't have, and it didn't come from me!"

"Keep my daughter out of this! I'll ask you again, why did you come here?"

The words came from a distance, but Natalie heard the heat behind them. It sounded like her mother and Beausoleil.

It had happened again. It seemed to happen often now, and there didn't seem to be anything she could do to stop it. She must have blacked out. Something soft cushioned her head and back.

Her lids were heavy, like weights over her eyes. She opened them. She did not know where she was, but it looked like part of another tent. Her section was swathed in heavy, red drapes and accented with gold-colored pillows. Like an Arabian room, she thought. She was lying on a cot of some kind, but it was covered with pillows and blankets and was quite comfortable considering it was just a cot.

"Hey," someone whispered.

It was Phillip. He was seated on an ottoman near the cot. "Shhhhh." He cocked his head towards the voices. They were on the other side of a thick curtain of material. Listen, his eyes said. She had to strain to hear, so she sat up on the cot to get a better sound.

"I came here to look for you." Beausoleil spoke now. "All of you."

"Why?" Serena asked. "Do you realize what you've done?"

"We've been hidden for a long time." It was Mrs. Stone speaking now. "We've worked hard to protect what we have."

"I'm sorry," Beausoleil said, "but you don't know what it's like out there. How can you all hide like this with everything that's going on?"

Natalie looked at Phillip. What was going on? Phillip shook his head.

"We have children we need to keep safe," Serena said.

"I had a wife and child to protect, too, but I didn't fare as well as you did."

There was a long pause. Finally Serena spoke.

"I know it's selfish to keep to ourselves like this..."

"You don't have to explain yourselves," Beausoleil interrupted. "I understand why you want to keep your family out of harm's way."

"We've suffered some of our own losses," Mrs. Stone said softly.

"Yes," Beausoleil said, "I know you have. I haven't come here to ruin what you have."

"Then why have you come?" someone said sharply.

A jolt went through Natalie. It was Mrs. Blaine!

"What's Mrs. Blaine doing there?" she asked Phillip.

"I don't know," Phillip said. "She was just there. Shhhhh!"

"I went into hiding myself after my wife and child..." Beausoleil's voice broke.

Natalie could not see what was happening, but her eyes welled up and became cloudy. Whatever they were talking about that had to do with *out there* was not good.

A sob broke from Beausoleil. It was a sob so deep it had no bottom, and it opened up a hole inside Natalie. Her insides crumpled and then filled with something sad—sadder than anything she had ever felt. And she sensed that whatever she was feeling, it was nowhere near the depths of what Beausoleil was experiencing now.

Phillip turned to her. The look in his eyes made her draw her breath. It was cavernous, filled with the same emotion as Beausoleil's sob. She saw that he knew what Beausoleil was feeling, understood it in a way she did not. He had suffered a loss at least as great as Beausoleil's, if not more, because Phillip did not know what had happened to his father.

There must have been something in her eyes because Phillip's expression changed into a scowl. His chin went up.

"We're getting answers," he hissed.

Natalie nodded. They strained to hear what else was being said.

There were no other sounds coming from the other section. Beausoleil must have collected himself. A few moments later he said, "Something has to be done about them. You know this. Your husband knew this."

"And he's gone because of it!" Mrs. Stone cried.

Phillip stiffened next to her, every muscle in his body homed in on what they would say next.

"Because he knew that you would not be safe forever. Because he knew the only way to keep you safe was to meet the danger head-on," Beausoleil said.

"He would want me to keep Phillip safe. It was something on which we both agreed," Mrs. Stone said.

"How long can you stay hidden like this?" Beausoleil asked. "Do you think you will always be safe here? You are all clearly very powerful. How long before they make it a point to find you and come after you?"

"How did you come to find us?" Mrs. Stone asked.

"I met your husband," Beausoleil said.

"Jack?" Mrs. Stone sounded shaken. "You saw Jack alive?"

"Yes."

Sobs came from Mrs. Stone. Phillip moved to get to his mother, his face a jumbled mass of emotions. Natalie grabbed hold of his arm.

"Don't you want to hear what they'll say?" she asked.

"What?" Phillip's expression was uncomprehending.

"Aren't you afraid they'll stop talking if you go in there?"

Phillip blinked at her in surprise. Natalie was also a little surprised. Why *was* she helping him?

"Isn't this what you want?" she asked, feeling a little cross. Phillip nodded. She let go of his arm.

"Are you feeling better?"

Natalie gasped. She and Phillip whipped around.

A girl had entered the tent behind them. I didn't even see an entrance there, Natalie thought. The tents had so much material!

"I'm sorry," the girl said softly, "I didn't mean to scare you. I just wanted to see if you were doing all right." She was around Natalie's age and wore jeans and an old sweater. Her hair was light, and her expression was shy, but her smile was warm and friendly. Natalie smiled in return. Phillip nodded, but shifted impatiently.

The girl waited for them to speak. They were stuck.

"I'm fine," Natalie said. "Thank you for asking."

"Oh, good," the girl said. "There was a lot of commotion when they brought you from the stage. Everyone was really worried."

"It was stupid," Natalie said, feeling somewhat embarrassed.

"What happened?" the girl asked.

How do you explain what happens to me, Natalie thought. She could not think of an answer, and her silence hung uncomfortably in the air.

"Natalie has fainting spells," Phillip blurted.

That was not an answer she would have given. She gave him a glare, but he gave a brusque shrug. What would you have said, his expression asked.

"I have fainting spells," Natalie said.

"Oh, you poor thing!" the girl said. "You must have a fragile disposition."

"What?" Natalie said. "I...no, no I don't. I don't know what's wrong." That, at least, was the truth.

"Oh, I'm sorry. I hope it's nothing serious."

"Yeah, me too," Natalie said.

There was another awkward lull before the girl said, "My name is Louisa. I'm the Great Beausoleil's daughter."

Beausoleil must have had two children, Natalie thought.

"I'm Natalie."

"I'm Phillip."

"Nice to meet you," Louisa said, with another warm smile.

"Louisa!" Beausoleil's head poked out from the other section. Phillip gave a little groan. There would be no informative conversation now. Beausoleil looked over the two of them. "We almost forgot you two were back here."

Serena, Mrs. Stone and Mrs. Blaine followed after Beausoleil. Mrs. Stone's eyes were a little red, but otherwise she was composed. Mrs. Blaine's face was stern, but there was nothing unusual about that.

Serena walked over to Natalie and put her hand on her head. "How are you feeling, darling?"

"Fine," Natalie mumbled.

The three ladies and Beausoleil considered Natalie for a few moments. They seemed to be collectively debating their next move with her. Natalie felt a bit like a butterfly pinned to a board.

"I'm okay, really!" Suddenly, she just wanted to be away from there. "Can we please go home, Mom?"

"Of course, sweetheart." Serena looked at the other adults. "We can talk some more later. I'd better get her home." She exchanged a glance with Mrs. Blaine, whose head moved in acknowledgment.

Natalie did not care much for that look. She did not know why, but she suspected it had to do with her.

"We'll see you later then," Mrs. Stone said. She hugged Natalie. "I hope you feel better, dear."

"See you later," Phillip said.

"Thank you for letting Natalie rest here," Serena said to Beausoleil and Louisa.

"It was no problem," Beausoleil said.

As Natalie and her mother moved to leave the tent, she heard Beausoleil say to Serena, "Please think about what I've said." His voice was low and urgent. Serena nodded curtly, put an arm around Natalie and steered her out of the tent.

Chapter Eight

The moon was full and high in the sky as Natalie and her mother departed the circus grounds. Natalie felt as though she had weights on her feet. It had been a long day, and although it had been fun earlier, it had turned into one she would rather forget.

The sounds of laughter and music from the circus faded as they walked. Under the bright moon, Natalie noticed a frown furrowed on her mother's face.

Serena put an arm across her shoulders. "You're awfully quiet," she said.

Natalie shrugged. Here it comes, she thought. But Serena said nothing. That was strange. Maybe her mother was just waiting until they got home. She did not know which was worse, her mother talking to her about things she did not want to talk about, or waiting for her to bring it up.

"It was quite a day, wasn't it?" Serena asked now. "At least you and Phillip seemed to be getting along well."

"I have fun with Phillip when he's not asking me too many questions," Natalie said cautiously.

Serena nodded. "Yes, I'm sure Phillip has a lot of questions for you. Do you want to talk about it?" Her tone was light, but Natalie sensed her mother testing the boundaries of her question.

Natalie sighed. No one would let her be.

"It's not like I can help him or anything." The words were out of Natalie's mouth before she could stop them.

Serena paused. Natalie clamped her mouth shut. It was a door she did not want to open, and here she'd gone and opened it.

"I don't want to talk about it," Natalie said. If there were a way to put up a stone wall with her voice, she would have done it. But Serena merely nodded, and they continued walking.

"I mean what's he going to do? Does he think he can go off and save his father or something?" Really, Natalie thought, this was getting out of hand! For some reason she could not seem to stop herself from talking about the very thing she did not want to talk about.

"Maybe Phillip is just looking for some hope," Serena said. "He misses his father very much. You'd miss me if I were gone, wouldn't you?"

Natalie stopped short. *Her mother gone like Phillip's dad?* The thought hit like a boulder, crashing into her and turning her whole world black. It was a feeling even worse than that horrible thing that took over her sometimes. Everything inside her started to shake.

"Don't say that," she cried.

"Oh, honey." Serena gathered her into her arms. "You don't have to be worried about that. Nothing is going to happen to me."

Phillip's father left him, though, Natalie thought. He did not want to but he felt he had to. She hugged her mother tighter.

"Do you believe me?" Serena asked.

"Yes." But even as Natalie said the word, her stomach twisted.

Serena pulled away and cupped Natalie's face between her hands, tilting it up to face her. Darkness cloaked the depths of her mother's eyes, but the brightness of the moon shone into Natalie's, revealing to her mother's penetrating gaze all the things she did not want to say or feel.

"Is there a reason you don't believe me?" her mother asked.

Natalie tried to pull her face away, but her mother's hold, though gentle, was firm.

"Sweetie, you have nothing to be afraid of."

Natalie ducked her head, and this time her mother released her. Natalie buried her head against her mother. She felt Serena's arms close around her, felt her breathe and exhale.

"It must have been pretty scary for you tonight," Serena whispered to her.

Natalie hesitated. "Why does everyone want me to talk about...things?" she asked softly. "They're so scary."

"Because we want to help. Because I want to help." Serena's breath rustled through her hair. "I don't like it when you're scared, sweetie. Maybe I can help make things less scary." Her mother paused for a long time. She tilted Natalie's face to hers again. "We're not like other people. You know that, don't you?"

Natalie wanted to pull away from her mother, to shut the door like she always did, but there was something in the way her mother held her, the way her fingers caressed her face and smoothed her hair back from her forehead. A night breeze drifted through the trees and the grass, kissing her face as it trailed past.

"Yeah, I guess." It was as if something she had propped up inside her crumbled and fell, and she was too tired to fight or care.

"Are you scared?" Serena asked.

"Yes. I don't know. I feel so tired, Mom."

"It's okay, sweetie." Her mother held her close again. "It's going to be fine." For a while they stood like that, swaying in the breeze, and that was fine with Natalie. It was the first time she had felt safe in a while.

Why she would feel safe now, though, she did not know. Because somehow, she knew things were going to get worse.

Chapter Nine

*N*ews of the storms trickled in over the next couple of days. People heard on the television and the radio about the fierce winds that blew throughout sections of the country. They were far and distant, though, and not much attention was paid.

But the storms continued to blow, and soon more reports came of their strange nature. They came without warning, sometimes lingering for days, sometimes disappearing as quickly as they came. Clouds were reported to circle and hover, never dispersing despite the winds that accompanied them. Sometimes there was thunder, sometimes lightning, sometimes both. Word of destruction came as well. There was talk of fire and debris and, alarmingly, of disappearances, but details were scarce.

Natalie sensed her mother's unease. Though their skies were clear and crisp, she caught Serena looking out their window every so often with pensive eyes, a frown crinkling her brow. Serena's customers had increased as well. Apprehension had settled over the town, and people were looking for reassurance, in whatever way they could.

Quiet conversations filtered throughout the area. When Natalie walked along the streets, or sat in the library, she heard snippets here and there of people exchanging news or rumors.

"I heard one town was completely leveled," one lady said to a group outside the pharmacy, while Natalie was running an errand for Serena.

"Three people disappeared in the storms," someone said to Mr. Mackey at the soda shop.

"It happens so quickly, no one has time to prepare," the butcher said to Serena and Natalie, while they were picking up an order.

"Strangest thing I've ever heard, I tell you," the librarian said to one of the patrons. "It's like our weather has changed completely. I don't remember it ever being this bad."

Even the circus was affected. Rather than risk hitting the storms on the road, or finding itself in a town suffering from the storms' destruction, it chose to settle in their town until further notice.

The surprising thing was that there had been no mention around town of what had happened to Natalie that day when Beausoleil brought out his living doll. She had mentioned it to her mother, and her mother had arched an eyebrow.

"What happened there has been forgotten," she finally said to Natalie.

"How could it just be forgotten?" Natalie had asked.

"Would you really like to know?" Serena had asked gently.

Natalie had felt like she was on the edge of a precipice. She had not backed away, but she had not quite been sure she was ready to step off the edge.

The phone had rung then, startling her, and she had reached out quickly to answer it. She caught Serena's smile out of the corner of her eye, as she managed, yet again, to avoid being drawn out by her mother.

It had been Mrs. Stone on the phone. She and her mother had been working together closely lately. Natalie did not pry, but whatever it had been, it had taken most of Serena's time, leaving Natalie with a lot of time on her hands alone. So when Serena asked her if she wanted to meet up with the Stones at the circus again, she had leapt at the opportunity.

"I guess you've been cooped up a little too long," Serena observed as Natalie danced along the path to Morton's Field."

"Yes," Natalie said, "it's been way too quiet. I was beginning to wonder if you forgot you even had a daughter."

Serena laughed at that. "Silly girl, as if I could ever forget you!"

The sounds of laughter and music from the circus spurred Natalie's excitement. The weather was not as nice as that first day; it was slightly cloudy, with no rain. Natalie did not care. They were out and doing something fun!

"I wanna try to win a prize at the arcade," she said, as her mother paid for the tickets. "Maybe one of those stuffed elephants!"

"It's pretty crowded today," Serena observed.

They had arrived at the arcade, and everywhere she turned she saw booths piled with people waiting to play. There were water games, racing cars, and shooting galleries. Sirens, horns and bells mingled with sounds of laughter and cheers and groans of frustration. Kids ran from booth to booth. A bell rang out behind Natalie, and when she looked, she saw a little girl jumping up and down, squealing in delight as her father handed her a stuffed toy.

"Serena! Natalie!"

Mrs. Stone and Phillip had joined them. Mrs. Stone was holding a blue and purple stuffed horse. Phillip's hands were shoved into his jeans pockets, but he gave Natalie and Serena a small smile.

"Hi, guys!" Serena said. "I see you already won a prize."

"Phillip won this." Mrs. Stone beamed at Phillip. "He gave his old mom a gift." Phillip looked embarrassed.

"Which game did you play?" Natalie asked him. "Was it hard to win?"

"Nah," Phillip said. "It was the one with the shotgun."

"Oh." She would not be good with a shotgun.

Serena chuckled. "Natalie was hoping to win a stuffed animal."

"Well, I'm sure Phillip could try to help win one for you," Mrs. Stone said.

Natalie shifted uncomfortably, as did Phillip.

"Why don't you two walk around a bit," Serena said. "Janet and I have some things we need to attend to." Natalie and Phillip nodded.

"Where do you want to go?" Phillip asked after Serena and Mrs. Stone had departed.

"I'm not sure," Natalie said. "What's an easy game?"

Phillip thought for a second. "Let's try the one where you knock the monkeys off the barrel with the bean bag."

She and Phillip headed towards the booth. The day was cloudy enough to trigger some of the circus lights. They lined the tents and ran along the booths, and their brightly colored glow gave the atmosphere a festive feel.

"Been doing anything interesting this week?" Phillip asked.

"Not really. What about you?" she asked.

"Yeah, sort of." He looked like he was about to say more, but they arrived at the booth.

"You kids wanna play?" the man in the booth asked.

Natalie nodded. She and Phillip gave the man money, and he set some bean bags down in front of them.

"The goal is pretty simple," the man said. "You have five chances to knock the monkeys off the barrel. But watch out, those monkeys are pretty tricky."

Natalie looked at Phillip, who shrugged. She picked up a bean bag, took aim at one of the monkeys, and threw it just as the monkey shifted to the side.

"Those are trick monkeys!" Natalie exclaimed. She picked up another bean bag and hurled it, then another, then another. She finished her pile of bean bags, but the monkeys remained on the barrel.

Phillip snickered. "Your aim is really bad."

"It is not! I'll bet you can't hit them either."

"Yeah, probably not." Phillip picked up his bean bag and tossed it around in his hand. He looked at the monkeys, took aim at one, narrowed his eyes, and whipped the bean bag. It knocked the monkey off the barrel right before it shifted direction.

Natalie's jaw dropped. The booth manager's head snapped in surprise. Even Phillip looked stunned.

"How did you do that?" Natalie asked.

Phillip looked at her, bemused. "I don't know. Luck?"

There was a loud clanging of bells and buzzers. A siren wailed while the booth manager called out, "A winner! We have a winner!" Lights flashed, and people's heads turned at the commotion.

Phillip looked like he wished he could shrink to about an inch tall. "Why is it so loud?" he asked aloud to no one.

"Congratulations, my boy!" the booth manager said. "You get to pick a prize!"

Phillip snuck a sidelong glance at Natalie. "The elephant," he mumbled. When the booth manager gave him his prize, Phillip held it out to Natalie.

Natalie took the elephant from him. "Thanks," she said. Her face felt as warm as a heat wave.

The booth manager grinned. "Aw, that's sweet. Pretty impressive, young man. Not every boy can win his girlfriend a prize."

"I'm not—" Natalie began, just as Phillip said,

"We're not—" and then they both stopped short.

Natalie almost wished she could give the elephant back. Phillip looked as though he wished she would.

"You want it back?" Natalie asked. But even as she offered, she gripped the elephant tighter.

"What am I gonna do with an elephant?" Phillip said with a scowl. "It's all pastel-like. You may as well keep it."

"If you're sure you don't want it." The elephant had her favorite colors: purple, pink with some shades of green, blue and yellow.

"Keep it."

"Thanks."

"You two have a lot to learn," grunted the booth manager, whose head had ricocheted from Natalie to Phillip during the exchange.

"Hey, Stone, you win something for your freak girlfriend?"

Natalie and Phillip spun around. Mike and Rory stood behind them, smirking.

"What do you want?" Phillip did not get along with Mike and his group either.

"Nothing," Mike said. "Just wanted to come over and see what two losers do in their spare time." He nudged Rory. "Aw, look, he gave her an *elly*. How cute!"

"Aren't you a sweetheart," Rory said.

"I don't see you winning anything," Natalie said to Mike. "But I guess there's no point when no one wants to be your girlfriend."

Mike's face hardened into a glare. "I'd rather have no girlfriend than have you as a girlfriend, Bristol. What loser would want you? Oh, wait." He looked at Phillip. "That explains a lot."

Phillip stepped in close to Mike's face. Oh no, Natalie thought.

"Tell you what," Phillip said. "Since I've already won two prizes, why don't I go ahead and win a third one and give it to Suzy Sherman?"

Mike stuck his face in closer to Phillip's. "Back off, Stone." He shoved Phillip, hard.

Phillip shoved back just as hard. "Make me."

Mike stumbled. He and Phillip glared for a few seconds, poised and tense. Then Mike lunged.

"No!" Natalie screamed.

There was a blur of fists and arms, and then both boys hit the dirt. Dust flew as Phillip and Mike wrestled and punched and rolled across the ground.

"Stop it!" Natalie yelled. She thought she saw Phillip get the upper hand, but then Rory moved to help Mike.

"No!" Natalie dropped her elephant and threw herself at Rory's back. She landed on him right before he got to Phillip, and they both tumbled next to the pile that was Phillip and Mike. Somehow Rory's arm and her leg ended up trapped beneath Rory's body with both their weights on it. Her body was just out of range of his elbow. Desperately, she wrapped her other leg around and hooked her legs together. She pulled his hair hard.

"Aauuggh!" screamed Rory.

Natalie managed to get her other arm around his neck, and she held on as tight as she could, while Rory struggled to free his arm and throw her off.

Dimly, she heard other people yelling. Feet trampled the ground around them, and then hands grabbed her and pulled her off Rory. Rory struggled free as she was hauled to her feet. He whirled around and launched himself at her, but hands reached out and held him in check. She glimpsed Phillip and Mike, already on their feet and held in place by what looked like a bunch of circus people. A crowd had gathered to watch.

"All right, you kids." Natalie looked up at the person holding her and saw a top hat and a bright green jacket. It was The Great Beausoleil, she realized in surprise.

Beausoleil was startled as well. He looked from her to Philip to the other boys. He pointed at Mike. "Cut that out right now."

Mike was struggling with the clown who was holding him, trying to get to Phillip, who was being held by the booth manager. Phillip, too, was struggling to get to Mike.

"That's enough, you two!" The loud roar of Beausoleil's voice was enough to quiet Phillip and Mike. They stared at him in surprise.

"He started it," yelled Mike.

"I did not!" Phillip yelled back.

"He did not!" Natalie yelled.

"He did too!" yelled Rory.

And the four of them started screaming at each other again.

"THAT IS ENOUGH NOW!"

Natalie had not thought it was possible for Beausoleil to sound any louder than he had before, but his words reverberated throughout the group and choked her words in her throat. The other boys stopped yelling as well, except for Mike, who managed to throw out some final insults.

"You two are freaks! You with your freaky, psychic mom and you with a dad who just vanished. You're both freaks!"

Beausoleil's hand tightened on her shoulder. Natalie winced. She shifted under Beausoleil's hold, and he recovered himself. He sent Mike a look that quelled him.

Beausoleil spoke again. "You four are clearly too hot around the collar to be around each other. Claude," he said, to the clown holding Mike, who nodded. "Harry," Beausoleil continued, and the man holding Rory nodded. "You two take those boys and try to find their parents. Explain what happened. In the meantime this young man," he nodded towards Phillip, "will stay here with me and this young lady while we wait for their parents."

But even as he spoke, Natalie saw both her mother and Phillip's hurrying over. Her stomach sank like a stone. She was in big trouble now.

"What is going on here?" Serena glanced, alarmed, at Mike and Rory leaving with their escorts. She observed the people holding Phillip and Natalie. Her eyes swept over Natalie, widening in disbelief.

Natalie looked down at her clothes. They were a mess. She tried to brush some of the dirt off her jeans.

"What happened?" Mrs. Stone asked Phillip. He was covered from head to toe with dust. He had scrapes on his arms and face, and his hair spiked up all over. His mouth was set in a mutinous line, but even he could not look at his mother.

Beausoleil answered. "It seems these two had a disagreement with the two who just left. I don't know what it was about, but it must have been something big, given how we had to pry them all off each other."

"Phillip!" Mrs. Stone's voice cracked like a whip.

"But Mom," Phillip protested.

"He didn't start it!" The explanation burst out of Natalie. "It was Mike!"

"That's enough, young lady!" Serena snapped.

The man from the booth spoke up. "If you don't mind my saying, I saw what happened. That other boy did his best to get under this boy's skin. This one has a quick temper, though, I have to admit."

"Mom," Phillip tried to explain. "He was really mean to Natalie."

"That is no reason to fight like that!" Mrs. Stone said angrily. "Why didn't you just walk away?"

"It's hard for a man to take when another man insults his girl," the booth manager observed.

"She's not my—" Phillip started just as Natalie said,

"I'm not his—" and then they both stopped short.

The booth manager rolled his eyes and chuckled. Once he did, the balloon of tension among the adults popped. Beausoleil chuckled as well, and smiles crossed the faces of the people who had gathered around. Serena and Mrs. Stone exchanged glances. Although their faces were serious, Serena's lips gave a little wriggle, and Mrs. Stone's eyes softened.

Natalie scowled. She did not see what was so funny.

"You and I are going to have a very serious discussion when we get home," Mrs. Stone warned Phillip.

"Those boys had some interesting things to say about these two," Beausoleil said to Serena. People were dispersing now that the excitement had passed.

"I'm sure they did," Serena said. Beausoleil looked as though he wanted to say more, but Serena's expression gave nothing away. He nodded and turned to leave, but then Serena said, "There is actually a matter we would like to discuss, if you have a moment."

Beausoleil turned back, surprised. "Of course."

His reply was smooth, but Natalie sensed that every part of him had sharpened, as if something he was waiting for had just arrived. She did not know what her mother wanted with him, but her stomach tightened.

Serena and Mrs. Stone took in Natalie and Phillip's disheveled state. They seemed to be at a loss about what to do with Natalie and Phillip when they had business to attend to.

Beausoleil followed their glances. He smiled. "Perhaps these two could wash up in my trailer? I'm sure Louisa would enjoy the company."

"You have a trailer?" Natalie blurted. "I thought you lived in tents." What was the fun of traveling in a circus if you just lived in plain old trailers?

Beausoleil chuckled. "Trailers are more convenient if you want to shower, do dishes, cook food, that kind of thing."

A tent sounded better, but Natalie did not think she could do without a bathroom either.

"That will be fine," Serena said.

"Papa!"

Louisa was hurrying through the crowd towards them. She wore bright blue circus pants with white suspenders and a red and yellow shirt. Natalie thought she looked like a miniature clown minus the heavy make-up and wig.

Beausoleil waved her over. "Your timing is perfect!" he said. Louisa wrapped her arms around Beausoleil's waist and gazed up at him. Beausoleil laid his hand on her head and smiled at her affectionately. For some reason Natalie could not stop staring. A sudden movement from her mother drew her glance.

Serena was watching her observe Beausoleil and his daughter. A strange emotion of some sort flashed in Serena's eyes, but it disappeared so quickly that Natalie wondered if she had imagined it.

"I heard there was a fight over here." Louisa was slightly breathless. "They said you were breaking it up. Are you all right?"

"It was nothing, just a few hot-headed kids." Beausoleil winked at Phillip who flushed in embarrassment. "You remember these people from a few nights ago, don't you?"

Louisa eyes widened as she took in Natalie and Phillip's bedraggled state. "Yes, you were the one who fainted," she said to Natalie.

Natalie felt the heat rush into her face. "Yes."

"We were wondering, my dear, if you wouldn't mind taking these two to the trailer so they can clean up while I talk to their mothers," Beausoleil said.

"Okay," Louisa said.

"You two go with Louisa. We'll pick you up later," Serena said. "I want you to stay out of trouble. Are we clear?"

"Yes," Natalie said. Darned Mike and Rory anyway! She rarely got into trouble with her mother, but whenever she did, it usually had to do with Mike and his gang.

Mrs. Stone had just finished giving Phillip a warning of his own. "Do you understand?" she asked him now.

"Yeah," Phillip grumbled, "I understand."

"Everyone all set?" Beausoleil asked. "Why don't you go on along?" he said to Louisa.

Louisa nodded. "We're over this way," she said to Natalie and Phillip. They fell into step behind her as she led them through the crowds of the circus.

Chapter Ten

"Were you the ones who got into the fight?" Louisa asked. She walked quickly, and Natalie had to jog a bit to keep up.

"Sort of," Natalie said. "The other guys started it."

"There were more of you?"

"Yeah," Phillip said. "You didn't think we'd fight each other, did you?"

"I only saw you two," Louisa said reasonably. "How many more were there?"

"Two boys," Natalie said. "Mike and Rory."

Louisa stopped short in her tracks. Natalie, who still had her momentum going, almost ran over Phillip. She stumbled and grabbed onto his arm. He held it steady as she regained her balance.

"Thanks," she said.

"You were in a fight with two other boys?" Louisa looked incredulous.

"They were ganging up on Phillip," Natalie said defensively. "It wasn't fair."

"I could have handled them." Phillip's brows had drawn together in a belligerent scowl.

Natalie rounded on him and placed her hands on her hips. "Oh, well, I'll just be sure to remember that next time then!"

Louisa's expression was puzzled. "I thought you had a fragile disposition."

Phillip snickered. After a moment, a chuckle escaped Natalie, and then they were both laughing.

Louisa eyebrows went up, but then a bemused smile broke from her lips as well. "We're over this way," she said.

They came to an area where there were only circus people; a group of clowns sat on equipment boxes, relaxing and talking, some with their wigs off, their big noses gone, and their suspenders down; tigers and bears in cages rolled in from the main grounds, their handlers barking orders as they wheeled through; some people ran by, pulling on costume pieces as they went. Natalie saw one man training a little monkey to do back flips on a box.

"Where are we?" Phillip asked.

"We're just outside the main circus grounds," Louisa said. "This is where we live."

People stared at them as they walked. Conversations stopped. Natalie had the uncomfortable feeling that they were seeing a part of the circus that was private and personal.

"Is it all right for us to be here?" she asked Louisa.

Louisa nodded. "Yes, don't worry about it. We don't get visitors very often, but it's allowed. People are just curious."

Natalie was not so sure. Maybe she was imagining it, but some of the glances were a bit wary, particularly when they shifted to Louisa. That's strange, thought Natalie. Why would they look at Louisa like that?

"Where have you been, Miss Louisa?" a voice demanded out of nowhere.

Natalie whirled about, startled, but there was no one there. Phillip looked confused as well. Well at least I'm not imagining things, she thought. Then the voice spoke again from behind.

"Down here!"

When she turned, there was a tiny man standing next to Louisa. Natalie had to blink to make sure she was really seeing what she was seeing.

It was indeed a tiny man. The top of his head barely hit Louisa's hip. He was dressed in a costume similar to Louisa's only, well, miniaturized.

The tiny man scowled. "What's wrong with the two of you? Never seen a tiny person at a circus before?"

Natalie shook her head. She tried not to stare, but she felt her eyeballs straining and realized she must have been looking rather wide-eyed.

Phillip stammered, "Well sort of...not real close...no...not really, I guess...sorry..." he ended with a grimace.

The tiny man glared in a way that made Natalie feel as though she might wither away on a vine.

Louisa's tone was mild. "Hercules, this is Natalie and Phillip. Papa said to take them to the trailer so they can get cleaned up."

"Cleaned up?" Hercules looked them over. "What happened?"

"They were in that fight we heard about."

Hercules' eyebrows rose. "These two are the culprits?" He shook his head. "Young people today have no sense of propriety."

Natalie thought that for such a little man, he was a large amount of grumpy.

"Natalie, Phillip, this is Hercules," Louisa said. "He's my best friend."

"Louisa, honestly, I am much too old to be your best friend," Hercules said, but his expression softened. It was obvious he was touched by Louisa's introduction.

"But you are," Louisa said. "No one looks after me the way you do."

"Well, I'm not much good at it when you run off the way you do. When we heard the news about the fight, I barely had time to think before you were off running." Hercules' scowl was back. "It's not like it's easy for me to keep up with you when you do that."

"I'm sorry, Hercules. I was just worried about Papa. He's been acting so strange lately, I was afraid there was trouble."

Hercules' expression changed again. Natalie could not put her finger on it, but it was as if a wiper blade had swiped off anything that might have been too revealing on his face.

"You're worrying over nothing, Louisa," he said.

"I don't think so." A stubborn look came over Louisa's face. "Papa's been acting really strange lately, like he thinks something bad is coming."

Natalie stiffened, and Phillip asked quickly, "Like what?"

Hercules' eyes snapped over to them. "Don't you start in on this, too! The last thing we need is some more imaginations running wild. Louisa, listen, there's nothing for you to worry about. Why don't you go on ahead and take these two culprits to get cleaned up?"

Natalie opened her mouth to protest being called a culprit, but Louisa shook her head at her and rolled her eyes. He's always like this, her look said.

Louisa smiled at Hercules. Natalie marveled at how good-natured Louisa was towards such a crotchety person.

"Hercules, can't you at least pretend to be a little friendly? Natalie and Phillip are guests, after all."

Hercules had the grace to look slightly shamefaced. "Of course. No offense to the two of you."

Natalie suspected that was as close to an apology as Hercules could get. She and Phillip nodded.

"Why don't you three get moving?" Hercules said. "I'll go speak with your father and check in with you later. Try not to cause any more havoc!" He spun on his heel and walked away, moving through the crowds like a beetle through grass.

"So much for being friendly," Phillip said in an undertone.

Louisa's face was apologetic. "You'll have to excuse Hercules. He's usually a little grouchy. Some days, he's really grouchy."

"We caught him on a bad day, huh?" Phillip said.

"Oh, no," Louisa grinned, "this is one of his good days."

At the looks on Natalie and Phillip's faces, Louisa laughed. "You get used to him. Once he gets to know you, he's pretty nice."

"How long have you known him?" Natalie asked.

"Since we've been with the circus."

"How long have you been with the circus?" Phillip asked.

"My whole life," Louisa said. "I think."

Phillip gave Louisa a strange look. "You think?"

Louisa's eyes widened. "That's not what I meant. You lose track of time when you travel as much as we do. We all spend so much time together that months with someone can feel like years. I don't know how long I've known Hercules, but I feel like I've known him all my life." She flashed Phillip a brilliant smile. Phillip blinked a couple of times and then smiled back. He looked a little thrown.

Louisa started walking. "Come on," she said over her shoulder, "we're this way."

Phillip still had a befuddled expression on his face.

"Come on," Natalie said irritably.

They came to a large area on which several trailers sat. Louisa stepped up to one of larger ones and held the door open so they could enter.

It was a basic trailer, somewhat cramped, with a small kitchen, an area in the back with a bathroom, and a bedroom with enough room for a bed and a small bunk on top. Still, there were little touches that made the trailer feel homey. Natalie suspected Louisa had set out the flowers that were lined up in vases along one of the window ledges, as well as the embroidered tablecloth that brightened up the kitchen.

Louisa pulled some washcloths out of a cabinet near the bedroom. "Here you go. You should be able to clean up with these. We have some disinfectant and band aids somewhere in here, too." She handed the washcloths to Natalie and went into the bathroom. Natalie heard her opening drawers and cabinets.

Phillip took one of the washcloths and wet it in the kitchen sink. There was a mirror hanging on one of the walls, and seeing her reflection, Natalie understood why her mother had been so dismayed. Her hair was matted and dusty, and dirt marked her face and neck. A scuff ran along her jaw, and small scratches streaked her cheek.

Phillip looked over. Her expression must have said it all, because he chuckled. "It might take more than a few wash cloths," he said.

Louisa came out with some alcohol, cotton balls, band aids, and a comb. "I found one with wide teeth," she said proudly.

"Is it okay if I use the bathroom?" Phillip asked.

"Sure," Louisa said.

Natalie put a washcloth under the faucet and went to work on cleaning off the dirt and the scrapes. Luckily, the scrapes did not require band aids, but there was quite a bit of sting with the alcohol.

"I could try to help you with your hair," Louisa said. "It's pretty tangled up."

"Do you mind?" Natalie asked.

"No, not at all. Just let me know if I pull too hard."

Natalie helped Louisa gather her hair in the back, and then Louisa started the arduous task of working the tangles through to the ends.

"What were you all fighting about?" Louisa asked.

"A couple of boys from town were acting like jerks," Natalie said.

"Do they do that a lot?"

"Whenever they can," Natalie said ruefully.

"Why do they pick on you?"

"They think I'm weird." Natalie felt the comb tug gently through her hair. It was actually quite soothing.

"You don't seem weird," Louisa said.

Phillip snorted from the bathroom. "Don't let her fool you. She's really weird!"

"Oh shut up!" Natalie retorted.

Phillip poked his head around the door. There was a marked difference in his appearance. He had cleaned off the dust and dirt from his face and arms, and he was using a cotton ball to apply the alcohol to a scrape on his arm.

"When you said your father was acting weird," he asked, "what did you mean?"

The tug of the comb stopped. Natalie twisted around to look at Louisa, who seemed to be giving it some thought.

"It's hard to say, exactly," Louisa said. "He's just more anxious than usual. It's like he looks at things around him more, looks harder. His mind seems to be in more places at once, like he can't stop thinking about things. And he's pretty anxious about me, always reminding me to stay close."

"Has he said anything to you?" Phillip asked.

Louisa shook her head and continued working on Natalie's hair. "No, but it seems to have started that last time you both were here."

Natalie glanced at Phillip. She wondered if he knew that no one else remembered that night. His eyes met hers, and the look in his told her he did.

"I wonder what the connection is." Phillip said.

"I've asked Hercules," Louisa said, "but he tells me I'm thinking nonsense."

"Ouch!" Natalie's head had yanked a little from the tug of the comb.

"Oh, I'm so sorry!" Louisa exclaimed. "I pulled too hard."

"That's okay, it wasn't too hard."

Louisa focused on the knots in Natalie's hair. Phillip went back into the bathroom.

"So how do you like living in a circus?" Natalie asked.

"It's fine, I guess," Louisa said. "I don't have anything to compare it to, but I like it. I have my papa and Hercules, and it's fun to be around the animals and to see the different people in all the different towns."

Phillip came out of the bathroom to join them. "It must be fun traveling everywhere."

Louisa nodded. "Sometimes, yes. It's fun being in different places all the time. There's always something going on, and whenever you get into town, people are always interested because we're the excitement." She shrugged. "Then there are times when it's hard to always be packing up and going. It's been nice staying here in one place for a while."

"Have you ever had to stay in one place for a long time before," Natalie asked.

Louisa shook her head. "Not that I can remember. I guess these storms are really unusual."

"My mom seems pretty worried about them," Natalie said.

"Yeah, so's my mom," Phillip said.

"My papa, too," Louisa said. She continued to work through Natalie's hair; she was almost at the top of her head now. "I wonder what your moms wanted to talk to him about."

"Yeah, I've been wondering about that, too," Phillip said.

Natalie groaned inside. Oh, great, she thought, here we go.

"Any idea where they might have gone?" Phillip tossed the question out casually, but Natalie was not fooled. "Maybe we can go check in on them."

"You mean listen in on them, don't you?" Natalie said.

Phillip grinned. "No, not at all. I'm just saying that we check in with them like we always do, and if we happen to catch anything they say, that's just unexpected information." Phillip's smile was so full of guile that Natalie found herself smiling in response.

Louisa giggled. "That's a funny way of looking at it." She gave a final tug on Natalie's hair, and smoothed the comb the rest of the way through her hair. "There! You're all detangled."

Natalie ran a hand through her hair. "Gosh, thanks, Louisa! It feels great."

"No problem." Louisa moved across the table from Natalie and sat down.

Natalie gazed around the trailer again. "It's nice in here. It's just you and your dad, right?"

Louisa nodded. "Yes."

"It's just me and my mom, too."

"What happened to your dad?" Louisa asked.

Natalie shrugged. "I don't know. He was gone before I was born, and my mom doesn't talk about him."

"Your mom is really pretty, and she seems really nice."

"She is." Natalie was finding it easy to talk to Louisa. She had an easy way about her. "Do you remember your mom?"

Louisa shook her head. "No, I must have been a baby when she died."

For a moment Natalie was thrown. "You don't...you don't know for sure?"

Louisa blinked. "No, no of course I do. I was a baby when she died, and I just don't remember her." She stood up then and started putting things away.

Natalie, surprised, rose to help her. Phillip looked at Natalie with raised eyebrows, and then proceeded to help as well.

"I hope I didn't make you mad or anything," Natalie said to Louisa.

Louisa reached out to take hold of Natalie's hand. "Don't be silly, I'm not mad at all." She released her hand, and continued to straighten up the trailer. "Do you guys want to go look for our parents?"

Phillip nodded. Natalie sighed and shrugged. No use fighting Phillip on this one. Truth be told, she was a little curious herself, and lately, her curiosity seemed to be getting the better of her!

Chapter Eleven

"Papa usually starts preparing for his show about now," Louisa said, when they stepped out of the trailer a few minutes later. "He likes to work in that area backstage where you were that last time. Not a lot of people go there, so Papa can concentrate on what he has to do for his show. He might have taken your moms there to talk."

"That sounds like a good place to start," Phillip said.

"Try to keep an eye out for Hercules," Louisa said.

Natalie looked around at the crowds. "That might be a little hard."

Louisa laughed. "With Hercules, sometimes all you have to do is listen."

Sure enough, as they drew near the tent of *The Magical World of the Great Beausoleil*, they heard Hercules yelling indignantly over the din of the crowd.

"Make way!" he cried. "Clear a path here! I've got to go check on little Louisa. Move along, why don't you? I don't have all day!"

"We won't have much time before Hercules sees we're not in the trailer," Phillip said.

Louisa nodded. "He'll probably come to the tent after."

They moved away from the sound of Hercules' voice and hurried towards the tent. Louisa took them around back to the entrance she had used the other night. She parted the folds of the tent, looked around, and nodded for them to follow.

Natalie recognized the room in which she had awoken the last time they were there. They moved as quietly as possible, listening for any signs of their parents. As they crossed the room, the faint murmur of quiet conversation floated into earshot.

Louisa held her finger up to her lips and tiptoed to one of the panels of heavy, velvet fabric. She grabbed one of the folds and pulled it back, revealing another set of heavy fabric. She stepped in behind it with great care, sliding along it sideways. She motioned for them to follow.

Natalie and Phillip slipped in beside her, and the fabric Louisa was holding fell back behind them. Without the double fabric to muffle the words, the conversation came through more clearly, though it was a bit of a strain to hear it.

"We're shielded for now, although Mrs. Blaine is not sure how much longer we'll be able to stay that way," Serena was saying.

"Not long I would think," Beausoleil said. "I'm surprised you've been able to stay hidden for as long as you have. They're getting stronger, I'm telling you."

"You haven't told us how you managed to escape detection," Mrs. Stone said.

"I found a way to contain my...gift in an object. To lock it away where only I can unlock it," Beausoleil explained. "I had to be vigilant, but whenever danger was near, I could shut it away, unnoticed, until the danger passed."

Gift. If Natalie had not been afraid of detection, she would have groaned. There was no getting away from the weirdness that followed them.

There was just enough light behind the curtain for her to see Phillip turn to her. He was trying to gauge her reaction, but she gazed back calmly. It seemed pointless now to keep struggling against all the information coming at them. Surprise flitted across Phillip's face, and then a small, shy smile formed on his lips.

A wall tumbled down in Natalie with that smile. For so long she had felt like a freak, different and alone. Now she wondered if this whole time Phillip had felt the same way, had been going through all the things she had. If she no longer hid from everything she feared, maybe she would no longer be alone. And maybe Phillip was happy that he no longer had to be alone as well.

As she gazed at Phillip, and he back at her, another feeling emerged. It was one she did not recognize, and she looked away in confusion. She heard, as if from a distance, Mrs. Stone's question to Beausoleil.

"Where do you lock it?"

And then Louisa sneezed.

The confused fog in Natalie's head cleared in an instant. She felt Phillip freeze beside her and then dive through the velvet folds, heading back from where they came. She followed with Louisa pushing her from behind. She heard puzzled exclamations and movement from the other room.

She fought her way out of the velvet folds and slammed into Phillip, who had halted once he had cleared them. She felt Louisa thud against her back, and Phillip's weight gave way as all three of them fell to the floor.

"Ugh!" Phillip grunted.

"Ack!" Louisa squealed.

"Get up, quick!" Natalie hissed.

They scrambled to their feet just as Beausoleil, Serena and Mrs. Stone stepped into the room. They all stared at one another.

"We just got here; we didn't hear a thing!" Louisa exclaimed.

Natalie groaned. Phillip's shoulders slumped, his head dropping onto his chest. Louisa looked over at them and grimaced in apology.

"I see," Beausoleil said.

"How long have you three been here?" Mrs. Stone asked.

"Not long," Phillip said.

"Did you hear us talking?" Mrs. Stone asked.

"We caught the tail end," Phillip mumbled.

Mrs. Stone nodded. She, Serena and Beausoleil exchanged a look that was a mixture of dismay, exasperation and concern. They looked as if they did not know what to say, and the sight was so strange, Natalie was not sure how to react.

Phillip, however, jumped at the opportunity. "Who's getting stronger?" he blurted out.

"Oh Phillip," Mrs. Stone said, "you really shouldn't..."

Beausoleil held up his hand. "If you don't mind my saying, it might be better to let the kids know what's going on. If they know what's going on, they might be able to avoid getting into trouble."

Natalie watched as Beausoleil's words sank in with her mother.

"You have a good point," Serena said, "but I think I'll need some time with my daughter. I don't want to overwhelm her, but you're right. They need to be prepared, just in case."

"Just in case what?" Natalie asked quickly.

"Nothing you need to worry about, darling." Serena reached out to smooth a strand of hair from her forehead. "You and I will talk later. It looks like you've both cleaned up from your fight earlier," she noted.

"Yeah, Louisa helped me with my hair," Natalie said.

"Thank you, Louisa," Serena said.

"It was no problem," Louisa said shyly.

Mrs. Stone was considering Phillip, but her tone was stern. "You look much better, but you and I have much to discuss tonight about fights and eavesdropping."

"Yes, Mom," Phillip groaned.

"We still have a few things to discuss," Serena said. "Why don't you all go enjoy the circus while we finish here? Come back in about a half hour, okay?"

Natalie nodded along with Louisa, but Phillip had a stubborn look on his face.

"Why can't we stay?" he asked.

"Phillip," Mrs. Stone said sharply, "you and I will talk later. For now, please do what Serena is asking."

Without a word, Phillip spun around and walked out of the tent.

"Phillip, wait up!" Natalie called. She and Louisa ran after him. He was walking very quickly, and they had to jog to catch up.

"I don't see why we couldn't hear what they had to discuss!" Phillip complained. He had not slowed down, and Natalie and Louisa were struggling to keep up. "I'm not afraid. I can take whatever they have to say! It's not fair!" Phillip's pace quickened, and soon they were bolting through the circus grounds.

"Phillip, stop, please!" Natalie sped up, trying not to lose sight of Phillip, who was dodging through the crowds. She heard Louisa's footsteps running behind her.

"Phillip!" Natalie yelled. What was wrong with him, she wondered. He was running like someone possessed. People jumped out of the way as they rushed by, but Phillip would not stop. "Where are you going?"

"Anywhere but here!" Phillip yelled.

They were already at the trailers, but still Phillip ran. Natalie was starting to get a stitch in her side. She heard Louisa gasping behind her. They ran past the trailers.

"Please!" Louisa called out. Her breathing was ragged. "We have to stop."

"So stop then," Phillip snapped.

"Where are you going, Louisa?" Hercules had spotted them, and he did not sound happy. Well, Natalie thought, even less happy than before.

"You kids stop right now!" Hercules barked, but it was like trying to stop a rolling train. Hercules and the circus faded behind them as she and Louisa charged behind Phillip through the open field towards the forest that lay at the end.

At the edge of the forest, Phillip finally started to run out of steam. He slowed, his arm wrapped around his side, gasping. Natalie stumbled up beside him and collapsed on the ground, her lungs crying out for air. Louisa flopped down on the grass next to Phillip. Phillip dropped to his knees and then fell on the ground between them. The three of them fought to catch their breath.

When she got her voice to work, Natalie yelled, "What is wrong with you?"

Phillip lay there staring at the sky, his breathing moving back to normal. The afternoon sky was starting to shift to dusk, the cloudy hues of gray fading as the day began its descent into the horizon.

"I don't know," Phillip said at last. "I just feel so mad."

"So you had to run a marathon?" Louisa asked.

"Yeah, sure, I guess." Phillip crossed his arms up over his forehead, as if to block out the world.

Natalie looked across him at Louisa who raised her eyebrows and shrugged.

It was several moments before Phillip spoke. "I don't understand you." He lifted his head to face Natalie. "I don't understand how you can bury your head in the sand. I don't understand why you're so scared about...things." He turned to Louisa. "You know what we are, don't you? You and your father are like us."

Louisa hesitated for a moment and then nodded. "Yes."

"But you're not scared, are you?"

"I grew up with it. I don't know anything else."

Natalie's muscles tensed. Was Phillip actually going to bring this up now?

He had dropped his head back to look at the sky, his arms behind his head. A breeze blew over them, and Natalie shivered.

"My mom says you're scared because you're really powerful," Phillip said. "She says that being that powerful can be scary, especially at first because the power can come on so strong, and you have no control. But Natalie," he spoke as if from the depths of his soul, "I would do anything for that kind of power."

"Phillip, you don't know what you're saying," Natalie said.

"Maybe not," Phillip said bitterly. "All I know is that we're here, with these...gifts, and we can't do anything with them. And my dad is out there somewhere, and no one seems to want to help him except me. And I don't have any way to help him myself—not yet. If I could have what you have, Natalie, I'd be out there, looking for a way to help him, not in here, hiding my head in the sand."

Natalie felt as if she had been slapped. "You have no idea what it's like," she cried. "And even if I could control what happens to me, what could we do? We're just kids!"

"That was really unfair, Phillip," Louisa said. "You can't say that to her."

Phillip sat up and buried both hands in his hair, his elbows resting on his knees. "You're right. I'm sorry, Natalie, I shouldn't have said that. I'm so sorry."

Natalie reeled under Phillip's words. They stung so hard it left her breathless. That he should feel the way he did about how she handled her abilities made her want to curl up with shame.

She pulled herself up off the ground and faced Phillip and Louisa. She tried to think of something to say, but the look on Louisa's face stopped her cold.

Louisa was staring at something in the sky behind Natalie. Her eyes were round as saucers, and her jaw had dropped.

"What's wrong?" The expression on Louisa's face sent Natalie's voice up an octave.

Phillip's head whipped up then. He looked at Louisa and followed her gaze. His eyes flickered with confusion, and then went wide.

Natalie whirled around. The sky had become a swirling mass. Clouds gathered from all corners of the horizon and formed a cavernous vortex that spun like a powerful whirlpool of dark gray and white. It was so large it ate up the sky.

Natalie's heart jumped into her throat. Even as she stared, more clouds moved along the sky to be sucked up into the giant funnel that had formed so quickly and was building larger still.

She heard Phillip slowly rise to his feet behind her, heard Louisa ask incredulously, "What is that?"

Words gathered on Natalie's lips, but when they came, they were in a hushed whisper.

"It's the storm."

Chapter Twelve

*T*he wind trickled slowly at first, tickling the tendrils of her hair like the touch of a ghost.

Phillip's hand slipped around her wrist. "It's moving this way," he said.

The light breeze quickly gathered into a gale. The force of it pressed against her face, gaining strength. The wind howled through the field. Natalie looked around and saw how the trees swayed and the grass billowed. Phillip was right.

She looked again at the clouds. They churned through the sky like a rolling wave, a single-minded force headed right for them.

Phillip gripped her wrist tighter. "We should get out of here!" he shouted.

"Louisa! Kids!"

It was Beausoleil. He was running down the field. As he drew close, the clouds whipped into a frenzy. Thunder roared and lightning shot through the sky.

"What's happening, Papa?" Louisa cried.

"Get back!" Beausoleil yelled. "Get back to the circus!"

Phillip pulled at her wrist. He grabbed Louisa's shirt and tugged her along. The gale had transformed into a tempest, tossing them off balance as they struggled to get to Beausoleil.

Beausoleil looked up at the clouds and all around, and stopped short. The expression on his face changed to a look of realization. Panic filled his face.

And then the wind was such that they could not move forward. Natalie pushed and pushed, but the force of the wind was like a wall.

"Papa!" Louisa screamed.

Through the storm, Natalie watched Beausoleil raise his hands and bow his head. The wind pulled at her from behind. I'm being sucked up, she thought in astonishment. She pushed forward again, but the wind was a solid wall. Her feet slid through the grass. Please don't let me fall, she prayed.

Something flashed to the left of her periphery, something large. Natalie strained to see what it was, but the wind flapped her hair against her face.

Now something else moved as well. The objects moved closer, and as they came into view, Natalie's knees buckled. Only Phillip's hold kept her from falling completely.

The trees were moving. Not blowing away, uprooted, but walking—if one could call it walking. They swayed one way, pulling up roots, then plunked back down, digging in the roots to buttress against the wind. Then they swayed the other way, hauling their roots, and planting it back into the ground. Each sway brought them closer and closer to where she, Phillip and Louisa stood.

Natalie's mind closed up. She opened her mouth and screamed. The wind muffled the sound, yet she was unable to stop; she screamed and screamed.

Phillip yanked her around. Louisa held on behind him, her arms around his waist. Phillip's other hand gripped Natalie's shoulder and shook her.

"Natalie! What's wrong with you?"

She gasped and pointed at the trees. They were almost upon them now, looming like giants as their roots slammed them in closer.

Phillip's face froze in shock. For a second he seemed incapable of movement. Then he screamed, "Run!" He whipped his arm around Natalie, wrapped his other arm around Louisa and pulled desperately against the wind.

"Stay where you are!" bellowed Beausoleil. He ran over and grabbed Louisa from Phillip. "Stay down. They'll protect us. Stay down." He moved his body so he stood over the three of them.

There was a crashing sound as one of the trees flipped its roots and dug in behind them. Natalie grabbed onto Phillip and held tight. She felt his heart beating fast through his shirt. Leaves jumbled and wood creaked as one, two, three, four more trees swayed round, forming a circle around the four of them. The howling sounds of the wind diminished as the trees leaned in, covering them completely.

"Listen quickly, children, we don't have much time," Beausoleil said.

"Wh...wha...what just happened?" Natalie cried out.

"There's no time to walk you through, child! You need to focus on me now." The urgency in Beausoleil snapped Natalie to attention.

"I brought the trees. They were the only things we had, but they won't hold for long. It's the storms. They're using the storms to take us!" Beausoleil said with an incredulous shake of his head. "I have no way to fight this one off."

"Mrs. Bristol said we were shielded," Phillip asked.

"You ran out of range," Beausoleil said.

Natalie's knees were shaking. Phillip's hold on her tightened, but he looked as if he had been hit in the gut.

"Papa!" Louisa cried.

"Shhhh," Beausoleil said. "You kids didn't know. It was what we were talking about, your mothers and I. We should have told you sooner. That was our fault, not yours.

"I brought the trees because that is my gift. I can make the inanimate animate. Sometimes I can make the inanimate look as if they have life."

The trees around them shook violently.

Beausoleil leaned in. "Listen, I can distract it. Neither of you has fully developed your gifts yet, so the storm will zoom in on me. When it does, you run. Run as fast as you can, back to the circus. Do not look back."

"I don't understand," Phillip said.

"There's no time!" Beausoleil snapped.

"No, Papa," Louisa sobbed.

Beausoleil put his hand on the back of her head. Almost immediately, her sobbing stopped and her expression settled into a blank calm.

"You know what you need to do, Louisa," he said quietly.

"Yes, Papa," Louisa's voice had become distant.

"Everything I have will be in you, so when they bring you back, you must keep yourself safe. Stay close to Hercules. Do everything you're told, but above all, stay hidden and protect what I give you."

"Yes, Papa."

The air crackled. Louisa's eyes blinked and then fixed on nothing. The warmth of her skin cooled and her joints straightened into stiff points.

There was a crash above them as the storm tore through the trees, snapping their trunks and ripping their roots from the ground. Natalie screamed as the leaves from the trees slapped across her face. The wind whipped around Beausoleil, but he closed his eyes and held tight to Louisa, whose skin was hardening to a beautiful porcelain.

"Oh, my god," Natalie whispered.

The wind jerked Beausoleil into the air. He screamed and threw the porcelain doll that was once Louisa down to Phillip.

"Run!" he screamed. "Run, now!"

For a moment Beausoleil hung suspended above them. He cast a final look at the doll, its transformation complete, before the wind yanked him through what was left of the trees, and flipped him, flailing head over heels, into the giant funnel of the storm.

Natalie felt as if her whole body screamed. Phillip dropped to his knees with the doll, but she reached down and dragged him back up.

"We have to run, now!" she yelled.

Phillip tried to pull away, but she grabbed his collar with both hands and hauled him back.

"He told us to run, Phillip! We have to do as he says! Come on! Run!"

Phillip spun about, and they tore through the fields. She heard the fall of Phillip's feet as he ran, saw him clutching the doll as they raced towards the circus.

"Natalie! Phillip!" It was Serena calling from far away. Natalie heard her mother's desperation. She picked up speed with Phillip keeping pace beside her. She did not look back.

A stitch developed in her side. Phillip stumbled with the doll, but she grasped him under his arms and pulled at him until he found his footing, and soon they were running again.

We're going to make it, she thought. Beausoleil had come for them, and now he was gone. They would make it because they had to. She felt a flicker deep in her belly. It spread up through her chest, covering her heart. It grew steadily into a flame as they drew closer to the bright lights of the circus.

Her mother swept her up as she and Phillip stumbled onto the circus grounds. Her mother's arms held her tight, tighter than any other time she had held her before. Natalie laid her head on her mother's shoulder and saw Mrs. Stone gather Phillip close.

They had made it.

Natalie closed her eyes. Images of the wind snatching Beausoleil, of Louisa shifting into porcelain, of the trees lumbering towards them, all ran like a movie through her mind. She was shaking.

"Thank goodness. Oh, thank goodness!" Serena's words were muffled in Natalie's hair as she held Natalie fast.

"Phillip!" Mrs. Stone cried. "Are you all right? Oh my dear boy..."

Natalie opened her eyes. Phillip stood as if numb in his mother's embrace, one hand holding the doll which hung limp beside him. He stared into space, and she wondered if he was seeing the same images that ran through her head. She closed her eyes again and buried her head into her mother's neck.

"Where are they? What happened? Tell me!"

It was Hercules, charging down the path. His eyes searched about and settled on the doll by Phillip's feet. His face fell. He toddled over and picked the doll up. It was almost as tall as he was, but he handled it easily.

"Where's Beausoleil?" he asked.

Serena shook her head in response. Natalie pulled away from her mother.

"He got pulled away by the storms. He said 'It's the storms. They're using the storms to take us.' He said he would distract it."

Serena started in surprise. "The storms? They're using the storms?"

"My god," Mrs. Stone said, shocked.

"What do we do?" Natalie cried. "How do we get him back?"

Serena and Mrs. Stone's expressions were solemn.

"I'm sorry, sweetie," Serena said. "There's nothing we can do. Not now."

"We have to!" Natalie said in disbelief.

"We can't just leave him!" Phillip chimed in.

"We don't know where he's been taken," Mrs. Stone said. "I'm so sorry, kids, I wish we did. I really do. I'm so sorry."

"No, I don't understand!" Natalie felt ready to climb out of her skin. How could there be nothing they could do?

"We'll explain it all to you. Not here though." Serena's head cast about to see if anyone was watching. "We should leave now."

Natalie wanted to protest, but her mother gave her a look of warning, so she kept quiet.

"What's this?" Mrs. Stone was staring at the doll.

"The doll is Louisa," Natalie said. "Beausoleil gave her something. He said she had to keep it safe for him. He said he could make the inanimate animate, and then he turned her into that doll!"

"He locked his gift up in the doll," Mrs. Stone said in wonder. "He did it so they wouldn't get it."

"So who wouldn't get it?" Phillip asked.

Mrs. Stone put a hand on Phillip's shoulder. "We need to talk about that, but now is not the time or the place."

"We should get going now," Serena said. "We need to get you two home. We will talk tomorrow."

"But what will we do about Louisa?" Natalie cried. "We have to protect her!"

Serena looked at Hercules who was clutching the doll close. He gave her a nod.

"Hercules will watch over her," she said.

"But we can't leave her like that!" Natalie protested.

"Sweetheart," Serena said, "that is what she is. She will be fine."

"She's a girl! She can't stay a doll."

"No, Natalie," Serena said, "she's a doll who looked like a girl."

"That's not true," Natalie said stubbornly. "She was crying out there. A doll can't pretend to cry like that!"

Serena considered her words for a moment. "Perhaps," she conceded. "In any case, there isn't anything we can do about it just now. Please, Natalie," she said, when Natalie opened her mouth to protest. "We just don't know how to bring her back. Beausoleil is the one who locked her up and only he has the key, so to speak. We will need some time, but we'll figure something out. She will be fine for now."

Natalie looked at the doll. She could not believe that only moments ago it had been Louisa. It just did not seem right to leave her.

"Beausoleil said he could make the inanimate animate," Phillip said to Natalie. "He turned the doll into the girl and then back again. It's okay, Natalie, that's how she started out."

"I'll take care of her." Hercules' eyes were bleak, but he spoke firmly. "I've looked after her like this. She'll be fine."

"Come on now," Serena said, "we need to leave. It's not good for us to linger here." She surveyed the field from where they had run. The storm had disappeared as quickly as it had come, but darkness had fallen, and Natalie could tell her mother was apprehensive. "We'll come back as soon as possible."

Natalie turned to Hercules, who had lifted the doll up and prepared to leave. "We'll see you then?" she asked him.

"Yes," Hercules said, "we'll be here.

Chapter Thirteen

*H*er stomach was churning. She was flailing in mid-air, the wind tossing her round and round as she flew towards the vortex, which spun ever larger to swallow her up...

Natalie surged up, her heart thumping hard, and felt the light of the sun fall softly on her face. No wind surrounded her. The familiar objects of her room came into focus. She was in her bed, and it was morning.

Her door opened. Serena crossed the room to sit on the edge of the mattress next to her. "Are you okay, darling? Were you dreaming?"

Natalie nodded, waiting for her heart to beat back to normal. "The winds blew me away. The storm clouds were going to swallow me."

"It's okay," Serena soothed. "It was only a dream."

After a while, Natalie leaned back onto her pillow. Her mother laid a hand on her cheek.

"I have never, in my whole life, been as scared as I was last night. For a moment, I thought I'd lost you. I don't know what I would have done if I had." Serena took Natalie's hand in hers and caressed her fingers.

"There are things you need to know, things I need to tell you to keep you safe. Things I know you don't want to hear..."

"Okay," Natalie murmured.

"Is it? I worry about how scared you are. I ask myself all the time what I can do to make things easier for you. I thought we had time, but suddenly it's run out, and as scared as I am to tell you, I'm even more afraid of what will happen to you if I don't."

"I understand," Natalie said. "I think I do."

"Do you?" Serena said, surprised.

"I was so scared last night. I couldn't do anything. I couldn't help Beausoleil."

"There's nothing you could have done. What happened to Beausoleil was beyond anything you could have done to help."

"Phillip said I'm powerful." Natalie bowed her head so that her hair hid her face. "He said if he had what I had, he wouldn't hide his head in the sand like me."

Serena raised her eyebrows. "Did he now?"

"Do you think I'm a coward?"

"Honey, no! You're just a child, and..." Serena paused as if choosing her words carefully, "...your experience can be frightening. It's natural to be afraid."

"Phillip doesn't seem to be afraid."

"Phillip hasn't experienced what you have. He's also a little more adventurous and motivated than most, especially when it comes to his father."

Natalie traced a pattern on her blanket. "Why don't you talk about my father?"

She heard a sharp intake of breath from Serena. Seconds passed before Natalie looked up from her blanket. There was a faraway look in Serena's eyes, and whatever she was seeing seemed to bring her sadness.

"Do I look like him?" Natalie asked tentatively.

Serena came back to the present. "You look like me, except your hair is brown and your eyes are like chocolate almonds. Can I have some? Mmmm..."

Natalie giggled as her mother leaned in and nuzzled her.

"Is he dead?" Natalie asked.

Serena shook her head. "I'm not too sure. At one time, our kind scattered and lost touch."

"People with gifts?"

"Yes," Serena said. "By now you know about that, right?"

"Beausoleil told us about his before the storm took him."

"Ah yes, I remember. Well, we all have gifts. We can do things other people can't."

"Like Beausoleil making the inanimate animate?"

"Yes, like that. We all have the ability to enhance our senses. To see, hear, smell, and touch more acutely than other people. But each individual also has something special, a gift that's greater than anyone else's. Some individuals have more than one gift. Some even have several."

"What do you have?" Natalie asked.

"I have several."

"What did my father have?"

Serena paused. "Several."

"Do I have several?" Natalie asked.

"I suspect you do, but we will have to see. You grow into your gifts, and the age can vary from person to person."

"What about Phillip?"

"Janet thinks he is starting to come into his, but it's early yet."

Natalie considered that for a moment. There were so many things to think about now.

"Who's coming after us?"

Serena sighed. "Years ago we all lived very peacefully. We were an organized people, content. We kept away from civilization, and lived in remote parts of the world, using our gifts to stay hidden. We avoided corruption. Our numbers don't grow very large, and we suspect it's nature's way of making sure we don't become overwhelmingly powerful. Power in the hands of corrupt men can cause destruction on a large scale.

"There was a man among us named Martin Reimer. He was one who had several gifts, and he worked tirelessly to enhance them all. Soon they were not enough. He grew curious about the gifts of others, tried to emulate those gifts, recreate them. But of course he couldn't; our gifts are an innate part of our very being, unique to each person alone.

"That should have been the end of that. But for Martin, it wasn't enough.

"Our problems started with one of the elders. Our health is always very good, so we were all puzzled as to why she was suddenly so drained of energy. She could give no explanation. When we asked questions she became unfocused.

"We looked into everything: history, lore, anything that could give us insight into what was wrong. Even our healers could not detect the problem. The elder just lay in her bed, fading further. And then one day she vanished."

"Vanished?" Natalie said.

"Yes. One of her family checked on her the night before. In the morning she was gone."

"What happened to her?"

Serena weighed Natalie with her eyes, and then laid a comforting hand on hers. "We found her body the following week. Her body had shriveled up, as if it had been drained of all its essence."

"That's just awful!" Natalie gasped.

"Her gift was one of purity," Serena continued. "She could restore anything that was spoiled, polluted—our water, the sky above us, our crops, all were clear, clean. We did our part to keep it that way, but anything we could not cover, she did. The strange thing was that none of that had changed. Our environment remained pure. We wondered how that could be.

"One by one, others developed the same symptoms. And always, somehow, their gifts flourished long after they had passed.

For the first time we panicked. Whatever was happening, we had no precedent."

Serena paused, seeming to choose her words carefully.

"Through a series of events, we discovered that it was Martin. He had somehow found a way to steal our gifts, at the very roots of our essence. With each success he was growing stronger and bolder. Once his deeds came to light, we became the hunted. We had no way to protect ourselves because Martin had planned well, and we were unprepared for that kind of onslaught. We had no choice but to run. We dispersed."

"So we came here?" Natalie said.

"Yes, I was pregnant with you, and I came with Janet, Cliff, Phillip and Mrs. Blaine."

Natalie started. "Mrs. Blaine?"

Serena hesitated. "Mrs. Blaine is your grandmother."

Shock ran through Natalie's body. "What?"

"Yes, it's true. When we came to this town, we thought it best to stay separate so as to avoid detection."

"I can't believe it. Mrs. Blaine?" If Natalie had not already been lying down, she would have needed to.

"Are you okay?" Serena asked. "I've given you a lot of information. I would have liked to have done this a little more slowly, but we don't have much time."

"Martin Reimer is still out there?" Natalie asked.

"Yes. He continues to collect people like us, to steal what we have."

"What does he do with all the gifts?"

"At this point it seems he is just building his power. What he will do after that is anyone's guess," Serena said.

Natalie was suddenly exhausted. It was all so overwhelming. She was afraid to ask the next question. "What will happen to Beausoleil?"

Serena's eyes were sad. "I don't know, sweetheart. Beausoleil locked his gift away, hid it out of sight so that Martin could not steal it. It's hard to say what Martin will try to do to get to it."

"He sounds like a horrible man," Natalie said with a shudder.

"Yes, he is a man without honor or mercy."

"Can anyone stop him?"

Serena hesitated. "It's hard to say."

"Did Phillip's dad try?"

"Yes, he did."

"And that's how he disappeared," Natalie said. "Does Phillip know?"

"If he doesn't, it will just be a matter of time."

"Does Martin Reimer know we're here?" Natalie asked.

Serena's expression was troubled. "It's just a matter of time."

"What are we going to do?"

"That is something we are trying to work out." Serena gave Natalie a squeeze and kissed her forehead. "First and foremost, you will have work to do."

"What?" Natalie said, startled. "What kind of work?"

Serena smiled. "It won't be so bad. You and Phillip will be working with your grandmother."

"Oh." She was not sure how she felt about that. Especially since she just found out that Mrs. Blaine, someone she never, in a million years, would have guessed was a blood relation, was, in fact, that grandmother.

"We need to try to get an idea of what kinds of gifts you both have," Serena said, "and your grandmother will be working with you to try to find that out. It will help us in trying to protect you. Your grandmother will also be able to answer any questions you might have. I'm sure more will come to mind as you think over what we've talked about."

"We're not just going to run?" Natalie asked.

Serena gave her a wry smile. "We've built strong protections here, but if we have to, we will run. We can run only for so long, though. The truth of the matter is that Martin has been growing stronger. Soon there won't be anywhere left for us to run. At some point we have to look at another way. We've managed to protect ourselves so far, but all the commotion we've had here is sure to draw some scrutiny. We have to be ready."

"I'm scared, Mom," Natalie said.

"I know, sweetheart." Serena reached out and caressed Natalie's cheek. "I am, too. But more than anything, I am absolutely determined to keep you safe. That is my driving force, and it overrides my fear. That's one thing to remember, darling. No matter how scared you are, hold tight to the people you love and the values you hold most important. Let that guide you through your fear."

Natalie bowed her head. Her shoulders slumped. That sounded easier said than done.

Serena chuckled. "You might surprise yourself." She ruffled Natalie's hair. "Now, do you have any other questions for me?"

There was one, but Natalie paused, uncertain.

"Go ahead," Serena urged. "You should ask me about anything that's weighing on you."

Natalie's fingers went back to the pattern on her blanket. "Did you love my father?"

Serena's breath seemed to catch.

"You don't have to—" Natalie said.

"Yes," Serena interrupted, "I did." Her smile was sad again. "Sometimes things don't work out between two people, but I would love him again a hundred times over. Of all the gifts I have, the greatest of them is you."

The sadness in Serena's smile disappeared to be replaced by pure happiness, and despite the heaviness in her stomach from that morning's revelations, Natalie felt her mother's radiance spill over her and smiled in return.

Chapter Fourteen

*T*hat evening Natalie lay across her bed, drifting. It was too early to go to bed, and yet the day had been so full she felt exhausted. Her brain simply could not take in any more of anything.

She and Serena had gone to visit Mrs. Blaine that afternoon. Natalie had not been sure how she felt about seeing the intimidating woman who was her grandmother so soon. Her mother had insisted, though, saying that Mrs. Blaine was anxious to see her.

It had turned out to be no less intimidating to see Mrs. Blaine as her grandmother than it had been before she knew her as such. Mrs. Blaine's demeanor was the same as it had always been. She did not embrace her warmly or smile fondly at her as her mother did. She was formal, oddly polite, and Natalie had felt like she had spent the afternoon at tea with the Queen. The only differences in Mrs. Blaine had been the slight softening of her expression whenever she asked Natalie a question, or the way she listened attentively to her whenever she spoke, as if every word she said was important to her. They did not talk about anything significant. The afternoon had been quiet and relaxed. It seemed to Natalie that her mother and Mrs. Blaine had been trying to provide her with an opportunity to adjust to the knowledge that she was now related to Mrs. Blaine.

Her mother had not pressed her as they walked home after, had merely strolled beside her with her arm around Natalie's shoulders. They had walked several blocks without speaking. It was the most relaxed Natalie had been all day.

Still, the worries of the past several hours sat on her like an ever-present weight on her chest. "Will it always be like this? Am I always going to wonder about what happened to Beausoleil and what will happen to Louisa?" she had asked her mother.

Her mother had not answered for a long time. After a while, she had wondered if her mother had just decided to ignore the question. But then she saw Serena swallow, as if there was a lump she could not clear from her throat; had seen pain in the tears that welled briefly in her mother's eyes only to be blinked away in a flash.

"Mom," she said shakily.

"I'm sorry, darling," Serena had answered. "It's just hard for me to speak. There are no words adequate enough to explain how badly I wish I could change what has happened these past several hours. I would do anything to take away your pain and fear and worry."

She had squeezed Natalie's shoulders, and they had walked a few more blocks before Serena spoke again.

"Our past is catching up with us, I'm afraid. We've managed to shield you from much of it all these years. Maybe that was wrong, but as your mother it was the only thing I wanted to do. Until the situation for us changes, it will be a struggle, and there will probably be more lessons and more pain. I'm so sorry."

As they had walked the rest of the way home, Natalie had remembered how she had felt in her bones, just a short time before, that things were going to get bad. Her gift, she had thought bitterly.

And so she now lay on her bed, letting her thoughts run and wishing she could clear them all from her mind and just be free from worry for a while. She contemplated how Phillip thought she was a coward. It seemed to her that it had been a very smart move on her part. Who wanted any part of this, after all?

A tapping at her window jolted her out of her thoughts. She sat up in bed, every nerve in her body snapping to attention. Was there someone out there? She opened her mouth to call for her mother, but then saw pebbles hit the window. Warily, she crossed to the window and peeked out the curtains so as not to be seen.

It was Phillip. He bent down to pick up some more pebbles, so she opened the window and stuck her head out. She did not call out, but held out her hands, palms up: what the heck was he doing? Without a word, Phillip crossed to the tree next to her balcony and climbed, as he had done before. Natalie shut her window and went to the balcony to open the door for him.

He came in and plopped on the floor, catching his breath.

"I wanted to see if you were here before I climbed up," he explained.

"Why didn't you just knock on the front door?" Natalie asked.

"Because your mom would call my mom, and I'd have to go back home."

"Are you running away?"

"No," Phillip said. "I just needed to get away for a while, and I don't want my mom to freak out."

"Don't you think she'll freak out when she finds you're gone?"

"It might be a while before she finds out. I might even be back before then."

"I think you're really mean to do this," Natalie said.

Phillip sighed and leaned his head back against the wall. "I had to do something, anything. Sitting around with my mom after everything that's happened was driving me crazy. At least coming here was a pretty safe decision."

"I guess," Natalie said. "But why would you want to come here?"

Phillip got off the floor. He walked to her desk and sat in the chair. He pulled over the frame with the picture of them all at the picnic and stared at it. Natalie perched at the edge of her bed.

"I shouldn't have said what I said to you in the field," he said.

"That's okay," Natalie said hastily. "Don't worry about it."

Phillip put the picture back in place. He leaned his elbow on the desk and buried his head in his hand. "It's my fault that we were out in the field. It's my fault that the storm found us and took Beausoleil. It's all my fault."

"No it's not," Natalie exclaimed. "You didn't know. None of us knew. We wouldn't have gone if we had. You can't blame yourself like that! But maybe you should stop taking off the way you do, you know? Kind of like what you're doing now?"

Phillip grimaced. "Oh, thanks a lot."

"Well? Look, things are pretty bad, and none of it is your fault."

"That's what my mom said, but I can't stop thinking about what happened to Beausoleil."

"Yeah, me neither."

Phillip looked up. "Did you and your mom talk?"

"Yeah, about everything, just about. Did you know Mrs. Blaine is my grandmother?"

Phillip nodded. "Yeah, kind of wild, huh?"

"Yeah, kind of."

A slow smile grew on Phillip's face. "I always knew you were kind of weird."

"Shut up!" Natalie exclaimed. She grabbed one of her pillows and threw it at him.

Phillip caught it and grinned. He threw it back, hitting her square in the face. Natalie gasped in surprise, giggling. Phillip grabbed another pillow, and soon they were standing in the middle of the room, engaged in battle.

Phillip chuckled as he swung out with his pillow, and for the first time in what seemed like ages, Natalie felt as if all the tension inside her dropped away. She gave a big swing of her pillow, and as it smacked Phillip, feathers popped and drifted around the room.

Phillip's eyes widened, his mouth opened in silent laughter, his expression filled with merriment. It was the most carefree she had seen him, and happiness tingled through her in response.

"You've done it now," Phillip said. He smacked her with his pillow, causing the feathers in his to spill out over the room as well.

Natalie could not help herself; she gave a scream of laughter as they both swung their pillows with renewed vigor.

"Natalie! What's going on in there?"

She and Phillip stopped dead. The feathers floated down around them. Natalie felt a brief surge of laughter, but quelled it as she realized her mother's voice was coming from the top of the landing, right down the hallway.

"Hide," she hissed to Phillip. Her mother's footsteps had started down the hallway towards her bedroom. Phillip jumped to the side of her bed and crouched just as Serena knocked on Natalie's door.

"Is everything all right?" Serena queried, and then opened the door.

The shock on Serena's face almost sent Natalie into another gale of laughter, but panic overrode it as she realized she had no way to explain the giant mess of feathers coating everything.

"What happened?" Serena's shock seemed to have kept her from stepping fully into the room.

Natalie tried to think of something, but all that came was a big blank nothing.

Serena's tone brooked no nonsense. "Natalie, what is going on?"

Something behind Natalie caught Serena's attention. Natalie turned, and saw Phillip stand up from where he had crouched by the bed. He had the pillow in his hand; feathers clung to his hair and dripped from the pillow.

"Phillip!" Serena exclaimed. "Your mother just called. She is out of her mind with worry! What are you doing here?"

Phillip hung his head. "Sorry, Mrs. Bristol. I just needed to get away for a little while."

"So you leave without telling your mother and let her go out of her mind with worry?" Serena scolded.

"She would have made me stay," Phillip protested.

"Yes, well, there's a reason for that, as you well know! Not only is this not the time to go wandering off on your own, but you were irresponsible about it. Phillip, I am disappointed in you."

Phillip had the decency to look ashamed.

Serena's eyes narrowed. "How did you get in here?" She looked at Natalie. "I didn't hear anyone knock."

Natalie struggled to find a good explanation that would not get Phillip into any more trouble, but aside from a lie, which she did not think was a good idea, nothing came to mind.

"You seem a little tongue-tied tonight, Natalie." There was a frown on her mother's face that told her she was going to be in hot water unless she had a good explanation.

Phillip sheepishly lifted his hand and pointed his finger at the balcony.

Serena's brows hit the top of her forehead. "You came in through the balcony? How is that possible?" She walked over to the balcony and stepped out, looking around. "Oh, my goodness, did you climb up that tree?"

"Yes," Phillip said.

Serena walked back into the room. Her expression was incredulous. "I can't even comment on this. I'm going to leave this one for your mother. We're going to give her a call right now. Phillip, you come with me."

As she walked out of the room, she said to Natalie, "You clean all this up, young lady."

Phillip followed after Serena. Before he left the room he set the pillow on Natalie's desk and gave Natalie a shrug. A smile played about the corners of his mouth. Natalie stifled a laugh and grimaced.

Phillip made to leave, but then hesitated. Natalie waited. She did not know what he wanted to say, but she was glad that whatever it was, it kept him there.

"See you later," Phillip said finally.

"Yeah," Natalie said, "see you later."

Chapter Fifteen

"Do you two have any questions for me?"

Natalie shook her head as did Phillip. Mrs. Blaine sat in front of them, leaning on her cane. She peered at them with blue eyes so penetrating, Natalie felt obliged to make up a question.

She and Phillip were to spend the morning with Mrs. Blaine. When they had arrived at her house, she had taken them out to her garden. It was a beautifully landscaped space, bordered with shrubbery that blocked out prying eyes. Various plants and multi-colored flowers speckled the lawn, and sturdy trees added scenic shade. A little path wove through it all. If Natalie had not been so intimidated by Mrs. Blaine, she would have enjoyed the grounds immensely. Whenever she had passed Mrs. Blaine's imposing house before, she had always wondered what went on inside and what Mrs. Blaine was really like. Now that she knew, it was a mix of not-what-she-had-expected, and even-more-than-she-could-have-imagined.

There was a table laid out for them with an assortment of pastries and jams, and some juice and milk. It was all very welcoming, but Natalie's stomach felt as if it had a cork stopped up in it. The look on Phillip's face said he had the same dilemma.

Still, they sat down and took some of the pastries onto their plates, and poured their juice while Mrs. Blaine sat with them and waited. Once they had their plates ready, she had asked them her question.

"I know your mothers have spoken with you," she continued, "so I won't reiterate what you've been told. This morning I'd like to try to see if I can get an idea of what kind of gift or gifts you each might be coming into."

"How are you going to do that?" Natalie asked nervously.

Mrs. Blaine's eyes softened a bit at Natalie's question. "You don't have to worry, child. Yes, it is a scary thing to feel your power when you have no control over it, but we will be going slowly. We will be exploring, but I will also be teaching you as we go along."

Phillip, who had been munching on a cherry strudel, looked like a child to whom Christmas had come early. "Mom said it's an honor to be taught by you."

Mrs. Blaine smiled. "Your mother is too kind."

Natalie sat up in her chair, nonplussed. How come Phillip knew more about her grandmother than she did?

"Your mother is my daughter so perhaps it's easier to take me for granted," Mrs. Blaine said with a twinkle. Only the words were not spoken aloud; Natalie heard them directly in her head.

She gave a little cry. The coffee cake she had picked up to nibble fell to the plate with a light thud, causing Phillip to look up from his strudel.

Mrs. Blaine reached across and patted her hand. "Don't panic, my dear. I just wanted to do a little test."

"What happened?" Phillip asked.

"One of the gifts of our family, Natalie's and mine, seems to be a variation on mind tricks. Reading thoughts, sending messages through the mind, influence. I was checking to see if Natalie might have inherited it as well, and it seems she has," Mrs. Blaine said. "I'm sorry to have surprised you, my dear, but when you first start coming into your gifts, they tend to start off when you're unaware. You've also spent considerable energy blocking yours, so I needed to put out feelers. Please forgive me."

Natalie rubbed her head. Nothing hurt, but she was not too happy about the intrusion.

"So you just did something with Natalie?" Phillip asked. "That's so cool!"

"Oh, fine for you, I'm sure!" Natalie said crossly.

"I will make sure to warn you next time, my dear," Mrs. Blaine said. "I know you don't like it, but I do ask that you keep your mind open to what we are doing here. It is important. I would not ask it of you otherwise."

"I don't mind," Phillip chimed in.

Mrs. Blaine gave a little laugh. It was a sound that transformed her, made her a little less intimidating, although Natalie did not think she would be throwing her arms around her in a hug anytime soon. Still, the sound of her laugh warmed Natalie.

"I could give it a try," she mumbled. She gave Phillip a little glare for being a suck-up, but he merely took a smug bite of his strudel and chewed contentedly.

"Phillip, do you know what your father's gift is?" Natalie noticed that Mrs. Blaine referred to Mr. Stone in the present tense.

Phillip's demeanor sobered. He studied his strudel. "I think it has to do with sketches."

"Not just sketches, but paintings and photographs as well," Mrs. Blaine said. "Your father could bring anything he wanted out of them."

"I don't understand," Natalie said.

"If my dad needed a hammer," Phillip explained, "he could draw a picture of one, and then he would have it in his hand."

"Wow," Natalie said. That sounded really cool, she had to admit.

"Do you know what your mother can do?" Mrs. Blaine asked Phillip.

"Something to do with sewing," he said.

"Yes, that is correct. There is something special about your mother's sewing projects. Everyone in the town wears something sewn by her, and it has helped us keep them and this town protected."

"What do you think I'll be able to do?" Phillip asked.

"Well, we'll have to do a little digging. You're about the right age, so it might only take a little prodding to see what's coming down the road for you," Mrs. Blaine said.

"What can my mom do?" Natalie asked in a small voice.

Mrs. Blaine smiled. "Your mom had a particularly hard time with hers, my dear. I suspect you will find yourself running into similar challenges, if you aren't already.

"Your mother is exceptionally gifted when it comes to mind tricks. She can do a number of them; she can read people's thoughts, influence them; at times she can even see where people's thoughts will take them. It's not quite predicting the future, although sometimes a flash of the future may come to her as well. Then there are variations on her gift, but that may vary from situation to situation."

"She can read our minds?" Phillip asked uneasily. He shot a quick look at Natalie and then down at the table. Mrs. Blaine's eyes glimmered in amusement.

Natalie, however, felt just as uneasy as Phillip looked. Had her mother been reading her mind her whole life?

"One of the challenges Serena had to master was controlling when to use her gift, and when not to use it," Mrs. Blaine said. "When we were at peace, she rarely used it at all. However, in our current situation, it has been very useful. I doubt she ever intrudes on anyone who doesn't want her in their heads. Not unless they want her to," she added.

A switch suddenly flipped in Natalie's head. "Like when she reads for people?"

Mrs. Blaine nodded. "When we came into this town, we were marked. We had to try to blend in and hide, but we knew we had a responsibility to keep this town and its citizens safe. When your mother opens shop, my dear, the customers give her insight as to what is going on in the town. People see and hear things they are not even aware of, some of which could be warning signs that danger is close. If we have warning, we can fortify, and that has happened on occasion."

It all made sense now. Natalie had always hated when her mother opened shop, had always wondered why she could not do something else. Now she saw that with Serena's work, her mother had her clients' blessing to see into them, to try to glean what might lie ahead for all of them. So much had been going on that she had not been aware of, had not wanted to know.

Mrs. Blaine leaned forward now. "Phillip, why don't we start with you?"

To Natalie's surprise Phillip looked slightly apprehensive.

"Not so easy when it's you, huh?" Natalie could not help teasing.

Phillip scowled. "Oh, be quiet. I'm not scared."

"It's natural to feel a little scared," Mrs. Blaine said. "As a matter of fact, it's a good sign that you are. Your gift is not something to be trifled with.

"I'd like you to try to think of a time, Phillip, when you felt something unusual. It could be anything: a rush you felt inside, maybe you were lightheaded for no reason, or the world looked different to you, somehow."

Phillip thought for a moment, but after a while he shook his head in disappointment. "I can't think of anything—sorry."

"What about that thing that happened when we were looking at your maps?" Natalie said.

Phillip looked at her, puzzled. "Huh?"

"Remember? We were looking at that big map in your room, and all of a sudden it was like the streets started to come alive or something."

"What are you talking about? That was the day you said my father was alive."

"Yes, but that part came after. Right before that, the thing with the map happened."

Mrs. Blaine listened with interest. "So you're saying, Natalie, that something strange happened while Phillip was showing you one of his maps?"

"Yes."

"I didn't know about that," Phillip said. "You never said anything."

"I guess I wasn't thinking about it," Natalie admitted. "It just came to mind now since we're talking about unusual things."

"Had you experienced anything like that before?" Mrs. Blaine asked.

"No," Natalie said, "it felt like something different."

Mrs. Blaine had a speculative look on her face. "You haven't experienced anything with the maps before?" she asked Phillip.

"No," Phillip said.

"And yet it was your map that you and Natalie were looking at," she mused. She stood suddenly with her cane. "Please come with me."

Natalie and Phillip rose and followed Mrs. Blaine into her house. She led them past the main room and opened the door to her office. At least Natalie assumed it was her office. Although it contained the requisite desk as well as bookshelves that ran up to the high ceiling, it had a decidedly feminine feel to it. The wood panels and bookshelves were painted white, and the walls were a light blue color. Lace curtains hung from the picture windows. The desk was all rounded corners instead of the standard sharp edges.

Mrs. Blaine crossed to one of the shelves and pulled out a thin leather-bound volume. She walked with it to her desk and beckoned them over. She opened the book, revealing pages of colorful maps.

"These are maps of our area," Phillip said.

"Yes." Mrs. Blaine flipped to a map and pointed to an area on it. "Do you know where this is?"

Phillip cocked his head to get a better look. "Yes, that's Parker's Field. We play baseball there."

"Let's see if you are your father's son." Mrs. Blaine opened up a drawer and pulled out another map. "Take this. It has my location on it. Do you recognize it?"

Phillip turned the map around in his hands. "Yes, I see it here."

"Good," Mrs. Blaine said. "Keep that copy with you." She watched as Phillip folded the map and put it in his back pocket.

"Now if you would, please come over here and look at that location for Parker's Field. Concentrate on it, and let's see if anything happens."

Phillip walked over to the map. He hesitated for a second, then took a deep breath and focused on the spot where Parker's Field lay. He stared for several seconds.

Natalie was not sure what they were waiting for, but nothing shook or stirred or vibrated around them.

Mrs. Blaine patted Phillip on the back. "That will do for now."

Phillip stepped back. His lips were a crooked line of disappointment.

"Nothing to be upset about," Mrs. Blaine said. "We just need to keep exploring. Sometimes it just takes time." She gestured Natalie over. "Why don't you give it a try, dear? Take the other map from Phillip."

Butterflies fluttered in Natalie's stomach. She took the map from Phillip and moved around the table. "What am I trying to do?"

"At this point I'm not too sure. I'm trying to recreate what happened when you said you felt something unusual with the maps."

"Great," Natalie muttered.

"Remember what I said. Please keep your mind open about what we are trying to accomplish. It's important," Mrs. Blaine said.

Natalie nodded. She focused on Parker's Field. She braced herself for something to happen, waited for the map to shift and evolve like it did before, but nothing did.

"That will do for now, dear," Mrs. Blaine said.

"Sorry," Natalie said.

Phillip looked relieved that he was not the only one who failed the test.

"Oh, honestly," Natalie said, exasperated, "could you want anything to happen more?"

Phillip chuckled. "Probably not," he admitted. "But I'm kind of glad the map thing didn't work for you. Maps are my thing."

"You are such a weirdo. Does it really matter what we can or can't do?"

Phillip looked as if she had sprouted horns. "You're kidding, right? I mean come on! I'll bet you can't even find your own house on a map."

Natalie did not have much of an argument there, but darned if she was going to admit that. She grabbed the map and searched it for her house. Unfortunately, all she could see was a series of criss-crossing lines and squiggles and none of it made any sense. She tilted her head this way and that, trying to make heads or tails, but it might as well have been a foreign language.

"Give up?" Phillip teased.

"Fine," Natalie said grudgingly.

"It's there." He pointed to a spot on the map. Natalie looked at where his finger was and recognized the street names as the ones surrounding her area.

"Oh." It was starting to make a little sense. "Which way do we go to get to your home?" she asked Phillip.

Phillip moved his finger down the map. Natalie looked at the street name.

"Cullom Lane," she said. "I get it now."

She followed with Phillip as his finger traced along the road they took to get to his home.

It was then that the map started to move. Cullom Lane had widened, become larger. Natalie blinked. Could her eyes be playing tricks on her?

But no, Cullom Lane was growing, shifting the other sections of the map aside and coming into sharp relief.

"What the..." she heard Phillip say.

Details emerged from the map. A sidewalk appeared, and then a stop sign. She recognized the fire hydrant she always passed when walking to Phillip's house. Street lights lined the sidewalk for blocks and blocks. There was the shrubbery from the Winterbell's house.

As the details appeared, they grew large—the way things grew big as you got close.

There was a rushing sound in her ears, as if a wave of water had crashed. A ball of heat slammed into her and then surrounded her in a warm cocoon, pulling her towards Cullom Lane. The Winterbell's shrubs loomed large, and her body glided towards them as if she were a plane coming in for a landing. She opened her mouth to scream, but there was a blinding flash of light. When the light receded, Mrs. Blaine's study had disappeared, and she was standing in the middle of the Winterbell's shrubs.

Her stomach dropped, her knees almost followed, but a hand clamped around her mouth just as she was about to cry out.

"Shhhh!" It was Phillip. He held a finger to his lips. He was pale, but his eyes glowed with delight and amazement. He pointed to a couple walking past the shrubs. Natalie and Phillip were well covered, but explaining why they were in the shrubs could become an issue.

The couple had paused in front of the shrubs. Natalie recognized Nathan and Erica Law, a young couple that had recently married. For a second they looked around as if they had heard something. Natalie shrunk further back into the shrubs with Phillip.

"Did...did you just hear something?" Nathan asked. He had unruly blond hair which only added to his flustered demeanor.

His wife, Erica, had brown hair and clear gray eyes that seemed to miss nothing as she scanned the area.

"I thought I did," she said, "but I'm not sure what."

They listened some more. Natalie held her breath and tried frantically to think of an excuse for why they were in the shrubs.

Luckily, Nathan shrugged and said, "Probably nothing." He put an arm around Erica. "Have I told you how beautiful you are today?"

"Well," Erica said with a small laugh, "aren't you the sweet one!" She wrapped an arm around him. "I'm one lucky gal."

"I'm the lucky one," Nathan said.

"Yes, you are."

"Hey!" Nathan exclaimed. He gave his wife a big kiss that went on for a long time. Heat spread across Natalie's cheeks as she and Phillip waited for the couple to leave. She was starting to think being discovered might be the better alternative when, finally, the couple broke apart and, arms wrapped around each other, they continued their sojourn down the street.

"That took long enough," Phillip whispered irritably. His cheeks were pink, but he peeked through the branches and nodded at Natalie. "All clear." He pushed through the shrubs, and Natalie followed him out into the open.

It was Cullom Lane all right. Natalie could hardly believe what she was seeing; one second they had been in Mrs. Blaine's office, and the next, they were standing in a completely different place.

"This is so awesome!" Phillip leaped up into the air with a big fist pump. His cry was exultant, his laughter free, and Natalie could not help but feel a rush of enthusiasm herself.

She walked to the sidewalk and looked up and down the street. Everything looked real at least.

"Did you do this?" Phillip asked.

"I don't think so," she said.

"I wonder what happened. We should get back to Mrs. Blaine's and see what she says." Phillip wheeled around and started down the sidewalk. He clearly could not wait to get back and learn some more from Mrs. Blaine. "We'll need to hurry," he said over his shoulder, "it's a bit of a walk."

"Hey, Phillip," Natalie called, "why don't we just use the map?" She pulled out the map she'd brought along and waved it.

Phillip's eyes lit up. "Oh yeah, that's why she had us take one with us."

They opened up the map, and with a quick nod to each other, Phillip located Mrs. Blaine's house on the map and pointed. They focused on the spot and once again, details sprang to life. There was a large hedge on Mrs. Blaine's lawn, and they glided in its direction. In the blink of an eye, they were back at Mrs. Blaine's, standing behind her hedge.

Phillip whooped again, and this time Natalie joined him, the two of them hugging in a jumping dance. What had she been afraid of? This was fun!

"Let's find Mrs. Blaine," Phillip said, and she ran with him up the steps to the front door.

It opened as they hit the top step. Mrs. Blaine stood there and ushered them inside. They crowded into the main room, and Natalie joined in with Phillip as they recounted their experiences traveling through the maps.

"Things started appearing on the map!"

"There was this whooshing sound!"

"All of sudden we were just there!"

"We did it again to get back here!"

"It was just so awesome!"

"It totally was!"

Mrs. Blaine listened as they talked, her head moving from Natalie to Phillip and back as their words spilled over each other in their enthusiasm. She leaned on her cane and smiled, although there was hesitancy to that smile that made Natalie wonder if there was something wrong.

"So what happened, exactly?" Phillip asked when the last of their excitement had faded. "I can't tell whose gift it was."

"Yes," Mrs. Blaine said, "it is a little hard to tell. I suspect it's your gift, Phillip. It would fit, given that it could be a variation on your father's gift. You have not fully come into it yet, but it seems it's there when Natalie works with you."

"Why?" Natalie said. "I don't get it."

"I'm not too sure about that either," Mrs. Blaine admitted. "It might have to do with whatever your gifts might be, my dear."

"What are my gifts then?"

Again, there was that hesitancy in Mrs. Blaine. "I believe you have gifts similar to your mother's. You have some of the same experiences she did. At the same time, you have experienced things unrelated to what one would think your gift would be. I would need more time to work with you to be sure."

"Do you have any ideas?" Natalie asked nervously. Mrs. Blaine did not sound reassuring at all.

Mrs. Blaine seemed to consider her words. "It's possible, my dear, that you might have the ability to take on other people's gifts, perhaps even to enhance them."

"Oh," Natalie said, "that doesn't sound *too* bad."

"Sounds pretty cool to me," Phillip said.

"Yes, it would be an asset." Something like worry flashed across Mrs. Blaine's face, but it was fleeting. She smiled at the two of them.

"Why didn't I experience anything that first time with Natalie when she told me about my dad?" Phillip asked.

"I would say that your gift was at a very early stage at that point, whereas Natalie's had developed enough to where she could take on yours enough to affect her. What happened today could be a sign that you will be coming into your gift soon, Phillip."

Now Phillip looked as if Christmas, Easter, Halloween and his birthday had arrived.

"I think you've both had enough excitement this morning," Mrs. Blaine said. "You are both free to go for today. I will let your mothers know what we've done so far.

"One word of caution," she added. "I know you might be excited by what you've discovered today, but you must refrain from experimenting until you have a good handle on what you can do and have learned to control it. It can be dangerous, so please exercise restraint."

"I guess it would be bad to travel through a map somewhere and forget to take a return map with you," Phillip commented.

"I sent the copy with you just in case, but we will be experimenting with that as well. Until we know more, however, I would hate for you to end up stuck somewhere with no easy means of making it back home," Mrs. Blaine said.

"Will we see you again tomorrow?" Phillip asked eagerly.

"Yes," Mrs. Blaine said, "how about the same time here?"

"Okay," Natalie said as Phillip nodded.

"Until tomorrow then." Mrs. Blaine put a hand on Phillip's shoulder, and then touched Natalie's cheek as she leaned over and kissed her forehead. It was a surprising gesture; Natalie still had a hard time remembering that Mrs. Blaine was her grandmother. But it warmed her, and she gave Mrs. Blaine a shy smile.

Chapter Sixteen

"So what did you think?" Phillip asked her on the walk to his home after departing Mrs. Blaine's.

It was now late morning, but the sky was blue and sunny, and the air fresh and cool. It was strange to think they had the ability to hop through the map, but even with that convenience, the walk felt good, and Natalie preferred it on a day like this.

"Pretty crazy," Natalie said.

"It was great! I can't wait until I get my gift. It would be so awesome if it was really the maps. I could go anywhere." Phillip fell silent then. Natalie wondered if he was thinking about his dad and wishing he knew where he was.

"Where would you go first?" she asked, hoping to distract him from his thoughts. "Didn't you want to go to China?"

"Yeah, but I'm gonna wait on that one. I'll go there with my dad."

"So where would you go instead?"

Phillip gave it some thought. "Probably Mount Rushmore. It would be cool to see those presidents' faces carved into the side of a mountain. Where would you go?"

"I don't know," Natalie said. "I haven't thought about it. There really isn't any place I'd like to go. I guess I'd want to stay here."

"My dad says that once you experience different places, you'll want to keep traveling. He always talked about all the cities he'd seen, what they were like, and which ones he'd like to go back to. He told me he'd take me with him." Phillip trailed off. "Anyway," he continued abruptly, "what are we going to do for the rest of the day?"

"I don't know." Natalie had not been aware that they were going to be doing anything for the rest of the day. "Maybe we could ask to go to the circus? We could check in on Louisa and Hercules."

Phillip brightened. "That's a good idea! We can ask my mom if we can go."

Mrs. Stone was waiting for them at the door when they arrived.

"Your mom asked if you could stay here for the afternoon," Mrs. Stone said to Natalie over Phillip's shoulder as she hugged him.

"Aw mom, c'mon!" Phillip complained from under his mother's arms.

Mrs. Stone stepped back, beaming with pride. "You are your father's son." Her eyes were a little misty. "I just got done talking to Mrs. Blaine, and she told me what you two did this afternoon."

"We're not too sure it's my gift," Phillip said.

"I'm willing to bet it is. And you, young lady," she hugged Natalie, "it looks like we'll have our hands full with you."

"We're not too sure," Natalie said. "I hope not."

Mrs. Stone put her hand on Natalie's head. "Well, we'll take it as it comes." The look in her eyes held the same concern Mrs. Blaine's had.

Natalie's unease grew over the reactions of both women. What was the problem with her gift? It was not like she would be eager to use it. It was, when you thought about it, pretty much wasted on her.

As it turned out, Mrs. Stone was more than happy to let them go to the circus.

"It's early enough and should be safe at this point," Mrs. Stone said. "But don't get into trouble, and make sure you're back by early this afternoon. And do not," she emphasized, "under any circumstances, leave the circus grounds unless it is to come straight back. I do not want you running off again or we will have problems. Are we clear on that, Phillip?"

"Yes, ma'am," Phillip mumbled.

"Good. Then if you don't mind, I have to work to do on a dress for Mrs. Milner. Why these ladies choose to do things at the last minute is beyond me." She kissed Phillip's cheek, hugged Natalie again, and bustled back inside.

Natalie started to leave, but Phillip said, "Hold up a sec, let me go grab something." He ran into the house and came back holding a map.

"Why are you bringing that?" Natalie asked suspiciously.

Phillip's face was all innocence. "You never know when we might need it."

Natalie put her hands on her hips. "We're not supposed to be doing that until we know more!"

"No," Phillip said, "we're supposed to exercise restraint."

"You don't know how to exercise restraint!"

"Ouch, I don't have an argument for that," Phillip said. He tucked the map into his jeans pocket. "Let's go ahead and get walking then. But I'll keep the map with us just in case," he said with a mischievous grin.

As they approached the circus, Natalie grew apprehensive about seeing Hercules and Louisa. It had been difficult, thinking about what had happened to them and Beausoleil, and now, coming to visit, she was not sure what to expect.

The circus was not as crowded as usual. Natalie supposed it was more like a fixture in the town now and had thus lost some of its allure. Still, there were people milling about, and bits of conversation floated around. The storms continued to be a hot topic.

"They say the storm hit close to here," someone at the concession stand was saying, "but for some reason, it didn't reach us."

"We are lucky," someone else replied. "Must be angels watching over us."

If they only knew, Natalie thought.

"Where do you think they are?" Phillip asked her now, as a clown wobbled by on stilts.

"Let's try Beausoleil's tent."

A placard seated on an easel greeted them at the entrance.

Canceled Until Further Notice

Phillip frowned at the sign. "What should we do now?"

"Let's look inside. Maybe Hercules is hanging around in there."

They parted the opening of the tent and walked in. The props were all gone, and the seats sat empty. Quiet filled every corner despite the muffled sounds of talking, yelling and laughter from outside.

"Hercules!" Natalie called out. "It's Natalie and Phillip, are you here?"

There was a rustle backstage and a flap parted. Hercules poked his head out.

"Hi, Hercules," Natalie said.

Hercules had dark circles under his eyes. He appeared too tired to even put on a grumpy face, but he nodded hello and waved his hand for them to come backstage.

"I'm just straightening up," Hercules said. Boxes were strewn about, and partially wrapped props waited to be packed away. "The manager wants Beausoleil's stuff cleared out so we can use the tent for other circus acts."

"What do they think happened to Beausoleil?" Natalie asked.

"They think he skipped town." Hercules frowned at a prop that would not fit into a box. "That happens in the circus; it can be a transient crowd. If he comes back, they'll try to fit him back in—if they don't replace him first. He was a good act." At that Hercules shoulders slumped, and he sighed.

"How's Louisa?" Phillip asked.

"See for yourself. She's over there."

Louisa stood in the corner, in doll's form. Natalie weaved her way through the boxes to her. The doll was just as entrancing as the first time she had seen it. She could see now how it resembled Louisa, but she never would have guessed that the beautiful porcelain skin could run warm, or that the stiff joints could bend and move as smoothly as her own. She knew Louisa was in there somewhere, but you never would have been able to tell from the way the doll was now.

"Why a doll?" she asked. Phillip had come up beside her to look as well. "Why did Beausoleil choose a doll? Why bring it to life like that?"

"It was a way to remind him of his daughter," Hercules said. "When he first made the doll, he poured every memory of her into its details. He did not want to forget a thing."

"He didn't really think bringing the doll to life would make it a good replacement for his daughter, did he?" Phillip asked, with a slight grimace.

"I don't know what a grieving father thinks in that circumstance," Hercules said simply. "I do think he was in a dark place when he brought the doll to life. Regardless, he wouldn't have hung on to that belief, if at all. I do think after he brought the doll to life, it occurred to him that it would be the perfect hiding place for his gift. When he returned the doll to form, he could fold his gift into it and keep it locked and safe."

"How could she seem so real?" Natalie asked.

Hercules tossed a prop into one of the boxes. "Knowing what you do now, do you think of Louisa as just a doll?"

Natalie shook her head. Phillip thought about it for a moment and then shook his head as well.

"Nor do I," Hercules said. "Even when she's in doll form, I think of her as Louisa. And when she's not a doll, she's as real to me as any human."

"Beausoleil seems to love her, too," Natalie said.

"In his own way," Hercules said. "It puts him in a strange place. He misses his daughter, and Louisa is real enough to be another child to him. But the doll also serves a very important purpose for him. When needed, he has to return it to form."

"It's all very strange and confusing," Phillip commented.

"How are you doing, Hercules?" Natalie asked.

"How do you think? These have been some of the worst days of my life. My friend Beausoleil is gone, and my dear Louisa is locked in a doll's form. I have no way to help them. I don't even know how to try. And I can't cover for them forever. It's all so stressful!"

"I'm sorry." Natalie could think of nothing else to say.

"Me too," Phillip said. "It's my fault."

"You stop that now," Hercules scolded. "You're too young to cause this kind of trouble—well, heaven forbid you ever cause this kind of trouble at your age. But this has been going on since before you were out of diapers. It's not your fault. I will say, though, that it would be nice if you could think before jumping in and doing whatever comes off the top of your head in the moment."

"Yeah," Natalie agreed, "that is something he needs to work on."

Phillip nodded grudgingly. "Yeah, I really do."

"Do you have any gifts, Hercules?" Natalie asked.

"Me? No." Hercules pulled himself onto a box and took out a handkerchief to mop his brow. "But Beausoleil's secrets, and yours by extension, are safe with me. Beausoleil saved my life, you see."

"How?" Phillip asked.

Hercules settled more comfortably on the box. "I was in a different circus at the time, and we were between cities. We had an unfortunate mishap, and some of the animals had gotten away. We organized several search parties to go after them, and I was one of the ones left behind.

"I happened to be alone by some of the empty cages when I heard a growl. When I turned around, it was one of the lions. It had come back, and it was stalking me."

Hercules shook his head at the memory. Natalie was sure her eyes were popping out of her head.

"Every time I moved in one direction, it would track me. I knew I didn't stand a chance running, and there was nowhere I could go; I was trapped. When it pulled back on its haunches, I figured this was it, I was a goner.

"But then, out of the corner of my eye, I saw something move. I glanced for a second, and I swear I nearly fainted.

"One of the cages was scurrying—I kid you not—scurrying across the gravel like a spider. It was the most unbelievable thing I'd ever seen. I thought for sure the lion had already grabbed me and that I was dead and stuck in some weird after-life.

"The lion was startled as well. It jerked in one direction, and then another. But then the spider cage leaped into the air and landed on top of it, caging it in.

"I really did faint after that." Hercules looked as if he felt like a bit of a fool. Natalie did not think he was; she would have died of fright.

"Before I fainted, though," Hercules continued, "I saw Beausoleil, standing at the edge of the field. He wasn't moving, but his attention was focused on that cage, and somehow I knew he was behind it. When I came to, he was gone.

"No one else had seen, of course, and when the search party returned and we had successfully captured the remaining animals, I kept my mouth shut. Who would believe such a crazy thing?

"That night, though, there was a commotion. Someone had been found taking food from our stores. When they dragged the culprit in front of us, I recognized Beausoleil as the man who had been standing in that field.

Food can get scarce when you travel, so everyone was angry. There was talk that perhaps this man had caused our mishap in order to steal from us. Sometimes an angry mob can lose all reason, and it was not looking good for Beausoleil.

"But I stepped forward and told them that I had told the man to help himself, that he had been looking for employment and that he had a good skill that would make good money for our show. I told them that I had been planning to bring him to our manager as soon as he had eaten.

"When they asked me what that skill was, I looked at Beausoleil and said, 'Magic and illusion.'"

Hercules laughed then, and Phillip and Natalie laughed along with him. He spread his arms wide and said, "And the rest is history. We became friends, and I learned his story, and we've stuck together ever since."

He sobered after that. "I just hope that wherever he is, he's doing all right."

Natalie could think of nothing to say. Phillip was solemn as well. After a moment she crossed to the doll.

"Is she okay like this?" she asked.

"Oh, yes," Hercules said, "this is normal. When we're able to bring her out, she will be the way she has always been."

"Is Beausoleil the only one who can bring her out?" Phillip asked.

"Yes," Hercules said, "he's the key to unlocking her."

Natalie reached out to touch the doll's hair. "Hey, Louisa," she said. She took the doll's hand.

The air crackled. A vibration hummed up her arm from the doll's hand. Oh no, she thought, not again!

"What are you doing?" Hercules cried out.

"Uh, oh," she heard Phillip say.

The porcelain softened and color ran like a river under it. The doll was changing.

"How are you doing that?" Hercules whispered.

Natalie did not answer. This was her curse.

The doll's joints loosened and became supple. The fingers on the hand Natalie held closed around hers. The doll became larger as the force inside it grew. Light came into the eyes, and they fluttered and focused. The mouth softened and parted into a sigh; Louisa was coming back.

And then, just as Natalie anticipated, the other part of her curse arrived.

The world faded as if a canvas had come up to cover it, and her mind floated free. She knew better, though. There was no freedom for her in this.

Awareness flickered along the edges of her consciousness. It curled up and around, enveloping her. It burned through the canvas that blanketed her from the world, slowly revealing another world for her to see.

Chapter Seventeen

It was dark, gloomy. Stone and metal surrounded her. She was in a room, a prison of some kind. Light filtered through a slit of windows set under the ceiling. They made it worse, somehow, those slivers of light. They accentuated the darkness of the room, and that darkness was enough to stamp out any hope those outside rays might bring.

A man hung in the middle of the room. Nothing tied him, yet his arms and legs were outstretched, pulled from his body by invisible bonds. Had these invisible bonds not held him, he would have fallen—every part of him ran slack. His chin bobbed onto his chest. His hair lay matted and dirty against his forehead. He gave a little groan and his head came up. It was Beausoleil.

Natalie felt a jolt inside. She tried to run to Beausoleil, but she had no body to take her there. It was as if only her mind hovered over the room, watching, only watching.

A light orb surrounded Beausoleil. It pulsed with an energy that seemed to eat at every living thing in the room.

Beausoleil gasped and licked his lips, which were caked and dry. "Please, no more. I have nothing you want."

"I find that hard to believe."

Natalie started. She had not seen anyone else in the room. Now a figure stepped into the orb, its back to her.

It was tall. A cloak covered its head and draped its form. Its voice was low and deep—a man's voice. He spoke leisurely, knowing he would have no problem being heard, certain that the hostage in front of him would cling to his every word. A panic froze Natalie's mind. This was a man to haunt her nightmares.

"I don't know why the storm picked me," Beausoleil cried. "It must have been mistaken!"

"I doubt that very much," the man said. "I can feel remnants of power flowing from you. I find it fascinating that that is all there is. It makes me wonder what else there was, and how on earth you have managed to hide it."

"I don't know what you're talking about!" Beausoleil insisted.

"Tsk, tsk, tsk." The man shook his head. "Haven't you learned by now that if you don't give me what I want, I am forced to go in and get it?"

The man reached out, his fingers stretched, spindly and claw-like. They fastened onto Beausoleil's chest and glowed as they pierced his flesh.

Beausoleil's face filled with a pain that tore through his entire body. A gasp filled Natalie, but she could only watch as Beausoleil's body arched in an agony too painful for cries or screams. When the man stepped back, Beausoleil fell slack, his body wracked.

"What do you want? Oh, please tell me what you want." Beausoleil was crying, at the breaking point.

Natalie felt every sob as if it were her own. "Stop," she said in silence, "please stop."

The man sighed. "I see one of us will need to search the area where you were found. Perhaps we can get more information that way. Sebastian, I think, will do for that mission."

His words galvanized Beausoleil. He yanked against his invisible bonds. "I have nothing you want!" he screamed. "Why can't you just let me go?" His body shook as sobs wracked him.

The man watched Beausoleil. "Yes," he said finally, "there is something there, I think, in the place we found you. Tell me what it is!"

"Nothing!" screamed Beausoleil.

The man shook his head. "You never learn." He put out his hands and latched them to Beausoleil's chest again. Natalie did not think it was possible, but Beausoleil's eyes translated a pain that was worse than the last time. It stiffened his body to a point that Natalie thought the pain would break him.

"Noooooooo," Natalie's mind screamed. "Nooooooo!"

The man stepped back from Beausoleil, his hands mid-air. Beausoleil's body fell, suspended only by his invisible bonds.

The man stood, stock still, transfixed and alert.

"What's this?" His head swiveled from one side, and then to the other. "What is this I feel?" He looked at Beausoleil. "There is something here."

Beausoleil was barely conscious, but he mumbled, "I don't know what you're talking about."

The man whispered, "I feel it. There is power here." His head tilted, feeling the room. "Not yet fully formed, but..." his head went up, inhaling deeply, "...yes, very powerful indeed."

The man peered into Beausoleil's face. "Is it yours? Did it come looking for you?"

There was no answer from Beausoleil; he had lost consciousness, his head slumped and hanging. The man straightened. Natalie watched as he toured the room, his face hidden by his cloak. He strolled as if he had all the time in the world.

"Where are you?" he crooned.

Natalie's blood froze.

"I can feel you here. Come out, come out wherever you are."

Fear choked her. She watched as the man circled, coming closer.

Please, she thought, I want to go. Please, let me leave.

But she could only watch as the man came to a halt in front of her. She sensed that he saw nothing, but felt much more.

"Hello," he cooed, "is this you I feel?"

He pulled his cloak back from his face, and Natalie screamed. Screamed and screamed as if she would never stop. She felt a yank from behind, and then she was flying, hurtling away from the room.

The man became a small dot in the distance, but not before she heard him say, "I'm coming for you. I will look for you, and I will find you."

Chapter Eighteen

Caught, she was caught. She struggled, but she was held fast. "Let go!" she cried. "Let me go, please. Nooo!" She was burning. She fought and kicked—to no avail. She sobbed.

"Natalie," a voice soothed. "Sweetheart, you're safe."

But she was not safe; she knew that deep inside. She struggled some more, until her mother came into her feverish view. Serena laid a hand on her forehead. She looked so far away.

"Mom," she croaked, "he's coming for me."

"Who, baby?" Her mother pulled her up into her arms. "Tell me who, please." She tried to stroke her hair, but Natalie pushed against her as pictures of Beausoleil, bound and tortured, flashed through her mind.

"No, please stop!"

She was dimly aware that her head rested on her pillow, but there was no comfort. That face had seen her, was here with her now. She screamed.

"Go away, leave me alone!"

The man's face, Beausoleil's torturer, rose before her, a misshapen mess—eye mismatched eye, nostril mismatched nostril; clumps of different features wedged into the man's face, molding it into a horrible hodgepodge of pieces; the forehead swelled at odd angles, pulled by the bones of many foreheads; the mouth leered and wriggled with the wails of many lips.

"I've seen you now," the lips whispered. "You cannot hide anymore."

She screamed.

Then a hand lay across her chest. It was warm, and Natalie felt a calm flow through her.

"Shhhh. Rest, child, rest now."

Mrs. Blaine, Natalie thought, Grandmother...

Her body loosened; peace rolled over her like a gentle wave. The terrible pictures faded, the face disappeared, and she fell back into the comforting blanket of sleep.

She heard Phillip speaking.

"Is she going to be all right?"

"Yes." It was her mother who answered. Her words were tinged with a ragged exhaustion.

Natalie tried to open her eyes, but her body would not let her. It's so nice like this, it seemed to say. He can't find us when we're here. Let's rest a while.

"Why won't she wake up?" Phillip asked now.

"She will," Serena said, after a pause. "She needs time."

"I'm sorry," Phillip said. "I didn't know what to do. It happened so fast. We were talking to Hercules, and she touched the doll to say hi. The next thing we knew, the doll changed into Louisa, and then this happened."

"Tell me again what happened, Phillip," Serena said.

"It was like two things happened at once," Phillip said. "The doll changed back to Louisa, but when I looked at Natalie, she was like she was that last time when she told me about my dad. She wasn't moving. She was staring into space like she was seeing something. But this time she was, I don't know—gone. She would jerk sometimes, like she wanted to move but couldn't. I think I heard her whisper 'no' once. And then she started to scream and she wouldn't stop. Louisa tried to hug her, but she kept screaming. I heard people starting to gather outside the tent. I didn't know what to do, so I just tackled her, and then it was like she blacked out. I didn't hurt her did I?"

"No, Phillip, you didn't," Serena said. "Do you have any idea at all about what she saw?"

"No, I'm sorry."

What did I see? Natalie wondered. Images started to form in her memory, and her body tensed, but then something inside her reared, and the images could not form; they remained a distant blur. That's so strange, she thought, as she drifted off again...

When she opened her eyes, sunlight dropped over them, peeking through the light fabric of her curtains. It's a pretty day, she thought. She lifted her head and looked around the room.

Serena sat in the chair next to her bed, observing her. There were dark gray smudges under her eyes, and tired lines etched across her face. Natalie frowned. What happened?

Then, in bits and pieces, parceled out in small spoonfuls like an unwanted soup, it all came back to her; Beausoleil, the man who held him captive, and all the terrible things that happened in that prison.

Her mother rose and cautiously sat on the edge of Natalie's mattress, her expression watchful.

Natalie sat up and backed into her headboard, away from her mother.

A sad look came into Serena's face. "The gifts can be so scary sometimes," she said. "We see things we don't want to see, do things we don't want to do. The most powerful of them seem to control us more than we control them and that can be the worst feeling. I know. I've been there."

Natalie looked away. She did not know why she was so angry at her mother, but somehow it sat there, in her chest and throat. She knew it was not her mother's fault, but everything felt so unfair and she did not know who else to blame.

"There are good things that come with it, sweetheart, trust me." Serena eyes were misty. "When you've learned more about how it works, you'll see. There is good in it."

"I hate it!" Natalie cried. "You don't know what I saw! I don't ever want to see like that again!" She pulled her pillow in front of her. She knew she was crying, but all she could do was sit and let the tears stream down her face as she glared at her mother.

For a moment Serena lost her composure; she blinked rapidly and looked away, her lip trembling. But she gathered herself and gazed at Natalie, her eyes soft.

Natalie held out her arms and reached for her. She buried her face in her mother's neck and sobbed as Serena's arms wrapped around her and hugged her close. She felt Serena kiss the back of her head and stroke her hair as she rocked her back and forth.

"It was awful!" Natalie cried. "I was so scared. Beausoleil kept screaming. He kept saying he had nothing, but the man wouldn't stop. He kept hurting him. Beausoleil was in so much pain. I couldn't stop watching him scream and scream." She sobbed harder, holding tight to her mother.

"And then the man sensed me. He talked to me. He said he would come after me. His face was horrible!" Her tears were coming from a bottomless well now. She cried and cried as the terror of what she had seen washed over her.

Another hand touched her shoulder. She pulled away from her mother, startled.

It was Mrs. Blaine. She smiled reassuringly and placed her hand on Natalie's chest. It was the same touch that had comforted her before. Calm flowed from her grandmother's hand and cooled the panic that blazed through her. Natalie felt her mother cradle her close, felt her grandmother smooth her hair from her face and kiss her forehead. And even though Natalie knew there was no safety for them now that the awful man was looking for her, for now, as she lay nestled between her mother and her grandmother, she let herself relax and feel safe.

"If you keep eating the batter, we won't have a cake to bake," her mother warned.

Natalie grinned over the mixing bowl and then went over to the sink to wash her hands. "I can't help it. It tastes so good!"

"Please bring me the chocolate chips," Serena said with a chuckle.

Natalie brought her the chocolate chips and watched as her mother folded them into the cake batter. It was her favorite cake, and Natalie knew that the house would soon be filled with the delicious smell of it baking it the oven. She was so happy she practically hugged herself.

Her mother and her grandmother had not asked her any more questions that morning. After Mrs. Blaine had gone, Serena had pulled Natalie out of bed and set about moving her into their household routine; they had done some cleaning, cooked their lunch, and then in the afternoon, they had started baking the cake. All in all, it had been a good day, Natalie thought.

A brief cloud settled over her, though, as she thought of Beausoleil. She wondered what he might be going through at the hands of the awful man. She saw her mother staring at her and dropped her eyes to the bowl, dipping her finger into the batter again.

Serena continued to mix the cake, but said, "I hate seeing you hurt, sweetheart. I wish I could make it all go away for you."

Natalie crossed her arms on the table and laid her head down. "I know."

"Things are happening so fast," Serena continued. "It's becoming more and more of a challenge to stay protected. You understand what I'm talking about, don't you?"

"Uh, huh," Natalie said, her head still in her arms.

"You're so vulnerable like this," Serena said. Natalie heard her pull the baking pan over to pour the batter. "It seems we've sprung leaks we don't even know about. It scares me to think that you're exposed in ways that we can't anticipate."

"I'm sorry."

"For what?" Serena said. "It's not your fault. But darling, can you please look at me?"

Natalie lifted her head. Serena was pouring the last of the cake batter into the baking pan, but she put the bowl down to speak to her.

"We need you—no, I need you—to try to look your gift in the eye. I need you to get to know it as much as you can. Knowing it gives you more control, and controlling it protects you. Your grandmother and I are going to do everything we can to keep us safe, and what we can do is considerable. But it's the things we can't see, can't anticipate that we need you to be prepared for."

"Is anything going to happen to you?" Natalie asked fearfully.

Her mother's lips tightened. "Not if I have anything to say about it. Don't worry about that, not a bit, okay?"

"Okay." Natalie could tell by the way Serena spoke that it would take something big to tear her mother away from her.

"Good." Serena picked up the bowl and finished putting the batter into the pan. "Why don't you go ahead and put this in the oven, and I'll start cleaning up.

"I know this has been scary for you," Serena said as she collected the bowls and spoons and put them in the sink. "To be honest, I don't think my experience was as scary as yours. Still, the first few times were not pleasant. But, Natalie, it does get better. Please promise me you'll try to learn about your gift."

Natalie put the baking pan in the oven and shut the oven door.

"I promise," she said.

Chapter Nineteen

O kay, Natalie, let's test out my theory from the other day," Mrs. Blaine said.

Natalie groaned. She and Phillip were seated on a sofa in Mrs. Blaine's living room. Mrs. Blaine stood over them, leaning on her cane.

"Now, now, dear, don't be like that," Mrs. Blaine smiled. "This is going to be fun! You remember I told you that mind tricks run in our family?"

Natalie nodded.

"Well, there are variations on that gift. One variation I have is the ability to alter reality. I can make things look different from how they really are."

"How does that work?" Phillip asked.

"Let's have a look." Mrs. Blaine walked over to a mural that took up a whole wall in the living room. Fields of wheat, golden yellow and kissed into glorious color by the sun, decorated that wall and brightened the entire room. The fields rose and dipped under a brilliant, blue sky, and in the distance there stood a cart, pulled by a horse.

Mrs. Blaine beckoned to Natalie. "Come stand here with me and look at this landscape, dear.

"I had mentioned before that I believe you might have the ability to take on other people's gifts in addition to your own. Let's have a look at that."

"Do I have to do anything?" Natalie asked.

"Not at the moment. We're just experimenting."

Mrs. Blaine put her hand on Natalie's shoulder, and together they admired the landscape. It was not long before Natalie felt the hair on her arms stand up on end.

Her breath caught in her throat. "I feel something." There was a tingling along her nerve endings, spreading from the tips of her fingers and toes to the top of her head. This was more powerful than what she had felt moving through the maps.

"It's okay." Mrs. Blaine squeezed Natalie's shoulder. "Keep looking."

The field of wheat swayed back and forth, as if a wind blew; the cart wheeled along the horizon; the leaves rustled.

"Wow," Phillip whispered.

"I'm the one who's doing this part," Mrs. Blaine said. "Natalie, I'd like you to add to the mural. Do anything you like."

"Like what?" Natalie asked.

"I can't recommend anything, dear," Mrs. Blaine said. "I need to be sure it's coming from you."

Natalie stared at the wall. If she had not known it was a mural, she would have thought they were standing in front of an open patio window; the view was that close to full life-like quality.

Natalie wondered if she could make it look even more real. She focused on expanding the horizon, and to her surprise, the field of vision unfurled from side to side.

"You'll need to make the sky bigger," Phillip suggested.

She concentrated on the sky, and watched as it spanned beyond the confines of the wall. I need to push the horizon back, she thought, and sure enough, it traveled further into the distance.

She made tweaks here and there, and soon, it looked as if the wall was right on the edge of a live field that reached out for miles. For good measure, she added a rainbow and some cows, and peppered the sky with clouds—the big, white, cottony kind.

"It looks so real!" Phillips said in awe. He walked up to the mural and tried to insert his hand into the scene. It hit the wall. Behind it, the landscape hummed with life.

"That is really cool," Phillip said. "Wow."

"You did a nice job with that, dear," Mrs. Blaine said. "I think we can stop there."

In the blink of an eye, the mural settled. Phillip's hand lay flat against the wall.

Mrs. Blaine patted Natalie's shoulder. "That wasn't so bad now, was it?"

Natalie shook her head. "No, not so bad."

"It seems my theory is correct, my dear. You have the ability to take on other people's gifts."

"So, she was able to bring Louisa back because Beausoleil's gift was stored inside her?" Phillip asked.

"Yes, that would support the theory."

"Maybe we could bring Louisa here to test the theory some more," Phillip said excitedly. "Beausoleil could make the inanimate animate, so that test could be a lot of fun!"

Mrs. Blaine chuckled. "You really enjoy this stuff, don't you Phillip?"

"A little too much," Natalie grumbled.

"I'd like to avoid exposing Natalie to Beausoleil's gifts for a while," Mrs. Blaine said. "At least until we get a better idea of what other gifts she has and how she can control them. Another gift seems to kick in as well, and that's one we need to look at."

"The one where I saw what happened to Beausoleil?" Natalie definitely did not want that one to kick in again if it did not have to.

"Yes," Mrs. Blaine said, "and Phillip's father as well."

"How is that happening?" Natalie asked.

"I've explained how our family has the ability, in a variety of ways, to see beyond what's normal. Each time you have been in proximity to someone, you have been able to see into their lives. Since your gift is not developed, it's not entirely consistent, although it did kick in when you were in proximity to other gifts, such as Phillip's and Beausoleil's."

"It didn't kick in with you, though," Natalie pointed out.

"Yes, well, I controlled myself, whereas Phillip has not yet developed control and Beausoleil was not around to exercise his."

"It's all so confusing," Natalie groaned. "How are we supposed to learn how to control things?"

"Don't worry, dear. You'll learn that things are much easier once you've gotten used to what you can do."

"Does this mean I can't see Louisa at all?" Natalie did not know if she was disappointed or relieved. On one hand, she wanted to see Louisa in human form again; on the other, she did not want to tell her about what she had seen of Beausoleil.

"It wouldn't be wise at this point," Mrs. Blaine said. "But perhaps we can talk to Janet to see if she can sew one of her creations for you. If it works, then you both can visit Louisa."

"I'm sure mom can do that!" Phillip said.

"We told Louisa and Hercules what happened to Beausoleil," Mrs. Blaine added, as if she had read Natalie's mind. Which she probably could, Natalie thought wryly.

"Was she upset about it?" Natalie asked

"We didn't go into too much detail," Mrs. Blaine said, "but yes, both she and Hercules were upset."

"I feel bad," Natalie murmured.

"Right now the best thing you can do is stay safe," Mrs. Blaine said. "That was what Beausoleil wanted.

"Now, that will do for today. We'll continue with this again tomorrow." Mrs. Blaine put a hand on Phillip's shoulder and kissed Natalie on the forehead. "You did very well today."

Chapter Twenty

On the walk back to Phillip's home, Phillip said, "Don't worry. My mom should be able to sew something we can use to go see Louisa."

"I'm kind of afraid to see her," Natalie said. "I don't know what to say."

"I think it will be okay," Phillip said.

"Does she even want to see me?"

"Of course she wants to see you. We were with her when everything happened."

"I don't know if I can answer her questions," Natalie said. "It would really hurt her if she knew what I saw, Phillip."

Phillip said nothing. They walked along in silence.

"I know you think I'm a coward," Natalie said.

Phillip stopped. "I don't think that. I know it's hard for you. It's just hard for me, too. And it's going to be hard for Louisa. But my mom said that I can't judge what you're going through. I'm sure it was pretty awful, what you saw."

Natalie's thoughts jumbled as they walked. She wanted to help so badly, but what could she do? All she could do was *see*, and that did nobody any good.

"If you could do what I do," she asked Phillip, "what would you do?"

Phillip grimaced. "You don't want to know."

"You're right. I don't, but tell me anyway."

"I'd probably keep trying to see, keep trying to get clues about where my dad or Beausoleil is. And then once I found out, I'd try to go there."

"Using your gift?"

Phillip nodded. "Oh, hey, do you wanna see what my mom made for me? It's really cool!"

"Sure."

Phillip motioned her to follow. They left the sidewalk and walked to a wooded area, out of view of the street. There, Phillip reached into his pocket and pulled out a piece of cloth that he had folded over twice. It was an antique beige color, and its ragged edges gave it the look of old parchment. It was small, even when unfolded, and had no stitching or designs to decorate it; it was plainer than plain. Phillip however, beamed with pride and barely concealed delight. He handed it to Natalie.

She turned it over in her hands and held it up to the light. I must be missing something, she thought, maybe a small pattern or stitch. But she saw nothing.

"Okay," she said, "I give up."

Natalie thought if Phillip's smile were any wider, it would swallow his face. He took the cloth from her and said,

"Paris, France."

From the beige of the fabric, a pattern emerged, as if rising out of water. Dark, brown lines crossed and ran parallel to one another in different patterns. Names and dots scattered along the lines. One word in bold letters sat in the center: *Paris*.

Natalie's jaw hit the ground. "Is that a map of Paris, France?"

"Yep." Phillip passed her the cloth. "Go ahead, take a look."

Natalie took the cloth and peered closely. It looked like a real map, all right. But the color of the cloth and its jagged edges gave it the look of one of those pirate maps from the movies.

"This has to be the coolest thing I have ever seen!" Natalie exclaimed.

"Look, I can even get maps from different periods of time." Phillip focused on the cloth and said, "Eastern Europe in the 1980s."

The lines sunk into the fabric; another pattern emerged. Bold letters rose as a banner at the top: *Eastern Europe*. There were now different names labeled for the different countries of Europe, as well as the larger cities.

"Dad said that Eastern Europe is different now, so I figured I'd give that time a try," Phillip said.

"That's a long time ago," Natalie commented.

"Yeah, I know, right?" Phillip examined at the map. "Yep, look. There's Yugoslavia. It's broken up now." He looked at Natalie, his eyes shining. "This has to be the coolest gift ever! And since it's cloth, I can bunch it up real small, and take it everywhere."

"And once your gift comes, you'll be able to travel wherever you want," Natalie said. "Gosh, that is so neat!"

"My mom's the best," Phillip said proudly.

"Can I try?" Natalie asked.

"The thing is, my mom made this so that I'm the only one who can speak to it—oh wait," he said, thinking. "With your gift, you might be able to. You could give it a try."

Natalie thought about what she would like to see.

"The Big Top Circus," she said.

Sure enough, the lines submerged and resurfaced. Pictures of the attractions and game booths and tents and concession stands appeared, with a path weaving through it all. The map spelled out the words: *Big Top Circus.*

Natalie and Phillip laughed.

"You are so lucky," Phillip said.

Natalie shook her head. "No, it's not always this fun."

"No, I guess not," Phillip said.

He looked down at the map and said, "Blank." The lines sunk into the cloth, and it was plain once more. When he looked back at Natalie, it was with an understanding smile.

Perhaps Phillip could not fully understand what she was going through, but at that moment, Natalie saw that he was trying, and it made her feel better.

Suddenly, a hand reached in and grabbed the cloth from Phillip.

"What are you two losers looking at?"

It was Mike. Rory and Larry were with him, and the three of them surrounded Natalie and Phillip. Natalie looked at Rory standing behind her. He scowled in reply.

"Give that back," Phillip said. He was trying to control himself, but his mother's gift meant a lot, and he was practically vibrating with anger.

"Take it easy, Stone, let's have a look here." Mike flipped the cloth over and gave Phillip a puzzled look. "What the heck is this? Hey, Larry, what would anyone want with a plain piece of cloth?"

"How would I know what a loser wants?" Larry asked.

"Hey, my little brother likes to hold on to one while he sucks his thumb," Rory offered.

Mike gave a hoot of laughter. "Is that what you use this for, Stone? Do you hold it while you suck your thumb?" He put his thumb in his mouth and rubbed the cloth against his cheek. "Is this what you do?" he taunted.

"You look way too comfortable doing that," said Phillip.

"Do you hug a teddy bear, too?" Natalie asked. There were times when Mike made it too easy.

Mike pulled his thumb out and glared at Natalie. He took a step towards her, but Phillip moved in front of him.

"What's the matter, Mike?" he said. "Did she hit too close to home? You got a teddy bear for when you go night-night?"

Mike looked ready to hit Phillip, but Phillip looked just as ready, so after a moment Mike stepped back. He looked at the cloth.

"You losers are awfully interested in this cloth. Maybe I should take it with me to see what's so special about it."

Phillip lunged for the cloth. "Give that back!"

Mike backed out of reach, a look of malicious glee on his face. "Well, look at that, guys." He circled Phillip and dangled the cloth in front of him. "He really wants it back."

Rory left Natalie and joined Larry to gather around Mike and Phillip, who were going round and round like two gladiators.

"Hey," Natalie yelled, "give that back! His mom made it for him."

Phillip stopped in his tracks and stared at her incredulously. Mike, Larry and Rory roared with laughter.

"Aw, poor baby," Mike taunted, "he wants his mommy's gift back."

Phillip tried another lunge which Mike sidestepped. The two circled again.

"Natalie, do me a favor," Phillip said, eyeing Mike as he passed her. "Don't try to help!"

"Sorry! I helped before, though. I handled Rory."

Rory glared at Natalie. "You took me by surprise!"

"What's the matter, Rory," Natalie said, "can't admit that a girl took you down?"

Rory's eyes narrowed. "You think so, huh? Why don't you try again? Come on!" He raised his hands and waved for her to come close.

She stayed where she was. "How did you explain getting beat up by a girl? Did you say anything, or did you keep it a secret?"

Rory left his post around Mike and Phillip and made his way over to her. "Let's see how you do when you're not taking someone by surprise," he said.

Natalie backed up, but Phillip did a quick dodge past Mike and rushed at Rory. He kicked Rory's legs out from under him and came to stand by her. Rory gave a howl and scrambled back to his feet.

"Not helping," Phillip muttered to her.

"It was three against one," Natalie mumbled back.

Mike, Rory, and Larry gathered in front of them.

Rory was enraged. "You're getting it now, Stone!"

"You're pretty sad, Rory, going after a girl," Phillip said.

"She's no girl, she's a freak."

"Just like you Stone," Mike added. He looked mean, but worse—he looked like he was having fun.

Larry stared at Natalie and Phillip without saying a word, but whenever his eyes landed on Natalie, she could tell he did not like her. Not one bit.

Mike, Rory and Larry formed another circle around them. Instinctively, Natalie shifted so that she was back-to-back with Phillip, facing Larry. His stoic, unblinking stare was downright unnerving.

"Geez, Mike," Phillip said, "three against two and one of us is a girl. Can't you fight your own fights?"

"I really don't care," Mike said. "Besides, Larry and Rory don't like you either. Why should I have all the fun?"

"Excuses, excuses," Phillip said.

This is not good, Natalie thought. It was not good at all and worse, she could see no way out. She and Phillip were surrounded and outnumbered.

"Let's see what you say when I make you eat this," Mike said. He twirled the cloth in front of Phillip's face. Phillip grabbed at it, but Mike snapped it away. Rory lunged and then stopped as Phillip wheeled about, but then Mike lunged and then stopped. Rory and Mike took turns, toying with Phillip.

Natalie mind raced. She and Phillip were not going to be able to hold them back for long. Ideas flew through her head and then were gone, except for one.

Her grandmother had said that mind tricks ran in her family. Should she try? What could she do? Desperation bubbled up and roiled inside her. She focused on a point behind Larry and concentrated.

"Hey Mike," she called out, "you might want to drop that cloth. It could catch fire."

"What?" Mike sneered. "You got something to say, Bristol?" Then he gave a surprised cry.

She heard Rory say, "What the...?"

There was a small commotion. Larry's attention was riveted by the clamor. She focused some more.

"Uh, oh, guys," she said, "aren't those the Riley's Rottweilers?"

Mike and Rory's cries stopped short. They were tense, listening...

"Run!" Larry screamed.

"Get away from me, get away!" Rory yelped.

"Help, it's got my pants!" Mike squealed, in a pitch as high as a piglet.

Natalie heard more cries and wails from the three boys, and the sounds of their feet slamming into the grass as they dodged this way and that. Then their footsteps scattered in different directions.

"Grab your cloth and run!" Natalie hissed. Phillip bent down to grab the cloth, and they were off; they charged onto the sidewalk and hightailed it down the street.

What did I just do, Natalie thought. What have I done?

They ran until they were sure they had ditched the other three, and then they stumbled onto a patch of grass off the sidewalk. Phillip threw himself down on the ground. Natalie leaned with her hands on her knees. They gasped for air.

"What did you do?" Phillip panted, when he had enough breath.

Natalie shook her head. Adrenaline and energy of another kind still streamed through her.

"Your eyes are about to pop out of your head," Phillip said. "You're scaring me." He put his arms around her in an awkward hug, patting her back while she put her head on his shoulder.

"I don't know what I did," she whispered. "I just thought really hard. I..." she struggled for the right words, "...I put thoughts out there, and they thought them, too."

"Mike dropped the cloth like it burned him," Phillip murmured. "They acted like the Rottweilers were bearing down on us. I heard everything you said, but I didn't see any of it."

"I was concentrating on them," Natalie said, still whispering, "just them. I thought they were really going to hurt us."

"Don't worry," Phillip said. "It's okay."

After a few minutes, Natalie straightened. "We should tell Mrs. Blaine, or my mom."

"Okay." Phillip checked their surroundings. "I think we're closer to your house." He felt around his pockets, and pulled out his mother's gift. He smoothed it out for inspection. "I know you're scared, but thanks for getting my map back. And thanks for getting us out of trouble back there."

Natalie nodded.

"Come on." Phillip put his map back in his pocket. "Let's go."

They were walking back onto the sidewalk when Natalie came to a halt.

"What's wrong?" Phillip asked.

"I'm not sure." A strange sensation had run through her and corralled her senses into high alert. She looked around.

Phillip surveyed the area as well. "I don't see anything."

"Maybe it was nothing," Natalie said.

They continued walking, but somehow she could not shake the feeling that someone or something had been watching them.

Chapter Twenty-One

*T*he next day, Mrs. Stone presented Natalie and Phillip with the sewing creations that would allow them to visit Louisa and Hercules.

"The pieces are simple," Mrs. Stone said, "but they should keep you shielded."

She had sewn them both jackets ("So that they're not easy to take off or lose," Mrs. Stone had laughed). Phillip's was a simple army green color with several pockets. Natalie's was a deep brown color with light ruffles down the front and on the end of the sleeves. Both jackets had their names sewn inside.

"When you wear these jackets," Mrs. Stone said, "any loose or random gifts should not affect you.

"However, keep in mind that these are merely designed as an additional shield to our regular protections. Safeguarding you from anyone purposefully using his or her gifts against you requires a different kind of defense: one beyond the scope of these jackets.

"Natalie, Mrs. Blaine mentioned that you can use your gift a little more at will now?"

"A little," Natalie said. She and Mrs. Blaine had discussed the incident with Mike, Rory and Larry. Her grandmother had been reassuring.

"Your gift might come to you in bits and spurts," Mrs. Blaine had said. "It's not uncommon for it to appear when your senses are heightened."

"What if I do something wrong or bad or hurt someone?" Natalie had asked.

"But you didn't," Mrs. Blaine had pointed out. "Have a little faith in yourself, Natalie. The fact that you are worried about it at all is a good thing. I would just caution you to watch when there are other people around. For now, let me worry about the three boys."

"If you choose to exercise your gifts when you come into them," Mrs. Stone was saying now, "these jackets won't prevent you from doing so."

"Thanks, Mom." Phillip pulled on his jacket. He put his map, which was never far from him these days, into one of the pockets, and put his hands in all the rest, testing them. "I can put a ton of stuff in these pockets!"

"I thought you'd like that," his mother said.

Natalie put on her jacket. When she looked in the mirror, her breath caught. It had to be the prettiest jacket she had ever owned. The ruffles gave it a dainty touch, but the style was very casual. Like a denim jacket only pretty and brown, Natalie thought.

"I love it! Thank you so much, Mrs. Stone!" she exclaimed.

Mrs. Stone laughed as Natalie hugged her. "I'm so glad you like it. Both of you should wear them whenever you're headed somewhere out on your own. Within range, of course," she warned.

"Yes, Mom, we know," Phillip grumbled.

"It always bears repeating, young man, especially with you."

"I get it," Phillip said.

"All right then, you two, off you go," Mrs. Stone said. "Enjoy the circus and give Louisa and Hercules my best."

The day was overcast, and the air bit a little harder than it had in the last few days, but the jacket kept Natalie warm, and its stylish look gave her step an extra spring. Phillip also seemed to be enjoying his jacket. He kept testing the pockets, and with the front buttoned up to the collar, he looked like a young soldier.

The crowd at the circus was noticeably thinner. Probably due to the weather, Natalie thought. The circus people managed to keep their festive energy, however, and cries of "Step right up!" and laughter and shouts of encouragement filled the air, kicking up the excitement for anyone who had chosen to attend. Despite everything that had happened, Natalie felt a thrill as she and Phillip arrived at the tent of the Magical World of the Great Beausoleil.

"Hello," Phillip called as they entered, "anybody here?"

There was an excited squeal as the flap to the backstage opened, and Louisa came running out to meet them.

She was the same as she had been before she had turned into the doll, Natalie marveled. There were no signs that the girl in front of them had once, just a short time ago, had the inert, vacant presence of a child's toy.

"You're here!" Louisa exclaimed. "I'm so happy to see you!" She threw her arms around Natalie and hugged her tight. She did the same for Phillip, who managed to take one hand out of his pocket to hug her back. "I wondered if you would come."

"Sorry we couldn't come sooner," Natalie said. "They didn't think it would be safe."

"But you're here now," Louisa said, her eyes shining. "Oh, your jacket is so pretty!"

"Thanks," Natalie said. "Phillip's mom made it for me. Do you like it?"

"I do!" Louisa said. "It's the color of your hair. It fits you so well!"

Pride, mixed with something else, rushed warm through Natalie. For the first time, there was another girl to whom she could talk about things like clothes. It was such a nice feeling.

"Louisa! Where are you? What are you doing?" The flap to the front of the tent opened, and Hercules stepped through. He did not look as tired as when they had last seen him, but he had regained his cantankerous disposition, which surprisingly, seemed to indicate he was happy. Perhaps, Natalie guessed, because it meant he was fretting over Louisa whom he was clearly glad to have back.

"I swear, Louisa!" Hercules said, "I don't know why it's so difficult for you to follow a simple rule. It's important that you stay close, or at least make sure I know where you are."

"I'm sorry, Hercules," Louisa said mildly. "I just wanted to spend some time in Papa's tent, and I forgot about the time."

Hercules' face softened. "Yes, of course, but please make sure I know where you are." His expression turned grumpy again as he looked at Natalie and Phillip. "So, are you two back to cause more trouble? You sure bring a lot of excitement whenever you come around."

Natalie wilted under his gaze. Phillip snatched his hands out of his pockets, as if standing to attention.

"Be nice, Hercules," Louisa said. "They're friends, and Natalie brought me back, remember?"

Hercules' expression could have withered flowers in high bloom.

"I just hope they don't do anything to send you back!" he said.

"Ouch," Phillip said under his breath to Natalie.

"I'm sorry, Hercules," Natalie said. "We won't stay long. We just wanted to see how you and Louisa were doing."

"No," Louisa cried, "don't let Hercules scare you away!" She shot a warning look to Hercules who harrumphed in reply. "Hercules, I'd like to spend some time with them, if that's okay. I promise we'll stay close."

"I don't know, Louisa," Hercules said. "I'd hate for anything unexpected to happen to you."

"Please." Louisa took Hercules' hand. "We'll stay right here, in Papa's tent, if that will make you feel better."

Hercules grumbled like a grouchy bear. He looked from Natalie to Phillip as if he wished he were a magician who could wave a wand and make them disappear.

"Fine," he said, "but stay out of trouble." He pointed at Natalie. "Whatever you have going on, tuck it away. I had a devil of a time explaining why someone was screaming like a banshee the last time you were here. We're on thin ice with the circus, and the last thing I need now is to have Louisa and me kicked out. Understand?"

Natalie nodded. "Yes, sir."

Hercules glared at Phillip.

Phillip gulped. "Yes, sir."

After Hercules departed, Louisa smiled in apology. "Sorry, he's been pretty stressed these past few days. He's glad I'm back, but he's worried that something will happen to me or that we'll be kicked out of the circus."

"Do you guys really think you'll be kicked out?" Natalie asked.

"Well, they're starting to wonder about what's happening. Why these storms are circling here, why Papa disappeared and left me behind. They were disturbed by your screaming the last time you were here. They're drawing their own conclusions, and even though they're off base, they're troubled by it."

"What kind of conclusions are they drawing," Phillip asked.

"They think there are bad things coming, and that we're the ones pulling it to them," Louisa said. "They're thinking about leaving town, but they don't know what to expect from the storms, so now they're thinking about kicking us out, and we can't afford to be on our own right now."

"You could always stay with us," Phillip offered.

"Thanks, but Hercules thinks you're a magnet for the problems, and he'd rather stay away. He doesn't blame you," Louisa said hastily, "not exactly, but he thinks some distance might be good."

Phillip looked as if he did not quite know what to say to that. Natalie thought Hercules might be right, even though trouble would probably come no matter what.

"So how are you doing?" Phillip asked.

"I'm okay," Louisa replied. "Mostly I just walk around the circus and try to help out. The others prefer I keep my distance, but sometimes they can't refuse help, so then I get a chance to do something. The worst part, really, is worrying about Papa." She looked down at her feet and blinked a few times.

A lump grew in Natalie's throat. She had hoped she might be able to keep guilt over knowing Beausoleil's current fate at bay, but standing here in front of Louisa, it bubbled to life, churning a hole of misery in her belly.

"I'm really sorry," Natalie said.

"Can you tell me anything?" Louisa asked tentatively. "I know we're not supposed to do anything to upset you, so you don't have to say anything you don't want, but if there is anything you can, could you please?"

"Louisa, I..." Natalie could not think of what to say. What she knew would hurt Louisa terribly. What would be the point?

Louisa must have sensed how bad it was, though, because she put her head down and sobbed. They were low, tortured sounds that shook her body, and Natalie's heart tore at each one.

Phillip walked over and put his arms around her. The expression on his face matched Louisa's, and it tore another hole in Natalie.

"I'm sorry," Phillip said.

Louisa pulled back, trying to collect herself. "You lost your father, too, right? You don't know where he is or what's become of him?"

Phillip met Natalie's eyes over Louisa. "He's alive."

"You know that?" Louisa asked in wonder. "You know that for sure?"

The guilt inside Natalie reared again, and she broke her eyes from Phillip's.

"I know it in my heart," he said.

"But he's been gone for a long time, hasn't he?" Louisa said.

"Yes."

"Does it get easier?" Louisa whispered, as if she knew the answer even as she asked the question.

Phillip swallowed and his mouth twisted into a painful grimace. A low moan escaped Louisa, and she wrapped her arms around Phillip. His arms came around her back as he buried his head in her shoulder and held her as she sobbed anew.

Natalie stood up then and quietly slipped away.

Chapter Twenty-Two

*I*t wasn't fair. Why did she have to be the one that had to *see*? It didn't help anyone!

The exit was ahead of her, and she broke into a run. She burst through the flap of the tent not knowing where to go, but feeling like anyplace was better than where she was.

She slammed into something hard. "Ouch!" someone cried. Natalie almost fell, but hands gripped her arms and held her steady. "Are you okay?"

Natalie squinted from the light, but when the colors settled, she saw the grip belonged to a boy of about sixteen. He had dark hair that hung down to his shoulders, and brown eyes that twinkled as Natalie swayed for balance. There was a wiry strength in the fingers that circled her arms. She stretched her head back to see him.

"Sorry," she cried. "I didn't mean to crash into you like that."

The boy laughed. He wore blue jeans, boots, and a dark flannel shirt over a white t-shirt. When he laughed, it was as if the cloudy day had turned sunny.

"No problem," he said. "It didn't hurt. Are you okay?"

"Yes, I'm fine."

"Are you sure? You looked a little upset when you rushed out of that tent."

"Yeah," Natalie said. "I just...nothing...I'm fine."

"Okay," the boy said. "I'm Saul, by the way." He held out his hand. His long fingers wrapped easily around Natalie's.

"I'm Natalie."

"Nice to meet you," Saul said. "Are you from around here?"

"Yes, my whole life."

"Seems like a nice town. I'm just passing through."

"Are you here with your family?" Natalie asked.

Saul shook his head. "No, no family. I just look for work when I get to a town and stay until it's time to move on. When I got here and saw this circus, I thought maybe this would be a good place to look."

"I know a couple of people who work here," Natalie offered. "Maybe you could ask them."

"That would be nice." Saul looked at Natalie as if he were trying to figure something out. "How old are you, Natalie?"

"Twelve," Natalie said. "Why?"

"Just curious. How old do you think I am?"

"Um, I don't know, fifteen or sixteen?"

Saul chuckled. "Good job. I'm really terrible about guessing people's ages."

"Did you guess mine?"

Saul shook his head. "Not even close."

"How old did you guess?" Natalie asked.

"Twenty-one."

"What?" Natalie exclaimed.

Saul cracked up. "You are too funny! Sorry, I couldn't resist."

"You're kind of weird, aren't you?"

"Yeah, I kind of am. You?"

"Yeah, me too," Natalie admitted.

Saul's head bobbed up and down as if to an invisible beat. "Cool," he said, as if he really thought so.

In spite of herself, Natalie grinned. Weird did not seem so bad when it sat on Saul.

Saul's head tilted. Surprise seemed to flash through him, but it disappeared so quickly that Natalie wondered if she had imagined it.

"Am I making you laugh?" Saul asked.

"Yes."

"Cool," Saul said, but he looked a little distracted now. "You have a pretty smile," he said abruptly.

The conversation felt like it had taken another strange turn, but Natalie could not put her finger on how.

"Are you being weird again?" she asked uncertainly.

"I think I am. Sorry, I'm like that sometimes." Saul looked around and then said, "I should probably get going. If I can't find anyone to give me a job here, I'll look to see about getting help from your friends. It was nice to meet you, Natalie. Maybe we can be friends if I stay here a while."

"Sure." Natalie did not know what to make of Saul. He was pretty interesting, but she could not tell if he was coming or going.

His head was tilted in that speculative way again. "That's a great jacket. It looks nice on you."

"Thanks," Natalie said. "My friend's mom made it for me."

"Really? How cool is that?" Saul reached for her hand and kissed it. "Until we meet again."

He really is a strange one, Natalie thought, as she watched him stroll away. He looked neither left nor right, but he gave the impression of being on perpetual alert, like a bloodhound sniffing for a new scent. Maybe that's what happened when you traveled a lot on your own, she reasoned.

"Hey."

She turned around. Phillip had come up behind her with Louisa. "You okay?"

"Yeah." Natalie wondered if she should bring up Saul, but Phillip and Louisa looked drained, so she decided against it. "How about you guys?"

Phillip and Louisa shared a glance. Something painful squeezed in Natalie's chest.

"I'm sorry, Natalie." Louisa reached out to hold Natalie's hand. "I shouldn't have cried like that. I didn't mean to make you feel bad."

"Why should I feel bad?" The words came out before Natalie could stop them.

Louisa blinked in surprise at her harsh tone. Phillip's head snapped to Natalie, startled.

"What happened to your father wasn't my fault," Natalie said. It was as if that pain in her heart pushed the words out of her mouth. "Don't get me wrong. I feel bad about it, and everything."

"I'm...I'm sorry," Louisa said. "Phillip thought..."

"Phillip thought wrong. He might want me to feel bad, but I'm not the one to blame. I'm not even the one who put your father in that position." She looked at Phillip. "That was you."

Phillip blanched. Natalie could not seem to help herself. It was as if she were two people; one who was driven by the pain, and another who stood by watching, helpless to do anything about the cruel words coming out of her mouth.

"And I'm not responsible for your father either," she told Phillip. "Just so we're clear on that."

"Got it." Phillip's lips were pressed together so tight they turned white.

Why she thought saying all that would make her feel better she did not know. She did not think she could feel any worse. She spun around to leave, but Louisa's hand held her fast.

"Natalie, please don't be angry. I didn't realize..."

"It's not your fault," Natalie said bleakly. She knew Louisa was not to blame, but that ache inside her throbbed, and she needed to get away. "I'll drop by to see you later."

"You will? Promise?"

Natalie withdrew her hand. "Yes, but I have to go now, please."

"I don't understand," she heard Louisa say as she walked away.

"It's not your fault." Phillip replied. His voice was jagged, like he had been hit in the gut.

Natalie's sight blurred as she rushed through the circus. Tears gathered in her eyes and slipped down her cheeks. People glanced curiously at her as she ran through the exit. She needed to get away as fast as she could.

She decided to cut through Morton's Field. It was still within bounds. She just wanted to get home.

Footsteps charged up behind her as she trudged through the field. She glanced over her shoulder. It was Phillip.

"What was that all about?" he demanded. He caught up and walked at her side, facing her.

"You know!" she snapped.

"No," he snapped back, "I don't. Could you have been any harsher? That was the meanest thing you've ever said to me!"

She stopped and faced him. All the anger, helplessness, fear and, most of all, guilt, raged inside her like a volcano about to erupt.

"I hate it when you give me the guilt treatment!" she yelled.

Phillip halted, stunned. "What the heck are you talking about?"

"Crying like that with Louisa!" She knew what she was saying was not rational, but she was on autopilot now. Everything she was feeling rolled off her like a train on rails.

"Are you crazy?" Phillip looked ready to blow a gasket. "She lost her father. She was upset. You don't know what the heck you're talking about!"

"Oh, and of course we all know you do!" Natalie said bitterly.

"What is wrong with you?" Phillip yelled. He reached out and grabbed Natalie's arm. She tried to yank it away, but when she could not, she pushed against him. Phillip stumbled and released her. He caught his balance and stared at her, stupefied.

"You know she's a doll, right? I mean she might walk and talk and act like a real person, but in the end, she's just a piece of painted porcelain." Natalie knew she was being spiteful, and shame of a different kind spread through her. She had been so afraid of not being a good person, yet she could not stop herself from proving exactly that.

"I know for a fact that's not how you think of her," Phillip said through gritted teeth. "If you're feeling guilty, that's your problem. All Louisa and I were doing was..." he broke off.

"What?" Natalie demanded.

"Missing our dads!" Phillip yelled. "If that makes you feel bad, don't take it out on us. It isn't about you!"

Natalie reeled under his words. She swung about and walked blindly in the direction of her house.

Phillip grabbed her wrist. She lashed out with her free arm, but he dodged it and grabbed her other wrist. She struggled to get free and tried pushing against him again, but he was ready this time.

They grappled and wrestled in an odd dance across the field. Natalie managed to yank one wrist free, and twisting her body, she wrested the other one from Phillip's grasp. She whirled around to face him. Their struggle had roiled her feelings into a wave of fury.

"I know what you think of me!" she shouted. "I know you think I'm a coward because I won't try to help you see where your father is. But you don't get it, Phillip! Everything I see is horrible. And I don't want to have to tell you if it is!"

"Natalie..."

"I don't want this! But you're always there, pushing, saying things, doing things that make me feel bad for not doing what you want. If you say you're not, then you're lying. Just admit it why don't you!"

Phillip looked shaken. His arms dropped, palms up, almost pleading. "Why are you acting like this?" he asked.

"Maybe you're right," he said. "Maybe I do resent the fact that you might be able to help me, but won't. Maybe I do think you're being selfish and cowardly.

"But don't you understand? All I want is my dad. All Louisa wants is her dad. What is so wrong about that, huh? Is that so wrong?"

"No," Natalie whispered.

Phillip's face was bitter. "I guess it's not something you can understand. It's not something you'll ever get. Maybe because you've never had a father."

Tears sprung into Natalie's eyes. All the anger drained out of her, and she sobbed. She wished she could disappear. Whenever her tears cleared enough to reveal Phillip, she could see the misery in his face, and the desire to take back what he said.

"I hate you," she choked. She turned and ran the rest of the way home.

Chapter Twenty-Three

*M*r. Mackey gave the key a final twist in the lock. After a long day at work in the soda shop, he was ready to go home. He tucked the pint of ice cream he was carrying under his arm more securely. His wife had made her delicious home-baked apple pie and had asked for the extra creamy vanilla-bean-flavored ice cream for the crowning touch. Mr. Mackey was only too happy to oblige. His wife's apple pie was one of his life's greatest pleasures.

The night air stung his cheeks, but Mr. Mackey wrapped his scarf tight around his neck and started his trek home. Fall evenings had become chilly this month, but it was not yet cold enough for snow. Good thing too, with the storms around the area, Mr. Mackey thought. It would not be pleasant to have rain storms turn into blizzards. It would interfere with his walk home, and he enjoyed using the stroll to unwind after his workday.

As he made his way down the street, he noticed that the light on the corner was out, and that a figure waited under it. Strange, thought Mr. Mackey, no bus stops there. He made out someone tall, but not much else.

"Hello, Sir," the figure said, as Mr. Mackey approached. It was a man who spoke, but he made no move to come into the lighter section of the street where Mr. Mackey could see him better.

"Good evening," Mr. Mackey replied. "It's gotten a bit chilly out, hasn't it?" He squinted to see if he recognized the man, but the shadows hid him.

"It has," the stranger agreed. "You all seem to be having an unusual fall out here."

"I suspect it has to do with the storms in the area," Mr. Mackey said. "I suppose you've heard of them?"

"Yes, they are quite the news nowadays, aren't they? They don't seem to be affecting this town, though."

"I guess we're having a bit of luck," Mr. Mackey said. "I take it you're not from around here, then?"

"No," the stranger said. "I'm not. I found myself here by accident."

"By accident?"

"This town slides under the radar, don't you think?" The stranger's tone was conversational, but there was something else to it that made Mr. Mackey feel like the stranger was not really having a conversation at all.

"It's almost too easy to miss," the stranger continued. "It slips out from under you unless you really want to find it."

"I'm not sure I know what you're talking about," Mr. Mackey said.

"No, I don't believe you do." The man took one step towards him. Mr. Mackey did not want to be impolite, but he instinctively took a step back.

"I've noticed that about the people who live here as well," the stranger continued. "There's something about you all that I, literally, cannot wrap my mind around. I should be able to read you, see everything about you, but," the man made a motion with his hands as if he was grasping at empty air, "you all seem just beyond my grasp."

A cold that was not a part of the fall air filled Mr. Mackey. He glanced around, but the street was empty. He had stayed at the soda shop later than usual, and everyone else had gone home.

"If you'll excuse me, I should be getting home now." Mr. Mackey backed away from the man.

"Have I made you uncomfortable?" the stranger asked. "I apologize. I just didn't expect to encounter such a puzzle here."

"What are you looking for?" Mr. Mackey asked.

The man paused. As the silence stretched, Mr. Mackey wondered if he should take the opportunity to hurry on home. But then a strange feeling stole into him. It was like fingers tickling along his skin, ruffling through his hair and burrowing into his head.

The ice cream he was holding dropped to the ground. He tried to move, but his limbs would not listen.

"You know," the man said softly, "I am actually not too sure you can help me. I don't think you know anything about what I am looking for. And yet there is something about you—it's maddening!"

The man's head moved then, as if he noticed something on Mr. Mackey. He took another step towards him, but not enough to pull him out of the shadows.

"Your scarf," he mused. "There's something about your scarf. Where did you get it?"

"One of our local stores." If Mr. Mackey could have moved his limbs, they would have shaken from fright.

"Does everyone shop there?"

"Yes, pretty much."

Again the man was silent.

"I'd like to leave, please," Mr. Mackey pleaded.

"Who owns this store?" the man asked.

Mr. Mackey hesitated. What if this man tried to visit Janet Stone? He could not send him to her.

The man stepped closer. Mr. Mackey stood captive.

"No answer for me? What's the name of the store?"

Mr. Mackey did not answer. Heaven help me, he thought.

The man sighed. "This makes it hard. It should have been easy to come in here and find out what I needed, but now I'm going to have to do some more work, and not all of it pleasant. Now," the man said, his voice growing hard, "I'm going to give you a chance to tell me what I need to know, before I start moving on to other methods. From which store did you buy the scarf, and who is the owner?"

Mr. Mackey closed his eyes. His heart sank. He sent a silent apology to his wife for not making it home with her ice cream. His eyes opened in time to see a hand reach for his scarf. He heard a roaring snap, and a bright light blinded him. He opened his mouth to scream, but then the world went black.

Chapter Twenty-Four

*T*he next few days were some of the worst Natalie had ever experienced. When she woke up in the mornings, all she wanted to do was pull the covers over her head and let the days pass without her.

Unfortunately, her mother had other plans. School had started again, and each day she got Natalie out of bed and packed her off to school. Natalie suspected her mother knew what had passed between her and Phillip, but chose not to push; she merely got Natalie into her normal activities and kept her busy.

School was no fun. Even though she and Phillip did not hang together at school, they passed each other on occasion, and it always helped with her day. Now she tried to avoid running into him, and it only increased the ache inside.

News of the storms continued to filter through conversations around town. Natalie's mother seemed particularly worried. Natalie had heard Serena talking to Mrs. Blaine the night before when they had gone to her house for a visit. They had done more of that lately since they no longer had to pretend they were not related.

"The storm is still circling us," her mother had said. "It won't be long before it draws attention, if it hasn't already."

"I'm afraid you're right," Mrs. Blaine had replied. "We're going to have to make a decision soon, in the next day or two if we can."

"This won't be good," Serena murmured.

"No, it won't." Mrs. Blaine said. "But we don't have a choice. We waited too long, and now we'll have to make the best of it."

Natalie tried to push all the worries and the pains away. When the weekend finally rolled around, she asked her mother if she could visit Louisa.

"On your own?" Serena asked. "Wouldn't you rather go with Phillip?"

"I'd rather go by myself."

Serena reached out and touched Natalie's cheek. "Don't you think it's time you two mended fences?"

"I'd rather not talk about it," Natalie mumbled.

"Are you sure? You've been pretty miserable."

"I'm okay."

"I'm not sure I'm comfortable with you going by yourself."

"I promise I'll stick to the main streets, and I'll wear my jacket," Natalie said. "I'll be careful, I swear. Please?"

Serena had relented, and Natalie walked on her own to the circus. She was nervous. She had been so awful to Louisa the last time she wondered if Louisa would even want to see her?

She arrived at Beausoleil's tent just as Louisa was entering. Thankfully, Louisa seemed as happy to see her as before.

"I was worried you weren't going to come," she exclaimed. "You seemed so angry that last time."

"I shouldn't have acted that way," Natalie said. "I was upset about everything, and I took it out on you guys. It was really selfish. I...I feel terrible. I'm so sorry."

Louisa's face was open and kind as she considered Natalie. For someone who was a doll, she had a heart bigger than most real people, thought Natalie. She marveled at the sheer human-ness of her. Today Louisa wore jeans and a fleece vest over a pink, long-sleeved shirt. She looked like any other kid at the circus.

"Was it something I did?" Louisa asked.

"No," Natalie reassured her. "It was me."

"Okay, I understand." Louisa opened the flap to the tent. "Would you like to come inside?"

Each time Natalie came back to the tent, it felt emptier and emptier. "Haven't they tried to put another act in here?" she asked.

"They planned to," Louisa said, "but now the crowds are getting smaller so there's no need. I'm okay with that. It means I get to come here and feel a little closer to Papa."

Louisa picked through Beausoleil's boxes backstage. A frown came over her face.

"What's wrong?" Natalie asked.

"I think someone's been through these boxes." Louisa sifted through the props, puzzled. "These are not how I left them."

"Maybe Hercules was looking through them," Natalie suggested.

"No," Louisa said. "The props are put in a certain way and these are out of order. Hercules would have put them in the right way."

"Is anything missing?" Natalie asked.

Louisa went through the boxes and examined their contents. She shook her head. "No, it looks like everything is here. Who would go through them?"

"Maybe someone from the circus?"

"I guess. Oh well, at least nothing's gone. I'd hate for any of Papa's things to be stolen." Louisa rearranged the contents and then sat down on a prop bench. Natalie joined her. They sat in companionable silence.

"Are you still mad at Phillip?" Louisa asked. When Natalie looked up in surprise, she said, "He stopped by a few times this past week."

"Oh? That's nice. I haven't seen him lately." Natalie hoped she did not sound bitter.

"That's what he said. He seemed upset about it. He wouldn't say what happened, just that you're both mad at each other. Are you?"

Natalie shrugged. "I guess. I don't think I'm really mad at him. It's just that...well...yeah, maybe I'm mad."

"That's too bad. You both seem close."

"We've known each other for a long time, but I don't know about close. I don't get him sometimes."

Louisa grinned. "Boys can be like that. At least you guys are friends. I don't know what I'd do if I didn't have Hercules for a friend."

"Don't you have other friends here?"

"Not really. We have to be careful about making friends. I think people can sense when something's a little off, and we kind of are, you know what I mean?"

"Yeah," Natalie said, "I know exactly what you mean."

She and Louisa smiled at each other. It was nice to have a friend who understands, Natalie thought.

"What's it like for you?" Natalie asked. "When you're a doll?"

Louisa thought for a moment. "When I'm hiding, it's like I've gone to sleep, I guess."

"Are you aware of anything?"

"At first, I wasn't, but a while ago, I started getting these flashes. I thought they were dreams, but they were actually bits and pieces of stuff that had happened while I was hiding. Hercules thinks I might have developed some awareness."

"Is it scary?"

"No, not at all." Louisa looked at Natalie. "What do you think of me?" she asked.

Louisa had the most straightforward eyes Natalie had ever seen. There was nothing hidden, nothing mean in them.

"I think you're my friend," Natalie said simply. "Probably my only friend."

"There's Phillip," Louisa pointed out.

"It doesn't feel like it right now."

"It will be okay." Louisa patted Natalie's arm. "I can tell he misses you."

"Yeah?" A lump had started to form in Natalie's throat. "Well, I guess I kind of miss him, too."

"Do you think you'll talk to him again?" Louisa asked.

"I don't know."

"You should. It's not easy finding good friends."

"I know. I'm glad we're friends, though."

Louisa's face brightened. "Me too!" She laughed, "See, it's not so hard making up. You were mad the last time we saw each other, but now we're okay."

"That was different," Natalie said.

Just then someone called from the outer tent.

"Louisa, are you here?" It was Phillip.

Louisa flashed Natalie a surprised look. "I'm back here," she called. "Natalie is here, too."

There was a long pause. Natalie's heart sank. Great, he doesn't want to see me, she thought.

"I can come back later," Phillip said.

"That's okay," Natalie called out. "It's about time for me to get going anyway."

"That's not true," Louisa whispered. "You should just talk to him."

"He doesn't want to talk to me," Natalie said.

"Don't be stubborn!"

But Natalie stood and walked into the main area. Phillip waited there with his hands tucked into his army green jacket. For a second Natalie thought about breaking the ice, but Phillip's eyes widened and shifted down, and her courage drained away. She walked past him without saying anything.

As she walked out of the tent, she heard Louisa ask Phillip, "Do you both have to be so stubborn?"

Natalie wandered around the circus, looking for a distraction from the dull pain squeezing in her chest. She meandered around the tents, and the rides, and the animals, blind to everything. Gradually, however, she became aware of some disturbing news running through people's conversations.

"The last time anyone saw him was two nights ago, after he left work. He locked up for the evening, but never made it home." One of the townspeople, Mrs. Evans, was speaking to a friend, as they waited for her daughter to finish her ride on the merry-go-round.

"The police haven't found any clues?" the friend asked.

"Nothing," Mrs. Evans said. "It's as if he vanished into thin air."

"I can't even begin to imagine what his wife is going through," the friend said. "The Mackeys are the last people you would want this to happen to."

Mr. Mackey disappeared! Natalie thought in dismay.

"First the magician, now Mr. Mackey," Mrs. Evans said.

"There's been a disappearance in the circus?" the friend exclaimed.

"Well, perhaps I'm speaking out of turn," Mrs. Evans amended. "There is speculation the magician might have just skipped town. People tend to come and go with the circus."

The conversation died as the friend's child finished with the ride. Natalie wondered if her mother and Mrs. Blaine knew about Mr. Mackey's disappearance. She hoped Mr. Mackey was okay. Even though he had not given her a job, she liked him very much.

The sounds of clanging bells and shrill whistles snapped her out of her thoughts. Lights flashed from one of the arcade booths, and two boys were slapping a high five. To her surprise she saw Saul handing a prize to one of the boys.

Saul's eyes lit up as she approached the booth. "Hey, Natalie, how are you?" He was dressed in circus garb: a black hat and pants, a white shirt with blue suspenders and a sequined bow tie.

"I'm fine," Natalie said. "So you got a job, huh?"

"I did!" Saul said, looking pleased. "I get to help man the booths. It's great! I love the games, so it's like I got my dream job."

"You're so lucky. I tried to get a job once, but no one would hire me."

"Why were you looking for a job?"

Natalie shrugged. "Times are tough." Her reasons back then for wanting a job seemed so far away. What she would not give to go back.

"Why do you look sad all of a sudden?" Saul asked.

"I didn't know I did. I'm not sad. I've just had a lot on my mind lately."

"What are you thinking about?"

"You ask a lot of questions," Natalie said.

Saul laughed. "I guess I do. I get curious about people, you know? Sorry, I don't mean any offense."

"That's okay." It was hard to stay mad at Saul when he smiled like that. Natalie did not think she had ever met anyone who seemed to go through life with a happy disposition the way Saul did. He was a strange one, all right.

Saul leaned towards her, his hands on the counter of the booth. "Hey, you want to shoot water at the ducks? You win a prize if you knock them down. I can spot you a round."

"You don't have to do that," Natalie protested. "I can pay."

Saul hooked his thumbs through his suspenders with a mischievous flair. "There's a method to my madness. I get you to play one game, and when you lose, you'll want to play more, and then we'll earn some money."

"What if I'm really good?"

"I think I'm safe."

"Hey!" Natalie exclaimed. "Give me the squirt gun."

For the next few minutes, Natalie proved Saul right. Hard as she tried, she could not shoot enough ducks to earn a prize, and not being able to do so just made her want to try more.

"I've run out of money," Natalie complained, as the last shot of water missed its mark.

Saul had a rueful look on his face. "I did try to stop you a while back there."

"I guess you were right," Natalie grumbled. "I just wanted to win."

"It happens to the best of us," Saul said.

"Oh, really?"

"Sure," Saul said. "Nobody likes to lose or admit defeat or think they've invested a lot of time and effort for nothing. It's easier to keep riding that train to nowhere, even though you know you should get off."

It was the closest thing to sad Saul had ever said. Even his demeanor had dimmed. Then he noticed Natalie staring at him, unsure of what to say.

"Tell you what." The cheerful glint was back in his eye. "Why don't I treat us to some hot dogs, since you have no money?"

"Rub it in, why don't you?" Natalie grumbled. She looked around. "I should be headed home. It's going to start to get dark soon."

"Please? I feel bad I made you spend your money. I promise I won't keep you long. It'll just be a hot dog."

"Aren't you supposed to be working?"

"I'm due for a break. Wait here a second while I go ask."

Natalie watched as Saul went to one of the circus people. The circus person scowled at first, but as Saul continued to talk, the scowl disappeared, and the man nodded. Saul came back, grinning.

"We're all set," he said.

"You have a way with people," Natalie said, as they walked to the main food court.

"Don't you?" Saul asked.

"No, I have the opposite effect."

"What? No way. You've been the nicest person I've met here."

Natalie was quiet with surprise. A warm feeling came over her, like a soothing balm. It was the first time in a long time that she felt good about herself.

She sensed Saul looking at her, and kept her face turned away.

"Hey." Saul reached out to touch her shoulder. "Are you okay?"

"Yeah, I'm okay, thanks." She was torn between wanting to hug him and wanting to hide. She smiled instead.

Something flickered in Saul's expression. He looked both puzzled and bemused.

"Don't you know you're nice?" he asked.

"I'm not really nice, Saul," she said.

Saul ordered two hot dogs and sodas, and they sat at one of the tables.

"So why don't you think you're nice?" Saul asked, after a few bites of his hotdog.

"I don't have the right personality, I guess," she said.

"Why, what's your personality like?"

Natalie finished her bite and took a sip of her drink. "I don't know. I get mad a lot. When people pick on me, I fight back, and I'm not very nice about it."

Saul froze, his hotdog halfway to his mouth. "You get picked on? Why?"

"I meant it before when I told you I was weird," she said.

"How are you weird?"

"Lots of ways."

"Like how?"

"You ask a lot of questions," Natalie said.

Saul looked at her shrewdly. "It bothers you?"

Natalie shrugged.

"Try telling me one thing," Saul challenged. "I'll bet there isn't anything you can say that will make me think you're as bad as all that."

Natalie took another bite of her hotdog as she contemplated how to answer. She did not want to give him the big reason, but she was not sure how to deflect his question.

"Well," she said slowly, "I don't have a father, that's one."

Natalie watched as Saul deliberately put his hotdog down and leaned back in his chair. He stared at her without speaking. The silence dragged so long that Natalie wondered if she should have chosen a different answer.

"What?" Her question was a sharp rasp.

Saul moved back off the chair to reach for his drink. He took a casual sip and asked, "Is that the worst you've got?"

"It seems like that was bad enough!"

Saul considered his drink. "No, that's not so bad. Did your mom ever mention your dad?"

"No."

"Maybe she didn't think he'd be good for you," Saul suggested.

"I guess," Natalie said. "It might have been nice, though. My friends love theirs. Don't you like having one?"

Saul took another sip. "It can be a mixed bag sometimes. Not all fathers are great." He gave her a look. "I thought you said you didn't have friends."

"I don't have many friends," Natalie corrected. "I have a couple. And you," she added.

Saul smiled his bright smile. "I'm glad you think of me as your friend, Natalie." He reached out and pinched her nose.

"Ow!" she said with a grimace.

"Are your friends as weird as you are?" Saul asked.

"You don't know the half of it," Natalie muttered.

Saul laughed, looking very amused. He put his elbows on the table, leaning his face against one of his hands. With his other hand, he reached out and fingered the ruffled hem of her sleeve.

"This is such a cool jacket," he murmured. "You said your friend's mother made it for you?"

"Yes." It felt strange to have Saul's hand so close, almost touching her. It had a hypnotic effect. She glanced down at his hand, at the long fingers running along the ruffle of her sleeve, and then up into his eyes. For a moment she had a sensation of drowning.

She gasped and yanked away.

"Is something wrong?" Saul asked, alarmed.

Natalie backed her chair away from the table, the metal clanking in protest, and stood up.

"What's wrong, Natalie?" Saul rose to his feet. He reached out to put a hand on her shoulder, but she stepped away.

"I'm okay." Natalie rooted through her mind to make sure her gift was not kicking in. For a second there, she thought it had, and to have had that happen in front of Saul would not have been good. She noticed a few people in the food court looking at them curiously, so she slowly sat down. Saul eased into his seat as well.

"Are you sure you're okay?" Saul asked.

Natalie felt Saul watching as she groped for an explanation. How was she going to talk herself out of this one?

"I'm fine," she said. "Sorry."

"What happened?"

"Um..." An answer came from out of the blue. "I have fainting spells."

"Fainting spells?"

"Yes, I have a fragile disposition."

Saul's eyebrows shot up. "You. You have a fragile disposition."

"Who would have guessed, huh?" Natalie forced a small laugh.

"Uh, huh." Saul nodded his head as if he really wanted to shake it. "So, what triggers it?"

"Um...well...sometimes...close contact?" That, at least, was somewhat true.

"Close contact makes you want to faint?" Saul said incredulously. "You mean, like, swooning?"

"Yes!" Natalie exclaimed. "That's it! I swooned." She stopped abruptly. Could she have swooned over Saul?

Saul looked thrown as well. For several seconds, neither one of them spoke. Natalie was starting to wish the ground would swallow her up.

"I should get going," she said a little desperately.

"Sure, I understand," Saul said, although he seemed a little perplexed.

Natalie felt as if her cheeks could turn the crisp air summery. "See you later."

"Will you be all right? Should I walk you home?" Saul asked.

"No!" Natalie turned around but kept moving backwards. "I'm good. Thanks, though. I'll see you later."

"See you later, Natalie," Saul replied.

Chapter Twenty-Five

Like she had promised her mother, Natalie stuck to the main streets as she headed home. She had stayed longer than she had thought, though, and the sky was starting to get dark. Her mom would not be happy with her.

The streets were quiet. Natalie figured people were at home getting ready for dinner. She thought about what had happened with Saul. Could she have actually swooned? It did not seem right. Saul was cute, but he was more of a friend, like an older cousin or something. So what had happened? Had her gift almost kicked in? It was reassuring to think that if it had, she had been able to stop it. Still, she was not sure.

Suddenly, she felt a tickle along her spine. She halted with a sharp intake of breath. Her senses gathered into high alert, like it had once before...

She whirled around. The street lights had kicked in, and it hit her again how quickly the days now headed into night. She scanned the street. No one was there.

She continued walking home, but that feeling was too strong. After a few steps she stopped and checked behind her. The prickling along her spine was starting to feel like a caterpillar racing up and down her back. She surveyed the street again, and then froze.

A couple of blocks down, across the street on the corner, someone stood under a darkened street lamp. Natalie craned her neck and squinted to make out who it was, but the figure was too far away. It waited without moving, but Natalie had the distinct impression that it was looking at her.

Her heart kick-started the blood through her veins. She moved down the street at a half run. After a couple of blocks, she stopped for quick look.

The figure had also moved and was standing on the next street corner under a street lamp which had now gone dark.

Abandoning all pretense, Natalie tore down the street. She did not look back again. Every nerve screamed like an emergency siren. She ran several blocks.

Please let me get home, she prayed.

She turned a corner onto the residential streets that would lead her home. She had a ways to go, and that shiver along her spine would not go away. She knew, deep in her bones, that the figure followed. How would she get away?

She rounded a street corner and grazed a body coming round the other direction. She heard a grunt, but she kept her balance and ran. Footsteps chased her, catching up close behind.

"Natalie!" It was Phillip. "Wait up. What's the matter with you?" He grabbed her arm, but she pulled him along.

"There's someone following me!" Fear filled her voice. Phillip must have heard it as well because he stopped pulling and fell into step behind her. A few blocks down she heard him stop.

She paused to run back and grab his arm. "Come on!"

Phillip was checking behind them. The figure stood on the corner under a dark street lamp, a couple of blocks down.

Phillip grabbed her hand and ran. He cut through a neighbor's lawn and crossed several backyards, crouching between houses.

"What are you doing?" Natalie hissed.

"We can't lead whoever that is home," Phillip whispered.

Terror poured through every cell in Natalie's body. She was not sure how much more she could stand.

"This way," Phillip said. He weaved through the neighborhood's backyards, keeping hidden through bushes, fences and
jungle gyms.

"Here," he said. He pulled Natalie up to a large tree with a tree
house camouflaged in the branches.

"We'll be trapped," she whispered.

"We just need time," he whispered back.

She squirreled her way up the trunk, branches scratching
against her, and dodged into the tree house, with Phillip close
behind. She sat on the floor and pulled her knees up to her chin.
Her teeth chattered. Phillip peeked out the square hole which
served as the window.

"I don't see him yet," he said.

He crouched beside Natalie and pulled a flashlight out of his
pocket.

"He'll see us," Natalie said.

"Shhh." Phillip pulled the cloth map his mother made him. He
gave Natalie a look. Terrified, she nodded.

"Natalie's house," Phillip whispered. After a couple of seconds,
he flashed on the light. He quickly found Natalie's house on the
map that had emerged in the darkness and put his finger on it.
Natalie pressed her finger with his and concentrated with all her
might.

The hair on the back of her neck stood on end.

"He's coming," she whispered.

"Keep focusing," Phillip said.

Every nerve in her body screamed the arrival of the stranger.
Natalie fought to block out everything except her house. Her
backyard came into focus. Phillip headed in its direction. Her
balcony beckoned them as they flew.

A footfall tapped on the wood of the tree; the branches shook;
the stranger was climbing. Natalie almost screamed, but Phillip
wrapped his arm around her head and slapped his hand over her

mouth. She closed her eyes. The air shifted, and a cold breeze chilled her.

She opened her eyes. They were no longer sheltered by the tree house. The rails of her balcony pressed against her back. The hair on her neck settled and the chills down her spine warmed. They had made it.

Phillip took a deep breath and pulled himself into a crouch. He peered through the rails, scoping the yard and the area around her house.

"I don't see anything," he said. "We must have lost him." He tucked his map and the flashlight back into his pockets.

"I think you're right," Natalie said. "It doesn't feel like we're being watched anymore."

It was now too dark to see Phillip's face, but she caught the outline of his head as it snapped around.

"You could sense him?" he asked.

"I just felt like someone was watching me." Natalie got to her feet. Her balcony was comfortingly familiar, and it helped ease the residual shakiness in her knees. "Let's go inside." She opened her balcony door and made a mental note to lock it from now on.

Natalie felt her way around her room and switched on the lamp by her bed. The warm glow eased her fears further, and she plopped down on the edge of her mattress. Phillip closed the door and settled into the chair by her desk.

"Do you know who it was?" he asked.

"No," she replied. "It was the same feeling I had that other time, after Mike, Rory and Larry, remember?"

"Yeah, you kept looking around, but there wasn't anyone there." Phillip was trying not to look worried, but he fidgeted in the chair and would not quite meet her eyes.

Natalie thought back over the last several days. There had not been any other time when she had sensed she was being watched.

"Did you know Mr. Mackey disappeared?" she asked Phillip.

Phillip's head shot up. "What?"

Natalie nodded. "I heard a couple of ladies talking about it at the circus. I'm surprised none of us heard about it. It was a couple of days ago."

Phillip shook his head. "That is weird. If our moms knew, there's no way we would have been let out of the house. I wonder why they never heard."

"What were you doing out in the street?" Natalie asked him.

Phillip reached out and fiddled with a pen that was sitting on her desk. "I had just come from here, actually."

"My house?"

Phillip shifted, his shoulders hunched. "Yeah, I was looking for you."

"Looking for me?"

"Louisa said I needed to stop being stubborn and just talk to you."

"Oh," Natalie said blankly.

"She...um...she kind of said you missed me."

"She what?"

Phillip looked up, startled. She was not sure if it was a trick of the light that made his cheeks look pink, but she felt a rising heat in hers.

"Why would she say that?" Natalie sputtered. "I thought she was a friend! Friends don't say that. They don't tell other people things that friends say in private!"

A ghost of a smile touched the corners of Phillip's lips causing a tidal wave of embarrassment to roll over her.

"What are you smiling at?" she cried.

The hint of a smile disappeared immediately. Phillip looked down at the pen he was holding and fiddled it until it fell off the desk.

"You're messing up my desk!" The pen had rolled towards her, and she picked it up and put it on her bedside table in a huff.

"Sorry." Phillip ran a hand through his hair. Natalie could have sworn it was an attempt to hide another smile.

This was really too much, she thought. She was going to have to have a talk with Louisa.

"Anyway," Phillip continued, "I was walking home when you came tearing around the corner."

Thoughts of the stranger under the dark street light chased away the mortification she felt at Louisa's well-meaning meddling.

"Phillip," she said quietly, "whoever it is has seen you now."

Phillip looked down at his hands. "Yeah, I know. But it was probably only a matter of time anyway."

"I don't know what I would have done if you hadn't shown up," she confessed.

Phillip shrugged. "Hey, it was an excuse to use my map," he said with a smile.

"You and your maps."

"They do have their uses," Phillip said.

"It definitely did tonight." She wondered what would have happened if they had not been able to get away. The thought was enough to give her shivers.

"We should tell your mom about this," Phillip said.

As if on cue, the door to Natalie's room opened. Serena stepped in, and from the look on her face, Natalie was in big trouble.

"I believe you assured me," Serena said deliberately, "that you would give me no reason to worry if I let you go to the circus. Where have you been, young lady?" Serena's question cracked like a whip, and Natalie's head shrunk into her shoulders. "I normally have a feel for where you are, but for some reason, you fell from my radar, and I have been out of my mind with worry. Phillip, your mother has been calling, also out of her mind with worry. Please tell me why I had to hear noises up here to guess you were home safe?"

"Something happened, Mom," Natalie whispered, "something bad."

Serena's eyes widened. They swept over her and Phillip. "Tell me," she said.

As Natalie recounted the evening's events, something seemed to sink in Serena's eyes. It was a look that stopped Natalie, it frightened her so, but Serena ordered her to continue. When she finished, the room was quiet.

Finally, her voice hard, Serena asked, "You have been home now how long, and you did not come to me right away to tell me?" Serena looked angrier than Natalie had ever seen her.

"I..." Natalie fumbled for an explanation, but it suddenly hit her that they had indeed been in her room talking when they should have reported what had happened right away. "...I didn't think," she stammered.

"No you didn't," Serena said. "I am appalled."

Natalie swallowed as if she had a pill stuck in her throat. Shame swept over her. She pleaded with her mother with her eyes, but her mother moved on.

"Phillip." Serena's tone told him right off the bat that she would take no guff. "In light of what's happened, you will stay here tonight. I will call your mother to let her know you are safe. Neither of you is to go anywhere outside of this house unless you are told. Do you understand?"

"Yes," Natalie said.

"Yes, ma'am," Phillip said.

"Clearly we have been too lenient with the both of you," Serena said. "The rules would have changed regardless, but the two of you need to know that if you don't behave responsibly, we, your parents, will have to manage you better. Are we clear?"

"Yes," Natalie whispered. Her mother had never spoken like this before, and it made her miserable.

"Yes, ma'am." Phillip sounded just as unhappy.

Serena turned to leave. "Natalie, prepare the guest room while I go inform Phillip's mother. You and I will have a discussion later."

After her mother left, Natalie avoided looking at Phillip, and quickly went down the hall to the linen closet to pull out towels and fresh sheets. Phillip padded down the hall behind her, but she went straight to the guest room and pulled the cover off the bed to change the sheets. It was all a watery blur, but she continued her task. She sniffled and wiped her eyes with her sleeve.

Phillip grabbed the end of the sheet and helped her pull it tight over the bed. His expression was bemused. He caught her glance and said softly, "Don't cry."

She shook her head and spread the blanket over the bed. Again Phillip grabbed the ends and helped pull it tight. They changed the pillow cases and folded the cover over the freshly changed sheets. When they were done, Phillip came to stand by her, and they surveyed their work. Natalie sniffled again.

"She's so mad," Natalie said.

"It's because she's really worried." Phillip stared straight ahead, as if watching her cry would drive him to tears as well.

"No, this is different."

"How?"

"I don't know, but it is," she insisted.

Phillip thought about it for a minute. "It will be all right."

Chapter Twenty-Six

Natalie tossed and turned that night. Serena had come up once during the evening to tell Phillip his mother had agreed to his staying at their house for the night. Natalie had hoped her mother would talk to her then, but Serena had locked herself in her study afterwards. Natalie and Phillip had been too anxious to talk, and had spent the evening watching TV, staring quietly at the screen, which could have been playing static for all Natalie cared. She had glanced several times in the direction of Serena's study, hoping to hear the door open, but it had stayed shut. By the time they had finally decided to turn in for the night, Natalie was a miserable mess.

Lying in bed, she waited for her mother. The way Serena talked to her made her feel as if she had been abandoned somehow, and she knew she would not be able to sleep until she could see her mother, talk to her, and know that everything was all right between them.

Natalie sat up. She strained her ears, trying to pick up any sound indicating that her mother was available to talk. Aside from its normal creaks and squeaks, the house stood silent. Natalie pushed back her covers and got out of bed; she could not take tossing and turning anymore.

Her mother sat on the couch in the living room, her elbow resting on the armrest, her hand supporting her forehead. Her body shook with silent sobs.

Natalie's heart jumped into her throat. She inched her way to the couch.

"Mom?"

Serena's head popped up. Her eyes and nose were red from crying. Natalie felt as though the whole day was a nightmare that would not end.

"I'm sorry, Mom." Her words wobbled as she tried to hold back tears. "Please don't be angry with me. I'll do better next time, I promise."

Serena reached out and ran her fingers along Natalie's cheek. The tender gesture released the dam of anxiety that had burdened Natalie all night, and she sobbed. Relief, pain, and fear all jumbled into a mishmash that flowed with the tears she wept.

"Shhh." Serena took her hand and sat her down on the coffee table. Natalie tried to stem her tears. She wiped her eyes with her sleeve and hiccupped.

Serena smiled and cupped her hand around Natalie's head. "I didn't want you to see me crying," she whispered. She leaned her forehead against Natalie's.

"Why are you crying?"

Serena sighed. "Because things are about to change. Everything we've worked for, everything we've built is about to crumble. I've been sitting here looking back at all the things I should have done to prepare, and it hasn't been enough. I've been complacent, overconfident, and it kills me how I've failed you."

"I don't understand," Natalie cried.

"Remember I told you about Martin Reimer? We believe that he, or one of his henchmen, has found us out, or is about to. Whoever came after you tonight has managed to stay hidden. While we've been wrapped up in our own plans, he has somehow found a way to block the signals that would have told us of his arrival. Mr. Mackey's disappearance was concealed from me; a reverse block of some kind, I don't know. But whoever this is, he knows what he is doing."

Serena hugged Natalie close. "He almost took you tonight," she whispered in her hair, "while I sat here, not knowing that we had been breached. We've managed to hold out for so long...it was arrogance on my part.

"You're not prepared Natalie. I've babied you; let you try to work things through in your own time when I should have been getting you ready for the worst. I've been blind, in denial, and because of that, you're in danger."

"Mom," Natalie said, alarmed.

Her mother's eyes became serious. She grasped Natalie's shoulders.

"I can't afford to soften things up for you anymore, Natalie. If you don't come to grips with how things are, I won't be able to protect you.

"You are very gifted," Serena said. "The nature of your gift gives you an inordinate amount of tools. You need to grasp them, control them so that you can use them to defend yourself, protect yourself. You cannot afford to deny them, not now."

Natalie's heart sank. Tears filled her eyes, obscuring her mother.

"I'm sorry it has to be like this, darling, but if I have to push you, kicking and screaming into acceptance to help keep you safe, then that is what I'll do." Serena squeezed Natalie so tight, the breath rushed out of her.

"You have to steel yourself, make yourself as strong as you can. You have to find it, Natalie. You have to.

"Phillip's father was right. Beausoleil was right. We lived with our heads buried in the sand, and now it's come to this."

"Can he be stopped?" Natalie asked tearfully. "Martin Reimer?"

"He has grown strong," Serena said, "and there are so few of us. But there is always hope."

Natalie's heart leaped. "What kind of hope?" Everything inside her grasped at the idea that there was something, anything that could help end the worry and despair that had fallen over them.

"That is a lesson for another time, darling." Serena seemed lost in her thoughts for a moment, but gathered herself quickly.

"You," she said, pulling Natalie up off the coffee table, "need to get back to bed. Your grandmother is coming tomorrow morning, and you will need to be ready."

Natalie walked back up to her room with her mother. She lay back in bed as her mother pulled the covers over her and sat on the edge of her mattress.

"I love you," her mother whispered to her. "Always remember that, Natalie, I love you so very dearly." As she bent forward and kissed her cheek goodnight, Natalie felt something wet fall on her face.

"I love you, Mom." She closed her eyes then. She felt her mother get up from the edge of the bed, heard her walk out her bedroom door and close it shut behind her.

Chapter Twenty-Seven

*T*he next morning a hand gripped her shoulder and shook her from the darkness of sleep.

"What?" She pushed the hair out of her eyes and rolled over to find Phillip standing by the bed. He was dressed in his clothes from the day before, but he looked fresh and ready to face the day.

"Your mom told me to wake you up." His eyes flicked over her face and what he saw made him frown.

"What?" Natalie asked grouchily, pulling up onto her arm; she could tell she was going to be dragging for most of the day.

"Your face looks splotchy. Were you crying last night?"

Her talk with her mother came back to her in a depressive wave, and she flopped back onto her pillow with a groan.

"You okay?" Phillip asked.

"No."

"Your mom didn't seem mad this morning," Phillip ventured. "I think you can relax."

Natalie sighed. "No, I can't do that."

"Why not? Did something happen?"

"Yes." Natalie told Phillip what had happened with her mother the night before. Phillip sat at her desk and listened, without interrupting. In the light of day, everything her mother told her did not hit as hard. Still, it was bleak news, and when Natalie finished, Phillip rested his chin on his hand, and stared into the distance.

"My dad used to talk to me about history," Phillip said after a while. "That's how I got into maps. He'd show me all the places where all these important points in history took place. Whenever he talked about wars, he'd sometimes say that you need an offense to have a good defense. I guess that's what was on his mind when he disappeared. He wanted to see what could be done to take Martin Reimer down before the situation got bad."

"It's not fair," Natalie cried. "All anyone wanted to do was live in peace, but he's taken all of that away."

Phillip opened his mouth to say something but changed his mind. He looked at her clock instead.

"You should probably get up." He stood up and headed out the door. "Your mom is cooking breakfast, and I'm really hungry." He grinned. "There might not be anything left if you don't hurry."

Natalie bounded out of bed and dressed quickly. She headed downstairs to find her mother bustling around the kitchen. Phillip was already seated and digging into a plate of pancakes and sausage. Natalie's stomach growled. She was hungrier than she thought.

Serena came over and kissed her forehead. There were dark circles under her eyes, but there was an excitement in them that had not been there last night.

"I told you your grandmother was coming over this morning, but the plans have changed. I'm heading out soon to meet with her and your mother, Phillip.

"You two are to remain here. Under no circumstances are you allowed to leave this house, do you understand? I cannot emphasize enough how dangerous it is for you to go out at this time. Do I have your word?"

"Yes," Natalie said.

"Yes, ma'am," Phillip said through a mouthful of sausages.

"As long as you stay here, you will not be detected. That's why you need to stay put."

"Why do you have to leave us?" Natalie asked.

Serena considered her words. "Your grandmother thinks she might have figured out a way to get us out of here safely."

Natalie's heart leaped with hope, but Phillip frowned.

"It won't do any good for long," he said. "We'd only be on the run."

Serena put her hand on Phillip's shoulder. "You are your father's son," she said with a smile. "You're right, just like your father was. But as it stands, we are sitting ducks, waiting for our defenses to be chipped away. If we can escape, we can retrench, and live to fight another day."

The answer seemed to satisfy Phillip. Serena settled Natalie in with her own plate of pancakes and sausage and then made to leave. The despair and defeat from last night no longer sat on her, and it lifted Natalie's mood to see her mother less burdened with it.

"How are you going to stay hidden?" Natalie asked, in a sudden burst of anxiety as her mother stood by the doorway.

"I have ways," Serena said. "And Janet made me a special scarf." She pulled a blue scarf from the pocket of her jacket. It was a lovely silk material with threads of purple and brown weaved through it. She winked at the both of them as she tossed the scarf around her neck and shoulders.

"Now do you remember what I told you?" she asked.

"Don't leave the house," Natalie and Phillip said in unison.

"Under any circumstances," Serena added.

"Under any circumstances," they repeated.

"Phillip?" Serena asked, with a warning lilt.

Once again Phillip answered with a mouth full of sausages. "I will not leave the house under any circumstances."

Serena nodded. "Good, I'll see you both later." With a twist of the door handle, she was gone.

Natalie got up from the table and went to the window. She watched as her mother went down the sidewalk and turned towards Mrs. Blaine's house.

"She'll be all right," Phillip said.

"I don't think I'll ever stop being afraid," Natalie said softly. Her mother had made it to the end of the block and continued across the street. Soon she would be too far for Natalie to track.

"It's not like there's anything you could do if anything happened anyway," came Phillip's reply.

Natalie sputtered in indignant surprise. She tried to think of a retort, but the teasing twinkle in Phillip's eyes was full of high spirits, and it turned her outrage into unexpected amusement.

Phillip's mouth was full of pancakes. "I'm just saying."

"Yeah, yeah, yeah." Natalie sat at the table and dug into her plate.

"I love your mom's pancakes," Phillip said contentedly.

"Watching you eat them is ruining my appetite."

Phillip's mouth clamped over the forkful he had just stuffed into his mouth, giving him the look of an offended chipmunk. Natalie snickered.

"So what are we going to do today?" Phillip asked. "I'm a guest here. How will you entertain me?"

"Excuse me?"

"Well, I have to spend a whole day here, and this is your house, so as the hostess, it's your job to make sure I'm entertained."

"Phillip," Natalie said, exasperated, "you're practically family. You can keep yourself entertained."

Phillip looked crestfallen. "You don't have anything special planned?"

Natalie nearly spit out her pancakes. "What?"

Phillip had an expectant look on his face, and she shook her head in wonder. What was he thinking?

"What about homework?" she suggested.

"I did mine on Friday."

"You did?"

"Didn't you?"

"Well, yeah, of course. I didn't think you would have."

"What's that supposed to mean?" Phillip asked indignantly.

"Nothing..."

Phillip scowled. "You're not a very good hostess."

"Oh, for goodness sake! Fine, what do you want to do?"

Phillip thought for a moment. "I have no idea."

"I give up."

"Well, what do you usually do?" he asked.

"Mom and I bake sometimes."

Phillip winced. Natalie rolled her eyes. "You are such a baby. Baking's fun, you'll like it."

"Please don't make me."

Despite Phillip's groaning and complaining, he obliged that afternoon when Natalie made him mix, beat, and fold ingredients into a bowl to make a cake. It really was a relaxing pastime, baking, Natalie thought. Indeed, even Phillip seemed unaware that he was humming as he poured sugar into the flour mixture and beat the egg whites for the frosting.

It happened suddenly, as Natalie was pouring the cake batter into the baking pan. The feeling tickled up her spine so quickly she barely had time to register it.

The kitchen faded and went dark, and a bright pinhole sparked in the distance. It burst forth, revealing the backstage of the Great Beausoleil's tent.

Oh no, Natalie thought. Here we go.

In the scene before her, Louisa lay prostrate on the ground. Natalie watched as she pulled herself into a sitting position. Tears fell down her face, and she sobbed, pleading, "Stop, please! I swear we don't know anything."

A voice, deep and hard said, "I am running out of patience with the both of you."

Natalie heard a snap and a cry of pain, and Hercules catapulted into view. He landed close to Louisa who grabbed at him and wrapped her arms around him as if to protect him. They shrank from the voice, which came from an area out of Natalie's view.

"You are his daughter, and his friend, and you are both lying."

The voice was not the one that had abused Beausoleil. This one was straightforward in a way that spread dread through Natalie's stomach; as if the person behind it knew what he needed to do and would have no problems doing it, even if it cost her friends pain.

A flash of light hit Hercules, who writhed as it buzzed into him. He opened his mouth to scream, but the voice said, "We can't have that, can we?" Hercules throat tightened. His chest heaved, but no sound came from his lungs.

"Hercules, oh, Hercules," Louisa wept. Another flash of light slammed the ground next to her, and she yelped in terror.

"Leave her alone," Hercules choked out. "She's only a young girl."

The voice was unyielding. "Then tell me what I want to know. Tell me how a gifted man like Beausoleil comes to us with hardly any sign of his gift."

"What is this gift you're talking about?" Hercules said. "We don't know what you mean!"

A flash of light hit Hercules, and the force of it tossed him against a large prop box. He bounced off it and landed on the ground, barely able to groan, his eyes scrunched tight in pain.

Louisa screamed. She pulled to her feet and charged for Hercules, but her momentum was cut short. She grasped her throat and gurgled.

"I believe I told you not to scream." The voice said. "It looks like I will need to take measures." There was a sound of movement, and then a force moved through her like a gentle breeze.

"There," the voice said, "that should block out the sound. It's unfortunate for you two, though, as now I don't have to hold back and can let you scream all you want."

The hold on Louisa dropped, and she fell to the ground, coughing. She tried to crawl to Hercules, but Hercules' warning cut like a cleaver between them.

"Don't move!" he ordered.

"You are both wearing my patience thin," the voice warned. "Let's try a different tack, shall we? What can you tell me about a girl named Natalie?"

Natalie's heart jumped into her throat. Was this the man who had come after her the other night? How did he know her name?

Louisa's eyes widened and Hercules bowed his head, the both of them too surprised by the question to hide.

"Ah." There was now a silky tone to the voice. "You do know her. What can you tell me about her? Where does she live?"

"We hardly know her," Hercules said. "We've seen her around the circus, but that's all."

There was an impatient burst from the voice. "This is maddening. I have never been in a town as well-fortified as this one. It is small, and finding a girl should not be hard, but it has been next to impossible. Now tell me what you know!"

Louisa moaned and pleaded, "We know nothing! Please believe us! If we knew we would tell you. Please, just stop!"

But Hercules' eyes bulged. His body rose into the air as he grasped at his throat.

"Noooooo!" Natalie screamed in silence. "Noooooo!"

She felt a yank from behind, and the scene receded to a pinprick. Her arms reached for it, but it disappeared with a snap.

She was back in the kitchen. The mixing bowl had fallen from her hands; batter spattered across the floor. Phillip's face was pale.

"You're back," he exclaimed. His hand gripped her arm. "What happened? What did you see?"

"He has Louisa and Hercules!" Natalie cried. "He's awful, Phillip. We have to do something!"

"Let's go!" Phillip ran to the door, but Natalie stopped him.

"We're not supposed to leave the house," she said.

"This is different! They need help."

"What are we supposed to do?" Natalie asked.

"I don't know, but we can't just sit here and do nothing!"

"I'm not saying we do nothing," Natalie said, agitated. "I'm saying we think of something besides barging over there and getting into trouble. Come on, Phillip! Think of something!"

Phillip's eyebrows screwed together. "Let's call Mrs. Blaine's house. She'll know what to do. What's her number?"

Natalie looked at him, mortified. "I don't know."

"How can you not know? She's your grandmother!"

"I only just found out," Natalie argued. "My mom always called her." She felt like an idiot, not knowing her grandmother's phone number. "Wait! The phone book!"

She ran to a drawer and pulled it out. She flipped through the pages as Phillip came to stand beside her. "Here it is!"

Phillip picked up the phone and dialed as she read the number. He let it ring several rings, but there was no answer. He slammed the phone down.

"How could they not be answering?" he yelled in frustration.

"Try your house! Maybe they went there."

Phillip dialed the number, but once again, after several rings, he let the line go.

"What are we going to do?" Natalie moaned. "He's hurting Hercules."

Phillip pulled out his map. "We use this."

"What? To go over there? Phillip we can't!"

"Then I'm going over there myself," Phillip said. "I'll run over, and you tell your mother when she gets back."

"You could get hurt! Phillip, he knows who I am. He asked Louisa and Hercules about me. If he knows about me, he must know about you."

"Maybe I can distract him, or maybe I can get someone to help."

"That won't do any good," she said softly. "He can do things."

Phillip understood. "I have to try."

"What good is it if he just gets you, too?"

"We got away from him before. I'll think of something." Phillip turned to leave the kitchen.

"No!" Natalie cried.

But Phillip left through the doorway Serena had used earlier, and headed down the walkway.

Natalie paced the kitchen. What should she do? She ran to the end of the hallway and grabbed her and Phillip's jackets, the ones Mrs. Stone made, and raced out the door after Phillip.

He had covered a good bit of ground by the time she hit the sidewalk, and she had to run fast to catch up.

"Phillip!" She did not want to draw attention by screaming his name, but he was moving quickly. "Phillip!" People who happened to be outside working in their yards or relaxing on their porches looked up, but must not have thought anything was unusual, and went back to what they were doing.

Phillip was almost two blocks down before he heard her and stopped short. He turned in surprise and waited as she ran to him.

"Here." She handed him his jacket. "You'll need this."

He took the jacket from her. "Thanks," he said, gratefully. "You'd better get back before you get into trouble." He looked around as he put the jacket on and put his map in the pocket.

"No," Natalie said, "it will be faster if we use your map."

Phillip shook his head. "I don't think you should go. I wasn't thinking earlier. This could get bad, and you shouldn't be there if it does."

Natalie hesitated. It was so tempting to just turn around and go back. Phillip had gotten her into so much trouble already, and after the reprimand they had gotten from her mother, she did not think he would hold it against her this time if she chose not to go.

But if anything happened to him, she would never forgive herself. And Phillip was right about one thing; it did not matter how much she hid her head in the sand, or how far they all ran. It was simply putting off the inevitable. At some point she would have to make a stand and use everything she had to do so.

"We stand a better chance if I go with you," she said. "It's not like you have the abilities I do, right?"

Phillip rolled his eyes. "Rub it in, why don't you?"

"You're the quick thinker, though," she pointed out. "You're the brains and I'm...I guess I'm the brawn, even though that's not saying much."

The corner of Phillip's mouth twitched. "I guess it's better than nothing." Still, he hesitated. "Natalie, I've already caused a lot of trouble, you know? You were right about me getting Beausoleil caught."

"I didn't mean..." Natalie started.

"No," Phillip interrupted, "I know this Reimer man is the real problem, but my mom always tells me I jump into things without thinking; that I need to think more, and she's right. I have to try to help Hercules and Louisa, but I don't want to get anyone else hurt."

"Okay then," Natalie said, "we won't just barge in. You take us somewhere safe, so we can get an idea of what's happening and come up with a plan. You'll think of something. You saved me from him before, remember?"

When Phillip did not move, she reached into his pocket and snatched his map.

"Hey!" Phillip grabbed for the map, but she held it out of reach, and then ran, looking for a place where they would not get caught using it. Phillip managed to grab her arm, but she slipped it loose and kept running.

"Natalie," Phillip hissed as she dodged his attempts to grab hold of her, "this isn't funny, give me my map!" They had hit the downtown area, and people were watching them with amusement. It must look like a game of keep away, Natalie thought.

"I'm looking for a place to use it," Natalie said. "Are you in or not?"

Phillip managed to snake in a hand and grab the map. "All right, I'm in." He shook his head and surveyed the area. "Let's go here." He checked to make sure no one was watching and ducked into an alleyway. Natalie followed as he turned into a back alley and crouched behind a dumpster.

He scanned the alley as she crouched beside him. "We should be all right here," he said. The alley was empty and the backs of the buildings had no windows to allow peeking eyes. Phillip pulled out the map and said, "The Big Top Circus."

As a map for The Big Top Circus emerged, Phillip paused and regarded her with serious eyes.

"Are you sure you want to do this?" he asked.

It was like standing with one foot in a boat and one foot on land. Natalie felt as if the boat was sailing away, and she could either take one foot out, or put the other foot in. She took her foot off land.

"Yes," she said.

Chapter Twenty-Eight

*P*hillip zoomed towards Beausoleil's trailer. The trailer lined up against the outskirts of the circus, so when they surfaced behind it—still within bounds of protection, Phillip noted—no one saw them. Natalie moved to sneak out from behind the trailer, but Phillip held her back.

"Can you see from here what's going on?" he asked.

"No." Natalie gave him a puzzled look. "What are you talking about? We can't see anything from back here."

"No, your vision, dork. Your gift."

"Oh." It was as if she had stepped into a vast desert with nothing before, behind, or beside her to help guide her through. She settled behind the trailer with Phillip, sliding down to sit on the ground. Phillip sat beside her. "I don't know. I've never tried it on my own. It just comes to me."

"You did something that one time with Mike, Rory and Larry," Phillip pointed out. "Why don't you give it a try and see what happens?"

"Okay." Natalie was not sure what to do, so for lack of a better idea, she pulled her knees to her chin, bowed her head and closed her eyes. She concentrated on Louisa, tried to focus every part of her being on her friend. She scrunched her eyes and pushed at her mind as hard as she could.

"It's not working," she said in frustration. She punched her knees with her hands balled into fists. "Of all the times for it not to happen, it has to be the one time I'd like it to!"

"It's okay." Phillip reached for her hand. He laid it into his other hand and gently worked her fist loose and clasped her fingers between his. He did not look at her as he did it, although his actions riveted Natalie's attention. She looked from their hands to his face and back. What was he doing?

"Do you remember when we went riding on the elephant that first day we came to the circus?" Phillip asked her.

"Yes."

"It was nice, wasn't it?"

"Yes."

Phillip leaned his head back against the trailer and closed his eyes. "When I was up there, I felt like I could see everything. And it was so peaceful, like I'd left everything else on the ground. Was it like that for you?"

"Yes."

"Let's go back there." Phillip gave her hand a shake. "Not to the ride, but let's close our eyes and go back. Try it."

"Okay." Natalie leaned her head back against the trailer with Phillip and closed her eyes, and remembered the time she was on the elephant—the breeze, the quiet from above, the bustle below, and the view all around. Her mind did a silent exhale, and the world opened up before her.

Louisa. The thought came unbidden. Her mind rushed forward, cutting through the circus to Beausoleil's tent and then inside.

Hercules lay on the ground, unconscious, his tiny body limp, almost lifeless. Louisa was a mess. Her hair was a tangled nest, her clothes dirty and torn, her body shaking as she sobbed over Hercules.

"Why won't you believe us?" she cried.

"Because I know for a fact that you're lying," the voice said. "There is something going on in this town. More than what has to do with your father. I can't put my finger on it. I sense it in everyone, but I sense it most of all in you, young lady. NOW TELL ME!"

Louisa grabbed at her neck. Her body lifted, first to her knees, and then to her ankles as they dragged the ground.

Natalie gave a giant heave and hurled her mind back to where Phillip waited, still holding her hand. She opened her eyes with a gasp and, releasing Phillip's hand, was up on her feet, running around the trailer, headed for Beausoleil's tent.

People from the circus gaped in surprise as she raced through the grounds. "Hey, what are you doing back here?" someone called out. She did not stop to answer.

"Natalie!" Phillip caught up to her. "What happened? What's going on?" He grabbed her arm, whirling her to a stop, and gave her a shake. "Stop it! Tell me!"

"He's hurting her bad! We have to go now!" She tried to run, but he held her fast.

"What are you going to do?" he demanded.

"That's not my job, it's yours!" With a yank, she pulled free and charged through the crowd.

"FIRE IN BEAUSOLEIL'S TENT!" Phillip yelled behind her.

Heads snapped around in surprise.

"Fire?"

"Did someone say 'fire'?"

"Beausoleil's tent!"

"Get the hoses! Get the buckets!"

The clamor grew as people swung into action. Without hesitation, Natalie threw out an idea from her mind, just as she had with Mike, Rory, and Larry. "I see smoke!" she hollered.

"Smoke?"

"Do you see smoke?"

"Yes, there's smoke in Beausoleil's tent!"

"Hurry, get over there now!"

By the time she arrived at Beausoleil's tent, people had gathered around, pointing, talking among themselves, watching with wide eyes and dropped jaws as smoke from Natalie's altered reality poured from Beausoleil's tent.

Soon after, it was chaos. Circus people scoured the tent, searching for the source of the smoke. Natalie scrambled through the entrance and ran for the backstage.

"Louisa!" she screamed. "Louisa!"

"Did you hear that?" someone yelled.

"There's a girl in there!"

"Get out of there!" someone screamed.

The flap to the entrance opened as people entered, looking for fire. Soon the main staging area was swarming with people. A hand grabbed her arm.

"Now who's not thinking?" It was Phillip, his face white, furious with her.

"Clear the area!" someone yelled.

"Natalie!" she heard Louisa cry. "Run, don't come in here!"

Natalie burst through the entrance to backstage with Phillip right behind. Louisa lay on the ground, gasping with her hand at her throat. Natalie moved to help her when a familiar feeling tickled up her spine. She stopped short and turned.

Hercules floated in a corner of the tent, his head and limbs hanging, like a puppet whose strings had been let go. Natalie took a step towards him.

"Don't," Louisa croaked. Phillip was kneeling beside her, supporting her battered body. She pointed her finger in Hercules' direction.

Natalie peered at Hercules. Her heart thumped a faster beat as she discerned a figure standing beside him, shrouded in the darkness of the corner. The tickling along Natalie's spine froze into ice. She stared at the stranger.

It was too dark to see him, but Natalie felt his presence clearly. He's the one, she thought, the one from the other night.

Voices gathered outside the entrance to backstage. The figure tensed. Natalie sensed he was calculating the time he had left before he had a crowd to contend with.

The air crackled and snapped. It crept along her skin, clawed its way around her, and somehow, she knew the stranger meant to take her.

She glanced at Phillip. His eyes were wide. He held out his arms and checked them; he, too, would be taken.

Despair coursed through her. What had they been thinking? What had made them think they could handle this? They had wanted to help, but now they were on the verge of being taken.

"Mom, I'm so scared," Natalie whispered. "I don't know what I'm doing." She pictured her mother's face. "I'm so sorry, Mom."

Her mother's words then came back to her.

"You are very gifted," Serena had said. "The nature of your gift gives you an inordinate amount of tools. You need to grasp them, control them so that you can use them to defend yourself, protect yourself. You cannot afford to deny them, not now."

Natalie looked at Phillip and then at Louisa. Poor, Louisa, who had tried to steer them away, even as she was beaten down; Louisa, who had held tight to her father's gift, even in the most torturous of circumstances.

Natalie bolted across the space between them and grabbed Louisa in a hug. A burst of power surged inside her. Her gift had kicked in.

The world around them started to dissolve; the stranger was taking them.

Natalie focused on one of the prop boxes. The wheels under it sprung to life. Its top opened like a giant mouth, and it rolled across the tent and took a flying leap onto the stranger. There was a clatter in the dark corner and a grunt of surprise. Natalie focused on the other boxes. Their lids opened, and props climbed out. Knives, cages, chains, saws, handkerchiefs, all sparked to life.

The knife flew across the tent into the corner. The stranger ducked, and the knife sliced a piece of the tent. The cages leaped from their perches. Their metal bars scurried to the corner to snap and clatter. They flew from the corner as the stranger hurled them away. The chains rolled off the boxes and unlinked to swarm and then gather to encircle the stranger. The saws paddled along their ridges, cutting a path along the ground to the corner.

The swarm proved to be too much. When the handkerchiefs soared across the tent and fastened to the stranger's face, the world clicked back into sharp relief.

Phillip and Louisa were staring, trance-like, at the props attacking the stranger.

"Run!" Natalie screamed.

Phillip and Louisa snapped out of the trance with a start. Natalie and Phillip grabbed Louisa's arms and hauled her to her feet. Phillip pulled her arm around his neck and dragged her to the flap leading to the main stage area.

"Hercules," Louisa protested, as Phillip disappeared with her under the flap. "I can't leave Hercules."

Natalie stopped and wheeled around. The pandemonium in the corner had intensified, and the stranger almost stepped into the light where she could see him. A white handkerchief covered his face as he tried to wrest it off. With a strong twist, he wrenched it off. She discerned the outline of his face, but it was still too covered in shadows to recognize.

His head scanned the tent. She did not have to see his eyes to get a feel for the fury that raged off him as he spied her. Terror clamped her in place.

A flurry of air startled her as the flap to the exit opened, and a hand reached in and yanked her out. She blinked as a man from the circus glared down at her.

"You shouldn't be in here," he growled. "Get out now."

He passed her on to the next man who passed her on to the next. She tried to protest, but the first man had already parted the flap, and he and the other men peeked in to inspect for fire.

Just then a flash ignited the backstage area like a mini explosion. The men jumped back from the opening, yelling and cursing.

"What was that?" someone yelled.

"Do you see anything?" Natalie heard one of the men ask.

A hand grasped her shoulder.

"We need to go now," Phillip whispered. His arm was wrapped around Louisa, supporting her exhausted body.

"Is she all right?" someone asked, nodding at Louisa.

"We're going to get her some help," Phillip said.

A path cleared for them. Louisa thanked people as they passed. Tears streaked down her cheeks. Natalie knew she was thinking about Hercules. She wished she could say something to make her feel better. There had not been time. The stranger had recovered quickly from the barrage of props, and would have even had a chance to deal with Natalie if the other circus people had not pulled her out.

"Where should we go?" They had exited the tent, and Phillip was looking around, trying to decide which direction was best.

"We should take Louisa home with us," Natalie said.

"I know, but will she make it home like this?"

"I can walk if we have to," Louisa said faintly.

Natalie shook her head. "Let's get back to her trailer. We can make a decision there."

"We can't wait too long," Phillip warned.

When they arrived at the trailer, Phillip helped Louisa sit at the table. Natalie went to the cabinets and pulled out the supplies they had used the last time they were there.

"Do you think she can move through the map if we hold on to her?" Natalie asked. She took a cotton ball and some alcohol and applied it to the scrapes and scratches on Louisa.

"I've been thinking about that." Phillip said, "I know we can take objects because I brought that flashlight the last time. Maybe it will work if you switch Louisa into a doll. We could always try her like this first, but I'd rather get it right the first time. We can't stay here. We need to get back to your house ASAP."

"What are you two talking about?" Louisa asked.

Natalie put down her cotton ball. "Phillip has a map, and we're able to travel through it. We haven't tried it yet with another person, but we might be able to bring you through if you're a doll."

Louisa's eyes widened. "Travel through a map?"

"Yes." Phillip showed her his map. "Right now I can only do it with Natalie, but we can do it for sure. It's how we got here once Natalie realized you were in danger."

"You knew Hercules and I were in trouble?" Louisa asked Natalie.

"I'm so sorry, Louisa," Tears started to brim in Natalie's eyes. "We would have come sooner if we could have. We weren't supposed to leave the house, and we had to figure out what to do."

Louisa put her head on Natalie's shoulder. "You didn't have to come. You shouldn't have. That man kept asking about you, and you put yourselves in danger by coming. Thank you, though. Thank you for saving me. I just hope Hercules is okay."

Louisa started to cry again, so Natalie wrapped her arms around her. "We'd like to get you to my house so we can tell our moms what happened," she said.

"If you need to change me into a doll, that's okay," Louisa said.

Natalie looked at Phillip, who nodded.

"Okay, I'm going to give it a try now. We need to move quickly." She tightened her arms around Louisa and felt her nod her head against her shoulder.

Natalie was not sure what to do, so she closed her eyes and tried to open her mind as she had with Phillip earlier. It did not take long this time. Everything inside her relaxed and spread wide. She focused on Louisa, and felt a shift in her arms. Her hold adjusted as Louisa's body stiffened became smaller.

"It worked," Phillip said.

Natalie opened her eyes. Louisa was once again a doll.

Phillip took a seat on the other side of Louisa. He smoothed out his map and called for Natalie's house.

They emerged behind a tall hedge on Natalie's lawn. Natalie checked Louisa. She had arrived intact. Natalie breathed a sigh of relief.

"Let's take her inside," Phillip said. He lifted Louisa, and they walked into the house.

Natalie had barely shut the door before a voice asked, "Where have you been?"

It was not a happy group waiting for them. Serena stood in front with her hands on her hips. Mrs. Stone was a step behind, glowering at Phillip. Mrs. Blaine sat in an armchair; she was once again stern Mrs. Blaine, and not the affectionate grandmother she had been for the past several days.

"There's been trouble," Natalie started to explain.

"Why does that not surprise me?" Mrs. Stone asked, with a look to Phillip.

"Is that the doll, Louisa?" Mrs. Blaine asked.

"Yes," Natalie said breathlessly, "we had to take her with us." She paused, wondering how the next sentence would fly. "We took her through the map."

Serena's eyebrows rose as did Mrs. Stone's. The air in the room seemed to contract with Natalie's information.

"I see you've been playing around with your gift," Mrs. Blaine said finally. "Please come in and explain."

Serena and Mrs. Stone stepped aside to let Natalie and Phillip enter the living room. They settled on the couch with Louisa between them.

"Should we leave Louisa like this?" Phillip asked.

Serena, Mrs. Stone and Mrs. Blaine exchanged glances. For the first time, there was an air of amusement among them, although they tempered it quickly.

"Please, by all means, change her back so we can get the full story," Mrs. Blaine said.

Natalie wrapped her arms around Louisa. Within seconds, Louisa was back to form as a girl.

Natalie saw Serena swallow hard, as if something had caught in her throat.

"It's getting easier to do these things," Natalie murmured.

Serena nodded. The nod was a mixture of pain and something else. Of what, Natalie was not sure.

Louisa blinked and sighed and stretched her limbs, wincing as her abused muscles protested. The first person she saw was Natalie, and she threw her arms around her.

"You did it!" she exclaimed. "We made it, didn't we?" She pulled back and noticed the three ladies. Her demeanor sobered.

"Hi, Mrs. Blaine, Mrs. Bristol and Mrs. Stone," she said.

After a pause Mrs. Stone said, "It looks like you've had quite an adventure."

"It wasn't an adventure, I'm afraid," Louisa said. "Phillip and Natalie saved me from something pretty horrible."

"Why don't you all tell us what happened," Mrs. Blaine said.

When they were finished, Mrs. Stone told them, "We were not where we could get to a telephone. We had agreed you would stay in the house. It was set up so we would know if there was any trouble here."

"I knew the second you left," Serena said. "We came right away, but you were gone. We've been trying to track you ever since, but your ability with the map is something we haven't mastered yet."

"Obviously, we will have to work on that," Mrs. Stone said. She looked at Phillip. "I should have known you would persuade Natalie to help you put it to good use."

"Serena, Janet, we should check our fortifications," Mrs. Blaine said now. "The children came by way of the map, which is actually a good thing, as it makes them harder to trace, but we need to make sure we are covered."

Serena and Mrs. Stone nodded. Serena walked over to Natalie and put a hand under her chin to tilt her face to hers.

"When I said you had to accept your gift and learn to use it, this isn't quite what I had in mind," she said. "I'm glad you're all right."

Mrs. Stone was having her own discussion with Phillip. From the looks of things, it was a much more stern conversation. Still, Mrs. Stone laid a hand on Phillip's head and ruffled his hair.

"C'mon, Mom," Phillip said gruffly.

After Serena and Mrs. Stone departed, Natalie, Phillip and Louisa sat under Mrs. Blaine's quiet scrutiny. Natalie squirmed slightly in her seat while Phillip looked down at his shoes. Louisa gave a tired sigh, though, and that ended the quiescence.

"Forgive me, Louisa," Mrs. Blaine exclaimed. "We should get you taken care of right away. I apologize for my lack of sensitivity. You should stay here tonight with Serena and Natalie. They will take good care of you, and as long as you stay in the house, you should be safe. I am sorry about Hercules. If there is anything that we can do, we will do it. I promise."

Louisa's eyes filled with tears, but she nodded.

"Natalie, Phillip, why don't you help Louisa settle in?" Mrs. Blaine picked up her cane and pulled to her feet. "We will talk later."

Natalie and Phillip helped Louisa off the couch. "Let's go upstairs," Natalie said. As they headed up the stairs, she glanced back at Mrs. Blaine.

She had moved towards the window and was staring out, but her expression was far away, and Natalie could tell she was not seeing anything outside.

"You guys go in my room," Natalie told Phillip. Phillip helped Louisa down the hall to Natalie's bedroom while Natalie ran to the bathroom to get a towel, bandages, and some alcohol.

"Here." She handed the supplies to Phillip. "I'm going downstairs to get some ice."

"What for?" Phillip asked.

"For some of those bruises."

Natalie went back downstairs. Mrs. Blaine still stood at the window. Natalie paused, unsure whether to pass through to the kitchen, when Mrs. Blaine turned.

"I'm getting some ice for Louisa," Natalie explained. "She got knocked around."

Mrs. Blaine's face was grave. "I can't imagine how frightening that would have been." She moved away from the window to step in closer to Natalie.

"Natalie," she said, "did you happen to get a look at the man who did this?"

"No, he was in the shadows so I couldn't see much."

"Did he do or say anything that stood out to you in any way?"

"Like what?" Natalie said uncertainly.

Mrs. Blaine dismissed her own question with a wave of her hand. "Nothing. There really wasn't anything you could observe, I'm sure. I just wondered what he might know, or how much he knows."

Natalie thought back on the encounter. "I think he knows enough to where he won't stop looking for answers."

Mrs. Blaine nodded. "Thank you, Natalie."

Natalie arrived back upstairs to find Louisa cleaned up of most of the dirt and patched up with a couple of band aids on her arms.

"Can you use this?" Natalie handed over an ice pack.

"Yes, on my knee." Louisa winced as she put the pack on the knot that had formed there.

"Was it the guy who chased us last night?" Phillip asked Natalie.

She took a seat at her desk. "Yes, but it's not the same guy from the last vision I had." Phillip's head gave a startled nod at her use of the word vision. "The other guy had mentioned sending someone, so it must be this one, the one in town."

"I couldn't see him at all, it was so dark in that corner," Phillip said. "Did you recognize him?" he asked Louisa.

"No, I had never seen him before. It was so weird, the way he stayed hidden like that. I never got a good look at him. I didn't even notice when he appeared. I was just sitting backstage when he spoke to me from the corner. It was so scary," Louisa said, shuddering.

"What did he say?" Natalie asked.

"He said I was an unusual girl." Louisa's brows furrowed as she tried to remember. "He said he could not get any sort of read on me at all, whatever that means. But then, I guess it would be hard to get anything typical off of me, right?" Louisa said with a small laugh.

"He kept asking questions about Papa, and how had Papa managed to hide, and where did he keep his most valuable possessions, things like that. I kept telling him I didn't know what he was talking about, but he didn't believe me."

Louisa tried to blink back tears. "I asked him where Papa was, what he had done with him, but he wouldn't answer. He was starting to get angry when Hercules arrived. And then it got worse.

"Hercules wouldn't answer any of his questions either, and when Hercules is angry...well, you know how he is when he's not angry," Louisa said.

Natalie nodded. It would not have gone well for Hercules if he had butted heads with the stranger.

"I wonder if he tried to stay hidden because he could be recognized," Phillip said. "Maybe it's someone we know?"

"If he looks like the other guy," Natalie said, "he would stand out."

"What do you mean?" Phillip asked.

An image of the man who had tortured Beausoleil popped into her mind. The thought of his patchwork face made her skin crawl. She shook the picture out of her head.

"His face, it's this mess of different...parts." She shot a surreptitious peek at Louisa, hoping that Louisa would not associate Natalie's knowledge with her father's fate. Luckily, Louisa did not seem to make the connection.

Phillip, however, picked up on her glance.

"How's that ice pack?" he asked Louisa.

"It's helping, thanks," Louisa said. "I'm pretty tired, though. Would it be all right if I got some rest?"

"Yes, I'm sorry!" Natalie jumped to her feet. "I'll get your room ready."

"I can do that." Phillip got up from the bed and walked to the door. He looked restless, as if he needed something to do. "I think I remember where the linens are. Should I just grab any one of them?"

"That's fine," Natalie said. "Are you sure?"

Phillip was already down the hallway. "Yes," he said.

Louisa had been holding up so well, but now all the energy had drained out of her. Her shoulders slumped low and her head drooped over. Her hand weakly lifted to her face to wipe her eyes.

Natalie moved to sit beside her on the bed and put her arms around her as Louisa's body started to shake with silent sobs.

Natalie did not know what else to do besides let Louisa cry. She heard Phillip's movement in the guest bedroom pause as the wracked sounds of Louisa sobbing increased. She heard him continue with his tasks while she rocked with Louisa on the bed.

"I'm so sorry, Louisa," she murmured.

Eventually she became aware of Phillip in the doorway. He waited with his hands in his pockets, peeking at them from under a flop of his sandy hair. Natalie looked at him helplessly above Louisa's head. He came to sit on the other side of Louisa, and patted softly at the sobbing girl's back.

It seemed Louisa had cried an ocean before the cries began to recede. Natalie continued to rock her until Louisa's sobbing ceased, and her body went slack from exhaustion. Natalie and Phillip helped her up, and walked her to the guest room. Natalie pulled back the covers from the bed as Phillip helped Louisa settle in. Natalie pulled the sheets over Louisa and sat on the edge of the bed and held her hand.

"Try to get some sleep," she told Louisa.

Louisa squeezed her hand. "Thank you for being good friends," she croaked, her voice hoarse from sobbing. She closed her eyes, and her hand relaxed.

Natalie stood up beside Phillip. She looked with him at Louisa's sleeping form and then turned to leave the room, closing the door behind them. She hoped that Louisa would avoid nightmares, and would instead have the kind of sleep that helped to heal the raw wounds that had been inflicted upon her.

Chapter Twenty-Nine

When Serena and Mrs. Stone returned, Phillip, his mother, and Mrs. Blaine all departed with reassurances that they would notify them of their safe arrival home.

"How is Louisa, darling," Serena asked her at dinner that evening.

"Not good, Mom," Natalie said. "Hercules took care of Louisa with Beausoleil gone. Now what is she going to do? What will the people at the circus think?"

"Naturally, she will stay here with us until we get things sorted out," Serena said. "She's one of us, so we will take care of her."

Natalie nodded. "Okay." They continued to eat without speaking, each of them lost in their own thoughts.

"Why hasn't anyone tried to stop him?" Natalie asked suddenly. "This Martin Reimer."

Serena set her fork down. "Have you ever heard of the phrase, 'divide and conquer'?"

"Yes."

"That's pretty much what Martin did. He managed to scatter us, and we lost touch, trying to stay hidden. As I've mentioned before, we were always peaceful, so we were blindsided by what happened. The scope of Martin's plan was beyond our comprehension.

"We should have organized, though. That should have been the route to take. Now, he is quite strong. It would take considerable planning, I think, to contain him." Serena shook her head, as if with great regret. She picked up her wine glass to take a sip.

"Do you think there are other people of our kind still out there that would want to try to organize?" Natalie asked.

The glass stopped on the way to Serena's lips. "Why do you ask?"

Natalie shrugged. "Maybe that's what we should do."

Serena laughed. "That sounds like something Phillip would say."

Natalie grinned. "I guess it does." She twirled her fork around her plate idly. "Maybe he'd be right." She snuck a peek at her mother to see what she thought.

Serena took a deep breath. "I'd worry about getting us out of here first." She set her glass back down without taking a sip.

"Oh, yeah, right," Natalie said. "That makes sense."

"There will be plenty of time to plan better once we're in a safer place."

"Do you think we're going to be able to?" Natalie asked. "Get to a safer place, I mean."

"Yes, there is a chance. We're working on it." Serena folded her napkin and leaned back in her chair. "So, I take it you're feeling more secure about your gifts?"

Natalie shrugged. "It helped when we had to help Louisa. I'm still getting used to it, I guess."

"Do you feel like you have more control?"

"I think so. Like if I try to ask for it, it comes to me a little easier now."

Serena nodded. "Try to be judicious in how you use your gifts. They're not toys, remember." She held up her hand when Natalie opened her mouth to protest. "I know you don't look at them that way, but it will always bear repeating, Natalie. The kind of talent you have can make a person giddy. You can never remind yourself too much, okay?"

"Okay, Mom," Natalie grumbled.

"Good." Serena rose and started clearing the table. "I should probably set aside a plate for Louisa, just in case." She paused, looking at the food. "Do you know, does she eat?"

Natalie had to think. "I don't know."

"Hmm," Serena said, "this is definitely not something you have to think about every day."

Natalie smiled. "No, but it's been like that with everything lately."

Later that night, Natalie lay awake in bed, watching the shadows play across her room. So much had happened, and her body could not come off high alert. She had flipped from one side of her mattress to the other, pulling her covers on and then kicking them off. Her mind gave her no peace as it raced through all the things that had happened these past few days. How could life have changed so quickly?

The sound of her door knob jiggling cut through her thoughts. She sat up in bed.

"Who's there?" she whispered in a panic.

"Natalie?" It was Louisa standing in the doorway. "I'm sorry. I didn't want to knock in case you were sleeping. I just thought I'd peek and then go if you were."

"That's okay," Natalie said, relieved. "Did you sleep well?"

"I guess," Louisa said. "I don't remember dreaming or anything, so I guess that's good."

"Do you want to stay here for a while?" Natalie asked.

"If you don't mind," Louisa said.

"No, come on in." Natalie scooted over to give her space. Louisa tiptoed across the room and crawled under the covers. She lay on her back, staring at the ceiling.

"It's so quiet here," Louisa murmured. "In the circus, people are up for hours. You can hear them talking or laughing or fighting. Sometimes you can hear the animals too."

"How do you get any sleep?" Natalie asked.

"You get used to it. You learn to block out the noise."

"You mentioned dreams earlier," Natalie said. "Do you? Dream, I mean."

Louisa turned to look at Natalie. "Yeah, when I'm not a doll, I do. Kind of weird, I guess, huh?"

"What kinds of things do you dream about?" Natalie wondered if they were any different for dolls.

"Things that happened during the day. Sometimes they're a little weird, too. Once I dreamed that Hercules was yelling at me, more than usual, when an elephant walked by and stepped on him. It carried him off, squashed under his foot. I screamed for help, but each time the elephant took a step, I could hear Hercules, still yelling at me from under the elephant's foot, as if nothing had happened."

Natalie giggled. "That sounds like something I'd dream about too."

"So it's true, what they said. You can take on other people's gifts? You saved me using Papa's?"

"Yeah, I guess it's true."

Louisa flipped on her side towards Natalie and propped her head up on her elbow. "You don't like it?"

"It's okay. I'm glad it helped us. It just takes getting used to."

"You need to be careful," Louisa said. "That man kept asking about you. Phillip too, but mostly you. It's like he knew something."

"Yeah," Natalie said. "He came after us the other night."

"What?" Louisa gasped.

Natalie explained what happened to Louisa, and watched, in the light of the moon streaming through the curtains, as Louisa's eyes grew round as saucers.

"He almost got you." Louisa shook her head in wonder. "It's a good thing Phillip showed up with his map."

"Yeah, he's a quick thinker. I don't know what I would have done. I mean, I'm the one with the gifts right now, but I wouldn't have been able to come up with anything to save myself."

"So he came after you and saved you," Louisa mused. She flopped onto her back and wrapped herself in a hug, giving an enraptured sigh. "He's your knight in shining armor!"

"What?" Natalie jackknifed onto her elbow, staring at Louisa in disbelief. "He is not! He's a pain in the neck!"

Louisa giggled. "I'm a doll, Natalie. I'm built for a world of princesses and evil witches and handsome princes. I know what a knight in shining armor is, and trust me, that's what Phillip is."

"That's so ridiculous!" Natalie exclaimed.

"You're blinder than I am when I'm in my doll suit," Louisa retorted with glee.

"Your doll suit?" squeaked Natalie.

"That's what I call it."

"Since when?"

"Since now!"

Natalie rolled back onto her pillow with laughter. Louisa's laugh echoed hers. Once they got started, they could not stop, and they clutched at their sides until they almost cried.

"You're so funny," Natalie said when their fit died down.

"You're easy to make laugh, compared to Hercules."

The thought of Louisa trying to make dour Hercules laugh started off another round of giggles. Natalie wondered at one point if her mother could hear them, but not a sound came from her mother's room, so they howled away.

This time, though, Louisa's laughter ended on a small sob.

"It'll be okay, Louisa." Natalie grabbed Louisa's hand and held it tight. "Hercules is really smart. I'm sure wherever he is, he'll know how to take care of himself."

Louisa used her other hand to wipe the tears from her eyes. "I don't know what I'll do if anything really bad happens to him,

Natalie." She squeezed Natalie's hand hard. "Hercules is my best friend. He's my knight in shining armor."

Natalie could not think of anything else to say, so she wrapped her arms around Louisa and held her tight. They both lay in silence until the light of dawn filled the room, and they finally fell asleep.

Chapter Thirty

Serena woke them up later that morning. She looked tired, but there was an indulgent smile on her face. Natalie guessed that she had heard their laughter last night. She kissed Natalie on the forehead, and patted Louisa's head.

"Good morning, girls," she said. "How are you feeling, Louisa?"

"A little better, Mrs. Bristol," Louisa replied, giving a little yawn.

"I don't know if Natalie had a chance to tell you, but you are welcome to stay with us until we get everything sorted out," Serena said.

"I'm sorry," Natalie said, "I forgot to mention it."

"I'd hate to be a bother," Louisa said.

"It's no bother at all," Serena said. "Your Papa was one of us, and we take care of each other. You would do it for Natalie, right?"

"Oh yes, absolutely!"

"Good, it's settled then. You can borrow some of Natalie's things until we can pick up yours. I'm afraid we won't be able to do that until later, though. I have a few things to take care of with Janet and Natalie's grandmother today.

"I'm keeping you home from school today, Natalie," Serena said. "I need to keep you close for now. I know you must be disappointed."

Natalie gave a big, contented sigh. "Oh, thank you," she breathed.

Serena laughed. "You silly girl. You might not think as highly of it when you find out what I have planned. I don't want either of you sitting around coming up with ways to get into trouble. I have a whole list of chores for you girls to do. I've been so busy that several things have been neglected around the house. Hopefully, helping me catch up on them will keep you two occupied."

Even Louisa's face fell at the prospect of chores.

"To think the day started out so well," Natalie grumbled, as she and Louisa crawled out of bed.

Despite what Natalie called "her recruitment into hard labor," Louisa seemed to fit into their household easily. As they went about dusting, vacuuming, cleaning bathrooms, and helping Serena with laundry, Natalie thought about how nice it was to have another girl her own age to talk to—and complain with—and even to laugh with during the rare times their troubles did not hang as heavily over their heads.

"This is actually not so bad," Louisa said, as they stood in the bathroom tub, scrubbing away at the tiles. "It's no worse than sweeping out the animal cages, anyway."

"I guess when you put it that way," Natalie said. "I'm just glad I don't have to do this by myself."

"You're a better cleaning partner than Hercules," Louisa said. "He usually just ordered me around, telling me which spots I missed, sometimes while sitting on a bucket." She gave a sad sigh at the memory.

"I don't mind sitting on a bucket giving you orders if that will make you feel more at home."

"Very funny!"

It was late afternoon when Natalie heard Mrs. Stone and Mrs. Blaine arrive. She and Louisa were finishing the last of their chores, and they scampered down the stairs, grateful for the distraction.

"Hi, girls!" Mrs. Stone said.

"It looks like you've been busy," Mrs. Blaine observed, taking in the clean house and breathing in the fresh scent.

"We cleaned the whole day," Natalie said.

Mrs. Stone laughed. "Phillip's been doing the same. It's the least amount of trouble he's been in for ages."

"He didn't come with you?" Natalie said.

"Not this time," Mrs. Stone said. "You two get into enough trouble as it is, so it was time to take a breather. He's under strict orders to stay put and finish his chores."

Natalie could only imagine what the day was like for Phillip, having to do chores on his own. At least she had had Louisa for company. Poor Phillip was probably climbing the walls.

"I put a recipe on the kitchen counter for you and Louisa to cook for dinner," Serena said. "Why don't you two start on that?"

"Aw, Mom," Natalie groaned. "We've been working the whole day!"

"And it's amazing how little trouble I've had today," Serena said. "But don't worry, you're almost through. The recipe isn't hard, and you'll have the whole evening to relax. I'm sure you must be exhausted."

"I don't think I've ever been this tired in my entire life," Natalie exclaimed.

The ladies laughed while Natalie scowled. Louisa, being new to the household, simply looked down at her feet, a small smile playing about her lips.

Just as Serena said, when Natalie and Louisa checked the recipe, they found it was a simple pasta dish.

"Oh, thank goodness!" Natalie said. "This one should be easy. Why don't you start gathering the ingredients while I put the trash in the bins?"

"Okay," Louisa said.

Serena, Mrs. Stone and Mrs. Blaine had gathered in Serena's study. Natalie made a quick sweep of the house to gather the rest of the trash and then stepped outside to put them in the bins. They had missed a whole day outside, Natalie thought grumpily, as she dragged the trash bags around the house. Not that it was a huge waste. The day was overcast with a slight nip in the air just this side of uncomfortable.

As she dragged the garbage bags, she noticed someone walk past the house and then halt upon seeing her.

"Natalie!" It was Saul. He looked like he had been out exploring. He wore a heavy jean jacket with a scarf and boots, and a backpack rested on his shoulder. Natalie envied his not being cooped up for the day like she and Louisa had.

"Hi, Saul!" After a whole day of chores it was nice to see his cheerful face.

"Here, let me help you." Saul ran up the walk to grab some of the garbage bags from her.

"You don't have to do that," she protested. "What are you doing around here?"

"It's no problem." Saul gave her a big smile that melted away the dissatisfactions of her day. "I've been out exploring the town. It's one of the things I like to do when I get to new places."

"Did you see anything interesting?" Natalie opened the bin and tossed in her trash bags.

"This whole town is interesting." Saul tossed his trash bags as she held the bin open. "It's a nice place. I just might stay here after the circus leaves."

"Is the circus leaving? The storms are still out there," Natalie said.

"Didn't you hear what happened yesterday?"

"You mean the fire?" Natalie asked hesitantly. She realized she was not sure how much she should divulge as far as her involvement was concerned.

"So you heard about it then? It was the weirdest thing. Everyone swore they saw enough smoke for a fire in one of the big tents, and some people said there was a small explosion, but in the end, there were no signs of either. No one knows what to think. I think it's gonna become one of those urban legends." Saul had a look of satisfied glee on his face.

"Anyway," he continued, "two people vanished: one of the little people, and the daughter of the magician, who, incidentally, disappeared himself not too long ago. I think the circus is planning to leave soon. The people are starting to freak out."

Just then, Louisa stuck her head out the door. "Natalie, is everything all right? Do you need help with the trash?"

Saul's eyebrows hit his forehead. "That's her. That's the magician's daughter."

"Um, she's a friend of the family," Natalie explained. Oh boy, she thought, this could get awkward. "She's staying with us until things get sorted out."

Saul looked at Louisa, then Natalie, then back to Louisa. Louisa looked at Natalie.

"Louisa, you've met Saul, haven't you?"

Louisa shook her head. "No, I haven't."

"I haven't been working at the circus long enough to meet you," Saul said. "I think we work in different areas. You watch over your father's tent, right?"

Louisa nodded. "Yes, that's right." She spoke to Natalie. "Sometimes people come and go so quickly in the circus that you might not have a chance to meet everyone."

"So how long have you guys known each other?" Saul asked.

"A while," Natalie said.

"People were asking about you," Saul said to Louisa. "You and the tiny person."

"Have you heard anything about him?" Louisa asked eagerly.

"Some stuff," Saul said. "I think it's mostly speculation. I wasn't listening too closely."

"Can you remember some of it?" Louisa asked.

"I can try," Saul offered.

"Would you like to come inside?" Natalie asked. "Louisa and I are about to cook dinner. I can ask my mom if you can join us. I don't think she'll mind."

"Sure!" Saul brightened at the invitation. "I don't want to be a bother, but if it's all right, I'd love to."

Natalie led Saul inside to the living room where he walked around, taking in the various knick knacks and pictures that decorated it. "You're lucky," she said. "Louisa and I were hard at work cleaning, so now you get to see the house all sparkly and neat."

Saul grinned. "You did a great job. It smells nice and lemony in here. I really like your house. Have you lived here a long time?" He picked up a picture of Natalie and Serena.

"Pretty much my whole life."

Saul set the picture back down. Natalie thought it rattled a little when he did, but then Saul turned to her abruptly. "Do you mind if I use your bathroom? I've been walking for most of the day."

"Sure, it's down the hall to your right."

Louisa waited until Saul clicked the bathroom door shut before she grabbed Natalie's arm. "When did you meet him? He's really cute!"

"A few days ago, I think." Natalie giggled. "Can I have my arm back?"

"Oh." Louisa released her arm. "Sorry."

"I'm surprised you haven't met him," Natalie said.

"Yeah, usually word travels if they're cute. To be honest, though, I've been pretty distracted."

"I'm sorry." Natalie touched Louisa's arm.

Just then the door to Serena's study opened.

"Natalie," Serena called, as she, Mrs. Stone and Mrs. Blaine walked into the living room, "we have to step out for a little while. Can you and Louisa stay out of trouble while we're gone?"

"Okay, Mom," Natalie said.

"Sorry I have to leave you. We won't be gone long. I should be back in time for dinner." Serena gave her a kiss on the forehead as they prepared to leave. "Same rules. Do not leave the house."

"Oh, hey Mom," Natalie asked as the three ladies headed for the door, "is it okay if my friend, Saul, joins us for dinner?"

It was like a domino effect. Serena stopped short followed by Mrs. Stone and Mrs. Blaine. The air took on the surprise of a gasp, but none of the ladies had taken a breath. If anything, it was as if the oxygen had been stolen from them.

"Who are you talking about, Natalie?" Serena's question was taut, almost disbelieving.

Natalie hesitated. Had she done anything wrong?

"Natalie," her mother said slowly, "who is Saul?"

"He's my friend from the circus."

"You've never mentioned Saul," Serena said.

Natalie searched her mind and was surprised to realize her mother was right; she had never mentioned Saul.

"I guess I forgot," she said softly. "Did I do something wrong?"

"I've been monitoring you closely, Natalie," Serena said. "I would have known if you had met someone I didn't know."

Serena exchanged a glance full of dismay with Mrs. Stone and Mrs. Blaine. Natalie's stomach dropped.

"You mentioned dinner, Natalie," Mrs. Blaine said now. "Have you spoken with him today?"

"He's in the house now," Natalie whispered. Her spine tickled in an all-too familiar feeling, and her head swiveled in the direction of the hall. Saul stood in the archway, leaning up against the side.

"Well, well, well." His voice had changed. The easy-going warmth had hardened into something cold and unyielding. A chill ran through Natalie as she recognized the voice from the stranger in the tent. "It looks like I've hit the trifecta. I've found Mama Blaine, Daughter Bristol, and the ever-loyal friend, Janet Stone."

Chapter Thirty-One

"Sebastian," Serena said.

"How are you, Serena?" the man named Sebastian asked. "It's been a long time."

"Mom," Natalie called to her mother in alarm.

"Come here, sweetheart." Serena held out her hand. Natalie ran over and her mother squeezed her to her side.

"Louisa," Mrs. Blaine called out, "come over here by Mrs. Stone, dear."

Louisa moved towards Mrs. Stone, tripping slightly as she did, but Sebastian held up a hand, and Louisa froze. Natalie saw fear fill up her eyes, and she cried out when Louisa did.

"I'm going to hang on to this one," Sebastian said. "I have a bit of unfinished business with her father."

"Leave her alone, Sebastian," Serena said sharply, "she's just a child."

"Is she really?" Sebastian said. "I've wondered about that. She doesn't read like any child I've ever seen. There's something not...I'm not even sure I know how to describe it...something not quite there with this one. It's quite a mystery, but then, I've always been good at solving those."

Tears fell from Louisa's eyes.

"Saul," Natalie cried, "I thought we were friends."

"Shhhh, Natalie," Serena warned.

Sebastian smiled. It amazed her that this time, it could send shards of fear through her.

"I would very much like to be your friend, Natalie. I thought we got along well, don't you think?"

"Who are you?" Natalie asked. "Who are you really?"

"I'm still your friend, Natalie, if you'd like me to be."

"Quit lying to her, Sebastian," Serena said. "Show yourself."

Sebastian's head inclined in assent. "If you insist."

Natalie nerves tingled; something was happening. Sebastian's face shifted; it had started to warp and wobble. The features gelled and pulled apart and gelled back together. As his face settled, it was changed. It was still Saul's, but it was a man that stared back at her. The jaw was chiseled, the lips had toughened into a tight line, and the eyes were hard and ruthless.

"Sorry for the deception," Sebastian said. "People are less threatened by a friendly young man."

"That's quite a handy trick you have there, Sebastian," Mrs. Blaine said dryly.

"It is, isn't it? I'm sure you recognize it."

"I do." Mrs. Blaine's voice hardened. "You have no conscience, do you?"

"It's nothing personal," Sebastian said coolly. "And we've developed a process that's much more humane. She hardly felt a thing."

"Is that what you tell yourself?" Mrs. Blaine asked.

"You haven't changed," Mrs. Stone said. "You are still a monster."

"Why are you doing this, Sebastian?" Serena asked. "You could have been better than all of this."

Something flashed across Sebastian's face that Natalie could not read. "You think so, do you, Serena?" His eyes narrowed, and Serena's body tightened. A strangled sound came out of her throat. Natalie opened her mouth to scream.

"Enough!" Mrs. Blaine's command cut across the room. There was a vibration and then a snap, and Serena's body was released. Serena grabbed hold of Natalie with a gasp, and when she looked at Sebastian, there was a fury that burned from her eyes to his.

"Try that again and I will destroy you," Serena said.

There was another vibration and a snap, and whatever chain held Louisa was released. The momentum propelled her across to Mrs. Stone's waiting arms.

Sebastian laughed. "I had forgotten how powerful you all were. I must say, Janet, your creations did an exemplary job of protecting people from my influence. It was quite frustrating. This whole town was so well hidden. I suppose that was your influence; Serena, with your mind tricks and the myriad of variations that come with it, and Mrs. Blaine, with all the limitless possibilities in your arsenal. You made my job extremely difficult.

"Of course, while you have all been hidden away, Martin and I have been quite busy ourselves. You now have no defense against what we have become."

He put up his hand, but not before Mrs. Stone gave a wave of her arms.

It was as if something invisible had dropped around them.

Sebastian's eyebrows went up. "Oh, this is going to be interesting. It's been a while since I've had a challenge like this."

He pushed out his hand, and it caused Mrs. Stone to push her arms out further as well. Her eyes narrowed in concentration, but whatever covered them shook with the effort.

Serena's grip on Natalie tightened. Her attention homed in on Sebastian. There was a flicker in Sebastian's eyes, and Mrs. Stone's shield gathered strength.

"Trying to get into my head, Serena?" Sebastian closed his eyes and once again, the power shifted.

Now Serena and Mrs. Stone closed their eyes. Their bodies tightened, their energies gathered and trained on a single purpose. Sebastian shook, pushing against the protection on which Mrs. Stone expended all her energies to fortify.

Mrs. Blaine lifted her hand, and the space around Sebastian slowly rearranged, like a puzzle whose pieces were pulled apart and then re-formed as another picture. Natalie did not understand what her grandmother was doing, but Sebastian opened his eyes and looked grimly at Mrs. Blaine.

"Trying to lock me away, are you?" he asked her. "It won't do any good. I'll escape and find you again, no matter what."

"I'm just looking for time," Mrs. Blaine replied.

Sebastian doubled his concentration. A vein popped in his head. It was as if the room was trapped in a vortex with two waves of power roaring through.

Sebastian must be very strong, Natalie thought. Her mother, Mrs. Stone and Mrs. Blaine brought all their resources to bear, but Sebastian would not give in.

Her glance had shifted to Louisa, clinging to Mrs. Stone, her eyes looking as though they would pop out of her head, when the idea struck Natalie.

Natalie focused on the furniture in the room and called them to life. The table reared on its legs, the carpet arched on its edge, the pillows leaped into the air, and the chairs clattered across the floor. Like soldiers in formation, they circled Sebastian.

"Have you come to join the party, Natalie?" Sebastian put up his other hand. The living room pieces had pitched forward, but now they halted, as if blocked. Natalie pushed with all her might, saw the table inch its way closer and the carpet slither around for an opening, but still Sebastian fought.

However, the division of his powers spread him thin. Serena, Mrs. Stone and Mrs. Blaine gained ground. The space around Sebastian formed quickly; a black hole crystallized behind him. Sebastian noticed it over his shoulder and shook his head.

Natalie felt some give in the force holding back the army of furniture. The power shifted to her mother, Mrs. Stone and Mrs. Blaine.

But then a piercing noise filled the room. It tore through her head and shattered her concentration. Serena, Mrs. Stone and Mrs.

Blaine grabbed their heads. Louisa released Mrs. Stone and cupped her hands over her ears. Natalie's hands pressed against her temple.

Through the pain, she saw a grim smile on Sebastian's face as the defenses against him fell, and the black hole rearranged and filled. The air snapped and crackled as it had in the tent. He was going to take them, Natalie realized. They were helpless against the pain of that sound.

Natalie muddled through the pain and stared at Sebastian. He was not affected by the sound.

Bit by painful bit she reached inside, to the very ends of her being, and marshaled all of its strength. She foraged along the edges of her consciousness and trickled through every crevice to latch onto whatever force Sebastian had at his disposal.

Then, like water through a burst dam, power rushed through her, snapping her head back. She threw out her arms, and the force that protected Sebastian slammed over the rest of them. Her mother, Mrs. Stone, Mrs. Blaine and Louisa pulled their hands from their heads, recovering in relief from the sonic onslaught; she sensed their surprise as the piercing sound wailed around them. She felt her mother staring at her.

The power raged through. It poured out of every cell as if everything around her could be contained by her very being. She stretched her fingers out, and Sebastian fell back from the force her movement unleashed.

"Oh, Natalie," her mother whispered.

Sebastian's face froze in astonishment. The piercing sound disappeared. He watched her as if she were a wild animal about to charge. He flicked his wrist and a wave soared over her, but she flicked her wrist, and it crashed back to Sebastian, who barely had enough time to sweep it aside. He sent another wave, and then another, but Natalie matched him wave for wave, and he struggled each time to dodge the rebound.

"My god," he said.

Natalie channeled her gift, and the black hole swirled once more behind Sebastian.

Sebastian looked at the hole, then at Mrs. Blaine, but Mrs. Blaine was staring at Natalie. Sebastian stared at Natalie.

It was as if every atom in the universe had come to stand at attention behind her. Every nerve inside her gathered to complete the goal of sending Sebastian away, and she felt as if nothing could stop her from doing that.

There was a flurry of movement next to Sebastian. Someone on her side of the room gasped. It was Mrs. Stone. As she sought the source of the movement, her heart sank.

Phillip stood there with his map in his hand. His expression shone with the wonder of discovery. A big grin covered his whole face. He gave a whoop and jumped in the air, punching with his fist.

"I did it!" he yelled. "I finally did it on my own!"

He whooped and jumped again, and then noticed the women standing across the room. He did not notice Sebastian standing behind him to the side.

"Oh, Mom," Phillip said in dismay. "I'm sorry, I know I was supposed to stay put, but I just felt something tonight. I just knew that I could do it, you know? I'm really sorry, but I had to try it. Am I grounded now?"

"Phillip," Mrs. Stone said with an anguished sob.

Natalie reared and tried to slam a protective cover over him, but Sebastian waved his arm, and Phillip was snatched into the air. His face turned red, and he grabbed at his throat.

Mrs. Stone screamed, but Sebastian cut her off.

"If you try anything," he warned, staring at Natalie, "that hold on his neck will tighten, and he will choke."

Natalie's mind raced in desperate circles. It moved so fast she could not take hold of anything, and despair started to wash over her.

"Let him go," Mrs. Stone pleaded. "Please, you can have me. I'm much more powerful."

But Sebastian continued to stare at Natalie. What he saw there made him nod in satisfaction. "No," he said, "I think I'll stick with this one. Unless, Natalie, you'd like to switch?" He waved his arm, and Phillip bobbed in the air like a tempting apple. "You for your friend here?"

Natalie almost let their protective cover drop, but Serena put a warning hand on her shoulder.

A voice popped into her head. It was Mrs. Blaine. "You cannot go with him, child. I'm sorry about Phillip, but we will get him back. But you cannot go with him, trust me."

"Phillip," Natalie cried.

"For pity's sake, they're just children!" Mrs. Stone exclaimed.

"You will not harm them!" Mrs. Blaine said. Her tone threatened worse if he tried.

Sebastian became serious. "I have no intention of harming them. From Natalie's reaction, Phillip is much more valuable to me alive. As to Natalie," he shook his head, "why would I want to harm her? She's magnificent. I am simply blown away. And she's so young and trainable. Martin will be pleased."

It was as if a cold hand had reached up from the ground to yank her under. Natalie shrunk against her mother whose arm tightened around her as well.

"Keep the shield up." Her mother's order sounded directly inside her head, taking her by surprise. Serena had never done that before, but, she reasoned, this was a whole different set of circumstances.

"Come on, Natalie," Sebastian said, "last call for tonight. Care to trade?"

Natalie looked at Phillip, suspended in mid-air next to Sebastian. His hands still gripped his throat, but his expression was mutinous. She opened a part of the shield to allow her to pass without compromising the others, and took a step forward, but another shield dropped to block her.

It was Mrs. Stone. Tears streamed down her cheeks, and the look she gave her son tore Natalie's heart in two, but she kept the shield fortified.

"Take me," she begged through gritted teeth. "Please."

"No," Sebastian said, "I think we're clear tonight about the prize I'm after." He gave Phillip another shake and addressed Natalie. "When you're ready to deal, Natalie, come look for us."

"Where will I find you?" Natalie asked quickly.

Sebastian opened his mouth to answer, but thought better of it. He indicated the three women, and gave a cunning smile. "You have vast resources in this room. Have them help you when you're ready."

With that, he gave a final wave of his arm. There was a blinding flash of light, and when it cleared, he and Phillip were gone.

Chapter Thirty-Two

"Phillip!" Natalie screamed. "Noooo..." She sobbed in her mother's arms. Serena's arms wrapped around her, her hands stroked her hair, but after a short time, they released her.

Serena and Mrs. Blaine approached Mrs. Stone. They gathered around her, reached out to soothe her, but Mrs. Stone's body vibrated like a guitar string stretched too tight. Natalie did not know how long Mrs. Stone could hold on before she snapped.

When she did, it was an avalanche of pain. Short sobs shook her shoulders and rolled down the rest of her body until it wracked and heaved with cries of agony. At times her pain bottled up fast and hard, only to be released seconds later in a wail of anguish. Natalie thought her own heart had been ripped out of her chest, but it was nothing compared to the torment Mrs. Stone suffered.

"We'll get him back, Janet, we'll get him back," Serena murmured.

"How?" Mrs. Stone cried. "There's no way to do it! Oh, Phillip. Phillip!" Her body slipped to the floor.

"We'll find a way," Mrs. Blaine said. "We will, Janet."

Louisa stood off to the side, her expression dazed. She glanced at Natalie and walked over. Her hand slid over Natalie's and gripped it tight.

How could this have happened, Natalie wondered. She thought Saul was a friend. How did she not realize he was anything but? How could she have let him take Phillip? Her vision blurred, and she wiped her hand across her face. Stupid. She had been so stupid!

Louisa's hand squeezed hers. "Natalie," she whispered. She motioned with her head. Something lay on the floor where Phillip had been. Serena and Mrs. Blaine were engrossed with comforting Mrs. Stone, so Natalie walked over to see what it was.

It was Phillip's map. Natalie's heart sank to the floor. What hope did Phillip have if he did not have his map? She was about to bring it to Mrs. Stone, but something made her stick the map in her pocket instead. She noticed Louisa watching, but Louisa did not say a word.

The rest of the night passed in a haze. For a long time it seemed no one could say anything. They each sat in their own tortured solitude.

"Why hasn't he come back?" Louisa asked once.

"He doesn't know the extent of what Natalie can do," Mrs. Blaine answered. "His best bet at this point is to wait for her to come to him."

That was the worst part. The idea of trading herself for Phillip scared Natalie to death, but knowing that Phillip could be suffering on her account filled her with a despair so deep, she feared she would never climb out.

"How do I do it?" Natalie asked. "How do I get Phillip back?"

"You can't do anything right now," Serena said. "If you go, Sebastian will keep you. You won't ever be able to escape."

"But I can't stay here like this while he's got Phillip," Natalie cried. "If he wants me, then I should go."

"It's not that simple, Natalie," Mrs. Blaine said. "You have no idea of size and scope of your gift. If you hand that to Sebastian and Martin, you give them limitless power, and heaven help us all if that happens."

"But they're already strong," Natalie said. "We could barely fight Sebastian."

"You almost defeated him single-handedly," Mrs. Blaine said. "Your gift tapped into Sebastian's and unleashed a power that surpassed the four of us. Sebastian sensed what you could do. It's why he wants you."

"Do you remember what you felt when you tapped into Sebastian's gift?" Serena asked her softly.

"Phillip helped me find a way to push my mind open." Natalie swallowed at the thought of Phillip. "I don't know how I did it this time; that sound was so horrible, but I did. I pushed my mind open. Then, I don't know, I just found it. Sebastian's gift. It's like it was there and it filled me up. I remember thinking that I could see everything; that I could handle whatever Sebastian threw at me."

"Were there any limits that you could discern?" Mrs. Blaine asked.

"I...I don't know what you mean." Natalie said.

"That's probably an advanced question. You'll have a better idea of what I mean as you come to know your gift more."

"If I came close to defeating Sebastian this time, maybe I could defeat him if I saw him again," Natalie suggested. "Maybe...maybe I could use my gift to get Phillip back."

"Let's not get ahead of ourselves," Serena said sharply. She glanced at Mrs. Stone and sighed, shaking her head. "I'm sorry, Janet, but sending her there now would be disastrous."

Mrs. Stone said nothing. Her grief seemed to have settled into a deep chasm of torment.

Natalie's guilt intensified. "But it's my fault! It's my fault Saul was in the house. It's my fault that Phillip got taken. It should have been me! I'm the one he wants!"

"And, unfortunately, you won't help him at all if you try to save him," Serena snapped. She ran her hand through her hair. Natalie noticed with surprise that her mother's hands shook.

"Your mother's right," Mrs. Blaine said. She touched Natalie's cheek and smoothed her hair back from her forehead. "You shouldn't blame yourself for Saul. He slipped past all of us. We did not anticipate where the danger might come, and that is our fault, not yours."

"I told Phillip to stay where he was," Mrs. Stone said tonelessly. "He is so like his father, wanting to run before he can walk, leaping before looking. I could have grounded him for a year, and he would have considered it worth it." She put her head into her hands and sobbed.

Mrs. Blaine moved over to Mrs. Stone and embraced her. Serena put her hand on Mrs. Stone's back and held her hand.

"You and Louisa should go to bed," Serena said.

Natalie and Louisa made their way to the stairs. At the bottom step, a thought occurred to Natalie.

"Should I set up a protective shield, kind of like I did today?" she asked.

Serena blinked in surprise, as did Mrs. Blaine.

"We've already set something up," Mrs. Blaine said, "but I guess the added protection couldn't hurt."

Remnants of Sebastian's gift still ran through her. Natalie reached for the protection she had used earlier and focused it around the house. At least if Sebastian tried to come, she thought, he would know. She was anticipating him and she would be ready.

Later that night, Natalie awoke to the sounds of raised voices. She turned on her pillow. Louisa lay across the way, sound asleep. She rose out of bed and tiptoed to her door and padded into the hallway. It sounded like her mother and Mrs. Blaine. The guest bedroom door was closed. Mrs. Stone must be sleeping there, she thought.

She crept to the stairwell and tried to hear what her mother and grandmother were saying.

"At some point you are going to have to accept this," Mrs. Blaine was saying.

"I don't," Serena snapped. "It's not something I ever have to accept."

"Then you will at least have to let go. We all will. If there is going to be any hope at all, we have to."

"Unless we find another way." It sounded as if Serena were squeezing her words through a jaw trapped shut.

"You saw what Sebastian could do," Mrs. Blaine said. "How much more will there be to contend with if Martin has the same abilities or more."

"We're powerful, too," Serena said. "We could be just as powerful."

"It would take years to build that kind of strength. Do you think we have that kind of time?"

"I don't know, Mother!" Serena exclaimed. "What I do know is that I'm not ready to give my daughter—your granddaughter—up to some cause, just because it looks like she may be the only one who can fight for it. She's just a child, my child, not some warrior to be groomed."

"They're going to come for her anyway," Mrs. Blaine warned. "You might want to keep her safe, but there won't be any safety for her now. Not for any of us. And she might be the only one who can change that."

"I don't care, Mother," Serena said vehemently. "No, no and no."

At that, Natalie stopped listening and snuck back to her room. She crawled into bed and lay awake for a long time, listening to the sounds of the night.

Chapter Thirty-Three

The next day, while Mrs. Blaine was out and Louisa was helping Serena in the kitchen after lunch, Natalie knocked on the guest bedroom door. Mrs. Stone had not joined them for breakfast or lunch, and even though Serena had suggested letting her be, Natalie knew she had to see her. So when Serena prepared a tray of food to bring to the room, Natalie begged to take it.

"Come in," Mrs. Stone called.

Negotiating the tray, Natalie opened the door and poked her head around. Mrs. Stone sat by the window, staring outside. She gave a little nod of her head when she saw Natalie, so Natalie brought the tray in and set it on the table by the bed.

"Mom thought you might be hungry," Natalie said.

Mrs. Stone's face was drawn, and there were dark circles etched under her eyes. "I'm not very hungry, dear, but thank you anyway."

Natalie sat down on the bed. "I wish I knew what to say," she said. Tears welled up and she brushed them away in frustration. What good are tears, she thought.

Mrs. Stone held out her arms, and Natalie folded into them.

"You don't have to say anything," Mrs. Stone murmured. "I know you care deeply."

"It's me he wants," Natalie cried.

"And it would be the worst thing, if he got you," Mrs. Stone said firmly. "Do not think about making a trade. It will only be worse for Phillip, everyone else, if you do. Don't even think about it." She rocked back and forth gently with Natalie, as they both cried for Phillip.

The whole day thoughts of Phillip crushed like a boulder on Natalie's chest. She could not find relief anywhere even though she and Louisa tried their best to keep busy. Mrs. Stone had finally come out of her room, and she and Serena had kept themselves locked up in Serena's study. Natalie assumed it was so that they could talk and plan their next moves.

We're all sitting here stuck, Natalie thought crossly. She plopped down at the kitchen table that evening and folded her head into her arms unable to bear her own thoughts.

She heard footsteps come into the kitchen. She did not bother to look up. A chair scraped the floor as someone pulled it back and sat across the corner of the table from her. A hand touched her back.

"Talk to me," Serena said.

Natalie shifted her head so she could see her mother. Her mother put her arm on the table and leaned her head on it so they were both eye level. She laid her other hand on Natalie's head and stroked her hair.

"Tell me," she said.

"I want to go get Phillip," Natalie said softly.

The hand stroking her hair paused. Serena sighed.

"It's too dangerous, sweetheart," she said. "You don't know what Sebastian can do, especially now that he's prepared. If you try to get Phillip, Sebastian will have a trap ready for you. You've never dealt with anything like this before. There's real danger here."

"Will you and Mrs. Blaine and Mrs. Stone be able to save him?"

"We're working on it."

"Do you think you'll be able to do it?" Natalie persisted.

"It's hard to say, sweetheart," Serena said. "Martin has stolen a lot of gifts. We don't know what we're up against. I don't know if we'll be able to."

"I think I can."

Serena's lips tightened. "You think it's that easy, do you? You took Sebastian by surprise before. It won't be easy for you from now on."

"We're sitting ducks anyway," Natalie argued. "It's not like we can leave. You haven't even figured out how we can get out of here. All we're doing is waiting, and if he's as powerful as you say, it's just a matter of time before he gets me anyway."

"Not if I can help it," Serena said adamantly.

"But you haven't been able to stop anything up to this point," Natalie cried.

"You don't know what we've done!" Serena snapped. "We've done more than you think we have, and we are still working on things. Don't make assumptions about things you know nothing about!"

Natalie buried her head back in her arms.

"I know you're frustrated." Serena's voice softened. "I know you're upset about Phillip, and I know you want to do something. But you cannot just barge on in and expect to come out victorious. Do you have a plan?"

Natalie had to shake her head.

"Do you know where to find Phillip?"

Natalie had to shake her head again.

"Do you know what to do if you find him? Do you have any idea what they might have in mind to trap you if you do decide to show?

"No."

"Do you see what I'm saying?" Serena asked.

"Yes."

"Trust me when I say we are working on things," Serena said.

Natalie kept her head buried in her arms. She could not argue with what her mother was saying, but it was so frustrating. How long did they have before Sebastian got tired of waiting and decided to attack again?

"Hey," Serena said, "come with me. I have something I want to give you." She patted Natalie's head and tugged at her gently. "Will you come?"

Natalie peeked up from under her arm. "What is it?"

"Well, come with me and you'll find out."

In Serena's bedroom, Serena pulled out a box from her dresser. She opened and poked through it until she found what she was looking for. She unfurled a chain from the box and held it up for Natalie. The chain glinted gold in the light, and hanging from it was a beautiful jeweled heart. Multi-colored stones accented the piece and sparkled in shades of blue, purple, pink and white. It was not a large piece, but the workmanship was exquisite.

"This was a gift to me from your father." Serena held the heart up against her palm so they could have a closer look. "We were walking at a market, and we were very much in love. I don't even remember much about the day, only that I was happy to be with him. We admired this necklace together, and at the end of the day, he presented it to me. How he managed to buy it without me knowing I don't know, but when he put it around my neck, he told me how much he loved me, and I was the happiest girl in the world."

"It's so beautiful," Natalie breathed. The stones twinkled at her, and she could almost feel the happiness that must have radiated between her mother and her father when he gave her the necklace.

"Here, try it on," Serena urged.

Natalie pulled up her hair, and Serena fastened the chain around her neck.

"It fits you perfectly," Serena exclaimed in delight. Her eyes grew wistful as she stared at the pendant hanging delicately from Natalie's neck.

"Why haven't you worn it?" Natalie asked. She traced the heart, feeling the fine filigree carved into the gold.

"When it didn't work out between us, it was too painful a memory," Serena said. "But I always knew I wanted to give it to you. It was given to me in love, never forget that, and I knew it would be lucky for you one day."

"Do you think my dad would have wanted me to have it?" It was all so wonderful and strange at the same time. She had never known her father, had hardly talked about him, and was not even aware of missing one, although deep down, she acknowledged she might have. Now, for the first time, she had tangible evidence of him, and all sorts of confused feelings crowded inside her.

Pain flashed in Serena's eyes. "Oh honey! What makes you say that? Of course he would want you to have it." She wrapped her arms around Natalie and nuzzled against her hair.

"Does he know about me?"

"I don't know, sweetheart. He might, but I don't know for sure."

"If he does, why doesn't he try to find us?" Natalie could not help asking the question.

Serena sighed. "Life can get pretty complicated, sweetheart. But I can tell you this, we loved each other very much, and you were the result. Anyone with the heart of the man I knew would love you without question if he came to know you."

She straightened the necklace around Natalie's neck. "Do you like it?" she asked, watching her in the mirror.

"Yes," Natalie answered, "I love it. I love you, Mom."

"I love you, Natalie."

Chapter Thirty-Four

*T*hat night, Natalie checked to make sure Louisa was asleep, and crept out of bed. She grabbed the coat she had snuck upstairs from the hall closet and stepped out onto her balcony. She pulled out Phillip's map and a flashlight from her robe before slinging the coat on over her nightclothes.

The moon was full, and between the numerous clouds that filled the sky, it cast a fractured light over the lawn. Natalie sat on the cold wood of the balcony and took a deep breath. She hoped what she was about to do would not cause any trouble, but she needed information.

She closed her eyes and pushed out her mind. She concentrated on Phillip. Show me Phillip, she asked. She focused for several minutes, and then her mind latched. A pinprick of light appeared, growing larger as it drew close...

She was back in the chamber, the one that had imprisoned Beausoleil. As her eyes grew accustomed to the darkness, she made out smaller chambers with bars set off to the side. Cells, she thought. She did a quick search of them with her mind.

Beausoleil sat in one, his back leaning up against the wall. He was thin, thinner than the last time she saw him. A beard hung from his chin, and his hair was matted and dirty. His eyes stared ahead, hollowed out, seeing nothing, but a noise in the next cell caught his attention.

It was Hercules. He knelt at the bars, trying to look around. He had a cut across his mouth, and bruises peppered his face, but his eyes flashed with a rebellious fire.

"Phillip!" he called in a fierce whisper, "are you doing okay over there?"

"Shhhh!" came the reply. Natalie quickly moved in its direction.

The cell on the other side of Beausoleil held Phillip. He was sitting on a bench with his knees pulled up to his chest. He did not look as badly handled as the other two, but his shoulders hung as if exhausted. He tilted his head to catch Hercules trying to get his attention, and his eyebrows crunched into frown. "You'll get into trouble if you keep that up," he whispered.

"Do you think I care?" Hercules asked.

"You should," someone else chimed. Natalie followed it and found Mr. Mackey in the cell next to Hercules. He was curled up on his bench, his arms wrapped round to keep warm. Poor Mr. Mackey, Natalie thought. He looked like he had aged with his hair all askew, and his clothes crumpled up and dirty. His voice was hoarse as he continued. "Why bring yourself more trouble?"

"Because it helps remind me that I would do just about anything to bring them ruin!" Hercules spat. "They have no shame, bringing a child here."

"They want Natalie," Phillip said. "They'll do anything to get her."

"I hope she has the good sense to stay put," Beausoleil said.

"What will happen to us, do you think? Mr. Mackey asked. "None of us have any more information for them. Why are they keeping us alive?"

Beausoleil swallowed. His lips were chapped and dry. "They probably believe they can get more out of me. As for the three of you, well, you're friends of Natalie so maybe they're hoping to use you for leverage. In any case, we're still alive. That's not a bad thing, is it?"

Mr. Mackey gave a humorous snort. "The circumstances could be a little better."

Natalie moved away from the cells and into the chamber where Beausoleil had been tortured. Chains sprawled across the middle of the floor, and the windows eked daylight in gloomy prisms throughout. A door stood at the opposite end of the chamber. She moved towards it, hoping to get an idea of what was on the other side, when it swung open.

Sounds scuffled from inside the cells. A hooded figure walked into the room. It was the man who had tortured Beausoleil. Sebastian followed, closing the door behind him as they advanced into the room.

"And how are we today?" the hooded figure asked the occupants of the cells.

"Good to see you as always, Martin," Beausoleil said. Natalie saw then that even though Beausoleil had looked abused and helpless, his spirit had not yet been broken. "Have you come to bring us good cheer?"

Martin laughed. "Still in good humor, I see. No, I came because I think we have a visitor, and I wanted to deliver a message to her myself."

It was as if an icicle had shot into her chest. The silence in the chamber was deafening.

"What do you mean?" Beausoleil finally asked.

"It seems Sebastian did the right thing, taking our young man over there," Martin said, gesturing towards Phillip. "The young lady cannot keep herself from checking in on how he is. I feel her in the room with us now."

"Natalie," she heard Phillip whisper, "go away now."

Martin laughed again. "So soon, my boy? It would be a shame if she left without anything to take back with her. I would like to make her a proposal."

He took his time walking around the room. Natalie knew he was trying to get a feel for where she was. The last thing she wanted to do was look at him, but rather than prolong the agony, she kept still and waited.

He came within inches of her, and when he stopped, he sighed in pleasure.

"So nice of you to come, my dear," he said. "I am amazed at the wonderful things Sebastian has told me about you. You are quite a find, I must say. Your mother and grandmother have probably told you about all the things I've done to our kind, and what I could do to you if I wanted, but I have a different proposition for you." He expanded his arms in an offer.

"I would like for you to come join me. I don't want to take anything from you, as I've found that taking gifts does not yield as effective a power for me as the one who originally held it. From what I've heard, your gift is formidable, and I would hate to dilute it in any way. What I would like to do is offer you an opportunity to use your power to its greatest potential.

"You won't get that chance living as you do among our kind. I could never understand why such a gifted race wanted to use so little of what they had. We could have such influence in the world."

"You mean control," Beausoleil said with contempt.

Martin laughed again. "You see? No imagination. I can offer you so much more. Among our kind your gifts would not reach its potential, and what a waste that would be! With me," Martin shook his head, "the possibilities would be endless.

"Think about it. If you come to me, I can let your friends go. Notice they are still alive. Now mind you, I had to torture them to get information, but now that I know about you, there is really no need for me to hurt them anymore. If you join me, that is."

Martin shook his head sadly. "Now I hate talking about what will happen if you choose not to come with me, because it really is a win-win situation if you do. But perhaps it is best to know so that you can make an informed decision."

He waved his arm, and suddenly there were gasps and muffled shrieks from the cells. When Natalie turned to look, Beausoleil, Hercules, Phillip and Mr. Mackey were all bowed over, their faces red with pain.

Natalie screamed then; a soundless scream that propelled her back to where she started...

The wood was cold beneath her, the night air chilled. A breeze nipped across her skin as she returned to the balcony with a gasp.

"Natalie?"

Louisa was crouched beside her. Her face looked pale, even in the moonlight. "Are you all right?" she asked. "I woke up and came to look for you. You must be so cold!" She took the blanket she had wrapped around her and laid it across Natalie's shoulders. "Come inside."

Natalie rose to her feet without argument and went with Louisa into the warmth of her bedroom. She sat on the bed as Louisa took a seat at her desk and waited. When Natalie did not speak, Louisa asked, "What were you doing?"

"I had to see how Phillip was."

"You used your gift?"

"Yes. I was there, Louisa, I saw all of them, your father, Hercules, Phillip, and Mr. Mackey, a man from town. They're still alive."

Louisa's hand flew to her mouth. "Alive? Oh thank goodness!" She threw her arms around Natalie and hugged her fiercely. "How are they?"

Natalie had been hoping she would not ask. "Not as bad as you would think. But Martin knew I was there."

"What?" Louisa drew back in surprise and gaped at Natalie. "How could he know you were there? Did he see you?"

"No, he didn't see me, but he could sense I was watching. I guess it's one of his gifts, or a gift he might have stolen from someone else. He sensed me. He even came to stand right in front of me."

"What did he say?"

Natalie hesitated. "He said he wouldn't hurt me if I joined him. He said he would let everyone go if I did."

Louisa's eyes grew wide. She sank onto the bed and slumped against the headboard. A mass of torn emotions tumbled over her face, but she said, "What a horrible man. You shouldn't do it."

Natalie fiddled with her robe. "He said he wouldn't hurt me."

Louisa sat up and grabbed Natalie's arm. "Natalie, he's evil! You don't know if he'll keep his word. Maybe he says he won't hurt you, but can you really say what he'll do to you? He wants to use you!"

"Maybe I could pretend I'll stay, but then escape," Natalie suggested.

Louisa looked skeptical. "Do you really think you could escape? Everyone says he's very powerful, and Natalie, he could sense you!"

"I'd like to try."

Louisa's head shook back and forth. "Oh, Natalie, you can't do that. It's a suicide mission."

"But whatever power Martin has, I would have," Natalie insisted. "Sebastian's, too. I could use what they have against them."

"If they're expecting you," Louisa argued, "they'll make sure you won't be able to use your gifts."

Natalie sighed. "Yes, you're probably right. Oh, Louisa! There's got to be some way. Help me think. Please!"

Louisa leaned back against the headboard. Natalie fell back on the mattress and stared at the ceiling. The rising tide of helplessness she felt made her want to scream. She had to help her friends somehow. She would not just leave them where they were.

"Maybe..." Louisa spoke quietly, as if thinking to herself. Natalie raised her head to listen. "Maybe we could take them by surprise."

"How?"

"They don't know what Papa did with his gift, right?"

Natalie shook her head. "It didn't seem like your father had given anything away."

"If you brought me with you, as a doll, then Papa would have his gifts back, and he could use them."

"I can't do that!" Natalie exclaimed. "It's way too dangerous. No, Louisa, that's not a good idea at all."

"Why not?" Louisa asked. "It's something they would never suspect. Papa would know how to help, and they would be completely surprised. It might give you a chance to use your gifts against them."

"I can't let you do that." There was no way she would allow Louisa to put herself in that kind of danger. It was not an option.

"Natalie," Louisa said, "it's my father and my best friend. We don't have any other ideas. Your mother and grandmother and Phillip's mother are working on something, but if any one of them tries to go, Martin and Sebastian will catch on right away, and they'll just get caught. We have an idea that could possibly work! Martin and Sebastian know Papa doesn't have his gift right now, and they don't know about me.

"You know how much you want Phillip back, right? Well, this is my father and my best friend, and I want them back just as much. Maybe even more! Don't you dare tell me I can't do this!"

It was the first time Natalie had heard her friend sound so angry. Louisa sat straight against the headboard, her breaths coming in quick succession from the heat of her emotions, her eyes flashing fiercely.

"What if something happens to you?" Natalie asked weakly.

"That's my choice, Natalie. It's what I want to do if it means a chance to get Papa, Hercules and Phillip back."

"Louisa, this is for real," Natalie protested. "You could be seriously hurt. I would never forgive myself!"

Louisa gave her a sad smile. "Dolls can be repaired. They can even be replaced."

Natalie stared at her, aghast. "You're not just a doll to me!"

"In the end, Natalie, a doll is exactly what I am," Louisa said firmly. "If you care about me, if you truly don't think of me as just a doll, then you'll let me do this, this one thing based on the closest aspect I have to being human.

"I feel love, Natalie. Love for my Papa, love for Hercules. And I care very much about Phillip."

All argument fell away from Natalie at Louisa's declaration. She shook her head, but there was nothing she could say in protest. Louisa reached over and took her hand and held it.

"Okay?" she asked.

Natalie nodded helplessly.

"Good. Now, do you have some kind of plan?"

"Sort of, but not a very good one. And worse, at this point, it's based on theory." Natalie stared miserably at Louisa. "We could really mess things up."

Louisa shrugged. "Maybe a half-baked plan will be the one they least expect. We should at least hear it out."

"We have Phillip's map," Natalie said. "I thought that maybe I could ask it to show me Phillip's location. Since it's his map, maybe it tracks him somehow. If it can do that, I can get us there. The map should be able to take us back too."

"Will it only work with you and Phillip, though?" Louisa asked.

"That's the other thing," Natalie said. "I'm not too sure. We haven't had a chance to see if we can pull people with us. We can do objects, and we pulled you as a doll."

"Why don't we try it now?" Louisa said. "Try it with me. I'm pretty close to human right now. Do you think that will be close enough?"

"I don't know," Natalie admitted. "We can try. Worse comes to worse we can get Phillip back, and Beausoleil will have his power. I can always stay and fight as well."

"Wow," Louisa said in a half whisper, "I guess you weren't kidding when you said half-baked."

"Should we do it, do you think?" Suddenly, Natalie was very frightened. The consequences were too scary to think about.

"Let's try the map first," Louisa suggested. "See if you can take me as I am."

"Okay. Let's try Phillip's home. No one is there right now."

"Should I do anything?"

"I don't think so." Natalie pulled out Phillip's map and said, "Phillip's room." As the map rose to the fore, she said to Louisa, "Give me your hand."

The map was an actual diagram of Phillip's home. She searched for Phillip's room and focused on that spot. Within a few seconds, she was there. His maps still hung on the wall; it was like he had never left.

A hand squeezed hers. Louisa had made it through.

"You did it!" Louisa said.

"It's happening much quicker now. That's probably a good thing. Let's see if I can bring you back without holding your hand this time. If it doesn't work, I'll come back for you."

Natalie spoke to the map, "My room." She pushed her mind out and folded it around her and Louisa. When the map showed her house, she focused on her bedroom. When she arrived in her room, she looked beside her, and there Louisa stood.

"Wow," Louisa breathed, "you seem really powerful, Natalie."

"Let's hope it works to our advantage," Natalie said grimly.

"So how do you think we should do this?"

Natalie considered this. "I'll take you over as a doll. You'll still have Beausoleil's gift, right?"

"Oh, yes. As a matter of fact, it will be even more protected that way."

"That's good. When we get there, I have to make sure you make it to Beausoleil. Does he have to be touching you or anything?"

"No. We have to be in proximity, but not necessarily touching."

"That helps," Natalie said.

"Are we doing this tonight?" Louisa asked.

It was a tough question. Natalie was anxious to help her friends, but she felt woefully unprepared for such an impossible task. Will I ever feel prepared, though, she wondered.

If they went tonight, they might have the element of surprise. It would be logical, after all, to report her findings to her mother, Mrs. Blaine and Mrs. Stone first, and to come up with a plan of attack for later.

She thought of Phillip and the rest, stuck in their cells. She thought of the pain Martin Reimer inflicted on them. She did not think she could rest another night with them imprisoned like that.

"Yes," she said, "we're going tonight."

Louisa nodded. She looked a mixture of nervous, terrified and resolute.

Natalie walked over to her desk and pulled out a piece of paper and pen. "I'm going to leave a note for my mom."

"I'll get dressed then," Louisa said, as Natalie settled to write.

Dear Mom,

I'm really sorry, but I have to try to help Phillip. I managed to see where he is. Beausoleil, Hercules and Mr. Mackey are there too. Louisa wanted to come. I think I can get there by Phillip's map. I know it's really dangerous, but I have to try.

Love,
Natalie

P.S. I was thinking, if we make it back, maybe we can use Phillip's map to find somewhere else to hide? Just a thought.

She set the letter on her desk where her mother could find it.

"May I write something as well?" Louisa asked. "I'd just like to thank your mother for everything. You know, just in case."

"Sure." Natalie hoped they would be back so that Louisa could thank Serena herself. She changed into jeans and a sweater while Louisa wrote a short note under Natalie's message.

"Are you ready?" Natalie asked when Louisa finished.

"Yes," Louisa said.

Natalie hugged her then and concentrated. She felt Louisa shift and shrink. A few moments later, it was as a doll that she held her.

Her heart thumping like a hammer against her chest, Natalie took Phillip's map and said, "Phillip's location."

Please let this work, she thought. Please let us come back safe and sound with everyone.

The map presented a floor plan that resembled the chamber that held her friends. Natalie stared at the plan for a few moments. Then she took a deep breath and plunged into the map.

Chapter Thirty-Five

Details emerged as she drew close: the dark gloom of the chamber, the bars of the cells, and her friends imprisoned behind them. She gathered her wits about her. First things first, she thought. Get Louisa to Beausoleil. She zoomed in on an area close to Beausoleil's and Phillip's cell.

But as she landed in the chamber, a forceful jerk yanked her around, causing Louisa to tumble from her arms. She heard exclamations and gasps, and then she was lifted off the ground. Her arms were tugged out to the sides, and her legs were gripped and pulled tight. She was trapped.

Her stomach sank. They had been prepared. She tried to see what held her, but there was nothing visible. She tried to move, but her bonds were firm. She was restrained and helpless, the way Beausoleil had been when he was tortured.

"Natalie!" Phillip exclaimed.

"You shouldn't have come!" Hercules shouted.

"Oh, my dear girl," Mr. Mackey groaned.

Beausoleil scoped wildly about the chamber. "Let her go!" he yelled.

The four of them were pressed against the bars of their cells, a mix of astonishment, dismay and fear on their faces.

Terror dug into her like claws. She had not expected to be contained so quickly. Where was Louisa? She desperately searched her out in the murky chamber and caught the barest glimpse of her arm in a shadowed corner near Phillip's cell, hidden. No one seemed to notice Natalie had been carrying her. How would Beausoleil reach her if no one knew she was there? Natalie tried to call out to Phillip, but her voice hit a block, as if she had been gagged.

She tried to cast about with her mind, but that too was bound; it was like pressing up against a steel wall. Panic rose inside her and she pulled and struggled frantically at the invisible bonds that held her.

"Natalie," Beausoleil called out, "it's okay. It's better if you don't struggle. Don't worry; it's just a way to hold you in place. Don't hurt yourself trying to pull out of it. Can you hear me?"

Natalie nodded. Her head, at least, had some range of motion.

"Can you talk?" Beausoleil asked.

Natalie shook her head.

The door to the chamber opened and the hooded figure of Martin Reimer walked in, followed by Sebastian.

Sebastian eyes swept from Natalie to the others in their cells and, finding everything to his satisfaction, he came to stand behind Martin.

"We can't risk having you communicate any silly plans you might have, my dear," Martin said. He waved his arm, and Natalie floated to where he waited in the middle of the chamber.

Never before had Natalie been so completely at someone's mercy. Her every nerve screamed and coiled with fright.

"Welcome, Natalie," Martin said. "I am so very happy that you have come to join us! I apologize for the precautions we have had to take, but until we understand your exact intentions, I cannot allow you an opportunity to use your considerable talents against us. You understand, of course.

"You cannot see what binds you, but it is a powerful invention of mine. It contains whatever gifts you have, and allows me to take whatever I want of them."

"Let her go!" Beausoleil said hoarsely.

Martin ignored him.

"You monstrous lunatic!" Hercules yelled. "What are you doing to her? She's just a young girl!"

Martin's chest moved, as if he had taken a deep breath. His shifted his attention to Hercules.

Hercules flew into the air. He tried to scream, but his cries choked off before they could pierce the dank air of the chamber.

"I don't like you much, little man," Martin said. "Since you're killing my excitement, let's start with you."

Hercules' cell door opened, and Hercules floated out to hang off to the side of Natalie, Martin and Sebastian.

"I'm going to release your voice," Martin told her, "but you are only to answer my questions. If you try to communicate anything other than a direct response to my question, Hercules will suffer. Do you understand what I'm saying, Natalie?"

Natalie nodded her head.

"Good," Martin said. "Now, I can tell you came by yourself. Why didn't your mother or grandmother come with you?"

Natalie started to speak, but before she could answer Martin's question, Hercules screamed. His body twisted awkwardly in the air as he writhed in pain.

Natalie cried out. Her voice was free. "What are you doing?" she shouted. "I haven't even said anything."

"I just thought a little warning might be good," Martin said. "I want to make sure it's clear to you that I won't hesitate to cause the little man pain if you try anything. Plus, I don't mind taking the opportunity to hurt him because I simply don't like him."

"It's mutual!" Hercules hollered.

"Be quiet, Hercules!" Beausoleil hissed.

Hercules whimpered a bit, but he was quiet.

"Good," Martin said. "Now, Natalie, would you please answer my question?"

"They don't know I'm here. They didn't want me to come," Natalie said miserably. This had all gone horribly wrong.

Martin's hooded figure gave a start. Sebastian looked surprised as well.

"How did you come here, then?" Martin asked.

Natalie hesitated. What would they do if they lost Phillip's map?

Hercules' body jerked, and he screamed again.

"Phillip's map!" Natalie cried. "I used Phillip's map!"

"Ah!" Martin clasped his hands together as if excited. "The young man's gift! Oh, I am so tempted to take it from him. It would be a wonderful addition to my collection.

"But," he held up his hands, "I know I made you an offer. I will leave Phillip intact as long as you've come to join me. You understand, of course, that I must make sure that is truly your intent."

He nodded at Sebastian who crossed to Natalie and began to search her. Martin stood by, and although he said nothing, his whole body emanated a malevolent glee that twisted Natalie's stomach into a pretzel.

Natalie glanced at Sebastian whose hands had suddenly stilled. When he raised his head, his face blazed with an intensity that took her by surprise. She begged him with her eyes to help her, but a shutter fell over his expression, rendering it impassive. He continued his search and discovered Phillip's map curled into her fist. He pried her fingers open, and pulled it out. He walked back to Martin and handed him the map.

Martin held it up. He flipped the cloth over and sighed in admiration. "Your mother is so gifted," he said to Phillip. "This is a magnificent piece of workmanship; so simple, yet so valuable." He handed the map back to Sebastian. "We will keep it safe for you."

"That's mine!" Phillip said through gritted teeth.

"Ah, but we can't have you using it to get out of here now, can we?" Martin said.

With their avenue to escape in Martin's hands, Louisa unnoticed in the dark corner, and her own power contained, Natalie's hopes started to sink like coins in a fountain.

"Please," she burst out.

Immediately Hercules screamed.

"I'm sorry!" Natalie sobbed. "Please stop!"

"I'm afraid it's all up to you to keep the little man out of pain. I quite enjoy his discomfort," Martin said.

Natalie kept silent.

"That's much better, my dear!" Martin said happily.

"You're a monster!" Mr. Mackey shouted.

Martin chose to ignore him. He took a leisurely stroll around Natalie.

"Have you decided to join us?" he asked her.

"Yes," Natalie said. "You said you'd let my friends go if I did."

"Ah, about that," Martin said. "I have to make a slight adjustment to our agreement."

"What do you mean?" Natalie asked in disbelief.

"Well, I think it's safe to let the old man and the little one go. They are not gifted, and I don't think they will present much of a problem. I'm afraid, though, that I will need to examine my friend Beausoleil here. He is supposed to be gifted, and yet he does not seem to be in possession of his gifts. It's a puzzle I have not been able to figure out, and I simply cannot let him go until I've solved it.

"As for your friend, Phillip, he will remain with us. You seem quite fond of him, and he will provide good insurance that you are indeed going to remain loyal to me."

Dismay flooded through Natalie. Beausoleil, Phillip and Mr. Mackey started yelling at Martin all at once, their words tumbling over each other in a mess of outrage.

"But you promised!" Natalie shouted. "You told me you wouldn't hurt them and that you would let them go."

Hercules gave an agonized shriek. This time the pain continued for a longer period of time. His body went stiff, and his face went from bright red to pale.

Natalie howled. Tears fell down her cheeks. She realized that Martin had always meant to betray her, and even though it had been her intention to betray him as well, having the tables turned twisted a knife of helplessness deep into her, threatening to kill all hope.

"I hate you!" she screamed.

"Perhaps," Martin said coolly, "but in time you will grow to love what we will accomplish together. You will be a force the world has never seen. Men will tremble at the thought of crossing you. People will bow down to you when they see you."

"I don't want that!" Natalie cried.

"You say that now," Martin replied, "but wait until you experience how satisfying ultimate power can be. I, myself, cannot say I have ultimate power, but what I have experienced so far has been extremely satisfying.

"I have spent much time inventing ways to acquire gifts, but you my dear, have the means of emulating them within yourself naturally, of even enhancing them, making those gifts greater than they are. That is simply incredible! Oh, what you could accomplish in the right hands!"

"In your hands, that would mean destruction! The world would be enslaved to your madness!" Beausoleil said.

Martin waved his hand, and Beausoleil fell to his knees, his hands gripping at his throat.

"You're bound to make enemies as you try to climb your way to the top," Martin told Natalie. "There will always be people who disagree with you, remember that. You have to believe in your vision. Do you think you could believe in my vision, Natalie?"

"Yes," Natalie whispered. "Yes, I could."

Martin threw up his hands in delight. "Why that's wonderful! This is going so much better than I thought."

"Don't do it, Natalie," Phillip yelled.

Martin waved his arm, and Phillip fell to his knees as well, red and choking. Natalie steeled herself and looked away.

"Such a smart girl," Martin cooed.

Natalie nodded her head, too tired to fight. She bowed her head to her chest.

"So smart and so brave, coming all alone to offer herself to me," Martin continued.

Natalie shook her head, no. Her head hung from her shoulders.

Martin and Sebastian froze; it was as if the air had contracted.

"Which part was no?" Sebastian asked sharply.

Natalie kept her head bowed, and soon her throat tightened. She snapped her head up, gasping at the air, searching for a breath.

Martin's hand grasped under her chin and held her face to his. His eyes were hidden by his cloak, but she saw the crooked bottom of his chin and the shadowy outline of his misshapen face under the hood.

"Be careful how you answer," he said. "I would like for you to join me, but not if you cause me more trouble than you are worth."

Natalie nodded desperately. The hold on her throat loosened a little to allow for air. She gasped it in gratefully.

"Now," Martin said, "did you come alone?"

Natalie shook her head. "No," she wheezed.

Martin stepped back abruptly. Sebastian wheeled around and surveyed the chamber for another person.

Louisa still lay in the corner, undetected.

Phillip, Beausoleil and Mr. Mackey all rose into the air. Natalie heard their cries and gasps.

"Do not try to outsmart me!" Martin's warning echoed through the chamber. "If you try anything, your friends will suffer!" He pulled back his hood, revealing his patchwork face. He leaned towards Natalie.

"Who came with you?" he hissed.

Natalie screamed in terror. She swerved her head from his as she shrieked and stared at Beausoleil.

"Louisa, I came with Louisa!"

Beausoleil's eyes went wide, and as Natalie saw realization fill them, he closed them shut. She continued to scream and shake her head.

"Silence!" Martin thundered. "Where is she?"

As Natalie's screams choked down to sobs, a voice called from the corner near Phillip's cell.

"I'm here."

Martin and Sebastian's heads whipped around to the corner as Louisa stepped from the shadows. She looked around, blinking at the surroundings. Her body stiffened as she saw Natalie hanging from her invisible prison and everyone else contained in cells.

Sebastian threw out his hands, and Louisa flew up into the air. She screamed, her legs kicking.

"Louisa!" Natalie yelled.

The bars from the cells started to vibrate. One by one each set tore itself from its hinges. The chains lying in the middle of the chamber wiggled up into the air like snakes dancing out of a basket. The legs from the benches in the cell shook and stomped.

Martin stared at the newly animated objects. His eyes narrowed and homed in on Louisa.

"It's the girl," he said.

Louisa's arms and legs were yanked straight; Martin was putting her into the same hold in which Natalie was locked.

The chains struck Martin then, like snakes snapping at prey. They clasped his hands in their shackles and wrapped around him tight. Martin's face filled with a surprised fury. With a swirl of his finger, he broke free of the chains. The chains continued to strike, undeterred.

The legs of the benches sprang into action and stormed from the cells. They split into two groups and charged at Martin and Sebastian. Four sets of cell bars crouched and ran across the chamber like spiders scurrying through a web. They rose up and slammed down on each side of Martin and Sebastian, locking them in with the benches and chains which charged and struck at them within the confines of their smaller prisons. Every time Martin and Sebastian attempted to destroy a bench or a chain, another would fly at them in distraction.

The distractions were enough. The shackles holding Natalie loosened. She tested her mind, and the boundaries swelled and expanded. She focused on Sebastian and Martin, who were using whatever they had at their disposal to fight off Beausoleil's attacks. Their powers poured through her veins and filled her.

Martin yelled, "The girl, Louisa! It comes from the girl!"

Sebastian whacked a bench into the bars of his cell and whipped his arm in Louisa's direction.

Louisa's floating body arched like a doll lifted by the small of its back. Louisa gave a startled cry, and then crumbled into thousands of little porcelain pieces.

A wave of shock rolled over the room. The chains and the benches dropped. Even Martin and Sebastian froze.

"Louisa," Beausoleil whispered.

"What was that?" Natalie heard Sebastian ask.

"That was not a little girl," Martin said in surprise.

Into the lull that followed, Hercules bellowed, "Noooooo!!!" It was a scream that held more agony than any of the torture he had suffered at Martin's hands.

Natalie snapped out of her shock. She felt as if hundreds of knives had just sliced through her heart, but she shifted her attention to Hercules and broke the bonds that held him. He fell to the floor, moaning, his body curled into a ball of pain.

Beausoleil, his eyes now sunken into deeper hollows, kept his gift trained on Martin and Sebastian. Natalie broke him, Phillip and Mr. Mackey free of Martin's hold. Phillip stumbled over to the scattered porcelain pieces and tried to gather them together. Natalie almost cried at the sight of him reaching out his arms to try to catch them all.

She faced Martin and Sebastian. Neither of them had moved. They watched as she casually pulled her arms down and freed her legs from the hold Martin had placed on her. She floated gently to the ground.

Martin's mismatched eyes glowed with exultant pleasure. "Sebastian was right. You are simply magnificent!" He took a deep breath and, with a wave of his arm, threw the benches, the chains and the bars off him and Sebastian. When they tried to rush him again, he put out his hands and blocked them. He nodded to Sebastian who moved to circle Natalie.

"Give me the map," Natalie said.

Martin laughed. "Oh, Natalie, why would I give you something that would take you away from me? Why don't we try to work something out?"

"I'd be an idiot to trust anything you say," Natalie said.

Sebastian made a move. The air crackled, but Natalie held up a hand, and the air settled.

Martin shook his head in delight. "The power coming from you is unbelievable! I don't think Sebastian and I can take you head-on.

"But, you are just a child. Do you really think, with all of our experience, that you will be able to hold out against us? We're very smart and very powerful. Don't you think we'll find a chink in your formidable armor?"

"Don't let them scare you, Natalie," Beausoleil said. He held the chains, benches and cell bars at the ready. He spoke to Martin and

Sebastian. "She won't be on her own. The rest of our kind won't sit by and let you have free reign anymore, Martin."

"I don't think there is much of our kind left anymore, Beausoleil," Martin replied.

"You are truly evil!" Beausoleil spat.

"But I am powerful, aren't I?" Martin said. "Just think, the whole potential of our kind, contained in me. Oh, what we could have done if only more of us had more ambition. It all would have been such a waste if it hadn't been for me."

"He is insane," Mr. Mackey said, appalled.

"Insane?" Martin mocked. "Well, I suppose genius straddles a fine line with insanity. In any case, you won't be able to escape from here. This place is another one of my inventions and it has been around for a long time, perhaps longer than these two," he said, indicating Natalie and Phillip. "It was built to contain our kind, and no one has ever escaped. Of course, this young man's gift is a new development, so Natalie and the—doll, is it?—slipped through, but that will not happen in the future."

"Give me the map," Natalie said again.

"No," Martin retorted.

"Give it to me!" Natalie yelled. She threw a hand out at Sebastian who held up his own to ward off her attack. Martin gave a swish of his arm, and Natalie felt a wave of current so powerful it caused her heart to race as she swung her own arm to avoid it.

"Natalie, do not lose your temper!" Beausoleil ordered. "You make yourself vulnerable if you do that."

Tears of frustration fell down Natalie's face. How would they get out of here without the map? They would be trapped in Martin's chamber, and Martin was right. How long could she fend them off?

A prickle of sensation hit the air so close to her that she gasped and quickly swirled her hands to shoot it back at Sebastian. His hands moved in front to block it.

"We're going to get even closer, Natalie," Martin taunted, "closer and closer, bit by bit. How long will you be able to hold out?"

Natalie gave a scream and shot a tidal wave of power strong enough to make Sebastian and Martin step back. Their arms shook as they fended off her attack. The three of them grappled for advantage, but Martin and Sebastian managed to stabilize their defenses, and soon they returned to a stalemate.

"I cannot believe how much you have evolved over such a short period of time," Martin mused. "Everything is fusing into a whole."

"What do you mean?" Natalie asked.

"It has been an interesting discovery, my dear, and at this point, it is still just a theory on my part based on experience. It seems that our individual gifts are all fractured parts of a harmonious whole—a river, or current, running through each of us, keeping us connected, but separate. Each gift I collect joins the others, and each time, the experience is transcendent and all that much more powerful."

"That might explain why our kind lived together peacefully," Beausoleil said angrily. "What we have should never have been abused."

"Were we supposed to just sit on what we had?" Martin asked incredulously. "We built our own little community and sat on it doing nothing!"

"We did no harm!" Beausoleil yelled.

"You did no good either!" Martin spat. "Can you really say it was that much better, living so removed from the rest of the world, using our gifts to create a little place for ourselves, sharing with no one?"

"And is this what you are planning to do? Share with everyone?" Beausoleil challenged. When Martin said nothing, Beausoleil continued. "That's why we lived apart. We saw the danger, the corruption that comes with absolute power."

"When you have a gift, you have a responsibility to let that gift become all that it can," Martin said.

"At the expense of those less powerful?" Beausoleil asked.

"That, my friend, is called destiny," Martin said. "It's what makes our dear Natalie here so interesting. She has the ability to absorb all our gifts into that harmonious whole so quickly. The grasp she has on the potential of our kind is limitless." He turned to Natalie. "How did you come about, my dear, and how will it play out? I think your place is with me. As I've told you before, I can help you make the most of the wonderful gift you have."

"As your weapon?" Natalie asked scornfully.

"It would be an exchange," Martin countered. "I am the one with vision, and under my tutelage, you would have the opportunity to be a part of true greatness."

"I'll never join you," Natalie said.

"Never say never," Martin said. "You would be surprised at what I am capable of."

"I don't think any of us would be surprised at what you're capable of," Beausoleil retorted.

"Enough of this!" Martin yelled. He set off a charge of currents towards Natalie. They gripped and latched to her, and her energy started to drain. Martin had moved so quickly, she thought. She was focusing on pushing the currents away when she noticed Sebastian twirl his fingers.

Beausoleil sicced the chains on Sebastian. They whipped around him, pulling his attention. The benches and the bars followed.

While Sebastian was distracted, Natalie fought against Martin's attempt to capture her. She searched for pockets in the currents and spread them out, pushing the currents away. She reached deeper into Martin's power with her mind as well. She saw Martin's eyes widen, and his power slammed shut.

The currents spiraled away, and they were back at stalemate.

"This is so much fun," Martin said with glee. "I'm enjoying learning so much about you, Natalie. It helps to know what you can do."

A flicker of panic rippled through her. The more Martin knew, the more he could use the information against her.

"Natalie," Phillip called suddenly. She stared at him in surprise. He had been so silent. He pointed to his feet and said, "Let's go home."

He stood over the porcelain pieces that were once Louisa. At first Natalie could not discern what he meant, but as she scrutinized the pieces, she noticed a pattern. She tried to sort out the lines and then realized, with a start, that Phillip had structured a map out of the porcelain pieces; he had mapped out the interior of her house.

She moved just as Martin and Sebastian sprang into action. The two men threw freshets of light at the map, trying to knock it apart, but Natalie threw a protective field over it. She spread the field to cover Phillip, Beausoleil and Mr. Mackey. Each blow from Martin and Sebastian illuminated the chamber with blinding light. Natalie had to adjust her vision through the light storm.

She worked the field over to her and Hercules, but Martin and Sebastian increased their efforts. The powerful streams became as intense as lightning bolts causing Natalie to shift some of her attention to preserving the map.

"Take Beausoleil and Mr. Mackey back," she screamed at Phillip.

"What about you and Hercules?" he yelled back.

"The less people they have to hold hostage, the better!" She searched frantically for Hercules. All Martin needed was one hostage. The sooner she could protect him, the better.

To her horror, she glimpsed Hercules crawling across the floor to Sebastian. Hercules was so small, and everyone so intent on the map Phillip had created, that no one except Natalie saw Hercules sneak up to Sebastian.

Phillip's map, the one gifted by his mother, stuck out of Sebastian's pocket, stuffed there by Sebastian once the excitement had started. Hercules had homed in on the map.

"Can I even bring them?" Phillip called to her. Natalie knew he meant Beausoleil and Mr. Mackey.

"Yes!" she said. "At least try!"

An especially bright stream hit the protective shield, causing a loud boom.

"Hurry!" Natalie screamed.

Beausoleil and Mr. Mackey gathered around Phillip.

"We'll come back with help!" Beausoleil yelled to her.

"Just get out of here!"

Martin and Sebastian redoubled their efforts. The lights flashed furiously.

With a snap of his wrist, Hercules snatched the map out of Sebastian's pocket. Sebastian grabbed for the map, distracted, and Natalie was able to fortify the protection around Phillip, Beausoleil, and Mr. Mackey. They were on their way.

Hercules ran to Natalie with Phillip's cloth map, his arm outstretched to hand it to her. Sebastian roared and made an arc with both arms. Hercules's back arched, his eyes widening in surprise. He searched out Natalie, and in that instant, she knew he was contained.

"Hercules!" she screamed. "No!"

Hercules face scrunched into one of the most disagreeable expressions she had ever seen on him, and he yanked his body another step closer.

Natalie shot a desperate look to Phillip, Beausoleil and Mr. Mackey. They were fading from view. She had to blink to be sure, but their figures were less distinct, the empty prison cells behind them showing through their forms. She could not remove their protection yet, and it required almost all of her resources, with Martin battling furiously to destroy the porcelain map.

Hercules, his body weakening, managed another couple of steps towards her. As the light behind his eyes started to fade, he pulled back his arm; Phillip's map was crumpled into a ball in his hand. With a final effort he hurled it at Natalie.

Phillip, Beausoleil and Mr. Mackey disappeared just as Natalie caught the map. Quick as lightening she shifted the protective shield over her and Hercules, who lay unmoving on the ground. Martin howled with rage. He and Sebastian shifted their attention to her.

Without the distraction of Beausoleil's gift, and with the collective wrath of both Martin and Sebastian, Natalie had to grapple hard against the attack leveled at her. Currents of energy rolled like a relentless army from all corners. It made it very difficult for her to put her request to Phillip's map.

"My living room," she whispered.

Martin's head reared. Frustration spewed from every atom, searing through the oppressive prison of the chamber. He took a breath deep enough to fill an ocean, and hurled everything he had at Natalie.

But Natalie had taken a deep breath as well, had taken in all the energy that flowed between the three of them. When Martin struck, the shield was fortified.

To Natalie's surprise, it captured the force of Martin's blow without disintegrating it. Ripples of Martin's power hovered around the edges of the shield like oil along the surface of water. Instinctively, Natalie reached out with her mind and gathered them together.

Martin threw up his hands, his fingers stretched, but Natalie pulled all that he had fired at her and launched a torrent straight at him. It hit him through and through. His robes fluttered as if a wind had swirled about, and his jaw dropped in surprise.

Consciousness ebbed from his eyes, and he fell without ceremony to the ground.

Natalie gaped at his inert form. She glanced at Sebastian, but he looked equally thrown. They eyed each other warily.

"Did I kill him?" Natalie asked, perplexed.

"If you threw his own blow back at him, I doubt it," Sebastian answered dryly. "The last thing he wants to do at this point is kill you."

Neither of them moved. Natalie knew she needed to escape through the map as quickly as possible, but something, she did not know what, held her there.

"I trusted you," she said finally to Sebastian.

Sebastian nodded. "I know. That was the plan."

"I thought you were a friend. I liked you." Natalie felt the sting of his betrayal as she spoke.

"I still like you, Natalie," Sebastian said gravely.

Natalie's words were bitter. "You're a liar."

"Yes," Sebastian said. A look Natalie could not read settled over his face. "I am a liar."

There was little else to say after that. Natalie prepared to leave when Sebastian suddenly asked,

"Did your mother ever talk to you about your father?"

"My father?" The question threw her. "What are you talking about?"

"Did she ever mention him in connection with that?" Sebastian pointed to her neck. "That necklace?"

"What do you mean?" Natalie put her hand over the jeweled heart her mother had given her. A touch of dread flittered in her stomach.

"I gave your mother that necklace," Sebastian said.

The world started to spin. It was as if she were being tumbled round, not knowing which end was up.

"You're lying," she whispered.

"I wanted to give her the world." Sebastian's lips had a wry twist. "But she didn't care much for what I had to offer."

"Stop it," Natalie cried, "stop talking! It's not true! She would never love anyone as horrible as you." The spinning would not stop. She was caught in a whirlpool, pulled down into murky depths of chaos.

"Did she tell you it was your father who gave her that necklace?" Sebastian searched her face closely. Natalie did not answer, but what he saw must have been an answer because he nodded.

"What are you going to do now?" Natalie asked.

The corner of Sebastian's mouth lifted without humor. "What would you like me to do?"

Tears prickled her eyes. She turned away from him and focused on the map. She wrapped her consciousness around Hercules and together they traveled through, leaving the hell of Martin's chamber and Sebastian behind.

Chapter Thirty-Six

𝒫 hillip, Beausoleil and Mr. Mackey were huddled in urgent conversation with Serena, Mrs. Stone and Mrs. Blaine when Natalie arrived with Hercules.

"Natalie!" Phillip yelled.

She did not try to move as everyone crowded around her. She could not find words to answer the questions that flew at her. It was as if every molecule in her body had been replaced by lead, and she had no will left to fight.

"Is she in some kind of shock?" she heard Beausoleil ask.

Natalie felt her mother hands checking her for injuries. They patted around her, lifting her arms, feeling around her head, trying to get a sense of what might be wrong with her.

"Why didn't you tell me?" Natalie asked her mother in a whisper.

Serena's hands fell from their inspection.

"What happened?" Serena whispered in reply.

Natalie did not speak, but Serena reeled slightly under the look Natalie gave her.

Hercules lay unmoving on the ground, but Beausoleil, who had knelt down beside him, looked up and exclaimed, "He's alive!"

Relief flooded through Natalie. After Louisa, it would have been more than she could have handled if Hercules had not made it as well.

"Let's put him on the couch for now," Mrs. Stone said. Phillip and Beausoleil lifted Hercules and carried him over to the couch.

"Natalie," Mrs. Blaine said urgently, "what happened with Martin and Sebastian? Where are they now?"

Natalie shook some of the numbness from her mind. "I managed to knock out Martin. Sebastian didn't do anything to stop me from leaving." She felt Serena listening beside her, watchful and observing.

"You knocked out Martin?" Beausoleil asked in wonder.

"We should move right away," Mrs. Stone said. "This is an unexpected opportunity."

"Janet is right," Mrs. Blaine said. "They'll need to regroup now that they know what Natalie can do. We might not have another chance like this one." She looked at Natalie. "You say Sebastian didn't try to stop you?"

For some reason, Natalie could not bring herself to look at Mrs. Blaine. She stared at Hercules lying on the couch and said, "No."

"How unusual," Mrs. Blaine murmured. Serena seemed to be avoiding Mrs. Blaine's glance as well.

"We should get organized," Mrs. Stone said. "We need to do this now!"

"There's actually a plan?" Phillip asked.

"Try not to sound too surprised, dear," Mrs. Blaine said tartly.

Natalie caught Mr. Mackey staring at her. He held out his arms, and she walked into them.

"Thank you so much, Natalie," Mr. Mackey said. "Beausoleil explained a lot to me while we were being held prisoner. I would not have believed any of it if I hadn't seen it with my own eyes. You shouldn't have put yourself at so much risk, but thank you for saving me."

Natalie saw Mrs. Blaine nod to her mother.

Serena came to stand by Mr. Mackey. She took his hand in both of hers and gazed directly into his eyes. "Mr. Mackey, you must be so tired."

Mr. Mackey shook his head, as if slightly confused. "I...why yes. You're right, of course, I am downright exhausted."

"Why don't I take you upstairs where you can lie down?" Serena suggested.

"Well, I guess that would be a good idea." Mr. Mackey did not protest when Serena took his arm and led him upstairs.

"It's best if he doesn't know what our plans are," Mrs. Blaine said to Natalie and Phillip and Beausoleil.

She addressed Natalie. "Your mother was quite upset when she found you had gone after Phillip and the rest. You should not have done that, child. It worked out well, but you risked a great deal."

"I know. I'm sorry." Natalie knew her grandmother was right. It had almost ended in disaster, and they had lost Louisa. Suddenly her heart was a load too big to carry, and she brushed her hand along her cheek to dry the damp paths that trailed it.

Phillip put his hand on her shoulder. "I brought some pieces back." He reached into his pocket and pulled out a handful of porcelain bits. "I couldn't pick all of them up, but I got some. Do you think that's okay?"

"I think so." Natalie sniffled as Phillip put the pieces in her hand. Her forehead rested against his as they bowed their heads over Louisa's remains. So many things had gone wrong with their plan at the start, yet Louisa's part of it had turned the tide. A giant hole carved out of Natalie's heart, and the trails on her cheeks became running streams.

"Hey, mom," Phillip said, "do you have any of your little bags with you?"

"In my purse on the chair," Mrs. Stone said.

Phillip went to look for Mrs. Stone's purse while Mrs. Blaine put out her hand and stroked Natalie's cheek, gently brushing at her tears.

"You have such a brave and generous spirit," she murmured to Natalie. "I'm not surprised, but it still takes my breath away."

"What good did it do?" Natalie cried bitterly. "We lost Louisa."

"I wish I could tell that you will never suffer any other losses in your life like this. A young girl like you should never have to. Unfortunately, where someone like Martin exists, there will always be that kind of possibility. I'm so sorry, Natalie." Mrs. Blaine reached out to cover the hand that held Louisa's remains.

"As long as there are brave people out there like Louisa," she said, squeezing her hand, "there will be victories like this one."

"It doesn't feel like a victory," Natalie said.

"Four people escaped alive from a place no one else has," Mrs. Blaine pointed out. "They were able to come back home, all because of her selfless sacrifice. That sacrifice was not in vain."

Phillip rejoined them then. "I found it." He held up a pouch, one of Mrs. Stones' creations. It was the color of sage and made of velvet fabric, with pink and yellow satin flowers sewn on the sides. A dark, green rope weaved along the top and pulled tight like a drawstring.

"What a lovely piece of work," Mrs. Blaine said.

Phillip pulled at the drawstring and held the pouch open. Natalie carefully poured in the pieces she held in her hand. When all the pieces were in, Phillip pulled the drawstring shut.

"It's perfect!" Natalie said.

"What's this plan you have?" Beausoleil asked, after Serena came back down.

"We've found a place to escape to," Mrs. Blaine said. "As you know, Martin's invention finds our people, and it has been circling our area now, waiting for us. Leaving without detection was impossible. Once we escape to a new area, we can work to blend in and set up more effective defenses."

"Can you use your influence to help everyone to accept your presence?" Beausoleil asked.

"I'd rather not use my influence that way," Serena said. "It would require constant vigilance. It's better to blend in using normal channels and leave the influence to things that require extraordinary means."

"Once we found a place," Mrs. Blaine continued, "the only piece missing was escaping undetected. Thanks to Natalie, we finally realized we have that piece with Phillip's gift." She smiled at Natalie and Phillip.

"We can put up as many of our defenses to avoid detection as possible beforehand, use Phillip's gift to escape, and then set up our new base," Mrs. Stone said. "We have to move quickly, though, before Martin and Sebastian are able to set up a way to work against Phillip's gift."

"What about after?" Beausoleil asked.

"After?" Mrs. Stone asked.

"Yes, after," Beausoleil said. "After we're safely away and set up in our new location. Do we sit there and wait for Martin and Sebastian to catch up with us again?"

"What would you have us do, Beausoleil?" Serena asked.

"Martin is insane," Beausoleil said bluntly. "He won't stop until he and Sebastian are the last of our kind standing. He intends to—how do I put it—influence the world with the powers he intends to amass. He has managed to annihilate most of our kind in his quest to gain as much power as he can. And he wants Natalie. He will do all he can to get her."

"Were you able to see how he strips us of our gifts, Beausoleil?" Mrs. Blaine asked.

"He has an invention of some kind," Beausoleil said. "Both Natalie and I experienced it."

Serena's head snapped to look at Natalie. There was anger and more than a little fear in her mother's expression.

"He could not strip me of my gifts as they were hidden in Louisa at the time," Beausoleil said, "and he did not strip Natalie of hers because, and this part is interesting, the gifts don't lend themselves to being as powerful with Martin as they do to the person with whom the gift originated. He would rather keep Natalie's gift at full power, and influence her to use it in whatever way he wants. That not only puts Natalie in danger, but everyone she is close to; whomever Martin can use to influence her. Think about it, Sebastian took Phillip, and Natalie came, just as they wanted, and fell into their trap."

"That's enough," Serena said sharply. She was staring at Natalie who felt as if a noose had been slung around her neck.

"I'm sorry," Beausoleil said, with an apologetic glance to Natalie. "I know you'd like to protect your daughter, but she has already seen things that most young people should never have to see. Both she and Phillip have."

"Regardless, that is not your call," Serena said. "My daughter left of her own volition to save her friend, what do you think she'll do if she thinks she is a danger to us all?" The anger behind Serena's voice rose with each word.

Beausoleil looked stricken. "I am truly sorry," he said. "Natalie and Phillip have been so brave that it is easy to think of them as more than children."

"They are still children, Beausoleil," Serena said, "and whatever you might think, Natalie is my daughter, and I will do whatever it takes to keep her safe."

"You kept your head hidden in the ground before," Beausoleil pointed out.

"I am aware of what I did before! I am aware of what she is capable of. I am aware of her value, not only to Martin, but to our kind as well. I am aware of all of that. Do not presume to know more about my daughter than I do, Beausoleil!"

The silence was deafening. Natalie stared at her mother in astonishment. She had never seen her so angry. But as her mother stood there with her color high and her eyes flashing with a grim set to her lips, Natalie realized that there were far more imply-cations than she had realized with her gifts, and that her mother saw them and was terribly afraid for her.

"I'm sorry, Serena," Beausoleil said again. "Everything I saw while in Martin's hands tells me that we cannot afford to just sit back and hope for the best. But you are right. I should not presume."

Serena nodded slowly. Natalie could see that her mother was torn about her situation, and that the argument was far from over.

"My suggestion," Mrs. Blaine interjected, "would be to worry first about getting out of our immediate predicament, and then we can give proper attention to the issues you have brought to the table, Beausoleil."

"I agree." Beausoleil seemed more than willing to drop the subject for now.

"Before we move on," Mrs. Stone cut in, "can you tell us, Beausoleil, what happens with the gifts? How does Martin retain them?"

"Amulets," Beausoleil said. "Martin invented them as a way to hold the gifts. The amulets are small. Sebastian wears his around his neck, but Martin has somehow managed to integrate his into his very body."

"What?" Mrs. Blaine exclaimed.

"It's an abomination," Beausoleil said. "I believe that's why his face looks like a molten mix of different features." He hesitated. "I suspect they represent the essences of the people whose gifts he has stolen."

"My god," Mrs. Stone said in horror.

"I wonder why Sebastian hasn't done the same," Serena said.

"Sebastian," Beausoleil said wryly, "the ever ruthless henchman. Martin could not have asked for a better son."

"Son?" Natalie exclaimed. "Sebastian is Martin's son?"

"Yes." Beausoleil gave Serena and Mrs. Blaine a puzzled look. "Didn't you know?"

"No," Serena said smoothly, "we haven't had a chance to mention that to her yet."

Anger rolled through Natalie. How many more surprises could there possibly be?

Beausoleil nodded slowly. "Yes, well, Sebastian is very much an integral part of Martin's plans. He's lucky to have someone as gifted as Sebastian on the same page. As it stands now, all Martin has to do is tell Sebastian what he needs, and the job gets done."

"So why hasn't Sebastian done what Martin has with his amulet?" Serena asked.

Beausoleil shrugged. "Maybe he's just not as insane as Martin."

"Why would he even want to be with Martin?" Phillip asked.

"Most likely the power," Beausoleil said. "If I hadn't just seen Natalie at work, I would have said the two of them were the most powerful of our kind that I had ever seen.

"I'm inclined to think that Martin's sold him on his grand master plan," Beausoleil continued. "Plus, with Martin being his father, there's probably a fair amount of loyalty as well."

"I had no idea there could be loyalty among thieves," Mrs. Stone murmured.

"Good point," Beausoleil said. "Maybe more of a paternal influence then."

"We should get organized," Mrs. Blaine said briskly. "Janet, Serena, why don't you pull together what we've prepared?"

"Okay," Janet said, but Serena shook her head.

"I'd like a moment to speak with Natalie."

"Can it wait, Serena?" Mrs. Blaine asked.

"No," Serena said firmly. "I need to have a word with her."

"Phillip, why don't you come with me?" Mrs. Stone put a hand to Phillip's shoulder as they went upstairs.

"I'll tend to Hercules," Beausoleil said.

Mrs. Blaine looked from Natalie to Serena and then said, "I need to get a few things done. I'll use your study, Serena."

Natalie waited as everyone went about their tasks. She and Serena would need to go somewhere private to speak.

"Beausoleil," she called out. Beausoleil looked up from where he had knelt beside Hercules on the couch. "There's a place in our yard, under one of our trees. It might be a good place for Louisa."

"That sounds very nice, Natalie," Beausoleil said with a sad nod of his head.

"I'll go dig up a place for her now," Natalie said.

"It's still dark out, Natalie," Serena said.

"I can find my way in the dark," Natalie said stubbornly.

Serena sighed. Natalie walked out the living room, into the kitchen and out the door leading to the backyard. Serena followed behind, grabbing a lantern from the kitchen pantry and a jacket hanging from a chair at the table as they passed. Neither one of them said anything as Natalie went to their tool shed and dug through it for a small shovel and spade.

"I know you're upset with me," Serena said. She wrapped the jacket around Natalie and held up the lantern for her as Natalie dug the shovel into the ground under one of her favorite trees. The leaves hung low over the yard, giving shelter to whomever sat under it.

"I'm so sorry," Serena said softly. "I should have told you, but I wasn't sure how. You've been through so much already."

"Why did you give me this necklace?" Natalie said. "Why now?"

"I hoped it might help you in a tough spot," Serena said. "And I guess I never really gave up hope in Sebastian. I thought that if the man I had loved was still in him, then he might do the right thing by you if you needed him to."

"Good heavens, Serena!" Natalie and Serena jumped in surprise. Mrs. Blaine had come to stand in the yard behind them without their noticing. "What were you thinking? You handed Natalie over to them on a silver platter!"

"Not now, Mother!" Serena said.

"How could you think he would change?" Mrs. Blaine walked up to them with her cane, and confronted Serena, an appalled expression on her face. "After everything he and his father have done, how could you have taken that chance?"

"I had my reasons," Serena said.

"You might see him as the young boy you fell in love with, but he is a man now, and responsible for so many terrible things."

"I am aware of that, Mother."

"Do you still love him?" Mrs. Blaine asked bluntly.

"No, I don't. It was over when I ended it."

"And yet you risked your daughter's life over what you had with Sebastian all those years ago?"

"That's enough, Mother!" Serena snapped. She took a deep breath. "It was only a matter of time before he found out."

Mrs. Blaine thought about that. "Perhaps. But I am still concerned about your motivation for revealing Natalie to him."

Serena rubbed her eyes wearily. "Yes, well, we can talk about that later. What's done is done, and now we just have to deal with it."

"Yes, you're right," Mrs. Blaine said. "We have more pressing matters now. I came out because I need your help. Would you please come in for a moment?"

"You should come inside as well, Natalie," Serena said.

"I think we're fine," Natalie said. "I don't feel Martin and Sebastian are close, and I want to finish this for Louisa."

Serena nodded in resignation. She hung the lantern from one of the branches to give Natalie light. "We'll come back out again soon. I'll bring everybody out so that we can say goodbye to Louisa. And then we need to go."

Before she left with Mrs. Blaine, she said quietly, "I'm sorry, Natalie."

After Serena and Mrs. Blaine departed, Natalie finished digging a special place for Louisa and stepped out from under the branches to stare up at the sky. Oh, how she would miss the view from their yard! The air was cold, but it cleared out the clouds that hung over her mind. She hoped that wherever they went, they would at least have the fall season. That would be something she could hold onto.

Thoughts of Louisa came to her then, and tears filled her eyes. For a short time she had had a friend whose spirit—because she did have a spirit, Natalie thought fiercely—was gentler than anyone else's, but who was also brave and strong and beautiful. The world needed more souls like Louisa, not Martin and Sebastian Reimer. Her father and grandfather, Natalie reminded herself bitterly.

She turned to go back inside the house, but a movement in the yard caught her attention. A fog rolled in from the edge between the trees and eddied into the middle of the lawn. Natalie looked around, but there was no fog in the sky or anywhere else in the neighborhood. Her heart began to hammer a louder beat in her chest.

Behind the fog, she heard the sound of footsteps crunching through the fallen leaves. She watched in silent fascination as the fog parted and swirled aside. Her eyes made out a figure walking up the middle towards her. It was Sebastian.

Before she could open her mouth to sound an alarm, Sebastian held a finger to his lips and then held his hands up in surrender. She shook her head in terror as a scream worked its way up from her chest.

In the blink of an eye, Sebastian was upon her. He clapped a hand over her mouth and steadied her head with his other hand at the back of her head, holding her securely.

"Don't scream." He released her as quickly as he had grabbed her and stepped back, once again putting his hands up in surrender. Natalie sputtered in surprise, but before she could gather her wits about her, he unzipped his dark coat, reached into his shirt and pulled out a chain.

At the end of the chain there was a glint of silver that shone in the moonlight. It had symbols Natalie could not read, and a deep power rolled off it. She stepped back to throw a shield between her and Sebastian. Her eyes felt much too large for her head as she glared at him.

Sebastian quickly removed the chain from around his neck and held it in front of him. "Do you know what this is?"

Natalie nodded. It had to be the amulet Beausoleil had mentioned.

"I am setting it to the side." Sebastian moved his arm out to his side and let the amulet fall to the ground. "Without it, I am at your mercy. You will still be able to take on its power, but without it, I only have my own gifts, which are no match for yours."

"I don't believe you." Natalie opened her mouth to shout for help, but Sebastian interrupted her.

"Please, I'm not here to hurt you."

"That's all you've ever done!" Natalie squeaked in disbelief. "To me, to all of us!"

"Shhhh!" The desperation in Sebastian's eyes checked her. As she stared at him in bewilderment, the corner of his mouth twisted in a wry movement. "You're right, I can't argue with you there."

After that he said nothing. Every nerve in Natalie's body shifted into high gear, but Sebastian simply stood there, unmoving. Natalie knew she should sound out an alarm, but Sebastian presented such a non-threatening picture, that she felt a moment's confusion.

"What are you going to do?" she demanded.

"I was hoping to talk to you."

"Why?"

"I was hoping you might consider coming back with me," Sebastian said.

"Are you kidding me?" Natalie practically screeched the words. Sebastian winced and looked up at the house.

"I think I'm going to have to phrase my words a little better," he said ruefully. "Outrage makes you loud."

"That isn't funny! I should warn everyone. You were crazy to come here. Crazy to think I would ever go with you. I would never, in a million trillion years, go with you or your horrible father! What made you think I would?

"Leave now." She gathered the power from Sebastian's amulet and prepared to defend herself. "Leave or else I'll make you leave."

Sebastian shifted uneasily as her power grew, but still, he did not reach for his amulet. He bowed his head and waited. When he lifted his head, there was just enough light from the lantern reflected on his face, and what Natalie saw took her by surprise.

Sebastian's face had always been stoic, as resolute as an assassin, save for the time when he was Saul. Now Natalie saw weariness and more than a little sadness on his face; he had the look of a man who had seen too much and done much worse. It was a look that threw her.

"All this time I never knew," Sebastian said. "A couple of times when you and I first talked, I thought there was something familiar about you. You look so much like your mother, but there was something else too. I suspected it when I discovered Serena was your mother, but it was when I searched you and saw your necklace that all the pieces fell into place."

He shook his head in wonder. He reached out his hand, and Natalie flinched before he touched her. His hand stilled, but then tentatively moved forward again. She was helpless to stop him as his fingers gently clasped her chin and tilted it towards the moonlight.

"Such a lovely little thing you are," he said quietly. "You could come with me, Natalie. We could get to know each other. I know I would like that. Haven't you ever wondered? Wondered what it would be like to have a father? To be adored by one?"

It was as though she were hypnotized. Sebastian's words were so warm, so inviting. She *had* wondered. Had always wondered...

"You could stay with us," she offered. The hope that grew in her heart surprised her.

An emotion Natalie could not read flashed through Sebastian eyes with an intensity that rooted her like one of the trees in her yard.

"That won't happen, I'm afraid."

"Why not?" Natalie asked urgently. "You don't like Martin anyway."

"You don't know that." Sebastian's tone held a warning.

"Am I wrong?"

"He's my father, and what he can offer is far greater than anything you can even begin to imagine, Natalie. Your gifts can take you so far, and he can help you with that."

"I don't want to have anything to do with him!" Natalie cried.

"And me?" Sebastian asked. "Do you not want to have anything to do with me?"

Before Natalie could answer, she heard her mother scream, "Natalie!"

Sebastian made a move for his amulet, but it was in Natalie's hand before he could grab it. Sebastian blinked at the empty spot on the ground where it had lain just a second before.

"I'm going to need you to give that to me," he said.

"So you can hurt more people?"

"No. Martin has done something very interesting with my amulet. He wanted to make sure I guarded it with my life, literally, so if I lose it, I die."

Shock coursed through Natalie. "How could your own father do that to you?"

Sebastian shrugged. "Power of this kind must be protected at all costs. Please," he held out his hand, "give it back."

"Don't do it, Natalie!" Beausoleil yelled. He, Serena, Phillip and Mrs. Stone ran to where they stood. Mrs. Blaine and, to Natalie's surprise, Hercules, followed after.

"Why are you here?" Serena demanded.

"Why do you think?" Sebastian drawled.

Just then, Natalie gasped. Her nerves prickled to attention.

"What's wrong?" Phillip asked her.

"That would be Martin," Sebastian answered. "He's probably conscious now and on his way to claim his prize." He was calm, almost leisurely, and it made Natalie uneasy. Did he have a plan up his sleeve that would prevent them from leaving?

"We have to go!" Mrs. Stone said. "We have to go now!" She had a coat in her arms, and she whipped the one Natalie was wearing off her shoulders and slung the new coat over her.

"I need my map," Phillip said to her. Natalie pulled Phillip's map out of her pocket and handed it to him.

A low vibration rumbled along the edges of Natalie's mind. Sebastian was right; Martin was coming.

"He's coming," Natalie cried. She waved her hand and lifted Sebastian into the air.

"Do what you can to shield us, Natalie," Mrs. Blaine urged.

"You know where to take us, Phillip?" Mrs. Stone asked.

"Yes." Phillip had the map out in front of him. By now he did not have to say anything. Their destination emerged almost immediately.

The vibration had become stronger. It was hard to tell from which direction it came; it seemed to come from everywhere. Dawn approached as well. Light peeked over the horizon, and the sky warmed to a lighter shade.

"Hurry, Phillip," Mrs. Stone said.

"I'll take my mom, Beausoleil and Hercules," Phillip said to Natalie.

"Okay." Natalie wrapped her mind around her mom and Mrs. Blaine.

The sound of the trees shaking filled the air. Leaves slid across the ground and whirled around their feet. Natalie looked to where Phillip pointed on his map. The details emerged; they were moving through.

Sebastian hung where Natalie held him suspended. He did not struggle, but watched as they made their escape. His outline started to blur; they were fading through the map. Sebastian's eyes met Natalie's, but there was no fury in them. At the last second, before they faded, Natalie threw his amulet at him and released him. He fell to the ground as they disappeared.

Chapter Thirty-Seven

They arrived in the new town. It had not yet awoken. The vibrations signaling Martin's arrival had vanished. A peaceful quiet greeted them.

"We can't stay here," Mrs. Blaine said. "We don't know what Sebastian saw. Use one of the backup towns."

Phillip looked at his map and made the request. Within moments they arrived at the next town.

"We have one more backup?" Mrs. Blaine asked. Serena and Mrs. Stone nodded. "Good, let's use that one."

Everyone agreed, and they arrived at the final town. They seemed to have gone west because the sky was brighter, and a little south because the fall air was warmer.

"Why in heaven's name did you give Sebastian the amulet?" Beausoleil demanded once they arrived.

"Martin had it rigged so that Sebastian would die if he lost it," Natalie said. "I couldn't have lived with myself if I had kept it from him."

"Even after all he's done?" Beausoleil exclaimed.

"A child should not have to make that choice," Mrs. Blaine cut in.

Beausoleil looked as if he thought that Sebastian not getting his amulet back was a missed opportunity, regardless of the consequences, but he kept his thoughts on the matter to himself.

"This looks quite nice," Mrs. Stone said of the town. They had arrived behind what looked like the main building downtown. The front of the building faced a quiet street lined with trees and quaint little homes that had been converted into boutique shops.

The town showed signs of waking, with an occasional car driving by, and a couple of beeping trucks making early morning deliveries. In more ways than one, it had the same feel of the town they had left behind.

"How does it feel here, Natalie?" Mrs. Blaine asked. "Did we make it?"

"I think we did," Natalie said.

"Our clothes should shield us for now," Mrs. Stone said.

"The preliminary groundwork we did here should keep us safe as well," Serena added.

"Preliminary groundwork?" Beausoleil said.

"Janet and I managed to set up a few safeguards in the towns we were considering. Janet had a few orders from these towns for her sewing projects, and we fit in a couple of deliveries. We learned about each town, and when we left, the customers had Janet's creations, and a bit of influence from me," Serena explained. "It wasn't the most foolproof plan, but every little bit helps. We won't be total strangers here."

"What should we do now?" Beausoleil asked.

"One of my clients mentioned a bed and breakfast," Mrs. Stone said. "From what I understand, the owner might allow us to take rooms early."

"Once we've got rooms," Serena said, "we can go about the business of settling in.

"Beausoleil, Hercules, we assumed you would escape with us," Serena said, "but we were not sure of your plans afterwards."

"I would like to hear what plans we make after we settle. I can decide from there," Beausoleil said. "I can understand you all wanting to hide and protect Natalie and Phillip, but after everything that's happened, I can't sit and wait."

"We understand," Mrs. Blaine said.

"I think it's best if I look for another circus," Hercules said.

"What? Why?" Phillip asked.

"We'd like you to stay with us," Natalie said.

"I think having a little person with you would draw attention." Hercules held up his hand as everyone jumped in to protest. "No, it's true. Martin and Sebastian will have an easier time if they hear about a town suddenly acquiring a resident little person. I can blend better in a circus. I would rather think of you all as safe, as Louisa would have wanted."

"They can just as easily find you in a circus, Hercules," Beausoleil pointed out.

"True," Hercules said, "but if Serena can use her influence to take away any information I have that might give you away..."

"Hercules," Serena said, "that would mean taking away all memory of us, of Beausoleil and Louisa."

A cloak of sadness seemed to drape over Hercules's shoulders. "Yes, but if it's the only way to keep us safe..."

"We can fight for you if you stay with us," Beausoleil said fiercely.

Hercules shook his head. "If you want to do this the right way, defeat this monster and then find me and give back everything that was taken from me to keep us all safe."

Beausoleil opened his mouth to protest, but Hercules held up his hand again. Beausoleil looked around at everyone and then nodded.

"I'll keep what we have of Louisa with me until I find you again," Beausoleil promised. His hand clasped Hercules' shoulder, and there was nothing left to be said.

They walked through the town in search of the bed and breakfast. Mrs. Stone led with Phillip, followed by Serena and Natalie. Beausoleil, Hercules and Mrs. Blaine picked up the rear, moving at a slower pace.

"Are you still angry with me?" Serena asked her.

"I...I don't think so," Natalie answered.

"How do you feel, knowing who your father is?"

Natalie shrugged. "A little confused, I guess."

"You didn't raise the alarm to warn us he was there," Serena pointed out. "You listened to what he had to say."

"I don't know why," she admitted. "He said he wouldn't hurt me. He put down his amulet and everything. I don't know why I believed him."

"He's a clever man." Serena put her arm across Natalie's shoulders and gave them a squeeze. "It's okay to want to know more about the man who is your father. It's natural, especially when he is nice to you, and genuinely seems to care about you and wants to know you. But with Sebastian, you have to be careful."

"I know," Natalie said defensively.

"I know you do, but..." Serena struggled with the words. "It's so hard to explain." She trailed off with the thought.

"Did you really think he might try to help me?" Natalie asked tentatively.

Serena's face grew troubled. "I think I was wrong to give you the necklace. My instincts were misplaced, and now he has a tool to use against you. I would have told you eventually about your father, but giving him the means to discover it so soon was an error in judgment on my part."

"You must have really loved him," Natalie said.

"We were both very young. We were at the age where we could have taken any path we wanted for our lives. When I found out the path he wanted, I knew I could never go with him. But yes, I loved him." Serena hesitated. "You liked him, didn't you? When he was Saul?"

"I thought he was my friend," Natalie said. "I thought he liked me."

"How could he not?" Serena said with a tender smile. "Be careful, Natalie. I wish I could tell you that blood trumps all, but it's not always the case. Do you understand?"

"Yes, I understand," Natalie said. But in her heart, she was a little bit afraid. She knew the kind of man Sebastian was. He was loyal to the most horrible man she had ever known, a man she now knew was her grandfather, and he had kidnapped her friends, tortured them, and destroyed Louisa. He had betrayed her friendship, and was a threat to everyone she knew and loved. Yet when he said he wanted to know her, asked her to come with him, everything felt so different. She just could not let him die.

"Like your grandmother says, you have a generous spirit. It's a wonderful trait. In the end you chose us over what Martin and Sebastian offered because you're strong. But in our situation, just..." Serena gave her shoulders another squeeze, "just be aware."

"Okay," Natalie said.

"Thank you for being so brave and for helping us to escape," Serena whispered.

Natalie put her arms around her mother as they walked.

The bed and breakfast was a lovely place, situated off the main street. The home was large with several rooms and a nice yard. They were lucky to find that the owner had room to house them all and was willing to give them lodging on short notice. They had made it in time for breakfast, and after they checked in, they sat down to a delicious buffet of eggs, sausage, pancakes, cereals and various pastries with jam and butter.

"Would you two like to come along, or would you rather stay here at the B&B?" Serena asked them as they ate. The plan was for Mrs. Stone to start house hunting, while Mrs. Blaine went to the bank. Beausoleil, Hercules and Serena were going to find which town had a circus. Hercules would then travel there by train. Serena would help with the final arrangements for him.

"Stay here," Natalie said. Phillip agreed through a mouthful of muffin.

"Can we trust you to stay out of trouble?" Mrs. Stone asked.

"Yes, Mom," Phillip grumbled.

"Don't wander around town," Serena said. "Stay here at the B&B for now."

After breakfast, Natalie and Phillip watched as the rest of their party separated for the morning. She and Phillip went out to the large front porch and sat on the chairs. The weather was cool, not cold yet, and she and Phillip sat quite comfortably, watching the people go by.

This town will be our new home, Natalie thought. "It's really not so bad here," she commented to Phillip.

"It's fine, I guess," he replied. "At least until they find us again."

"What can we do?" she asked.

"I know what I'm going to do. Now that I've got my gift, I'm going to look for my father."

"How?" Natalie asked. She would not even know where to begin.

"I'll figure something out," Phillip said. "My dad wanted to do more about Martin and Sebastian. He didn't want to just sit and wait for them to find us. I think that's how we have to look at it. Beausoleil knows this, too. I'm sure he'll have ideas. I'm going to be a part of that. What about you?" he asked. The question seemed like a challenge.

"I could try to help you find your father," Natalie offered. "I'm too tired to think about anything else."

"Would you really?" Phillip asked excitedly. "Having you around to help would be huge."

"I'm not sure how much use I'll be."

"What do you mean? Look at everything you did."

"Yes, but now that Martin and Sebastian know about me, I don't think it will be easy."

"At least we have some hope," Phillip said.

Natalie sat quietly in her chair and took in the town. She did not want to have to think of anything. Right now she had a chance to feel, even for a minute, that her life was the way it was before the circus had first rolled into town. There would be time enough to worry about being discovered, to plan how to handle Martin and Sebastian, and to help Phillip find his father. But for now, she could sit back and enjoy the pleasant feel of a fall breeze over her skin.

"Do you want to throw a football?" Phillip asked suddenly. "I see one out there in the bushes."

"I don't know how to throw one," Natalie said.

"I can teach you. Come on, it will be fun." Phillip got to his feet and jumped down the stairs onto the grass. He picked the football out of the bushes and tossed it around in his hands.

"Are you in?" he asked.

Natalie let thoughts of Louisa, Hercules, Martin and Sebastian cross her mind; let them run through and then filter out. As her last thoughts of them faded, she stood up and skipped down the stairs to Phillip.

"Yes," she said, "I'm in."

Acknowledgements

As is usual with most things in my life, I owe my family a thank you too big for words on a page. Their love, support, and encouragement are a constant buoy as I navigate this crazy, wonderful world of writing.

Thank you to my mom and dad for brainstorming the title with me. My dad brightened my day by cracking us up with his... creative attempts. My mom brought me tremendous relief by coming up with the perfect title. They are troopers who make my heart swell with gratitude.

Thank you also to my mom for clearing aside time to read one of the earliest drafts as well as the final one, sometimes pushing aside her own exhaustion and staying up until the wee hours of the morning to do so. In my eyes, she exemplifies all the wonderful things we say about mothers and more.

Thank you to my sister, Mel, for her support. I can always count on her to be absolutely honest with me, and I freakin' love her for that!

Thank you to my brother-in-law, Tyler, for setting me up with a big computer screen when my small laptop reduced me to squints and bleary eyes. When the writing starts to crowd and blur, those little things mean the world!

My friend, Anne, took time out of her busy schedule to read one of my early drafts. It was a longer tome then, yet she plowed through and endured my long list of questions after. My thank you to her goes beyond the novel and encompasses years of invaluable friendship and support. Anyone who knows her will not be surprised when I say she is one in a million.

Thank you to editor/author Susan Helene Gottfried for her suggested edits to the prologue and part of the first chapter. I cannot wait to have her dig into more of my stories in the future.

Thank you to Jean Boles for helping me format the manuscript for print, and for the final proofread. I can be stubborn about doing things on my own, but in this case, I was more than happy to leave all that to a true professional.

Thank you to Candace Foy Chabot for her work on the cover, and for her talent and friendly professionalism. I so appreciate what she brings to her art and what she brought to this project.

Writing my first novel was a long journey, and I would not have known where to begin if it had not been for instructors like Uma Krishnaswami, Gloria Kempton and Dennis Foley. I am forever grateful for the guidance and encouragement I found in their classes on Writers.com.

Thank you to Ranjit Souri. His workshop with the sketch comedy group Stir-Friday Night! was where the writing pieces really started to fall into place. He is a wonderful teacher and a consummate artist.

About the Author

M.L. Roble's desire to write a children's novel stems from the nostalgia of her own middle grade reading years where she first experienced books like *The Chronicles of Narnia* and *The Shattered Stone*. There have been different books and genres since, but those years fueled an enchantment for story that never died.

Ms. Roble currently lives in the Chicago area, where each winter she vows to move to a warmer climate.

Please visit her blog at **www.mlroble** for updates and news about past, current and future projects.

CPSIA information can be obtained
at www.ICGtesting.com
Printed in the USA
LVOW01s0825191216
517913LV00020B/1339/P